For Tony

## Acknowledgements

Grateful acknowledgement is made to Faber and Faber Ltd for permission to use the quotation from W H Auden's 'Your Sleeping Head' which appears in his Collected Poems (Faber and Faber). The 'twitch upon the thread' mentioned in the text appears in The Innocence of Father Brown by G. K. Chesterton. I found The Flamenco Guitar by David George (Society of Spanish Studies, Madrid, 1969) extremely helpful for information about the guitar in Spain.

**Orange Bitter, Orange Sweet** Anthony McDonald
First published in 2001 by Gay Men's Press, part of the Millivres Prowler Group,
PO Box 3220, Brighton BN2 5AU, East Sussex, England

For more information see www.gaymenspress.co.uk

World Copyright © 2001 Anthony McDonald

Anthony McDonald has asserted his right to be identified as the author of
this work in accordance with the Copyright, Designs and Patents Act 1988

A CIP catalogue record for this book is available from the British Library

ISBN 1 902852 28 1

Distributed in Europe by Central Books,
99 Wallis Road, London  E9 5LN

Distributed in North America by Consortium
Book Sales and Distribution, 1045 Westgate Drive,
Suite 90, Saint Paul, MN 55114-1065, USA

Distributed in Australia by Bulldog Books,
PO Box 300, Beaconsfield, NSW 2014

Printed and bound in the EU by WS Bookwell, Juva, Finland

# Orange Bitter, Orange Sweet

Anthony McDonald

GAY MEN'S PRESS

# One

On her arrival at Seville airport, Pippa had planned to take a taxi. Her luggage was bulky and she didn't fancy being drenched by the rain. But no taxis were to be seen so she joined the queue for the bus into the city centre. Night fell swiftly and the rain, as abruptly, stopped.

The approach to the city was unpromising. Even in the dusk it was impossible not to see how gardenless the suburban wastelands were and how barrack-like the apartment blocks; impossible to miss the neon-lit hideousness of the Coca-Cola plant. But then, as the bus bounced over the hump of a railway bridge, a transformation came about. Now the dark streets were lined with orange trees and the trees were hung with fruit. Half-concealed in dense foliage, the oranges borrowed a dim luminosity from the street-lamps. They reminded Pippa of something homely yet magical; Christmas tree baubles lit by firelight. Beneath the trees were groups of people – men mostly – emerging after the rain and standing, slouching or sauntering about, each one attended by the red firefly of a cigarette. They were shadow-people who would not have substance until tomorrow. Tonight, only their Spanish cigarette-smoke made them human. It came in through the bus's windows, crept beneath the door; you breathed it second-hand; it was like an energy-source, fuelling the city.

When the bus stopped, Pippa did have to take a taxi but now she found one easily. As she was sliding into it, her attention was caught by two young men who passed by on the pavement. They seemed not much older than herself and were both attractive in their different ways. One was tall and broad-shouldered with curly, rope-coloured hair – probably from northern Europe, Pippa thought. The other was smaller, Spanish-looking, with the aristocratic bearing and features that she half-knew from the paintings of El Greco. She was startled to hear the taller one say in English: "But how could you possibly lose a window?" as the taxi door shut and they disappeared from view.

The address Pippa had given the taxi-driver was only a couple of blocks from the bus-stop and in a matter of seconds she was peering through a wrought-iron grill into an ill-lit stairwell and pulling the bell-cord. A young woman came down almost immediately and let her in. "Hallo Pippa," she said. "I'm Jeannette. We spoke on the phone. Welcome to Seville."

Jeannette had a pleasant enough face though it was somewhat sharp-featured. Her eyes were bright blue but challenging. Pippa could not decide whether she was going to like her or not.

"I'll show you round the flat and we'll have a coffee."

Pippa looked down at her two bulging cases.

"Don't worry. We can get them later." And Jeannette led the way upstairs. "Your cousin's asked us over on Saturday," she said. "She's dying to see you."

"I haven't seen Sophie since I was a child. The family always called her eccentric. Is she?"

Jeannette thought for a moment. "If leaving your country behind and marrying a foreigner is eccentric then I suppose she is. She's certainly individual. And since Pablo died she's... I suppose she's been working at turning herself into what her generation would call a character."

"I've brought her some Bisto and Bird's Custard."

Jeannette's eyebrows rose expressively. "Did she ask you to?"

2

Pippa laughed. "Of course. I'd hardly have thought up presents like that on my own."

"No, I suppose not. Sophie does excellent Spanish and French-style cooking. I hadn't imagined her hankering after instant gravy and custard. And yet people sometimes miss the most unexpected things... Now, I think the water's boiling. Can you pass that pair of pliers?"

"Pliers?" Pippa found them and handed them over a little uncertainly.

"The gas turns on easily enough," said Jeannette. "But you need the pliers to turn it off."

Later Pippa accepted Jeannette's offer of an omelette and a glass of wine but when they had eaten and drunk she excused herself to unpack before going to bed. "See you tomorrow, then," Jeannette said.

Tomorrow. Tomorrow the sun would shine on the oranges nestling in the dark trees. Pippa wondered whether they would be ripe at this time of year. It was the end of October and apples were already well-ripe in England, but about Seville oranges, she had no idea. Tomorrow the cigarette-smoking men would step out from the shadows and show their faces to the light. Pippa settled into her bed – it was rather hard and narrow but still comforting – and wondered what the men here would be like. She remembered the two who had passed her when she was getting into the taxi, saying something non-sensical about a window. She tried to imagine who they might be, wondered if one of them would be for her. Tomorrow... Her thoughts seized on the word as she drowned in a cocktail of tiredness and expectation. Whatever tomorrow might throw at her she promised herself she would not fumble it. Holding fast to this crucial thought she drifted into sleep.

When tomorrow came, it brought with it sunshine and a deep blue sky. The only signs of yesterday's weather were the broad puddles in the streets. They presented mirror-images of the city's splendours as if out of consideration for the first-time visitor who might otherwise get her feet wet while trying to look up. Pippa turned left at the bull-ring as she had been told to and found herself on a wide riverfront promenade among tall date-palms and massive beds of flowering shrubs. Here there was a light silvery mist that hid the river itself, the Guadalquivir, from view. Ahead of her the Torre del Oro stood, its top half bathed in sunshine and living up to its golden name, its lower half still veiled in mist. It was as if the city, which had cloaked itself on Pippa's arrival with dark and rain, was trying to hold out a little longer before exposing itself fully to her eager gaze.

Pippa felt relaxed. Although she was on her way to her new place of work, she would not actually start until Monday. And Monday, seen from the vantage-point of Friday, was a weekend and an age away. When she arrived after a few more minutes' walk she was pleased to be met by Jeannette who explained that all her other colleagues-to-be were then in class. She introduced Pippa to the principal, Ignacio, showed her the shut doors of classrooms, went through the library and helped her with a stack of form-filling in Spanish, explaining everything down to the minutest detail. Pippa appreciated this. But when lunchtime came and Jeannette took her to a café and proved just as voluble on the subjects of her boyfriend Felipe, the price of clothes in Seville compared to Edinburgh and the impossibility of finding a decent cup of tea outside Scotland (England scoring no higher in this regard than Spain or France) Pippa began to feel less grateful for her companionship.

"And another thing," Jeannette said. "There'll be a do this evening since it's payday. Not to be missed. Everyone'll be there."

Pippa drew breath to make an excuse but, fortunately for her, Jeannette didn't give her a chance to make it. "I'll be able to take you there and introduce you round but I'm afraid I can't stay long. Felipe wants us to go to the football."

Pippa hastily recomposed her features and asked where the 'do' was to take place.

"In Santander, in the Bodegón."

"Santander?" Pippa imagined, momentarily, the Basque seaside town.

Jeannette smiled. "Calle Santander. The street, not the town. We always meet up there. It's by the Torre del Oro. The Bodegón's a great barn of a place, full of barrels and pillars. I'll show you anyway."

Pippa thanked her then she got up to leave. "I could do with a siesta," she said. "Then maybe I'll get some sunshine while it lasts."

Jeannette looked out and upward. "Well, don't leave it too long. They say it's going to rain later."

*

The rain slashed suddenly against the face of the sun and within a second or two had extinguished it entirely, before wrapping it, as an extra precaution, in an asbestos-grey blanket of cloud. Mop-headed palm trees quivered under the sudden attack. Harpoons of water punctured the soft surface of the Guadalquivir then instantly became one with it as the lightning does with earth.

Umbrellas flowered magically along the Avenida de la Constitución while the herds of shoppers who did not have them stampeded into the wide entrance of the main post office. Cornered now, they could only peer through the downpour at a truncated slab of cathedral, one palm-fringed corner of the Archive of the Indies and at the front door of the Oficina de Turismo from which Borja had chosen this precise moment to emerge.

He mouthed a swear-word to himself: it was not possible to see which one. Then it occurred to him that his umbrella, which he had not used or even seen in half a year, had as good a chance of being here where he worked as at home. So he went back in to look for it.

Ten years ago he would have simply closed his eyes and seen it – seen the umbrella exactly where it was at that moment – and known precisely where to find it. It was an unusual ability and Borja had been extremely proud of it, although secretive about it as well. But then, as suddenly as he had acquired it, he lost the knack in his late teens. Still, in the present instance it was not needed: within a couple of minutes the crowds marooned in the post-office entrance saw Borja re-stage his exit, this time plus umbrella. Then he disappeared from their sight into the Plaza San Francisco.

Secure under his umbrella, where he imagined himself as a bird sheltering under the great leaves of a dragon tree, he began to whistle a tune from Rigoletto. Crossing the Plaza on a diagonal, he set his course for home in the neighbouring Plaza del Salvador. All around him other umbrellas sheltered men in suits, women in smart skirts and vertiginously high heels, and a few small dogs on leads. And then something strange happened to Borja. Despite the security of his umbrella, despite his whistling and despite the fact that this, his journey home, was one of the best moments of his day, he was seized by an overwhelming consciousness of death. Death was all around him suddenly, integral with the scurrying crowds. It was not exactly a vision – a transfiguration of clothed humanity into putrefying flesh and whitening bone – it was more abstract than that: a feeling in what he would have called his heart that life was the illusion and that it was death that was real. Nobody else around him seemed to share the moment; everyone hurried on oblivious to the fact that they were merely the future's ghosts. 'The lilies of the field that bloom today and shall feed the furnaces tomorrow,' he thought. He made the sign of the cross under his umbrella with his free hand.

James recognised the umbrella from the window of the third-floor flat. It was not the colour, which was non-descript – umbrella-colour, that drew it to his attention, but the way it moved, bounding forward at twice the rate of any other and making a bee-line for him. Whatever intimations of mortality might be fermenting beneath it, James recognised from above the loveliest, liveliest, most life-affirming umbrella in the square, if not in all Seville.

A moment later and Borja stood in the room with him, shaking the dripping umbrella.

"That's very bad luck," said James.

"What?"

"You should fold it up as you come through the door and not open it again until you are in the street."

"But what happens to the water in that case?" Borja asked, shaking huge droplets over the television and bookshelves. He laid the half-furled accessory carefully on top of the fruit basket where it rested uneasily on the top of a mound of oranges and grapes, kissed James matter-of-factly on the cheek and sat himself tidily in one of the two cane armchairs.

"I've really no idea what happens to the water," said James, settling himself in the other armchair. "I got hake again. OK?"

"Hake's fine," said Borja. "Before the Bodegón or after?"

"Oh, after."

"Well so long as we remember to eat it. You know what happened last time." Then he added: "I've just seen death again."

James drew in his breath. "Yours? Anyone in particular's? Or just death in general?"

"Not the full picture this time, just the general idea. Death in general. In the Plaza San Francisco."

"Remind me not to go there."

"Don't joke."

James smiled. "All right, I won't. But everyone has to die. It doesn't serve a lot of purpose to go thinking about it."

"I don't go thinking about it. I wish I never think about it. It's more like... death is thinking about me."

"So it's more as if you feel your ears burning." James hoped Borja would not find his tone too flippant. He crossed the floor to where Borja sat and cuddled him roughly like a dog.

Borja shook himself free. "Why do I have thoughts like this?"

"I don't know. But forget them. As quickly as you can. 'Cowards die many times before their deaths. The valiant taste of death but once.'"

"I'm not a coward."

"I know that," said James and was silent for a moment. Borja had left his family home to live with James. In Franco's Spain, even in its last days, that had not been the action of a coward.

James walked over to the window. "Apart from that, went the day well?"

This made Borja grin because he loved the game of inserting Shakespeare into ordinary conversation – even if he was not so adept at it as James was. "We had some problems with some Americans," he said. "They took all day complaining. They had booked a coach to Vejér but the coach broke down and couldn't take them."

"So what did you do?"

"Nothing. What could we do? There was no other coach. Nowhere else we could send them. They just hanged around the tourist office all day."

"Hung around."

"And complained."

"I'm not surprised they complained. Surely you could have done something?"

"No," said Borja quite firmly and changed the subject. "There were some Swedishers. Very tall, very blond, with back-packs. You would have liked them. They spoke a very good English."

"It's actually Swedes," James pointed out, a little apologetically. Borja's English was so superior to James' Spanish that pots and kettles always came to his mind when he corrected it. Yet Borja liked to be corrected, insisted on it even, while James preferred Borja to correct him only when absolutely essential, in order to avoid too much damage to his self-esteem.

"I thought swedes was something you ate."

"It is too, but don't worry about it. Swedes can be either people or turnips."

"These were definitely people."

"I'm glad to hear it," said James.

"And how was it with thee?" Borja asked.

"Friday bliss. There's a new teacher starting Monday."

"Boy or girl?"

"Girl. So you needn't worry. I haven't met her yet anyway. Nothing else much. Oh yes. Señor Ybarra wants me to do some work for him. Privately."

"Teaching?"

"No. I don't know what it is. Some sort of translating, I suppose. I may have to go to Jerez on a couple of Saturdays."

"All the way to Jerez for translating? Ybarra's crazy. You can do it here."

"Well, I don't know. I only guessed it was translating. It might be confidential documents that can't leave the office for all I know. Or interpreting. You know, simultaneous translation."

Borja spluttered a laugh. "You? I'd like to see you try!"

James smiled. "All right. Well I don't know what he wants."

"I do. Ybarra is maricón."

"He isn't."

"He isn't married."

"What does that mean? Loads of people aren't married. They aren't all maricón."

"Ybarra is."

"You've hardly met him," said James. "You can't possibly know."

"Each year at your staff-student party he makes straight for me. He guesses exactly who I am. He tries to chat me up."

"Start to worry when middle-aged men don't chat you up." James was six months older than Borja. Sometimes it showed.

"Be careful of him anyway," said Borja. "I know that kind of man."

"Yes: Spanish," taunted James.

Borja dived at him. James caught him by the wrists then folded him in a hug and their shared laughter was stifled in a confusion of clothes and hair.

\*

"Ignacio doesn't pay us until nearly midnight," Jeannette explained as they walked together towards Calle Santander. "So on the last day of the month it's a tradition to get together in the Bodegón. Everyone eats and drinks something then goes round the block to get paid and returns to the Bodegón to settle up."

"Why does Ignacio pay everyone so late?"

"Partly it's the Latin habit of leaving everything to the last possible moment. Partly it's his preoccupation with the school's cash-flow. The longer the money stays in his hands the better as far as he's concerned."

"But he must get the cash from the bank during the afternoon," Pippa objected. "The last few hours can't possibly make any difference to the interest."

"Don't forget that the Spanish afternoon doesn't begin till the English one is as good as over," said Jeannette. "But I see your point. Maybe it just makes him feel better."

"Or else he's got shares in the Bodegón."

They arrived at large wood and glass doors and pushed hard. Pippa found herself in a vaulted cavern of an interior in which a sea of tables, about half of them occupied, stretched away into the distance. To their right a wooden counter that seemed as long as a station platform led the eye to a far-off kitchen. Signed photographs of bull-fighters in action adorned the walls and pillars; a bull's mounted head glowered down from over an archway. Above their heads a multitude of smoke-dark hams hung from black beams like a colony of giant bats. White-aproned, silver-haired waiters stood behind the counter and watched impassively as they approached. Jeannette ordered herself a coffee and Pippa, although she would have preferred some-thing stronger, followed suit. The waiter, still impassive, took a stick of chalk from behind his ear and wrote the price on the counter in front of them, then mechanically replaced the chalk and shambled away.

"Hallo," said a voice at Pippa's elbow, "I'm Sarah."

"Hallo," said another, "I'm Dave."

At first Pippa supposed that the swarm of new colleagues homing in on them were just anxious to exchange news with Jeannette. But soon she realised that it was she, Pippa, who was the centre of attention. She was the news and the small expatriate community into which she had been thrust was hungry for her. They wanted to know everything she could tell them about England – shows, fashions, politics – and were as avid for the latest gossip as Sophie apparently was for Bisto and Bird's Custard.

Pippa was astute enough to realise that this interest in her would not last long – would probably not outlive the night – and determined to make the most of the discovery that here, now, amidst palms and Moorish palaces, in a land of djinns and caliphs, it was she, the visitor from banal and chilly England, who wore a whiff of the exotic.

Her coffee was soon followed by a tumbler of red wine and soon after that her new acquaintances were pulling tables together and settling into convivial eating mode. Pippa had her first encounter with tapas and raciónes: portions of olives, fried anchovies, squid in batter, kidneys and kebabs that were handed up and down the tables and dipped into by everyone with fingers, forks and egg-sized loaves of bread. Earthenware jugs of wine were circulating. Pippa never saw them refilled and yet they never seemed to empty.

Looking around the group she calculated quickly that three-quarters of her new colleagues were female, an imbalance that served to focus her attention more urgently on the men. The most attractive male on the scene was bright-eyed and Spanish and would have been well worth getting to know, she thought, but for the fact that he was clearly spoken for by the bubbly-blonde haired girl who sat next to him. Second best was a tall fair-haired man in a check shirt. He had only just arrived and Pippa was beginning to think that he looked vaguely familiar, when he was joined by another new arrival. Then she recognised them as the pair she had seen from the taxi last night.

*Anthony McDonald*

She turned to Jeannette. "Who are those two?"

Only it wasn't Jeannette next to her. Her place had just that minute been taken by a man. She must have seen him earlier but he had somehow escaped her serious scrutiny. "Which two?" he said. His voice was soft and his accent American.

"Oh, it doesn't matter. I thought you were Jeannette. Sorry."

"Don't be. I think you're Pippa. Right? My name's Mark." He smiled, displaying neat white teeth with a gap between the two front ones. "But back to your question. You want the low-down on the guys round here. Right? Now which two did you have in mind?"

Pippa saw that there was no point in pretending and so she said boldly: "The tall one with curls and the El Greco character."

"Their names are James and Borja."

"Borrkha?"

"That's how it sounds, only its written with a 'j'. Can you figure out which one of them is English?"

"I could make an intelligent guess."

"James is a colleague of yours – least he will be on Monday – and his friend works in the tourist office. Good guys."

The penny dropped with a dull clink of disappointment. "Are they..." Pippa hesitated, unwilling to make a choice of word.

"Another intelligent guess. They're a couple, yes. Er... That a disappointment to you?"

"Could be." Then, because the wine was giving her confidence, she added: "Is it a disappointment to you?"

"No," he said without hesitation. "A lot of my friends are gay but I'm not."

"Well, that's... ahem." Pippa managed just in time to turn a too-revealing expression of satisfaction into a cough and then adjusted the conversation's heading by a degree or two. "You said James was a colleague of mine rather than one of yours. Does that mean you're not one of my colleagues?"

"Well I am. And then again I'm not."

Pippa paused before replying. Mark was clearly someone you chose your words carefully for. This might become a source of irritation in time. But then she noticed that his nose was small and up-turned and sprinkled rather winsomely with neat freckles. "Will you be my colleague on Monday, for example?"

"No." Mark's eyelashes flickered across his eyes as he spoke. The lashes were long and dark. Pippa thought they were the longest she had seen on a man.

"On Tuesday or Wednesday?"

"Tuesday no, Wednesday yes."

"Would I be right in thinking you teach part-time, then?"

"You would."

"And would it be indiscreet to ask what you do with the other part?"

"It would not." Mark's eyes opened very wide for a moment. They were large, dark green, flecked with gold. Pippa could not think why she had not noticed them before.

"Then what do you do?"

"You'll laugh."

"I won't."

"Promise you won't?"

"I promise."

"Cross your heart and hope to die?"

Pippa obliged.

"All right then. I'm a poet."

"A port? A porter?"

"A poet. P.O.E.T. I write poems."

Pippa laughed.

"You laughed," said Mark.

"I didn't," said Pippa. "I mean I didn't laugh at your profession. I laughed at my mistake: hearing port for poet."

"You're forgiven," said Mark. "For being English."

"You being...?"

13

Mark smiled. "I won't subject you to any more guessing games. I'm American-born, with an American father. But my mother was Spanish."

Pippa registered the 'was' but let it go for the moment.

"So," said Mark, "Seville's all new to you."

"Yes. Jeannette's promised to show me the sights over the weekend." She managed to shade her tone just enough to give Mark a little encouragement.

"Is that how you'd really like to discover Seville?"

"Well..."

"What about telling Jeannette you have a subsequent engagement?" Mark did not wait for an answer. "You are gonna love this place, I know it. The Alcázar, the gardens, the Giralda... Did you know you can climb the tower on horseback? Right to the top?"

At that moment James arrived next to them and, having introduced himself to Pippa, said to Mark: "I'm wondering if you can do me a favour. A bit of work's come my way: some translating for Paco Ybarra in Jerez. Good money. For some reason Borja doesn't want me to do it – I don't understand why. Do you think you could take it on? It's just for a couple of Saturdays."

"Sure," said Mark. "Hey, it's time we went and got paid." For some time now people had been leaving in ones and twos to return a few minutes later clutching small square manilla envelopes. "You can tell me about it as we walk." He stood up. "Hey, Borja," he called, and beckoned him over. "Sit here. Meet Pippa and keep her company." He turned back to her. "We'll only be a minute." Then he muttered something in rapid Spanish to Borja which Pippa thought she understood as: "Don't let her leave before I'm back." Then he was gone.

"Tell me, Pippa," said Borja, running soulful eyes over her face like gentle fingers, "where are you from?"

"How well do you know England?"

"I haven't been there. At least, not yet."

"Well, I come from a place called New Maldon." It always embarrassed Pippa to say this. It seemed even worse now, here in Seville.

"It's really a suburb of London but London's so big that it feels a long way from the centre. And you. From here?"

Borja shook his head and smiled. "No. From far away. Near Salamanca in the north."

"What brought you all the way to Seville?"

"That's a long story. Perhaps I'll tell you when I know you better."

"Perhaps I can guess though."

"Perhaps you can guess, yes – in part." He let the afterthought dangle teasingly for a moment and then changed the subject. "What books do you like? Which authors?"

"English ones?"

"Any ones."

"It's difficult to say. I have to read so much for my studies in Spanish and French. Lorca, Machado, Victor Hugo... It's all a bit of a whirl at the moment."

"Yes, but who do you like, I mean really like?"

"All of them. Though I also admit to liking Raymond Chandler."

Borja did not know Raymond Chandler. "For my part I like especially Virginia Woolf."

Pippa felt herself outgunned and changed the subject. "Did you find the missing window?"

Borja looked at her incredulously. "You mean you're looking for it too?"

This in turn startled Pippa. "No, no," she said. "I'm not looking for a window. I thought you might be, that's all."

"Me! Looking for a window? All this is crazy."

Pippa tried to stabilise the conversation. "I think you may have misunderstood. Or else I did. It's just that I saw you in the street yesterday evening, not knowing who you were, and I thought I heard James say something to you about a lost window. I didn't mean to eavesdrop. I'm sorry..."

"I see," said Borja. "You make sense now. But you know, it was an odd thing. Very strange."

"Then tell me."

"Yesterday evening I was home from work before James. An old woman rang the bell. She demanded to see the window in the room at the front because hers was stolen or something and she thought I might have it. I can not think why. She said she was looking in other apartments too. She started to examine the woodwork and the metal..."

At that point James and Mark returned with their pay-packets. Pippa insisted Borja be allowed to finish the story.

"In the end she seemed satisfied it was not hers. I did explain I knew the window was there for three years certainly and it looked like it was there many years before also. So she went to check in some other flat."

"But what about her window?" Pippa wanted to know. "Did she have a great gaping hole in the wall or what?"

"She didn't say." Borja shrugged.

"And he didn't ask," put in James. He tweaked Borja's shoulder playfully. "Couldn't you just kill him sometimes?"

"That's a great story," Mark said. "It's maybe better not to know if the lady had a hole in her wall. Better just to imagine."

Borja was beginning to make going home signs to James. "He turns into a pumpkin at midnight," James explained.

"It's just that I have to work tomorrow," said Borja, slightly ruffled by James' teasing.

Pippa looked about her, wondering if this was the moment for her exit too, but Mark was quick to tell her that the night was young and to promise that he would see her safely home in due course. Did Pippa imagine it or did Borja give her an old-fashioned look as James and he left for home and their hake?

When the party finally did break up, Pippa was not permitted to pay for anything. She was the newcomer, the honoured guest. Another time, people said. A forest of chalk-marks and slips of paper were reckoned up and divided in a hit-and-miss attempt at fairness whose shortcomings, Pippa was happy to see, bothered no-one. Her friends at university, she thought, would have been recalculating the wine-bill till the place closed.

As they stepped out of the Bodegón into the warm night, Mark said to everyone, though for Pippa's sole benefit: "Stand still a moment and listen. Somewhere you'll hear a guitar. Always, in this city, a guitar is playing somewhere."

They stood. They listened. And then, just across the street, a shutter that had not been properly fastened slipped open. A stream of light bled out and on it rode – not the expected sound of a guitar – but the solemn cavalcade of chords that introduces the slow movement of Beethoven's Sonata Appassionata.

"My God," said Mark, "I never heard a piano playing here before. Least, not played like that."

Goodnights were said and people drifted off on their various roads home. Pippa and Mark walked together towards the river, and the ghostly variations on Beethoven's theme followed them a little way like a puckish will-o'-the-wisp.

## Two

It was probably the only Bechstein in Seville, Alexa thought. Almost certainly it was the only one of its type: a turn-of-the-century six-foot-niner, veneered in glowing rosewood with a French-polished finish that caused it to glow like a hologram. It had machine-turned legs, each with twelve facets that returned the sun's stare impudently like the faces of a cut gem. The music-desk was a fretted sunburst while the cheek-pieces scrolled as satisfyingly as a trill in Mozart. Only a black and sepia cigarette-burn on a corner of the lid testified to a working life of nearly a century.

But sunshine posed a problem for the Bechstein. A creature hatched in northern latitudes, it craved the shade of drawn shutters on sunny days. And, except for the last two days when the town had seemed to be in danger of being swept away by rain, sunny days had been the norm since Alexa's arrival. And she had gleaned from various sources that these would mount up to an impressive total in the course of a year.

She wanted that. Unlike her instrument she would have preferred to work with shutters and window-panes flung wide, letting the southern warmth soak its way into her muscles like a linament – for six hours a day of Beethoven was no five-finger exercise – and irradiate her playing with a new dispensation of light.

It was out of the question of course. Andalucíans shut their windows to keep cool as well as to preserve the colour of their furniture. Nobody else's shutters were thrown back even though the autumn was well advanced. And, the heat apart, there was the matter of noise... which in Alexa's case was a double problem. On the one hand the street outside was a perpetual cacaphony. There was traffic, there were pneumatic drills, there were radios tuned to a peacock's tail of stations that seemed to be competing in a stridency sweepstake, there were men who coughed like horses, and women whose voices seemed to have been developed for the role of Turandot, though without the qualities of beauty and refinement that would be thought necessary in an opera house. It was as if Spain abhorred the vacuum of silence and felt uneasy with the insipidity of a noise level that was merely moderate.

On the other hand, how would Alexa's neighbours have taken to the sound of the Bechstein? Would they have accepted the chime of its treble, the boom of its bass, harnessed up to Beethoven and Liszt, hours at a time every day, surging in through their windows from the narrow street? Alexa doubted this and so she had worked for the most part since her arrival in artificial light with the shutters pulled to.

Not so when she went for her lesson. (Consultation, Eulogio called it.) Eulogio's piano-room opened onto his own flower-filled inner patio; his villa stood in a smart suburb at a soundproof distance from his neighbours. It was very different from his teaching-room at the London College. But one thing had come with him. Alexa recognised the familiar framed print of a Hoffnung cartoon on the wall: the one in which the concert platform is transformed into the arena of a bull-ring; the grand piano, centre-stage and solitary, has become a fighting bull with lowered head; and the pianist making his lonely way towards it is a matador, his tail-coat a sequinned suit of lights. For Eulogio the cartoon was a metaphor both for his profession and for life itself.

Alexa played Beethoven at this first lesson in Spain: his fourth sonata. "Yes," said Eulogio, "it's very nice. But where are the guitars?"

"Which guitars?" Alexa asked.

"I'll show you," her teacher said. He sat down at his Steinway and played the soaring, vibrant, passage that climaxes the first movement. Alexa heard the guitars all right. "You're in Spain now," Eulogio said. "Profit. Go to the Barrio Santa Cruz. Sit. Wait. Then listen." He smiled through his monumental moustache; it parted and rode up like an opera curtain. "Learn."

Alexa got off the bus two stops before her own and made her way into Santa Cruz.

*

"If it's all the same to you," Pippa had said over unbuttered toast and honey earlier that Saturday, "I'd rather wander around on my own today."

Jeannette responded to this with a rather stony look though she said: "Sure. Go ahead if that's what you'd prefer. I just thought you might like to have someone with you who knew the city, that's all."

Which did make Pippa feel a little bad. Still, she told herself, it would have hurt Jeannette more had she explained that she had found a guide whose company appealed to her vastly more than her flatmate's. Jeannette reminded her that they were to dine with her cousin Sophie that evening. Pippa promised to be back in good time and stepped out into the sunshine.

She met Mark as they had arranged, by the bull-ring. He greeted her with a peck on the cheek. He had wished her goodnight with something similar outside her door the previous night. As they set off he recited the names of the streets they were going to explore: Lirio, Virgenes, Fabiola... There was a street whose name meant Snakes, another one meant Eagles, another was Air and there was one called Water.

They circumnavigated the cathedral. They had agreed to explore the interior another day. "It's not the place to start," said Mark. "You'll see." Flying buttresses beetled like crags overhead, changing perspective as they walked, while falcons wheeled and darted among gothic tracery. Then the clifflike walls changed their texture, were pierced by Moorish arches that opened into a grove of orange trees. Still their circuit continued until Pippa began to see the scale of the building as a metaphor for eternity itself.

Mark, reading her thoughts correctly, wrenched them away leftward, out of the giant building's gravitational pull and, passing through a keyhole archway, they found themselves in another, differently-scaled world. Monolithic, Christian Spain was behind them and all around were the human-size perspectives of the Moors.

They stood in the Patio de Banderas, more like a private garden than a public square. Orange trees in rows grew from its sandy floor. White and ochre houses stood little higher than the orange trees and over their miniature battlements peered feathery date-palms and the gilded weather-vane of the Giralda. To Pippa it seemed that the past two days had been just a prelude and that her real contact with Spain was going to date from now. Skirting the fountain that wept in the centre, they left the Patio through another archway that became a vault-roofed street and tunnelled its way, zig-zag, beneath the houses. 'Judería' proclaimed the ceramic street-sign: the medieval Jewish quarter. At last its twists and turns expelled them into the Barrio Santa Cruz and into a passage so narrow that an armchair would have blocked it: Agua, the street named water. They found a café where bougainvillea and jasmine had been encouraged to cross the street on a latticework of wires to give a canopy of shade and scent and installed themselves at one of the tables. Mark said: "Now tell me everything."

"Everything?" Pippa smiled but felt a certain alarm all the same. "About what?"

"Yourself of course."

"I'm not sure I'd want to tell you absolutely everything even if I knew it myself. Though of course it's nice to be asked. Would a few edited highlights do?"

"To be going on with," Mark answered and then, quickly establishing eye-contact with a passing waiter, ordered two manzanillas without asking Pippa whether that was what she wanted and called the waiter by name in order to impress her. And although Pippa was not especially impressed – because anybody could learn off the names of a few waiters – she was somehow stirred by the realisation that impress her was what he wanted to do. As a result she told him in the next few minutes rather more than she had been meaning to a moment before. It was not that her life had been eventful; it was the thought that counted.

"I have to do another year at Leicester after this," Pippa explained. "If you study languages you have to take your third year out and work in a foreign country before finishing your degree in the fourth year."

"Doesn't that mean that most of your friends will have graduated and left by the time you get back?"

"Some of them," said Pippa, "though the ones who're also doing languages will be in the same boat as me." Earlier she had dropped the name David into the conversation; she had not said whether he was reading languages or not. Mark would have to wait for another opportunity to find out. However Pippa fixed him with a mock-serious look at that moment and added: "But life's at least as much about making new friends as it is about keeping up with old ones, don't you agree?"

*

Later, in the afternoon, they returned to Santa Cruz; its labyrinth of alleys formed the heart of Seville after all. Pippa was in a daze: she thought she had never seen so much colour, so much beauty in all her life; had never felt before quite what she felt this afternoon. So, as she sat with Mark in a tiny shaded square, she was not especially pleased when a young woman leaned across from the next table where she had been sitting alone, nursing a glass of coffee, and said to her: "I couldn't help overhearing. I've also just arrived to work here for a year.

I'm sorry to butt in like this but in five days you're the first people I've heard talking English." The stranger had a pleasant face with determined features though attention was distracted from these by a mane of pre-Raphaelite hair that Pippa would have died for. "My name's Alexa," she said and added that she was alone in Seville except for a grand piano.

Mark said to her: "You live in Calle Santander, on the corner with Temprado."

Alexa was surprised but sounded pleased as well. "Have you heard the piano from the street?"

"Last night. We heard you playing. It sounded terrific. It was the slow movement from the Appassionata." Mark took a sip of manzanilla and then looked up to receive the smile that Alexa not unnaturally gave him for having both praised her playing and correctly identified the piece.

"So are we neighbours?" Alexa asked.

"We don't exactly live in Calle Santander," Pippa explained. (Mark made a note of the 'we'.) "But we work just round the corner. At least Mark does. I start on Monday."

"The Bodegón Torre del Oro. Know it?" said Mark. "That's our hangout. You'll have to come in and find us there some time... between the variations."

"Thank you," said Alexa.

Three teenage boys emerged from a narrow alley. They wore light grey denims like a uniform and each carried a six-stringed guitar. A little diffidently they shuffled into the Plaza, took up a position and began to play.

"Is that flamenco," Alexa asked, "or is flamenco something different? Doesn't someone have to sing and dance for it to be real flamenco?"

"I've always called it flamenco myself," said Mark, "though maybe there are more precise words. For the experts. I mean for people like you... I mean musicians." He tailed off.

"The reason I'm here this afternoon is because of my teacher. He's Spanish; he's just come back here from London to retire. He says I should listen to the local guitarists and get some of their southern-ness into my playing. He thinks my temperament is a bit northern. Though I can't help it if I like playing Beethoven."

"Being a north European didn't seem to do him any harm," said Mark helpfully.

"Vienna's hardly the north," said Pippa.

"He was born in Bonn," said Alexa, more brusquely than she meant to. She changed the subject back again. "I'd like to know what I'm listening to. I mean, if I'm going to listen to Spanish music I'd like to have some terms of reference – a framework."

"I can't help you there," said Mark. "But I know who can. A guy called Karsten Bäcker."

"He doesn't sound too Spanish."

"He's German. But he teaches the guitar. He also speaks English. I'll introduce you some time."

At that moment one of the three boys embarked on a song in a rough tenor voice, accompanying himself with only the occasional plucked chord and allowing the other two to extemporise more elaborate lines on their instruments. Two more songs followed. After that the singer stepped forward, turned his guitar upside down and handed it round the tables to do duty as a collection plate, his friends meanwhile strumming something noncommittal but encouraging. The captive audience paid up quite willingly: by the time he had finished collecting the cherry-coloured back of his guitar was quite hidden. Efficiently he slid the coins into a cloth bag and the trio obliged with an encore. Mark leaned over to Alexa. "Any problem identifying that one?" She laughed. It was 'Bridge Over Troubled Water'.

Pippa was not too pleased when Alexa invited them then and there to see her flat. Natural curiosity struggled with the desire not to be upstaged at this precise juncture. But Mark accepted with a casual 'why not?' and so Pippa allowed her curiosity to win.

The flat was comfortable and spacious with big windows that afforded an excellent view of the comings and goings at the Bodegón opposite. Alexa led them up to the roof-garden at the top of the building. "It's fantastically secluded," said Pippa.

"Yes," said Alexa. "You could sunbathe nude up here and nobody would know."

But the thing that most occupied the visitors' attention was the piano. "How on earth did you get it here?" Mark asked.

"It's quite a story," Alexa said. "I'll tell you."

Eulogio had had no idea if it would be possible to hire a Steinway in Seville. He had had his own Steinway in the villa for so long that he could not remember where it had come from let alone how it had got there. Alexa had made enquiries in Seville and so had her father but they had drawn a blank. Madrid had been more promising, except in the matter of cost. "Outrageous," said her father. "It would be cheaper to take your own Bechstein on the back of a lorry."

So that was what happened.

Colin and George had moved the piano once before, to a concert where Alexa had performed the Emperor Concerto with the local youth orchestra. What's more, they had returned it in one piece. The two young men operated a small haulage business with their father. They would happily take off into any part of Europe with one-way payloads and tout for a return freight when they got there. They were popular with clients because they were punctual, drove fast and were happy to operate in cash.

Still, taking a piano to southern Spain was a new experience even for them. A price was negotiated. Alexa's father volunteered to pay it. Alexa decided it would be diplomatic to chip in the money she had earmarked for the airfare and travel down with Colin and George in the van. This bothered her father a little at first. Apart from the obvious discomfort of the journey, it did seem a long time for his daughter to be cooped up in a van with two young men. He could not help noticing that Colin actually had a tattoo on each muscular forearm while George, though un-tattooed, was equally muscular and wore an earring. But at least they were brothers and their father knew Alexa's; it was a business trip, not a holiday; Alexa's travelling with them would shave a fair amount off the eventual bill; and they would be staying in decent accommodation on the way. Or so her father thought.

Colin explained the economics to Alexa. It did not make sense at the prices they charged, he said, to do other than drive non-stop to their destination, taking the wheel and sleeping, turn and turn about. Obviously Alexa did not have to drive but she would still have to take her turn with the sleeping space. This consisted of a wide plank behind the front, and only, row of seats. Two people could sit upright next to the driver or one could curl up there in a ball while the other stretched out behind on the plank, depending whether it was day or night.

At least, Alexa had thought, trying to make the best out of the realisation that comfort and undressing were out of the question, only one full night was involved – they started out well before daybreak – and the tight schedule would leave little room for rape.

Once they were under way it was the piano that occupied her mind. It lay on its side in the back of the lorry, bound and tethered like a powerful animal under sedation. Though invisible it was at times all too audible. Alarming creaks and bangs came from it on the road to Newhaven and occasionally it heaved a little musical sigh as if unearthly fingers were dabbling among its strings. It was a relief, once they had arrived, to get up on the deck of the ferry and to hear the sound of gulls and sea, wind and rigging – things for which she was not responsible – rather than to have to listen to the cries of her suffering instrument below.

It was George's turn to sleep through the first chunk of France. He was going to take the wheel around midnight. So Alexa sat next to Colin, making a little conversation though not much, while Colin played a tape – some rock music which she did not recognise – at full volume. Alexa watched the road – Rouen, Evreux, Chartres – and then they stopped for supper near Tours: steak, chips and red wine, dirt-cheap, in a Relais-Routier. They stopped again an hour later in the middle of nowhere. A puncture.

It was on the offside and as Colin worked the jack the van began to tilt alarmingly: the camber of the road being very steep already. The piano stirred and sighed in the depths of the van. What happened next got edited out of the story when Alexa told it to Pippa and Mark. "You're quite sure it won't topple over?" Alexa had asked. Something on the faces of the two men – they had exchanged glances before replying to her question – suggested that they wished the question unasked. Nevertheless, George answered. He put both arms around Alexa and breathed a distillation of vin de table into her face, brushing her cheek with his lips so that it was through an unwished-for kiss that he whispered: "No worry, girl. You just don't worry about a thing."

Alexa had felt her body go rigid involuntarily and George must have sensed this because he withdrew his arms and breath, although a little reluctantly. A few minutes later they were on the road again, heading south. Alexa was now quite ready to sleep but it was with some apprehension that she lay down on the plank behind the driving-seat.

At four o'clock in the morning she changed places with Colin to allow him a chance to stretch full-length himself, so that she now found herself sitting upright in the darkness next to George: the one who had tried to kiss her a few hours before. This darkness seemed deeper than any she had known before and Colin's snores, coming from just behind her, only served to heighten the impression. There was no cassette, no conversation; even the Bechstein seemed, mercifully, to have gone to sleep. Only the lorry's engine fought against the silence. Only its headlights, peering now left, now right, sweeping the night, struggled with the darkness. Up, up they climbed among the Pyrenees. You could not see the mountains in the dark but you certainly knew they were there. The engine groaned, the gear-changes grated and the whole lorry shook with the strain of the ascent. Now the headlights seemed lost and afraid; there seemed a desperation in their sweeping gestures: their beam the white stick of a blind person in an unfamiliar part of darkness.

Alexa, cold now and feeling very much alone, began to ask herself why she had ever thought to come here to this inhospitable place. Why Spain, when she did not speak the language? Why so much expense? Why so much energy? Why play the piano at all when so many other people – too, too many – played it better? Questions crowded in on her as George put the shuddering lorry into bottom gear. "Runceval," he said. The name meant: valley of the thorns.

Then George took the gear-lever again and changed up. Into second. Into third. Alexa felt a wave of tiredness suddenly. It was as if she had never felt more tired in her life. Then George nudged the gear-lever into fourth and the whole world tilted forwards, shifted downhill, slid into the future.

At that moment something began to happen to George. He began to take shape, though not all at once. It started with his left cheek which, second by second, discovered contours: ridges, crevasses. His earring came into focus: cold and white at first then suddenly gold. His hair, curly like Cherubino's, took on the bright brown of hazel bushes in spring, lit by an advance party of rays from the morning sun. And just for a moment Alexa had felt that George, earringed, rugged, unwashed beside her, his hands on the wheel and his eyes on the road that was now falling precipitously away before them, was infinitely more lovely than the Bechstein in the back of the lorry, lovelier than Bach, Scarlatti, Brahms and Mozart, brighter than her future career, more golden than her art.

To her confusion her inward thoughts found an unlooked-for public expression in a noisy flood of tears. She tried to choke them back but could not. She spluttered and gasped and the drops ran down her cheeks so fast that they formed a stream. What would George think? Say? Do?

George did not take his eyes off the road. Not even to glance in her direction. But he did speak. "Don't worry about anything," he said. "It's all going to work out great. Everything's going to go fine."

The tears continued to run down Alexa's cheeks, but quietly now, as she thought that, just occasionally, men could behave better than you ever dreamed possible and the lorry continued, but quietly now, its descent from the Pyrenean passes while in front the light of a Spanish dawn, Alexa's first, rolled like a wave of gold across the vast plain. George flicked a tape into the cassette-player and together – George and Alexa, the sleeping Colin and the bound and gagged Bechstein in the back – they had made their triumphal entry into Spain.

Telling the tale to Pippa and Mark, Alexa excised the emotional outburst as well as the kiss. "It was a special moment though," she finished. "Seeing Spain first at first light." Mark nodded his approval.

Pippa looked at her watch and announced that they must go: she had a dinner invitation. And Mark, though he had no dinner invitation himself, obediently stood up to leave with her. He would not forget, he told Alexa, his promise to introduce her to Karsten.

\*

There was some stiffness in Jeannette's manner and a little awkwardness in Pippa's when they set out together for Sophie's apartment. Pippa had actually caught sight of Jeannette at one point during the afternoon as she and Mark were turning a street corner. She was fairly certain that Jeannette had not seen them, but not quite. It annoyed her to think that you told a white lie purely in order to spare someone's feelings and then saddled yourself with the trappings of guilt and concealment. She had not mentioned any of this to Mark.

Sophie lived in a modern apartment block a manageable walk from the city centre. There was even a lift. Sophie, who greeted them with a flurry of hugs and kisses, managed somehow to be both small and matronly. She wore a knitted white shawl over a shiny mauve dress, had her froth of honey-blonde hair whipped up on the top of her head like meringue and sported a pair of hoop-earrings big enough to go over a curtain-pole. The overall impression – the product of twenty years cultivating an image more Spanish than the Spanish – was memorable. She was delighted that Pippa had remembered the Bisto and the custard powder.

Sophie's living-room, smartly furnished though it was – in contrast to the one Pippa shared with Jeannette, struck Pippa as spartan. All her life she had lived with carpets and deep-upholstered sofas, with curtains and pelmets: the English sitting-room as a cosy padded cell. Spain offered nothing of this. Two or three plain mats, only, relieved the uniformity of the pearly tiled floor. Three abstract paintings blazed primary colours from the walls. The room was made for hot weather, not cold. Above all, Pippa thought, it lacked... clutter. Her mind went back to other rooms she had seen that day: the jewel-like apartments Mark had shown her in the Casa Pilatos, palace rooms that sparkled with blue tiles in the gold half-light...

"Have a drink, dear," Sophie was saying. She held out a small glass of purplish liquor. It exactly matched her dress, Pippa noticed. She tasted it. It was aniseed, plummy...

"It's called Pacharan," said Sophie. "Now tell me: what do you make of Spain?"

Pippa stared at her for a moment open-mouthed, as if suspecting either a trap or a hidden profundity in the trite question.

"Difficult to answer," said Sophie. "I know, dear. I understand completely. Meeting Spain is like meeting a new lover."

"It's wonderful," Pippa blurted.

Sophie asked her about her journey from England. Her what? Her flight, just two days ago. Yes, of course. Pippa had almost forgotten it. They had had to change planes at Valencia.

"You usually do. You must have had marvellous views."

Pippa tried to remember. "Not really. It was a very rainy day, I think. Oh, but we had a glimpse of Hampton Court – as we were climbing up from Heathrow, I mean."

Jeannette looked a little disappointed at this, having probably expected the Pyrenees or a first sight of the Mediterranean. She asked Pippa how she had spent her day. Pippa gave a stumbling account. She thought it as well to mention that she had bumped into a colleague-to-be (called Mark if she remembered rightly) and seen some of the sights with him though she avoided catching Jeannette's eye while saying this. But, trying to describe the places she had seen, she found herself failing to bring them to life. All she could see were the glimmering lights in the chambers of the Casa Pilatos and the twisting stairway where she and Mark had kissed for the first time in the half-darkness before emerging onto the sunlit gallery and into an explosion of scent and colour.

Throughout the meal Pippa's mood fluctuated wildly. One moment she would be burbling with incoherent enthusiasm about the wonders of Spain and all things Spanish, the next sunk in a mire of introspection in which she had difficulty keeping up with the conversation or even hearing the questions put to her.

"Of course," said Sophie at one point, "Seville is not just a place for falling in love with Spain. It's for falling in love with people too. That above all." Pippa jumped slightly and hoped the others didn't see.

But Sophie turned to Jeannette. "Isn't that right?"

Jeannette did not rise to this. "Sophie must speak for herself," she said to Pippa. "It wasn't me, after all, who ran away from their parents during a family holiday to marry a waiter."

Sophie laughed. "You know very well Pablo's parents owned the hotel. He wasn't just a waiter."

Pippa, whose jaw had dropped open at this revelation, now recovered her powers of speech – up to a point. "I'd no idea," she said.

"Sophie could write a book," said Jeannette.

"But has no intention of doing so," Sophie said firmly.

"The family never said anything about a waiter," said Pippa.

"Families never do," said Sophie. "Now coffee." She got up to make it but had not meant to change the subject entirely. "I'm not unique, you know. Far from it." She looked at Jeannette meaningfully.

Jeannette looked uncomfortable. "Now then," she said, "we're not going to discuss me and Felipe."

"No," said Sophie, "but I did introduce you and I know what's what. I only mean," she turned back to Pippa, "Seville is like that."

"Well, it did seem to have an effect on Borja and James," said Jeannette, seizing the opportunity to turn the spotlight away from her own relationship. "Three years they've been together, against all the odds. And here they are, still absurdly happy."

Sophie shook her head. "You've chosen a risky example to back up my point," she said. "I could have pointed to a hundred better ones. But that's a dodgy example." She liked the word. "Decidedly dodgy."

"Why?" asked Pippa.

"Because they're men, quite simply. Oh I know they're charming boys but..."

"But what?"

"One day you'll both learn what a full-time job it is to keep a man settled. It's a woman's nature to settle, to keep. It's a man's nature to pull apart and fly away. We're like the two different ends of a magnet. But it's the woman's job to win. She's got to."

"I don't think relationships should be like that," objected Pippa. "At least, not modern ones."

"Don't you, my dear? You will," said Sophie matter-of-factly. "Two men together don't stand a chance. How can they? When both are set up by nature to... pull apart."

"To be promiscuous, you mean," said Jeannette.

Sophie smiled. "I wasn't going to put it quite like that. I wish them well, of course I do. But I'm not very optimistic. Sorry, but I've lived just a little too long. Now to happier things. Who are we going to fix Pippa up with? What about that lovely boy from Germany who plays the guitar?"

Pippa grimaced. Jeannette said: "Sophie, you're impossible."

Sophie ignored them. "Of course he is a bit of an artist. Pippa might be looking for something more solid. Or even," she looked mischievously at Pippa, "she might have found it already. Now let's see if that coffee's ready."

# Three

Borja left work the following Monday an hour before James. They were going to meet in the Casa Morales but in the meantime there was a slice of early evening to enjoy. Although plenty of sunshine had come flooding through the windows of the tourist office during the course of the day, Borja had been missing the fresh air that had stayed firmly on the other side of the glass. Now as dusk fell he walked down Santander towards the river. Early joggers loped past in the cooling air under the palm trees. Mostly they wore shiny jockey-shorts – red, green or blue – that gave their firm buttocks the appearance of Christmas-wrapped gifts. At least it seemed so to Borja. As they passed to and fro, not too fast, they shot each other little glances – sometimes of recognition, sometimes admiring, sometimes competitive. Theirs was a relatively new pastime here – an all-male, all-jogging variant on the traditional evening paseo that took place just two metres away, parallel, nearer the river, and like the more traditional promenade it had its rituals. Like the paseo its element of healthy excercise was incidental to its real purpose which was to parade, to see, to be seen.

Borja had no illusions about the parade passing before him. Though the joggers were as eager for each other's admiring looks as they were for those of the girls who stood in groups of three or four, pretending to be interested only in their own conversations, none of them was gay. That was one difference between Borja and them. But there were others.

For one, Borja was wearing a suit. It was the only one he had and he lavished much attention on it with brush and iron. Indeed, even on the occasional days when he did not retire to bed sober, he would take care to put it on a hanger to prevent its disciplined creases from forming a breakaway set on their own. And even if – which did happen sometimes – he awoke with a hangover he would check the creases carefully in the morning just in case his judgement had let him down the night before. And although James told Borja often enough that he looked really nice in shorts (here Borja privately agreed) he was disinclined to compete with the jogging boys. Instead he kept his modest musculature firm and well-defined by doing press-ups and sit-ups when nobody was looking, though he would never have dreamed of admitting this; he detested any kind of hearty, communal athletic show. So there was something almost defiant in the way he strode, besuited, through the ranks of sport-attired joggers.

And then Borja was not a native. Not a real Sevillano, not an Andaluz. Many of the joggers had been at school together, or at university; they had a past in common that he did not share. Few of them even knew him by sight; his work brought him into contact with tourists rather than locals. He had told Pippa that he came from Salamanca in Castille. In fact he he had grown up a few miles outside the city on his parents' hill-farm. He had been a solitary child. Despite having a number of brothers and sisters, he preferred to play imagination games by himself or to write, and draw fantastic shapes and pictures, in the dust. Later, because he was a bright boy, he had gone to university in Salamanca but had then departed for the south when it finally became clear to him that there were two kinds of people in the world and that his family and almost everyone else belonged to one kind and he to the other.

Writing in the dust. Jesus had written in the dust when men lined up to stone the woman caught in adultery; when they saw what he had written they dropped their stones and went shamefaced away.

When Borja had followed his master's example the effects were even more dramatic. At the age of twelve, in a moment of religious fervour, he had taken a stick and written in the dust of the village square the names of six members of the village council who were having extra-marital affairs at the time. He had added the word 'adulterers', which he had just learned, as a caption at the top of the list. There was nothing revelatory about this. Everyone knew. It was the fact of its being written down that caused the frisson. Borja was quite surprised by all the fuss. He had not acted out of malice. It was simply – as he explained to his parents, the priest and the mayor – what God had told him to do. They all told him that he was a good boy and one whom God must love very much but, even at that age, he detected a certain unease behind their assurances.

One year later God told him to write quite a long list of the injustices inflicted on his fellow men by the Caudillo, Generalísimo Francisco Franco. This command came one market day in Salamanca while his father was negotiating the sale of some ewes. Here the writing on the wall caused even more consternation than before and the whole family had to spend the rest of the day at the police station. It took the bishop to sort things out this time. Fortunately he was something of a family friend; Borja's parents had more or less ear-marked him for a career in the church and vocations were already in short supply, even in rural Castille. The bishop managed to explain that God's message had become a little scrambled in transmission, though through no deliberate fault of Borja's. But it was generally regretted that Borja had graduated from sticks in the dust to the cans of anti-rust spray paint that his father used on the tractors. It took a lot of scrubbing to erase the message and, even after it had ceased to be recognisable as words, traces of Borja's work, in the form of brown blobs and streaks, survived long enough to outlast the dictator himself.

To the relief of his parents and the establishment in general, God lost interest in Borja as a channel of communication when he reached fourteen. But Borja was not to be left alone entirely. From this time on he began to be shown, on an almost daily basis, a vision of how the people he rubbed shoulders with would look a few decades after their deaths. In time he got used to this though the first time it happened – when his mother was putting a dish of baked meat on the table – and the second – when the priest was just about to give him communion – it precipitated a fit of hysterics that Borja found difficult to explain. Although Borja learned to deal with the fits as he grew older, his parents did not. They were relieved when he went away to study in the city and not too sorry, though they would never have admitted this, when he left home altogether.

Eventually the fits had stopped. But the visions of death continued, though they became less frequent as the years passed. And now, even as he looked admiringly at the young men jogging along the riverfront under the palm trees, they lost their tanned skins, their smiles and their taut muscles, and Borja saw them clearly in the lamplight just as they would be in fifty years from then, shrunk to dry meat and bone and clad in rags: the future's skeletons, tomorrow's dead. Borja turned from them a little sadly and comforted himself with the weedy smell of plumbago flowers that shared their beds along the paseo with spiky oleanders and red-hot pokers, glowing dully now in the artificial light. He found himself at a pedestrian crossing, one which cut across eight lanes of traffic without the security of a halfway island, and hearing the eight queues of vehicles revving their engines in anticipation of the changing lights, sprinted suddenly across the road with a speed and energy that would have surprised the now skeletal joggers that he had left behind.

Borja made his way up Calle Dos de Mayo, away from the river. There was still some time before James would arrive at the Casa Morales and Borja hesitated at the next crossroads as he weighed the rival merits of a stop-off at the Bar del Arco, where peanuts in their shells were served along with the orange wine that was the house's speciality, and the chapel of the Charity Hospital. Borja was not a great drinker by inclination though he found that, living with James, he drank considerably more than he would have done otherwise. He suspected that James, on the other hand, might have been a much heavier drinker were he not living with Borja. He made for the chapel.

The Charity Hospital had been built by one Don Miguel Manara, an eighteenth-century playboy and philanderer whose life had suddenly changed direction when he was brought up short in the streets of Seville by the sight of his own funeral procession passing by, all in black. Understandably Borja thought of Don Miguel as something of a kindred spirit.

He bowed his head as he entered the chapel. He knew its contents by heart. The six Murillos that hung upon its sombre walls were like old friends and as he walked round, not too fast, not too slow, he stopped a moment in front of each to pay his respects. Finally he halted before the Triumph of Death paintings by Valdés Leal. Here stood Death himself in a black cowl through whose sleeves protruded skeleton hands, an hourglass in one, a scythe in the other. Nearby a scroll of parchment bore the stark and sober caption: 'In Ictu Oculi', in the blink of an eye. For some minutes Borja stood contemplating his last end while, from Leal's dark canvas, Death stared unflinchingly back.

An oldish woman in black shuffled up to him. "Are you a priest, young man?" she asked in a throaty Andalucian accent. He shook his head, willing her away from this private moment, out of his personal space. "Too young, perhaps," she qualified. And then persisted. "But a student for the priesthood?"

"No," he said, politeness finally obliging him to speak.

Borja turned towards her, not unkindly. "Soy maricón," he enunciated in his best Castillian accent: I'm queer.

The old lady appeared horror-struck. Her features crumpled like a cellophane bag thrown on a fire. She shrivelled and stepped back. Borja immediately felt sorry for her and wished he had held his tongue. Silence was nearly always better than speech, he reflected. What deadly power a word could have. For his interlocutor, reduced to genuflecting and repeatedly crossing herself in the aisle, seemed shocked to death. In Ictu Oculi. Amen.

Borja left the chapel and cut through an alley into Calle Vinuesa, heading back towards the cathedral as far as the Casa Morales where he pushed open the ancient door and walked in. The bar was less sumptuous than the chapel he had just left but no less gloomy. It was divided into two sections: one for sitting down in, one for standing up. Neither was particularly comfortable. The sit-down section was furnished with decrepit canvas-backed folding chairs and some half-dozen earthenware wine-jars about fifteen feet tall. Three naked light-bulbs of assorted wattage dangled on an unlikely arrangement of wires from the darkness above. This evening Borja chose the stand-up section. He liked the feel of the sawdust underfoot and the company of sixty-year-old brandy advertisements and took pleasure in the smoked ochre paintwork and brass light-switches that might have dated from the same time.

He ordered a manzanilla. It arrived cool and cloudy from one of the amphorae in the other room, covered with a small saucer (a tapa) on which two olives nestled like pigeons' eggs. The barman knew him by sight and greeted him with a slight, silent bow. Borja placed his money on the counter; it had been landscaped like a butcher's block by the passage of countless coins. Behind the bar stood a gigantic cash-register that had been old when Franco came to power and next to it, on a high stool, sat the elderly proprietor of the establishment. He wore a Basque beret and fingerless gloves in readiness for the oncoming winter. He kept the till drawer open and in the long intervals between arrivals of staff with cash to put in it he kept himself entertained by emptying its compartments, stacking the coins in regimented piles, counting them, admiring their symmetry and returning them to their proper place. Borja was watching this entertainment for want of anything better to do when the door opened and James sailed in on a sudden blast of wind.

"Sorry I'm late. Manzanilla? – Dos mazanillas, por favor." He threw an arm around Borja's shoulder: loving, protective.

Borja squirmed at this intimacy and wriggled free from the arm, as James knew he would. Sometimes things were easier for James. As a real outsider, less was expected of him in the way of conformity to Spanish social mores. In addition, his ignorance of some nuances of Spanish language and behaviour allowed him to be unaffected by reactions in word or look that could be wounding to Borja. For Spain was the only home that Borja had; there was nowhere to go back to if he didn't like it. So he was punctillious in observing the requirements of Spanish society, one of which was was that you did not fondle your same-sex lover in a bar like Morales. At least, not unless you really looked forward to fist-fights in dark alleyways at times not of your choosing.

"Hola," he said. "What news from Gothenburg?"

"Wasn't it Wittenberg?" queried James. "Oh I don't know. There's good news and bad if you like. One, I can't get out of going to Jerez. There's this new thing in Mark's life – called a woman – and he's not prepared to sacrifice the smallest part of a Saturday just at this stage. On the other hand it looks like being only one Saturday so you needn't worry too much about my virtue."

"The new teacher, Peeper?" said Borja. "Yes, I thought that would happen. She seemed... how can I say... ready for something as soon as she arrived. And Mark for a long time has seemed... Do I make sense?"

"Couldn't have put it better myself. Mark seems completely besotted. She can't even walk to the book cupboard without him getting up to help her. They seem to have spent most of the weekend together. Apparently Pippa's a relative of that crazy Englishwoman, Sophie."

"Crazy? She seemed quite normal to me. For an Englishwoman."

"And she – Sophie that is – is all excited about the two of them. I ran into her in the street. She thinks it's the best news in Seville."

"All a bit quick, no? They only met on Friday."

"And since then they've met up with another Englishwoman. She's just arrived with a grand piano and installed it in a flat opposite the Bodegón."

"Now that is crazy," said Borja. "OK. And the result of all this is that you have to go to Jerez to see Ybarra after all."

"I really don't understand why the man's name gets you so spiky," said James. "He's a middle-aged, overweight businessman. There's no way I could possibly be interested in him."

"But he could be interested in you."

"Could be. Yes, could be. He could be interested in graphology or steam-engines. There's just as much evidence: none. And I actually don't care. If he *is* interested in me it makes no difference."

For a second the chink-chink of the bar-owner's coin-counting operation was the only sound to be heard.

"Anyway," James resumed, "this is what it's all about. I'm going to Jerez next Saturday – one day only, as I said – to look at some new publicity material for O'Donnell's sherry. It's in English and they want to get the views of an English person on it. You know: the style, the feel of it..."

"And you're supposed to be the best judge? O'Donnell's is full of English people."

"Yes. Aged fifty or more. But they want to target the younger British market. And that's where I come in."

"I still don't see why it has to be you. I mean, are you sure you're young enough? You're going to be twenty-five, remember." Borja laughed. "OK. I suppose I don't mind if you have a nice day out in Jerez. And if they pay you for it that's great. Even much better. But don't drink too much sherry. I would not like you to make a fool of yourself in front of Ybarra."

"Oh come off it. Look, why don't you come with me? We could make a day of it. Have an outing."

At that moment, the keeper of the cash-register climbed down from his perch and embarked on a tour of his domain. In contrast to most landlords who make this an indoor event, an opportunity to chat to the customers, this one emerged from behind his counter, picked his way among the amphorae and went out into the street. Then, walking round the outside of the building, he paused at each dusty window and peered in, cupping his hands between glass and temple in order to see more clearly.

"Have you seen him do that before?" James broke off to ask.

"Yes. So have you. Many times. You just never noticed."

"Well, it's a bit weird don't you think? Disconcerting for the customers."

Borja shrugged. The old man peered at them, gimlet-eyed.

"I mean," James went on, "it's as if you had a goldfish and it suddenly left its bowl to take a turn round the garden, peering in at you through the bay-windows."

Borja laughed out loud. "You're right. That's loverly." (Borja always pronounced that word as three syllables. James hoped he would never learn not to.) Then he recomposed his features into their more usual, serious expression. "A very English picture. I want to see English gardens one day. You know."

"Yes. I know. One day. Soon. When we've both got a bit more money. Meanwhile – next Saturday – Jerez. Are you on?"

"OK. I'll come. Just to keep you out of trouble."

"And Jerez is halfway to England, you know."

"So everybody says."

"Spain's still ten times better. But you'll see England one day. If only to discover how well-off you've been here."

The proprietor returned from his ramble and repositioned himself behind the cash-desk. He began slowly to count the copper coins.

\*

In the end Borja, was asked to work on Saturday and could not go to Jerez. James took the train alone. He liked train travel. He was just old enough to remember steam trains: the black, hissing dragons of childhood that had carried him on their backs to magic holiday kingdoms – Weston-super-Mare, Penzance – across landscapes filled with sparks and noise. And then, more recently, it had been on a train that he had had the greatest piece of luck of his life.

That train had been travelling from Salamanca to Madrid. It was crowded and hot. Mile after mile he had sat face to face, almost knee to knee, with the young man who had at first attracted him and then turned out to be Borja. The silent offer of a drink from a bottle of water – the most tentative of openings but James had made it – led to an exchange of smiles, then talk. They were both travelling in search of work: Borja going for an interview in Madrid, James going on to Andalucía to look for teaching work 'on spec'. He remembered having to explain to Borja what the expression meant. As they both had to spend a night in Madrid they decided to pool their resources and take a room in a hostel together. This experience was an exquisite torture for James. He found his companion so beautiful, soulful, poetic and yet...

In Britain James would have known exactly how to play it, what signs to look for, and these days you could actually ask someone straight out if they were gay without the atmosphere turning sour if the answer was no. But here James was out of his depth. He had no idea how you discovered whether a Spanish boy shared your sexuality or not and Borja, perhaps deliberately, gave him no clues. The night was tensely uneventful. But when they parted the next morning on the pavement outside the hostel, Borja, now dressed impeccably in suit and tie, shook his hand formally and said: "I think I am crazy. And you will think me crazy. Last night I wished to sleep with you. That's all now. Goodbye."

James had seized Borja's hand with both of his own. "That's not crazy. I wanted you too. What's crazy is that we didn't. Hell! Stay another night. We'll get this right..."

Borja had torn away, visibly distressed. "No, it's not right. Two men."

"It's right for me. I know that. I'm comfy with it." Even now, three years later, James felt his face go hot at his stumbling choice of words. Borja, not even speaking his mother tongue, had done better.

"But not right for me. Simple. 'Bye."

Somehow James saved it. "OK. I respect that. And always will. At least give me your address. I'll give you mine."

"But you have not one," said Borja, coolly logical. "And neither have I. We both begin new lives, remember."

"Give me your parents' address," James practically begged. "I'll give you the address of mine." With James hardly daring to believe it, Borja took out pen and paper and obliged. James followed suit. When Borja went James sat down involuntarily on the pavement – he caught his back jarringly against the wall as he did so – and cried.

The train to Jerez today was crowded too. But no future love of his life sat opposite. Instead, a large schoolgirl of about sixteen lay across two seats, talking over the seatback behind her to a friend who reclined in the same position, out of sight except for the head, which appeared in the gap between seatback and window, and the feet which stretched across the aisle. Two foreigners came through the carriage: a man and a woman, middle-aged, German possibly or British, carrying suitcases. The man asked with gestures if they could sit down. The two young people shook their heads and pointed towards the next carriage. Meekly the new arrivals left.

James spoke to the girl in Spanish. "There was room. Why did you do that?"

"They are just tourists," said the girl.

"Like you," added the face behind her. James could not tell if it was boy or girl.

"They pay the same price for their seats as you," said James.

"The price is easy for them. Not for us. You people are rich," said the girl. Then she rearranged her face as if for a kiss and aimed a large pink balloon of bubble-gum towards him to indicate that the conversation was closed. James looked at the woman next to him for support but she was asleep, or else pretending to be.

He turned his attention to the window and the landscape beyond it instead. Low hills of baked beige soil and olive scrub rolled past, empty except for the occasional hoopoe flashing between olive trees, a flying confection of pink and zebra stripes. At last the olives gave way to undulating seas of vines; the giant logos of the sherry houses crowned the hills – the Sandeman Don, the Osborne bull – and Jerez came in sight.

Despite its bacchic associations Jerez presented a distinctly sober face, James thought, to the arrival from Seville. Perhaps most places did. Even the palm trees had a tamer look than their counterparts in the larger city. James made his way across the central square to the premises of O'Donnell, first impressions of which were of a long wall stretching down a sidestreet and an alcoholic reek which grew in intensity as he approached – a little alarming to the stomach at ten o'clock in the morning. James passed through the entrance gateway and found his way to reception where he waited till Señor Ybarra arrived. When he did arrive he looked somewhat sheepish: an expression James had not seen him wear before. "Sorry to make you wait," he said and then suddenly thrust forward a mop-headed young man who had entered behind him. "This is William who has come to work with us. We begin (shall we begin?) with a tour of the bodega."

Ybarra led the two of them through long barns stacked rafter-high with time-blackened barrels. Doorways let the sun in from flower-filled courtyards. Men in white boiler-suits pumped wine from barrel to barrel through nozzled hoses like petrol-station attendants and, from time to time, tiny chocolate-coloured mice, high on sherry fumes, would sprint across their path from the shade of one stack of barrels to another. Ybarra meanwhile delivered an uninterruptible monologue on sherry production that went from bud-burst on the albariza hills to blending and shipping and the current state of the market. James was wondering who or what William might be but exchanged no words with him and studiously avoided eye-contact.

When the tour was finished Ybarra led the two of them up to his office. At least he called it an office. It looked more like a stationery cupboard. Anything in the way of filing seemed to have ceased for good with the death of Franco. But there was a fridge. Ybarra opened it, said "Please call me Paco", and lifted out a half-bottle of sherry after checking the time on his watch for form's sake. He ran two glasses to earth between two box-files on a high shelf but had to excuse himself and leave the room to look for a third.

Left alone together the two Englishmen could not remain silent. "Maybe I'm being obtuse," said William, "but I'm not at all sure what we're both supposed to be doing here."

"Neither am I – now. I was asked to come here – I thought – to look over some publicity material and check for mistakes in the English."

An expression of amazement settled on William's face. "You are here to check my English?"

"Hell, surely not. I mean, of course not. I was expecting something translated from Spanish."

"And I've just been employed here to write all the English copy myself. I started on Monday. Do you work for O'Donnell's too?"

"No, I don't. Ybarra – sorry, Paco – was a student of mine in Seville. Then out of the blue he asked me to come all the way over here to do this job... whatever it is, today."

"Paco your student? Of what?"

"Of English. I'm an English teacher."

"Then you're not a..."

Paco came back just then, carrying a glass in triumph. He sat James and William in two chairs side by side like an audience while he stood before them. "Of course you are getting to know each other. That is good. To have friends when you live in a strange country is very important. I worked in Argentina ten years ago and, far from home, my friends were very..." Vocabulary failed him at this point and he resorted to waving his hands about like someone splashing water into his face from a basin. "Well, so try this one. Fino: Solera 1868." He turned and poured from the half-bottle with great concentration.

"So you're not an advertising copywriter?" William asked James cautiously.

"No," said James. "Never have been."

"Thank God for that," said William under his breath. "Neither was I before Monday."

"Of course," said Paco, handing them a glass each, "not all of it is from 1868. It is simply that this blend was started in that year. Added to and taken from every year but the barrels never emptied. So in your glass is some wine, at least, from every year between then and now. From 1868 there would not be a spoonful, not even a drop, just a few molecules. But it is there. Salud."

"Salud," said James. "You make us feel very privileged."

"Salud," said William. "Hey, that's got something."

Paco sat down suddenly on the edge of his desk; there was only room for a couple of inches of him, it was so cluttered. He looked closely at the two young men opposite him. "I just realise something. You two boys look so much similar. You can be brothers."

"Could be." Without thinking, James corrected his former pupil. Then he turned, rather awkwardly, to face William. It was true that they were both tall, had blue eyes, fair curly hair and a tendency to sunburn. Apart from that though, James thought, they did not look that much alike. But the comparison unsettled him; it opened up the crucial question: which of us is the better-looking?

"So," said Paco to James. "Now you have met William. What do you think?"

Startled by the question and unsure what Paco meant, James felt himself redden. Paco went on: "Do you think he can do something for the image of sherry with the young British?"

James felt relief and almost laughed. At least he knew now what Paco was talking about. O'Donnell's must be desperate, he caught himself thinking. "Well... his English is certainly good enough," he answered, hoping that William would catch his tongue-in-cheek tone and that Paco would not. He then considered asking what he was actually supposed to be doing in Jerez today when there seemed no logical reason for him to be there at all, but quickly remembered that he was being paid to be there whether anything constructive was done

48

or not and so left the question unasked. William seemed equally tongue-tied.

"Interesting," said Paco musingly. "The names you have. William and James. Orangeman and Jacobite."

"You're very well informed about British history," said James.

"No I am not," said Paco. "I know only the history of my company. If you think for a moment you will remember that O'Donnell is not a typically Spanish name." Then he looked at his watch and at the half-bottle of Solera 1868. There appeared to be only enough for one glassful left. He was silent for a moment. There was clearly a decision to be made. "So," he said finally, "I have one or two small tasks to finish before we have lunch. Maybe if we say, you come back in half an hour?... No. You meet me in the square by the Alcázar. Then I take you to lunch. Good?" And James, with William, was ushered out into the sunshine.

"I'm baffled," said James to his new acquaintance. "Can you explain what's happening?"

"Probably not," said William.

"But what was I dragged all the way over from Seville for? Not just for a glass of sherry, surely? Isn't there supposed to be some business to discuss or something? Or will that be this afternoon?"

"I doubt it. Anyway, I thought you knew Paco. It's always like this."

"I only know him as a student, sitting in a classroom. I've never seen him at work before."

"Well, now you have. And I know I've only been here a week but I'd say this morning was fairly typical. It's been like that since I got here. There are meetings to arrange other meetings. But nothing happens. I write drafts of publicity material, type them out, give them to Paco and they disappear, never to be seen again or even referred to. He's chaotic. The whole place is. Probably when he asked you to come here today he'd forgotten I was coming to work here. Then when he realised, he felt he'd lose face if he un-invited you so you had to come anyway. Even if there was nothing to do."

"It's a possibility at least. It certainly sounds very Spanish. Well, given that it's so chaotic, how long do you think you'll last here?"

"Too early to say. On present form I'd say there were two possibilities: one, they'll get fed up with me after a couple of months and chuck me out or, two, I'll just become so much a part of the furniture during that time that no-one'll think of getting rid of me or even ask me what I'm supposed to be doing here for the rest of my life, assuming I want to stay that long."

A red admiral butterfly skimmed between them and settled on a palm-trunk.

"Could be a nice life," said James.

"Anyway, what brought you to Spain?" William asked.

James thought for a moment. "The pursuit of freedom?"

"Freedom from what?"

"You know, I never thought of freedom as being from something. It's not like an escape. I'm not escaping from anything."

"Aren't you?" said William. "I am."

"From what?"

"From everything: family, Britain, myself. Especially from the grown-up me. William as an adult. Huh. I'm twenty-three but I don't feel it. How old are you?"

"Twenty-four."

"Ancient."

James aimed a mock punch at William's stomach. "How's your Spanish?"

"So-so."

"It'll soon improve. Three months is all it'll take. You'll soon get to know people."

"Yes, but at first it's a bit..." William stopped and peered sideways, cautiously, into James' eyes.

"Yeah, I know," said James, meeting the look for just an instant then turning to look at his watch. "Fancy a beer before lunch?" Now he knew he was the older one it became easier to take the lead.

They found pavement tables in a patch of sunshine and sat there, ordering a beer when someone eventually shambled out from a dark doorway to serve them. Their conversation might easily have taken an autobiographical turn but it did not. Instead they talked inconsequentially, exchanging only the parings of their lives – information that could be offered without danger or loss: snippets of information about bars in Seville and Jerez, characters they had met in them, funny things that had happened in the streets and shops. They laughed a lot. William seemed something of a chatterbox, James thought, until he realised that he had probably not spoken English to anyone of his own age for over a week. Anybody could become a chatterbox after a little social deprivation. James also decided, before his glass was quite empty, that William was rather good-looking and completely forgot that they were supposed to look like brothers. He drained his glass.

"You got through that quickly," commented William.

"So did you. Come on. Time to meet Paco."

Paco's loquacity seemed quite restored by the time they caught up with him in the shadow of the old Alcázar and he shepherded them directly to a restaurant where they received all the fuss and attention that is usually reserved for only the most loyal of customers. If the main course was somewhat predictable – chicken cooked in sherry with raisins and onions – it hardly mattered since it tasted delicious. Paco talked energetically about the bullfight, about the water shortage, about the Jerez riding-school, about almost everything under the sun in fact, but he never said another word about advertising copy, English or translation. It was past four o'clock by the time the meal was finally over and so too, evidently, was the day's business, just as William had predicted it would be. Paco made this clear to James by shaking his hand at the door of the restaurant and presenting him with a small sealed envelope.

William said: "Are you going to the station? I'll walk with you." Then he too took his leave of Paco and set off down the hill with James. "Look, do you have to go back just yet?" William's face was flushed, probably with the brandy that had concluded the meal, but James thought he looked excited, eager in some way.

"'Fraid so," said James. "I'm meeting someone." But he did not say who and, for a disloyal half-second, guiltily wished he were not.

"You're gay, aren't you?" was the next thing William said.

"Yes," said James. "Does it show?"

"No, not at all. At least not outwardly. It was just a feeling I had. An intuition."

"So – what about you?"

William laughed. "I'm not. At least, I don't think I am."

An answer and a half, James thought. "You don't think you are! What's that meant to mean?"

"Tell you some other time. I don't think you'd want my life story. At least, not just yet." (Want a bet? thought James.) "Look, Jacobite, give me your phone number." He took out a pen and scribbled down his own on a scrap of paper. They swapped. And arrived at the station.

"See you again then," said William.

"Right," said James, "see you again." And they parted.

Yes, thought James, there would be another time. Certainly there would.

When he had met Borja three years ago – met him only to lose him in Madrid – there had been no such sense of certainty about another meeting. Instead, James had felt a kind of desperate exhilaration. Within a few days of arriving in Seville he had secured a job and an address. And having an address he had immediately written to Borja, care of his family home. It was the longest letter of his life. James surprised himself. Folded up it was as thick as a cheque-book. He had a job to seal the envelope. Then he waited. Six weeks. Hoping. Then a letter had arrived. It was polite but distant. Borja had not got the job in Madrid and was in Granada, staying with an aunt and looking for work in the south. It was not easy. He had enjoyed meeting James and would remember him in his prayers.

Granada. Half a day's train journey away but still twice as near as Madrid. James carried the letter in his pocket for three weeks and four days. Then came the second letter. Borja had been offered an interview at the Seville tourist office. He would be staying in such and such a hostel. Might they meet for a drink?

Might they? Might the Guadalquivir foam with champagne. Might the palm trees kneel down and sing in praise of good fortune and the horses dance in the streets.

When at last they met, one long week and three long phonecalls later, it was as two boys already in love. James waited outside the tourist office from an absurdly early hour and caught Borja as he arrived. Borja never even went looking for the hostel he had booked into. But he got the job. And had kept it ever since. Plus James.

James' return to Seville was uneventful. He spent the train journey trying to compose an account of his day that would make it sound purposeful and businesslike and not accord too prominent a role to William – which was not easy. Arriving relatively early in Seville he made straight for the tourist office. He had surprise on his side: Borja would still be at work. Only Borja was not at work. One of his colleagues, Angel, occupied his usual place. "He had to leave work about an hour ago," Angel explained. "There was a phonecall. Some problem at your flat."

"What kind of problem?" James wanted to know but Angel had no further information.

With a sense of alarm, James left the tourist office and headed straight for the Plaza del Salvador. Soon he could make out the front wall of the flat in the distance, beyond ice-cream parlours with their sun-shades and the red-brick front of the great church of the Saviour. And even as he approached, James could see what was wrong. Where the front window of their living-room should have been was now a great, gaping, squarish hole in the wall.

# Four


When her doorbell rang Alexa was working on the opening movement of her Beethoven sonata, on the fifty-first bar. She had always taken the first note in the top line with her left hand: it was safer that way in view of the great leap that followed it. But when Eulogio had demonstrated the passage at her last lesson he had used his right hand and then jumped at lightning speed to take the following high F. It had looked and sounded brilliant. Alexa tried it... and missed. The doorbell rang again. "Shit," she said.

It was never for her anyway. When it rang it was always a mistake: it was the old lady downstairs who was wanted. And in the end she would always shuffle forth and answer it. Praying that on this occasion the old lady would not be long, Alexa tried to refocus her concentration. She began the lead-in, this time approaching the dangerous leap a little more slowly. The bell rang a third time. Alexa's startled hand shot up to F sharp. She stood up in a fury and slammed the keyboard lid shut. The bell rang once more as she stalked out of the room and down the stairs.

Beyond the wrought-iron grill that separated the cool hallway from the brilliant street stood a short but commanding-looking woman, draped in an enormous black, lace-edged shawl and wearing outsize pendant earrings that looked to Alexa like a pair of chestnuts still in their spiky shells.

"I heard you playing the piano," said the woman brightly, in English.

This was the last thing that Alexa's ears, still ringing with the unfortunate F sharp, wanted to hear. "Oh yes?" she snapped.

"I'm sorry that my ringing upset you... because it obviously did."

Alexa felt slightly mollified. At least the woman had a little sensitivity. Her face relaxed, almost smiled. Encouraged, the woman continued:

"I think you must be Alexa. My name's Sophie. I'm a distant cousin of Pippa's"

"Oh, Pippa. With the nice-looking American, Mark."

"Indeed, yes," said Sophie.

"Look, come in," Alexa said. She was not used to talking to people through wrought-iron and she suddenly realised that it must seem unfriendly of her not to open the gate just because she could see her visitor through it. She pressed the button and swung it open.

"I won't come in. I really didn't want to disturb you. Only I'd like to ask you to dinner. Pippa is coming on Friday with Mark and I wondered... Of course, if you have something else..."

"Actually I don't. And it's very sweet of you. I haven't met many people since I came here and... Look, do come up."

"No, really. But you will come on Friday?" She took a card from under the voluminous shawl and handed it to Alexa. "It's not very far. You'll find it easily. And I'm also inviting another guest. There's a young man I'd very much like you to... I mean, whom I think you would like to meet."

"Oh, right." Alexa was surprised but, she discovered a moment later, not unpleasantly so. By then her caller had turned smartly and, with a flurry of shawl, bustled back into the street.

Alexa returned upstairs. The room was not very tidy. Perhaps it was just as well her visitor had not come up. But when she sat down at the piano again she acheived her high F at the first attempt.

It could be a lonely life. The piano demanded your full attention.

Before, there had always been family and friends, fellow-students from the college. Now there were only waiters in cafés to talk to in rudimentary Spanish. Alexa had not run into Pippa or Mark again since their first meeting over a week ago though she had visited the Bodegón from time to time. She liked to sit over a coffee and to silence Beethoven with the undemanding sounds of the espresso machine and background chatter. Going to and from her lessons with Eulogio, she always lingered now in the Barrio Santa Cruz to listen to the busking guitars and to soak up the atmosphere in general. She had an idea that 'southern-ness', whatever that was, might somehow creep into her playing. If she could only – one day – play like Eulogio.

"Not bad," said Eulogio, when she played the Beethoven to him again the following Friday. "You manage that difficult jump very nicely. Next week bring me the third movement. There are guitars there too, you know, in the trio section."

Walking back through Santa Cruz, this time her attention was caught by the sound of a guitar drifting out from a café at a point where two thread-thin streets were spliced into one. There was something different about this playing, she thought: something that marked it out from the strumming of the boys in the plazas. So she walked in at the pitch-dark doorway.

Inside, thanks to one of the tricks that light plays in sunny climates, she found herself not in the stygian blackness she had seen from outside, but in a realm of clear, cool light, refracted through windows of coloured glass and playing off walls that were covered with jewel-like, Moorish, azuelo tiles. The room was bare except for a few dark wood tables and chairs, and empty of people except for the guitar player; and he seemed scarcely to be in the room at all. He was perched in the deep window-recess, his feet a little higher than the table-tops. He was a small, wiry young man in faded denims, with curly hair and a little beard. The rest of his face was not available for scrutiny as his head was bent over his instrument and he did not look up when Alexa came in. And though he did look up briefly when the piece came to an end, his eyes did not focus on his surroundings. His thoughts were still engaged with music and soon his head had dropped again and his fingers were back in action along the strings. This time he played something that Alexa already knew as a keyboard piece: it was a stately Handel sarabande. Alexa was now sitting at one of the tables listening; when a waiter arrived to take her order she seemed not to understand what he was doing there and looked at him with such puzzlement that he shrugged and walked away.

After Handel, Scarlatti. The perching figure embarked, after the shortest of pauses, on a brilliant virtuoso sonata: one that, again, Alexa knew in its original, keyboard incarnation. Played on piano or harpsichord it demanded dexterity enough; to manage it on the guitar seemed to require magic. To Alexa the sound became almost tangible, radiating, pattern-like from the instrument, to merge and form yet more complex patterns with the filtered sunlight and the interweaving intricacies of the Moorish tiles. The senses of sight and hearing had fused and for a few minutes Alexa sat, not in a café but in a rainbow of light and sound.

The piece came to an end. The colours faded slowly, as rainbows do. The artist looked up. This time his eyes, a penetrating maritime blue, focused directly on Alexa. He smiled. Then, to her astonishment – for though she had learnt a little German in her musical studies she had never spoken a word of it – she heard herself say: "Bist du Karsten?" After that it seemed less surprising when the man's smile broadened and he replied in English: "Mark didn't tell me you spoke German, Alexa."

A second later he had jumped down from his window-seat, ordered two beers, ignoring Alexa's plea that she would prefer a coffee, and joined her at the table. "Do you play that Scarlatti... on your Bechstein?"

"Heavens – you even know the make of my piano. Mark again? No, I don't play that sonata. Some of my college friends played it." She paused before adding, seriously, "but not as impressively as that."

Karsten gave an infinitessimal bow and said: "Thank you." Then he reached inside the neck of his T-shirt and extracted a packet of cigarettes. This came as a relief to Alexa who had been slightly worried by the hump on his left shoulder. He held out the packet towards her – an offer she declined – before lighting up himself. "You will soon see that Seville is a quite small society. But for now, welcome to the Gitanilla, the gipsy bar."

Then they began to talk, about music, interrupting and overlapping each other, catching up on the way with each other's life stories so far. Karsten was five years older than Alexa and he had done something similar, a few years ago, to what she was doing now. His parents were both music teachers in the classical mode: his mother taught piano, his father singing. In order to demonstrate his independence of mind, therefore, the teenage Karsten had bought himself an electric guitar and joined a rock band. His parents were chagrined – as he had, unconsciously, intended them to be. But a year or two on he had felt a lack of something in his new branch of music and took himself off to Andalucía to find something else; a chance hearing of a record of Segovia's had sparked his interest. He found himself a teacher in Córdoba where he studied for six years in both the classical and the flamenco traditions. Then, last year, he had come to Seville, "where now I am myself a teacher."

"And do Andalucíans take kindly to having a German teach them their national instrument?" Alexa could not help asking.

"Naturally, some do not. But I do not need to teach all of them in order to earn my life. There are more than enough who are willing to learn what they do not yet know from someone who does, wherever he comes from. Sometimes an owl can be welcome in Athens." Alexa found this last observation intriguingly enigmatic but Karsten moved on to a new thought. "Do you feel like having a walk?"

"Why not?" Alexa answered. "Anywhere in particular?"

"I thought, maybe, the gardens of the Alcázar. I know one of the... guardians, is that right? We would not have to pay."

It took them only a few minutes to wind their way through the crannies of Santa Cruz and into the gardens through an unassuming archway. Alexa had been here before, via the proper entrance, and found the place enchanting. It was a garden of surprises and corners in which no part was quite the same as another. Here was a carved stone basin full of carp with Neptune and other amphibious gods painted on a blue and rustic wall behind; there, a courtyard with a fruiting grapefruit tree in the centre; down below, a hundred metre staircase of cascading water in which a thousand spider-plants bathed their tresses. At one point, as they turned a corner in the path between two cypresses, they were startled by a grasshopper the size of a chicken drumstick that took off with a rattle of wings from almost beneath their feet.

"Do you mind insects?" asked Karsten.

"Not at all. Snakes though..."

"Me too. Although men do not usually admit to such things."

"I know. Why is that?"

"I don't know. One of the mysteries of sex? Like why do men write better music and women better books? And women are better at acting? And are all these things connected?"

"They're very sweeping generalisations," Alexa protested.

"And like all generalisations, not to be taken too seriously. Just because I am a German you must not take me too serious in everything. You can take me with a pinch of sugar sometimes." It sounded better, just this once, Alexa thought, than salt. "Listen, are you doing anything this evening?" He interrupted himself. "Oh bloody hell! I just remembered something."

"Do you always swear in English?" Alexa asked, curious.

"Whenever possible. English has such a powerful repertoire of words like that. All those gradations."

"You wouldn't think it very varied if you heard our London population swearing. All the same, I see what you mean. But, as for this evening, if you've just remembered you're not free, well, neither am I as it happens. I've been invited to a dinner. It's the first invitation I've had since I've been here. A most peculiar woman..." She stopped as a thought struck her. "Oh dear, you might know her. Mark and Pippa will be there."

Karsten laughed extravagantly.

"What?"

"It's too good. Too funny. You will find me at Sophie's dinner too. She told me..." he hesitated, "... there was a young lady she wanted me to meet."

"And she told me there was a young man I had to meet."

"It might be me, I'm afraid. She does have a rather terrible reputation. As a... I don't know what the word is in English."

"As a matchmaker?" Alexa offered.

"Possibly. Hallo Dolly? Yes, that's it."

They had wandered into an open part of the garden where a pagoda-like building was surrounded by tile-ornamented stone seats. Low hedges of box and myrtle scented the warm air. Ripe pomegranates hung over them, russet-coloured, dangling from spindly branches. Nearby was a carefully tended maze of myrtle with cypresses standing sentinel at its many corners. It was waiting for its next appointment with the clippers and its recent filmy growth gave it an out-of-focus look, as if viewed through someone else's spectacles.

"Please do me the honour of playing for me soon," said Karsten, sitting down. "But you can not do that just here. So may I play for you?"

This time he chose flamenco: a sevillana and then a beautiful rondeña. The gardens had not seemed full of visitors; Alexa had noticed only a few twos and threes. But now people began to appear, squeezing past clumps of oleander, emerging from behind mock-rustic walls. Some sat on the stone benches, others on the ground, and some just stood where they arrived. Karsten played another sevillana and a rumba. Then he did what Alexa had seen the boys in the plazas do: he walked round with his guitar outstretched and invited his audience to deposit coins on the back of it. Only this time Alexa was viewing the scene from behind. No longer a spectator, she was part of the act. He returned to her, counted the coins and put them in a cloth bag which he fished from a trouser pocket. "That was good," he said. "I shall treat you to tea and dough-nuts opposite the cathedral."

Alexa had seldom seen music and money go together so unashamedly, so naturally. In her world they hardly ever did. There was her father's money, of course, and there was the scholarship she had won to study with Eulogio. But playing concerts, when and if she ever did, still lay some years ahead. And she knew already that classical concerts seldom covered costs.

"Some things must be easier for guitarists," she said.

"I know. The piano is an expensive thing to drag around. Do you not sometimes wish you played the flute? Now I have just thought of something. Come with me."

They got up and went towards the palaces of the Alcázar, approaching them in reverse, against the tide of all the paying visitors coming the other way. They walked through cool, fountained courts, beneath horseshoe arches and cedar ceilings carved with the intricate detail of snowflakes while the gardens, ever present, breathed and rustled at the open windows.

The last room they came to was of a later, heavier style than the others: no longer Moorish but echoing the formal tastes of later Christian kings and – until recently – part of the state apartments of the caudillo. Vast tapestries cloaked the ochre walls and at one end, on a low dais, stood a full-length grand piano.

"A Blüthner," said Alexa in surprise, inspecting it. "I never came into this room before."

"Play it," said Karsten. Alexa looked doubtful. "It's OK. I'll make sure of it."

Alexa lifted the lid, thought for a second and then plunged into

one of the grander preludes by Bach. A uniformed official came up
to Karsten. "She can not..." he began.

"Oh but she can," said Karsten. "Listen to that."

\*

With a varnished fingernail Sophie trawled her wineglass for
imaginary pieces of cork. "I'm so happy for you both." She was talking to Pippa and Mark. She turned to Alexa and Karsten. "Aren't you?"

Pippa would be moving in the morning: out of the flat she shared
with Jeannette and into Mark's quite spacious but, until now,
bachelor apartment. She had visited the place for the first time ten
days ago. It had been dinner for two and no direct suggestion had
come from Mark that the invitation might include an overnight stay.
Pippa had been impressed by that delicacy of feeling. But all the
signals had been set between them: the eye-contacts, the half-finished
gestures, that indicated that next time the meal would not be the
climax of the evening. And three days later it so proved. All naked,
Mark looked even better than Pippa had dared to hope and as a lover
she found him... lovely: neither too much the fumbling amateur nor
too alarmingly expert a Don Juan. As for Mark, the event had the
quality of a revelation. His experience was not extensive and he now
saw with the blinding clarity that comparison offered that his two
previous conquests had been merely dutiful in their participation.
Whereas Pippa abandoned her twenty-year-old body to the experience
so completely that he had no choice but to conclude that she was the
first and only female who really wanted him. For him the moment
was a turning-point and better than any of his poems.

Pippa had not been able to help noticing the attractive qualities of
Mark's flat. Though ramshackle it had large rooms and windows, a
terrace near roof-top height, and it occupied two floors. It was easily
big enough for two. There were some alarming disadvantages, though.
The kitchen made Jeannette's (where pliers were required to turn the

gas-tap) seem modern and there was no glass, only bars, at its high-up window. The bathroom was little better, the shower being prone to evil mossy sproutings and the U-bend below the basin was slender and dubious as that in a wine-maker's air-lock. But who needed glazing this sunny November? And weren't fresh air and sun the very best guarantors of hygiene? The other rooms had been made attractive, not by spending money but simply by being inhabited for some time by a person of refined taste and sensibility. And the person was Mark. She loved him now, there was no doubt about it. And here was where Mark lived. She was not entirely sorry, either, to be getting away from Jeannette, who had not yet forgiven her for lying to her that first weekend.

"I've had another chat with Jeannette," Sophie was saying. "Of course she'll miss the rent for a bit. Such a pity Felipe can't move in with her but that's Spanish families for you. Anyway, I've promised to help her find someone else as quickly as we can. And she entirely saw my point: how important it is for you to be together on your own. Thank goodness it's possible for you now. Children of today, I take my hat off. You have done what we never did: taken by storm the freedoms we only dreamed of."

"You except yourself, of course," Karsten said.

"Indeed I must. I had to make up my own rules, as you know. And it didn't go down too well in some quarters." She nodded meaningfully at Pippa as representative of the family she referred to. "Well, you must all make the most of it." She looked at everyone in turn. "Young people don't know how lucky they are." Catching herself, she stopped. "Oh what an old auntie I do sound!" She changed the subject. "Now you two." She wagged a forefinger at Alexa and Karsten in mock-reproach. "I consider it most unsporting of you to spoil my little arrangement this evening. And Seville such a big city! Of all the people you might have run into this afternoon..."

"I still don't know how the two of you recognised each other," Pippa said. She turned to Mark. "Did you describe them to each other?"

"No. Though, come to think of it, I may have mentioned Alexa's red hair..."

Karsten, catching the look that Pippa shot Mark and the beginnings of a blush on the latter's cheeks, leaped in quickly with: "But that wouldn't explain how she knew me."

Quick as a flash, Pippa said: "Alexa had just been told she was going to meet an interesting young man this evening. She'd slso been promised an introduction to someone called Karsten. Maybe she put two and two together... subconsciously..." She faltered. "Or something."

Sophie sniffed the air. "I think my little casserole is ready. Do come through and help me eat it."

Later, when the most urgent pangs of hunger were assuaged and conversation was starting up again, the subject of Borja and James and their window arose. "It's the most extraordinary thing I ever heard," said Sophie. "And so inconvenient for the pair of them."

"It was certainly that," said Mark. "James said they were stuck in the flat for the whole weekend."

"To keep the place secure," added Pippa.

"Fortunately the money side was their landlord's reponsibility," Mark continued. "And, remarkably for Seville, he sent a builder round first thing on Monday. All the same, James had to take most of Monday off."

"He said they were pretty well living in public all weekend," said Pippa. "Somebody lent them some plastic sheeting..."

"...But it drew one hell of a lot of attention from the plaza."

(Only ten days, Alexa thought, and they're finishing each other's sentences already.)

"I can imagine," said Sophie. "It must have been difficult. People like them must surely want to blend into the background, not to stick out like a pair of sore thumbs."

"People like what?" Alexa asked innocently, having assumed that Borja was the name of a woman.

"People like that, dear," Sophie explained concisely.

"Two boys who live together," said Karsten. He issued a bulletin of approval. "I have met them. They are both very fine."

"And as much in love as two people can be," Mark added. He spoke with new-found authority.

"Has it been in the papers?" Pippa asked.

Nobody quite followed.

"The thing about the window. Is it a gang going round stealing them for sale?"

"Could be," said Mark.

"Well, if it hasn't been in the press," said Pippa, "maybe you could research it, write it up and get it there. Your Spanish is native standard, after all, and you are a writer."

Mark squirmed. "Yes, I know..."

Again Karsten came to the rescue. "Do not be sure that Borja and James will want to be in the newspaper together. Remember that homosexual actions are not legal here, even in private."

Sophie intervened. "This is about a theft, not homosexual actions – even in private."

Mark was giggling. "I think it's acts, not actions."

Sophie took no notice. "Two men live at the same address. What of it? Whose business is anything else?"

"I think it is never so simple," said Karsten evenly. "You said that people like them – same-sexers – want to blend in, not to look differ-ent." He shrugged. "But it is not for me to say. You must ask Borja and James."

"Well," said Mark, "it's a great story, newspaper or not. I mean, now that my friends are no longer inconvenienced," he added quickly. "Stolen windows. It's like, so mysterious because it's so... pointless."

"If it's such a good story," said Pippa brusquely, "why don't you do what I said? Just go ahead and write it." This sent a ripple round the room and the conversation drifted away to other topics.

Later, when the party had broken up, the four young people found themselves walking along the street together.

"Your aunt's a good cook," said Alexa.

"She's a kind of cousin really," Pippa answered. "My grandmother was her aunt, so whatever that makes her..."

"Are all your family like her?" Karsten asked.

"Hardly. They're a pretty conventional lot mostly. But she's from heaven."

"She's certainly been amazingly good to us," said Mark. "So supportive. Smoothing things over with Jeannette like that. For someone of her age she's pretty... liberated."

"She seems to love young people very much," said Alexa.

"Maybe she just loves love," suggested Karsten.

At the corner of the street their ways diverged. "I'll walk you back to your flat if you like," Karsten offered Alexa, and they said their goodnights to Pippa and Mark.

"Strange," said Alexa. A cat stared at them from the barred window of a derelict building.

"What is strange?"

"The feeling I get about Sophie. All this freedom our generation has struggled for – and I include the freedom to move in with some-one you've only known a fortnight. We ought to be really pleased. And yet, when it's served up to you on a plate by someone of that generation – Sophie seems to have almost pushed them into bed together – it doesn't quite seem... I don't know. But why should I have this feeling? Is it because we prefer to take our freedom than be given it?"

"Maybe the fact of taking it defines it as freedom," said Karsten. "And if it's given to you it's not freedom but something else. Interesting."

They turned the corner into Calle Temprano. A blast of jasmine scent met them and a dog barked at them from the safety of iron railings. They were almost at Alexa's building. Karsten read an inscription on a high wall. "Domus Pauperum et Scala Coeli." It was the Charity Hospital where Borja liked to pay his respects to Death in the chapel. "I never saw that before."

"I can read it from the window of my kitchen," said Alexa. "The house of the poor and the ladder of heaven. It seems somehow comforting."

"Does it really? I don't think so." Karsten's voice had hardened.

"Explain." Alexa had no objection to an argument.

"It says – or implies – that poor people are close to God. In other words, that being poor is good for you. It's a cruel trick practised by all religions and then supported by authority as a means of controlling the masses."

"You sound very certain of that," said Alexa. "I can't say whether I'd agree or not. I'm just an Anglican. That, in case you don't know, means never having to say you're sure of anything. At least, not in religious matters."

"Well, I was brought up a Catholic. In Germany at least you have to think these things through."

"So you now reject the whole lot?"

"Naturally."

They turned the corner into Calle Santander. "Well, this is where I live," said Alexa. "Can I make you a coffee or anything?"

Karsten hesitated. "No. Another time. I would want to hear you play again and that would not be fair so late. Also," a mischievous look came into his eyes, "you might think I was going to move in within a fortnight."

# Five

James answered the telephone. Borja was in the shower.

"Hi there, this is William," said the voice at the other end and then, without drawing breath, ran on: "Are you doing anything on Saturday? Like to come over?"

"Yes, sure," said James. His answer had come like a reflex. "That'd be fine."

"Get the same train you got last time. I'll meet you at the station. OK?"

"OK."

"See you on Saturday then. Bye now."

"'Bye." James put the phone down. It had been extraordinarily brief. Had William guessed that a longer exchange might have been domestically inconvenient?

Borja emerged, naked and dripping. "Who was that?"

"I've got to go to Jerez again on Saturday. Some more translation." It was the first time he had ever told Borja a direct lie. To his surprise it had slipped out quite easily, as if he had been rehearsing the moment for years.

"Ybarra?"

"No, it was one of his assistants phoned. Give me the towel." James took it and dried Borja affectionately all over. After that he considered helping him on with his clothes but in the end, and with a little help from Borja, he took his own off instead.

Sex had always been good between them. At first Borja's religious scruples had created problems – not, fortunately, in performance, only in discussion afterwards. Then Borja's eventual compromise with himself – that sex with James was a sacrament, comparable to Christian marriage – had alarmed James a little with its seriousness. But soon he had learned to be not only flattered by Borja's intensity but also confirmed in his own belief that his relationship with the young Castillian was the most important thing in his life, not only up to now but for the future as well. Three years on, he had had no cause to change his mind.

Borja accepted James' need to revisit Jerez without surprise or protest. James had hardly spoken about his first visit. His return had coincided with the emergency of the stolen window and there had been more important things to discuss. After that the Jerez trip seemed to have slipped Borja's mind; he never questioned James about it and James didn't specially want to bring the matter up himself.

The morning was warm for November and James toyed with the idea of setting out in shorts before remembering that he was supposed to be going on a business trip. He compromised and wore a pair of bum-hugging jeans, light blue, and a collarless white shirt, a combination which he knew flattered him. When he arrived at Jerez station the first person he saw was William, from behind, looking towards the wrong end of the train and apparently biting his nails. Tactically advantaged, James went up to him and clapped him on the shoulder. William turned, startled. He was wearing an identical collarless shirt, open like James' to the third button, and the same blue jeans. "Wow," he said, registering the coincidence, then modified the greeting: "So how are you, Jacobite?"

"Never better, Orange." James gave him a second clap on the shoulder.

"Listen. I've got a car. It's a nice day. We could go to the beach."

"You have a car now? You didn't say. You could have come to Seville."

William looked at him quizzically. "Something told me that might have complicated life for you. Right?"

"I suppose so," admitted James.

"Well you can tell me all about that later. Fancy a beer before we go?"

William selected a bar at random and led the way in. He evidently hadn't visited it before. It was a rough place full of card-playing railwaymen enveloped in a fug of cigarette-smoke that seemed as thick and tangible as moss. Conversation ceased abruptly on the Englishmen's entrance and William's command of the situation evaporated, for the moment, just as quickly. It was left to James to find a table and order the beer. "At least we can say whatever we like without being understood," he said. "So tell me: how come the car?"

"It's one of Paco's. Or one of O'Donnell's. I don't know which. Anyway, Paco says I can use it whenever I want so it's more or less become mine."

"Very generous of Paco."

"Perhaps he fancies me," suggested William playfully.

"I hope he does," said James. "It'll be a relief to my boyfriend. He's afraid that Paco's after me."

"One wouldn't rule the other out, surely? Anyway, you do have a boyfriend – as I guessed when you had to hurry home so soon after our first meeting. Tell me about him." William lit a cigarette.

"What do you want to know?"

"Name, nationality, how long together, personality, looks, how you met... that sort of thing. You can leave out your sex-life if you want."

"Thank you. I was going to. Salud." He took a mouthful of beer. "OK then. He's called Borja and he's beautiful. Castillian. We've been together three years..."

"Man, that's a long time," William interrupted.

"It doesn't seem like it," James said a little coolly.

"Time flies when you're having a good one, I suppose. How did you meet?"

James was slightly surprised, slightly distrustful of William's insistent curiosity but he felt flattered by it so he told him the story: the meeting on the train, Madrid, his subsequent courtship by letter and phone, and Borja's eventual arrival in Seville.

William shook his head slowly from side to side. "That's really romantic. Quite fantastic." He paused before asking: "Are you really sure it happened like that?"

James gave a puzzled sort of laugh. "Of course I bloody am. Why should I invent a story for you?"

"OK, I believe you. But what about his religion then? Meaning, if he's gay and such a devout Catholic?"

"That's still a problem for him. He has visions sometimes."

"Visions?"

"He sees death sometimes. Hell opening up all around him. That sort of thing."

"You mean like an Hieronymus Bosch painting? Sounds intriguing." Restored to his usual equanimity (for the silence around them had not lasted long) William semaphored towards a waiter and ordered a second beer.

"Maybe it's something like Bosch," James said. "Remember it's not me that sees it. I'm just telling you. But he's not a weirdo," he added hastily. "It's just that he sees things that the rest of us can't."

"For instance?" The beers arrived. William delved for coins.

"For instance, if you wake him up in the morning and ask him the time, he'll shut his eyes again for a moment, visualise his watch-face and tell you the time to the minute. It's uncanny but it's true. Never fails."

"Oh, hey. Anything else?"

"Yes. One thing – at least that I know of. If you're driving with him, and you're the driver I mean, and you're driving into a blind bend, sometimes he'll yell out: 'Car coming!' and sure enough, there always is."

Driving with Borja. He hadn't often. Driving, let alone keeping, a car in central Seville would have been madness. But on summer holidays they would hire one. Borja, when it was his turn to take the wheel, would exhibit a lust for speed and danger that belied his otherwise sober approach to life. "Don't forget," he would say, "I grew up on a hill farm." He talked about driving tractors across slopes so steep that you had to lean sideways like a yachtsman to stop rolling over, about backing four-wheeled trailers up twisting sheep-tracks. Last year, on an idyllic holiday in the Sierra Morena, Borja's nerve on mountain roads had left James both envious and breathtaken. And grateful too when, in the course of his own more circumspect turns at the wheel, Borja's cry of "car coming" had turned more than one head-on day of reckoning into a mere near miss.

"I can't explain how it works," James said. "Only that it does."

"Doesn't it worry you sometimes?"

"No. Why?"

"Well, like what else might he be able to see but not tell you about? How would you know? Like, does he know what you're doing when you're not with him? Does he know where you are today, for example?"

"He knows where I am," James began carefully, then stopped, feeling suddenly uncomfortable, remembering Borja's lack of curiosity about his last visit to Jerez and his uncurious acceptance of this one.

"Does he know I exist?"

"No." James began to sound annoyed. "I hardly know you exist. It's only the second time we've met."

"Sorry. I didn't mean..."

"No. I'm sorry. Forget it."

The glasses were empty. "Shall we hit the road?" said William.

"Suits me." James had not used the expression 'hit the road' for three years. Of course his friends at university had talked like that but he and Borja never did: their conversation, however intimate, always had, of necessity, a rarefied, literary quality. 'Hit the road' didn't feature. A sudden, surprising tidal-wave of home-sickness, past-sickness, broke over him and for an astonishing half-second he thought he was going to cry. He fought to put the feeling behind him. "Hit the road, Orange," he said.

Jerez did not fray at the edges like Seville, petering out into graceless suburbs. Instead it came to an end abruptly with a fringe of palm trees which lingered for some time in the driving-mirrors like a mirage or oasis. From then on, the road to the coast lay over rolling, vine-clad hills: they were monotonous if you didn't like sherry, magical if you did.

"Do you know Chipiona?" William asked. Chipiona, according to the signposts, was their destination.

"Yes," said James. "Borja and I spend weekends here in the summer." He remembered the last one: making love on the beach after night had fallen and the holidaymakers gone indoors; the lap of the waves on the rocks beside them; the winking lights of ships funnelling into the estuary, so close that you could almost stroke them... "The city gets too hot."

"I can imagine. I drove there last weekend. First time I had the car. But on my own... you know."

James did know. He felt keenly the difference between his own visits with Borja, in love, wrapped together, mutually sufficient, and William's, last weekend. William's loneliness became suddenly very clear to James. He imagined him alone on the beach at Chipiona, like the evening star in Turner's painting: reflected, but not accompanied, along the mud-flats. The image beckoned him. He wanted to say how much he understood and how deeply but he could find neither the words nor the right register. Then he caught sight of something that changed his line of thought. "I don't want to worry you," he said, "but have you looked at the temperature gauge recently?"

William looked at it. "Sod it. We'd better stop, I suppose." He pulled over and switched off.

"Can't see any steam," said James. "... Or hear any."

"That could be good news or bad. Better check it out." William made a move to get out of the car.

"No, wait. Give it a few minutes to cool down. You could burn yourself." Instinctively James had caught William's hand to restrain him, just as he would have done with Borja. William made no attempt to pull away. His sleeve was not rolled up but unbuttoned at the cuff. By way of experiment James ran his hand up over William's wrist. The skin felt soft and warm. William exhaled involuntarily with a little noise which he managed to turn into a laugh. James kept his hand on William's forearm for a second longer, then withdrew it. "Let's get out of the car anyway, though," he said. "It's getting bloody hot in here." They both laughed.

When they unscrewed the radiator cap a few minutes later, they found the water at a reasonable level and no sign of overheating. "Must be the gauge," said James. "Turn on the ignition." William obeyed and the temperature needle climbed immediately into the red sector. "Faulty gauge," said James authoritatively. "No problem. We can get going."

"Are you good with cars?" asked William.

"No," said James. "Not at all. But sometimes I can pretend to be." They drove on and in what seemed like no time came to the brow of a hill that fell away to reveal a long ribbon of sea, blue and sparkling, dead ahead. Another sparkling sea of glasshouses filled the foreground and over to the left the salt-white houses of Chipiona shimmered in the heat. Towering over them a lighthouse stood, tall and slender as a minaret. "To the lighthouse, man," said James.

*

"The question is," said William, after they had had an initial stroll along the sea-front, "do we want to go for lunch somewhere or do we just take some bread and a largish bottle down to the beach with us?"

"I like the second idea," said James. "Especially the largish bottle. We'll get some fizzy water too, otherwise..."

"Yeah," said William. "Don't I know."

The beach was a long, long crescent of sand. There were few people on it, just one or two dog-walkers and a few young men playing frisbee. The fingers of foreign tourism had not yet reached out to Chipiona, while for most Spanish people sea-bathing and beach activities came to an abrupt stop on the twenty-first of September.

William had a way of walking, James noticed, that involved lifting the heel with each stride so that he seemed to bounce along on the balls of his feet. There was something joyous and puppyish about it. James thought it looked nice.

"Swim?" queried William when they got down to the beach.

"I don't think so," said James. "The Atlantic. Mid-November. Anyway I didn't bring my bathers. I was supposed to be going to a business meeting, after all."

"Is that what you told Borja?"

"I sort of let him assume it," James answered awkwardly. He was trying to erase the memory of his outright lie from his consciousness. "Look, if we're not swimming let's get that bottle open. Oh hell." The obvious had struck him. "No corkscrew."

"Don't you believe it." William flourished one from a pocket. "Never knowingly without one."

James smiled, took the implement from William's hand and dealt with the cork. "Now," he said, "it's time you told me who you are."

"Oh really?"

"Yes. I answered a question for you the first time we met which you wouldn't answer for me. You said your life story had to wait for next time. So that when you rang to ask me here today you knew I'd come."

"Did I?"

"Certainly you did."

"So who am I? Big question."

"Big answer?"

"No, not really. I come from a highly respectable family. Too highly respectable actually. My father's a bishop."

"A Catholic one?"

"Ha-bloody-ha. C. of E. And my mother's a doctor."

"I see what you mean about respectable. How do you deal with that?"

"I don't. Or rather, I did. I was at boarding-school but I left. People say 'ran away' but I didn't run away. I just walked out. It was near the sea. Lots of ships from the Baltic. I didn't fancy that: it sounded too cold. But one day there was a Dutch coaster in. I simply walked up and asked if they could use an extra hand. That was that. They wanted to know if I had a passport but apart from that, no questions. I was seventeen."

"Jesus," said James. "That's quite a story. What about your parents?"

"I didn't need to feel too bad. I've got five brothers and sisters and I was kind of destined for the role of black sheep of the family anyway. I sent them a card to say I was alive and well but taking a few months off to see the world. See you at Christmas – that sort of thing."

"And did you see the world?"

"Not as much as I'd hoped to. I saw Rotterdam, Ipswich, Antwerp and Ramsgate. But I got to know them bloody well."

"Then what?"

"Three months was about enough. I couldn't go back to the same school, obviously. My father sent me to a crammer to fail my 'A'-levels."

"That must have cost a bit."

"It did. I retook them at the local tech and went to work in a bank. That lasted about a year. I was sharing a flat with some old school-friends. Then I met a girl from London and moved there to be with her. It was good while it lasted."

"How long?" James asked.

"Three years."

"Three years," James echoed.

"I did bar work in night-clubs. Finally..." he paused and looked carefully at James, "... we split up six months ago." Another pause, then he ran on. "It was her flat of course. But one of my mother's practice-partners knew someone at O'Donnell's. And that's how I'm here. I'm supposed to be making good or something. In the end you never escape your parents altogether." William took a long pull from the wine bottle as if to signal that this was the end of the story.

"Does your father have a cathedral then?" James heard the question sounding idiotic as he uttered it but he was finding William's family background difficult to picture.

"Sorry to disappoint you. He's not the Archbishop of York. He's what they call a suffragan bishop. It's really an admin job."

"White-collar work," James couldn't resist adding.

"All right. No more bishop jokes. That's a rule around me."

"Sorry."

They had bought ready-made boccadillos rather than face tussling knifelessly with hunks of bread and sausage. Now seemed the right moment to eat them. It did not take long. Then, with only the bottle to carry, they moved on, rounding the sharp corner under the light-house. No longer facing out across the Atlantic, they looked now over the estuary of the Guadalquivir. Here the beach was segmented by rocky outcrops which the sea broke in upon to form a series of lagoons that might once have been saltpans. Beyond the waves container ships, a biscuit's throw away, stole up the estuary towards Seville. Opposite lay another shore, the Coto Doñana, a flat, unpeopled expanse of sand and trees.

Lazily they skimmed stones, played noughts and crosses in the sand, sat about on the rocks. They both had their shirts off now. William, James noted carefully, had a broad and muscular chest just like his own, sprinkled with a few – a very few – sun-catching blond hairs. Unlike Borja's. Which swam suddenly into James' mind. Slender but taut, it wore a plume of soft black fur which fountained from the navel in a thick dark spring, fanning out above the solar plexus with wonderful symmetry across his rib-cage like a palm tree.

"Was Borja your first?" William asked casually, as if he had been a party to James' thoughts.

James answered slowly. "No – and yes. There'd been boys at university – you were supposed to say men but we were only boys really – who seemed important at the time. Now I know they weren't. Only sex. Well, sex and friendship. With Borja it was – it is – different. Really." He stopped.

"Smoke?" William offered.

"No. Used to, but now hardly ever."

William produced a small leather purse from his trouser pocket. "Not even silly ones?" Unzipping it he showed James a small block of resin nestling inside.

"You're a conjuror," said James. "OK. Why not? What else have you got in your pockets? No, don't answer."

They shared the joint. William blew smoke rings. James tried but failed. "I had a girlfriend once," he said. "I was sixteen. It didn't really work. I think I knew it wouldn't, even then."

"Did you...?"

"Nearly. Once..." James remembered an evening, late summer, after the cinema, "... but no."

William gave a soft chuckle and lay back on the sand.

"Curiosity's not enough, is it?" James went on. "Other boys had an urgency, an enthusiasm I just didn't have – in that direction."

"Oh I don't know. A little curiosity can get you a long way." This gave James' consciousness a jolt. William's life-story, though full of incident, had been disappointingly lacking in any signs of sexual ambiguity. But now, was he saying something else? Or was James' mind, now moving towards a more fluid state, playing tricks? William stretched out, cat-like. One hand came within reach of James' own. James grasped it for the second time that day.

Neither of them made another move. There were small

fair-weather clouds above them, white and so filmy that their passage across the sun scarcely dimmed its light. "Look at that one," said William. "It's like a kiwi."

"More like a plane," said James.

"The other one, you wally."

"Then it's like an oil-can."

"Now it is."

James hardly dared to breathe. Any second William would take his hand away. Like someone watching a wild creature at unexpectedly close quarters, James dreaded being the cause of its departure.

"That one's like a beetle," William said.

"A butterfly."

"With one wing?"

"Its wings are folded," said James. "It's asleep."

"Then it'll fall out of the sky."

"And envelop us with... with... with what?"

"I had a boyfriend once too, Jacobite."

Startled, it was James who withdrew his hand. "How come? When did you have time?"

"Funny boy. I met him on the boat."

"So he was Dutch?"

"Named Pieter. We shared a cabin. Then became lovers almost without thought. It seemed so natural with him. It wouldn't have done," he added with plonking carefulness, "with almost anybody else."

"What happened when you left the ship?"

"We kept in touch for about a year. Met and made love sometimes at first. Then gradually less often. I was interested in girls as well, of course. The competition simply grew too fierce."

"How sad for Pieter. What happened to him?"

"Don't be sorry for him. I heard from him last year. An invitation to his wedding. Just a printed one, you know. Nothing written in by hand. Nothing personalised. I didn't go, of course."

"That's painfully sad. But I would think that, being me."

"Being you." William repeated this two or three times as if he had stumbled on a new and profound concept. "Being you. Do you want me to change the ending, then?"

"No, not if it's not true. What would be the point?

"No, not if it's true. It's true, Jacobite."

James turned towards William, propped himself up on one elbow and with his other hand stroked his hair. Emboldened by William's stillness he traced the outline of his cheek with his forefinger, then ran it down the middle of his chest. William did not stir.

"And that's as far as it goes." James waited for the words. In his experience that was what straight, or relatively straight, men always said at this point. But William remained mute, his eyes half-shut, possum-like.

All the same, James did leave it at that and sat up. "We'll have to go soon if I'm going to get back in one piece," he said.

"Shame," said William, "but understood. Back in Jerez, can I show you where I live?"

James couldn't quite believe that William had said that.

William's driving, as they left the town, was wildly erratic. If Borja drove fircely he at least brought something of a professional quality to his cornering and racing; William simply drove without care or thinking. James half-noticed this – but decided not to care. Twice they mounted the kerb on corners, laughed and carried on. In the open country things got better, though the temperature gauge behaved surreally, drifting at intervals slowly up and down. Then, coming into Jerez – "Jesus Christ Almighty!" James shouted, the tail-gate of a parked lorry passing within six inches of his face at fifty miles an hour. An alarming crack. The wing-mirror had gone.

William slowed and stopped the car. "I'm sorry, really sorry," he said, pulled James' head towards him and kissed him lightly on the top of it.

"The mirror glass is broken," James observed.

"Then let's declare seven years' good luck," said William. "Buck the trend."

Where William lived was a little ramshackle but attractive: the top floor of an old house, reached by an outside stair alongside which an immense crimson bougainvillea swarmed up the stonework. "But I can use the main staircase of the house if there's an emergency," explained William.

"What sort of emergency?"

"Oh I don't know. There hasn't been one. A fire, maybe, or a hailstorm."

The steps brought them to a terrace with flower-pots on it and William reached under one of them for the key to let them inside. Although near the centre of town there were views, through television aerials and washing, of the surrounding hills. Inside was a kitchen, a bathroom and a spacious main room that was bedroom at one end and living-room at the other. It was equipped with a large stereo system and a small TV. "I'm getting there," William said, "but I need some pictures on the wall."

"I'll bring some posters next time I come," James heard himself say. "I've got loads to spare. You could make your own selection or..." he faltered, "... or just dump the lot if you didn't like them."

"If you liked them they'd be good enough for me, wouldn't they?" William seemed surprised at James' doubt, his expression of trust striking James as almost childlike. "Do you have time for a beer before your train? There's a couple in the fridge." He went out to the kitchen.

Left alone for a moment, James explored the end of the room with William's bed in it. It reminded him of Van Gogh's picture of his bedroom in Arles, spartan but sunny and oddly cheerful. On the shelf opposite the bed was a small round mirror. Sitting on the bed, your face was neatly framed in it. A mirror for one. Sitting on William's bed, confronting himself thus, James could not hide from himself what he really wanted to do. He got up quickly and made for the fresh air on the balcony where William joined him a second later with two beer cans. "Ten minutes to your train," he said, looking at his watch. It took just three to drink the beer.

"Seven minutes," James said, draining his can. "Now I must go." They walked indoors together. "Let me phone you next time. It's... less complicated." William stood facing him, saying nothing. His eyes gazed fixedly into James'. "You're trembling," said James.

"So are you."

Then they were locked in an embrace that neither seemed to initiate and neither had the will to break. At last, almost roughly, James tore himself away. "Five minutes," he said, then leaped down the stairs and, without stopping, ran all the way downhill to the station and into the waiting train.

He dozed on the journey, waking sometimes with a start to wonder whether he had imagined the events of the day, especially the last one which was already taking on the insubstantial quality of a dream. But each time, the train wheels resolved his uncertainty, speaking to him in English and Spanish, albeit with a question of their own. "Qué haces tú?" What are you doing? Over and over again.

\*

"Saw you the sun today?" Borja quoted. "Your nose is red."

Involuntarily James' hand went to it. He thought of Pinnochio. "There wasn't much work to do." He sought refuge in half-truth. "We all went to the beach."

"Oh marvellous," said Borja. "Leaving me to deal with the police."

"Again? I thought we'd done all that?"

"Plus your friend Mark."

"What do you mean? What's been happening?"

"Oh nothing. Just that the police sent their fingerprint people. Just two weeks late. After everything is cleared up. Why didn't they tell us they would do that. God, your breath smells. And who's 'we all', anyway?"

"Ybarra has some assistants. Very good English. Hardly anything for me to do. Ybarra lends them a car." (Safety in plurals.) "You come too next time," he added recklessly.

"How much have you had?" asked Borja.

"Not that much. I smoked a few cigarettes though. Not used to it any more. Makes me light-headed. It's all right; I didn't drive." He thought back to the brush with the lorry.

"I'm glad to hear it."

"What did Mark want, anyway. He wasn't with the police, surely?"

"He can be an idiot sometimes. He wanted to write the whole story up for the press. I told him: no." Borja spoke firmly but then, more doubtfully: "Did I do right?"

"Of course you did." For the second time that day James was close to tears. "It's Pippa putting him up to it, you know. He'd never think of anything so enterprising on his own. "I'm sorry you had to cope, darling." He kissed Borja.

James was a strange, marvellous creature, Borja thought: the blond handsome northerner who had entered his life like a shooting-star three years before; who still dazzled him with his looks, his love, his careless, arrogant charm; and that touch of the unexpected: Borja's typically extrovert, muscular Englishman had the untypical habit of shedding frequent tears, a welling-up of emotion that Borja found intriguing as well as beautiful. He was aware of their imminence now, though they didn't actually come.

"Look, let's eat out tonight. My treat." James felt he had been mean and selfish. He wanted everything to be right between them.

"Like a saying-sorry present?"

"Exactly that."

Borja smiled. "I accept then. But get a shower and use some mouthwash."

James thought that he had never loved Borja more than now. He hugged him. How small and vulnerable he felt. He put the palms of his hands up under his T-shirt and felt his furry chest. It was just as he had remembered it, feeling it with his mind's fingers earlier that day on the beach while looking at William. He would never, ever, see William again.

"You stink," laughed Borja. "Get in the bloody shower."

That night James could not sleep. His mood swung wildly, like the car's temperature needle earlier in the day. Arriving at Seville station, back from Jerez, he had wanted with a mad thirsty desperation to phone William before returning home. But to say what? Thank you for a pleasant day? I can't live without you? There seemed to be nothing in between. But, for God's sake, nothing had happened! It had only been a kiss between friends. Hardly grounds for soul-searching, let alone divorce. William would not give it another moment's thought. Next time they met it wouldn't even be referred to. Where was William now? In bed. Alone. Asleep. Awake?

Borja stirred beside James. A restless dream. He murmured something. You had to watch your dreams, James recollected: the wrong name or endearment whispered in half-sleep... Borja rolled towards him, flopped an arm across his chest and muttered something again. It was a single word, of two syllables, but what it was James could not make out.

# Six

Pastora scuttled down the alley dressed in her skimpy black widow's dress. "Frio, frio," she greeted Pippa, rubbing her hands together to underline the point. Pippa, who had only known English Novembers until now, thought it quite pleasantly warm. Martins still wheeled in the cobalt-blue overhead, chased by the grey and chestnut kestrels that lived among the pinnacles of the cathedral.

Life had become very settled very quickly for Pippa. At first, moving in with Mark, living with someone she was in love with for the first time in her life, she had hardly been able to believe it was all happening. Yet now, just three weeks later, life had a routine quality that she had hardly anticipated. Nothing negative about the idea of routine. Everything about Seville was spell-binding: the atmospheric walks through the crumbling streets; the piropos or compliments addressed to women by members of the opposite sex as they passed by; getting to know little by the little the Spanish people and what made them tick; learning the language. But a routine it was all the same. There were visits to, and visits from, her cousin Sophie who took such a keen interest in her welfare and in Mark's. There was the school, teaching – but not too many hours a week, shopping and cooking, the Bodegón after work, and then her life with Mark, the most important thing of all. That part of the routine seemed perfect, no doubt at all. The only thing... There always was an only thing. The only thing was his writing, his poetry. Pippa had been disappointed at Mark's abandoning the story of the window so easily. This was because James and Borja had been surprisingly timid – or old-fashioned – about letting their names into the newspapers together. Surely Mark could have tried just a little bit harder to persuade them? But far more than this, Pippa was concerned about his poems. For hours each day he shut himself away and worked on them. She respected him for that. But what were the results of all these labours? Nothing that she could see, apparently. Had he ever had any published, she had very soon wanted to know? No, not since he was fifteen and that in a school magazine which hardly counted. Were there any that she could read for herself or that he could read to her? She imagined that this might take place in bed, or on the terrace under a starry sky. But again, no. None of his work was ready, he said. When would it be? He didn't know. How could he be expected to know? he said. He only knew that when it was ready he would know that it was ready. It was not a very satisfying answer.

Pippa was on her way to work. Though it was mid-afternoon she would be teaching till nine in the evening and she was planning to call on Alexa on her way in. Alexa was very different from herself, she felt, yet they had grown friendly through the bond of being new in Seville. And they respected each other, realising that they both knew exactly what they wanted, however different their goals might be.

Pippa turned right, out of the absurdly narrow street in which she lived, into Calle San Esteban. Her new address was Virgen de la Luz. Mark said that they lived like lizards in a crack in a wall and indeed Calle Virgen de la Luz did seem almost that dark and narrow, belying its luciferous name. The name was full of resonance though, combining the two greatest symbols of purity that western civilisation had come up with, and it had made Pippa smile to find them united in a metre-wide alley, and one that was her own address.

A moment later she was passing the Casa Pilatos in whose jewel-like courts and chambers she had fallen in love with Mark – and Spain

– so short a time ago. She saw the building now as an old friend. A mere huddle of roofs from the outside, it gave no clue as to the beauty it offered up within. There were books like that at home – the note-books in which Mark wrote his poems. She had never thought to breach his trust by opening one.

Her way cut through some seedy byways: Calle Aquila, Almirante Hoyos, Argote de Molina. She clutched her shoulder-bag tightly, wall-side. It was the tourists that the biking bag-thieves went for: they seemed to be able to smell them. Still, you couldn't be too careful.

"It does all sound véry quaint," Alexa had said when Pippa had first described the place where she lived. "Yes, quaint's the word," Pippa had agreed. (Though Alexa had at once regretted her choice. Quaint was the word her mother would have used; she had made a mental note not to sound like Mother in future.) Pippa had been telling her about one peculiar aspect of their domestic arrangements. Pastora, who was both caretaker and agent for the landlord (her nephew as it happened), required that the occupant of the flat she now shared with Mark should make the beds of two lorry-drivers who lived on the ground-floor. It was a condition of the tenancy that, for all anyone knew, went back centuries. So every morning Mark religiously entered the fetid downstairs room and pulled up the sheets on the mouldering double bed. Happily it was not his responsibility to launder the sheets as well. Mostly the lorry-drivers were away. You knew when they were not by the sepulchral coughing that echoed up from their quarters. "They don't keep the door locked, then?" Alexa had asked. "Nothing worth stealing," Pippa parroted Mark's own answer. "They don't have a bean between them."

Pippa emerged from the web-like street-plan of the old town into the cathedral square where the drivers of horse-carts lined up hopefully, waiting to whisk nervous tourists off on un-budgeted tours of the city. The orange trees that lined the square now showed their fruits half-ripened, streaked green and gilt. A zig-zag round the crenellated cathedral walls brought her to the tourist-office – she waved automatically just in case Borja was looking out through the plate-glass window at that moment – then she crossed the main road and dived down Calle Santander towards Alexa's flat.

Alexa was a reassuring person to talk to about Mark. She saw nothing alarming in Mark's reticence on the subject of his poems, his failure to have anything yet in print, the silence of his firmly shut note-books. It was the same with her, she said. She could not – or would not – perform a piece of music until it was ready. "But at least you do play. You've played to me," Pippa had said. It had only happened once in fact but it had been an impressive event. "Yes," Alexa had said, " but on my terms, not yours." Pippa had pursued the matter. Surely, when Alexa played to her teacher that was on his terms? Alexa had agreed but said that that was a condition of the special relationship between teacher and student. As far as she knew, poets didn't have teachers. Yes, it was good to talk to Alexa.

Pippa arrived at her door now. Alexa was pleased to see her. Conversations with visitors – though strictly limited in number – made a welcome change from the rather one-way communications of Beethoven. But she could not give Pippa much of her time on this occasion. Karsten had surprised her by asking for a piano lesson. (He had actually said: "I wonder if I might have the temerity to play some-thing to you." She had winced at his choice of phrase.) He was due any moment.

"I didn't know he played the piano," Pippa said.

"Oh, I did," said Alexa, sounding perhaps a little too proprietorial, because Pippa added quickly:

"Well of course, you would. I mean..."

"Don't mean too much," Alexa warned. "We have a wonderful relationship in music. I think his guitar-playing is up there with the best. But that's all. There's no love story about to happen."

"I see," said Pippa. "I hadn't actually drawn that conclusion..."

"But you might have done if I hadn't stopped you. What are you doing at Christmas?"

"Christmas?" The change of subject gave Pippa a jolt. "I see what you mean. It's only four weeks away, isn't it? I was thinking of – or rather, I was putting off thinking of – taking Mark to meet my parents. Sort of officialise things."

Alexa stared at her. "Officialise. Is that a word?"

"I don't know. Maybe not."

"Do your parents know?"

Now Pippa stared.

"I meant about Mark."

"They know he exists. Not that we live together."

"Well, at some point they're going to find out, assuming you stay together. What about his parents?"

"That's easier. They're dead. Mark's an orphan." She liked the sound of the last phrase and was pleased to have the opportunity to use it.

"An orphan," echoed Alexa. Like Pippa, she had never before met one under the age of about forty. "Yes, that must make things easier."

"His parents died in a car-crash in the States. Before that they'd lived in Seville. His father was the US consul here for six years. Mark was twenty when they died but as soon as he finished college he came back here and has been here ever since."

"He must have loved Seville very much."

"He did. He does. Of course, he did inherit a bit of money. The family solicitor collects the rent on his parents' house as well."

"Enabling him to devote some of his time to poetry. I see. Perhaps you'll find the inheritance will be something in his favour when it comes to introducing him to your parents."

At that point the doorbell rang, announcing Karsten who came bounding up the stairs with his guitar over his shoulder as usual but, less typically, carrying an old leather music-case as well. Pippa would have loved to have been a fly on the wall at the ensuing lesson but, pointing out the imminence of her own next class, withdrew and left them to it.

Karsten took a well-thumbed volume of Mozart from his leather case, spread it open on the Bechstein's music-desk and, sitting down, launched into the familiar theme and variations from the Sonata in A. Alexa was apprehensive both as to the quality of the performance and to the reaction that would be expected of her. But she was soon able to relax. Karsten played competently and attractively with just a few wrong notes – as if to reassure Alexa that he didn't take his pianism too seriously. Still, the extra something – the magic or whatever it was that made his guitar playing special – did not transfer to the other instrument. Nor was it something, Alexa realised at that moment, that it was in her power to give. It was her first ever experience of teaching and her simultaneous discovery of its greatest limitation. Nevertheless, when he had finished and smiled rather nervously towards her, she was able to manage more than mere encouraging noises: she gave him some constructive suggestions about dynamics and especially about the pedal. "It's just too much," she said. "You don't have your foot on a sustaining pedal when you play the guitar, do you? Well, you hardly need it on the piano either, when you play Mozart." She sat down and played a little of the piece to him to show another way it could be done while he sat a little way off, listening and watching her feet intently.

A little later, when they were sitting over a coffee, he asked her about her plans for Christmas. Spending a few days with her parents, she said.

"I'm thinking, myself, of going to Morocco. I've always thought that Christmas in a non-Christian country must be good fun." He invested the words 'good fun' with great earnestness. "I won't go about the bush. I would like you to come with me."

There was a second or two's silence while Alexa digested the proposition. Then, "Yes," she said, deliberately. "I think I'd like that. But right now there's something I'd like to ask you. I've never held a guitar in my hands. Could you show me how?"

"Yes, of course." Karsten was more than ready to oblige. "You never, ever...?"

"I was a terribly serious teenager. The piano took up most of my time. As for my second study at college, that was the viola."

"OK then." Karsten drew the piano stool into the centre of the room, motioned Alexa to sit on it and then presented her with his guitar quite ceremoniously as if it were an award. "Now. Fingers here, here and here. And now make it sound."

Alexa drew her right thumb across the strings. "D major," she said, pleased with herself.

"Not bad. Now louder. Make it ring. OK. Now take your hand away and find the chord again yourself."

Instinctively Alexa turned the instrument upwards so that she could see the position of her fingers on the strings.

"Ha," said Karsten. "Don't do that." He affected smugness. "Do you watch your feet on the pedals when you play the piano?"

\*

On her way in to the school, Pippa saw James with his back to her at the reception desk. He was leaning over it and talking into the telephone. The principal's wife, who worked as secretary, administrator and receptionist, was not in her usual seat. James was standing on one foot, rubbing the other shoe agitatedly up and down his calf. He took no notice of Pippa and she wondered idly for a moment what could be making him look so ill-at-ease, before making her way towards her classroom.

James was returning a phone-call from Paco Ybarra which had come while he was in class. Only the return call had been answered not by Paco but by William.

"Great," William had said when James had given his name. "Glad I was here when you rang back." He sounded breezy, matey. James was partially relieved. There was a pause and then William said: "Aren't phones a bummer?"

James could not have agreed more. "Look, I wanted to call you..."

"Don't worry. I understand."

"Yeah, but there's a few things..."

"Listen," William interrupted. "There's an invitation for you. And Borja. And me."

"Oh Jesus Christ."

"It's all perfectly OK."

"I've got to tell you..."

"It's a Chamber of Commerce do. The Federación de Comercio in Jerez – which effectively means the sherry companies – together with the regional tourist board. In Seville. Thursday week. You'll both get official invitations in the post."

"What? As a couple?" James was aghast.

"No, no. Nothing so crass. Paco knows what he's doing. And look, there's another thing. He wants English lessons again. From you. In the bodega here in Jerez. Lessons for himself plus anyone else who wants to learn English. He says he intends to set a good example to the staff."

"You have to be joking."

"No, it's serious. He's already asked the school to release you on Thursdays. He was discussing it just now while you were working. All paid. Starting this week." He paused then, a little less confidently, said: "You won't say no, will you?"

"This is madness, William. Paco must be going out of his mind. Borja would..."

"I miss you," said William softly.

James looked up and glanced around the reception area. He was the only person there. "I miss you too," he said in a voice of resignation. Then, "Yes, I'll come." And as he half-listened to William giving details and times he found himself back in the train from Jerez, hearing the dull insistent questions of the wheels: "Qué haces tú, qué dices tú – What are you doing, what are you saying?"

\*

Some days of the week, James met Borja for lunch but because of their respective schedules Thursday was not usually one of them. And, as he would naturally look in at the school on his way to the station and again on the way back, there seemed no real necessity to tell Borja that he was going on somewhere else betweenwhiles. It was just part of school business; you did not detail it all, classroom by classroom: that would bore any lover. Of course, if Borja asked (or discovered) where he was going he would tell him. But for the moment there seemed no need. Borja had such an unaccountable aversion to Paco; why should James re-arouse his suspicions needlessly? So James went to Jerez on Thursday without telling Borja.

Paco was not in his office when James arrived. William was there instead, speaking in Spanish, to James' surprise, on the telephone. "Hi, there," he said with a smile as he put the phone down. "Look, there's good news and bad news. Bad news: Paco couldn't drum up anyone else interested in lessons, at least not for today. Also, he won't be buying you lunch today; he's not back till two and he wants his own lesson then. The good news is, you get paid for the full day, you only have one lesson to give..."

"And I'm free till two o'clock."

There was a pause in which they looked at each other. Then, "And so am I," said William. There was another pause. "I've got my own office now. Want to see it?"

It was just down the corridor from Paco's. If anything it was smaller and even more untidy. James had just enough time to wonder – struggling to keep his thoughts in neutral – where all the chaotic stacks of papers and files had come from: surely not all produced by William during his own five-week tenure? – when William turned abruptly to face him. He felt the blood punching through his veins, and then they were back to where they had been at the end of their last meeting, locked in each other's arms. They each explored, just for a second, the other's trouser-front, then pulled apart.

"We could go over to my place," said William, struggling for an even tone. "Crack a bottle of something."

"Remember I've got to teach this afternoon." It was not too late, James thought, to put an end to this nonsense.

William put his head on one side. "So?"

James shrugged. "Lead the way, Orange."

A three-minute walk in the sunshine. They could have a drink, surely, James told himself. Nothing that he didn't want would happen. He'd make sure.

William took the key from under the flower-pot and let them into the cool interior. It was just as James remembered it. Remembered it? Hadn't been able to get it out of his mind. "Oh hell," he said. "I forgot the posters."

"Next time," said William, and put a hand on his shoulder. "Do we really want to open a bottle? I mean, just yet?"

"Maybe... not just yet." With both hands James caught William's open-necked shirt, pulled him slowly towards himself and began to undo the remaining buttons.

\*

Without any prompting from Pippa, Mark said: "Let's get out of town this weekend." He suggested Cádiz, on the coast, while autumn lingered and before the winter sea-fogs could spoil what he said was the best sunset in the world.

Cádiz, Pippa vaguely remembered, was where Drake had 'singed the King of Spain's beard' though she couldn't recall how or why. Mark needed some prompting to remember who Drake was. They set off quite early on Saturday. Mark had planned to stop off at Jerez on the way and look round a bodega. Everybody had to do that once, he said. He had a scooter on which he buzzed around Seville and Pippa, defying all the laws of physics and commonsense, sometimes rode pillion with him. There was no question, though, of taking the rusting machine on a two-hundred-mile round-trip so they went by train.

Jerez seemed to be shut. "Dammit, I should have thought," Mark said. Saturday had made him look a fool in front of Pippa. One by one the great sherry-houses – Domecq, González Byass – announced: 'Visitas, lunes – viernes'. But not Saturday. However, one of the big sleepy drink factories was open: O'Donnell's. A crowd of visitors was streaming in through the gates.

"Might as well tag along," said Mark. "See what happens. I know a guy who works here as a matter of fact. He's pretty high up. He had some lessons at the school during the last few years. Ybarra, his name was. Come to think of it, I nearly came over here to do some translating for him. Only I met you and James went instead. I forgot to ask him how it went. Be funny if Ybarra's doing the guided tour."

The crowd they had joined was American. "Compatriots," said Pippa incautiously.

"Semi-so," Mark answered, displeased. He was all-American when it suited him, fiercely Spanish when it did not. Their guide was not Paco but a smiling young man with an English accent and blue eyes. He did his job with some panache. "Probably an out-of-work actor," Mark said. He dealt with questions with charm and a flow of statistics that seemed almost too impressive. Mark couldn't help thinking that he was making a lot of them up. Pippa and Mark would have liked to talked to him afterwards and found out what brought him to Jerez. But he was beset by the swarm of tourists and they had a train to aim for so, after their free samples of O'Donnell's Fino and Oloroso Seco, they made their way out through the geranium-bright courtyards.

"He reminded me of someone, that guide," said Mark.

"James," said Pippa. "He looked like James."

Cádiz appeared first across the water, a medieval fortress islanded save for a long spit of sand and sardine canneries which ran parallel to the coast. The train wound round and doubled back across salt-pans where avocets and plovers delved, self-absorbed, for worms in the mud, then headed north along the isthmus. It seemed as if only an act of faith, namely that high tides would never run more than a metre above today's level, enabled anyone to reach Cádiz at all.

At its narrowest, at the neck of the old town, Cádiz was barely a hundred metres wide: the lagoon on one side, the Atlantic on the other. They booked into a hostel right there near the station, the two seas and just about everything else – for old Cádiz was very small. It was also very old. Pippa fancied that the buildings were held together by a crust of salt and that a hefty rainshower would dissolve them and tumble them back to the sea. She felt she had to tiptoe round the streets. Mark had another image in mind. "It's Miss Havisham's wedding-cake and we're infesting it."

Their hostel, unpretentious from the outside, was ranged around a centre-court so grand that it was as if the sterns of four galleons had been pulled together to form a square and you were looking up the light-well thus formed. Drying sheets spread out like mainsails and officers hollered information from poop-deck windows. Late at night, Pippa thought, with a little imagination the whole hostel might seem to be afloat.

They watched the sunset from the Atlantic side of the citadel. The sun dropped hissing into the sea, just as Mark said it would – on its way to America, he added. It was a gigantic, wasteful spread of red and gold. They kissed, as lovers never fail to, sharing the wastefulness, the abundance, of the moment.

They dined (muy típico Mark said) at a simple eating-house just around the corner from their hostel. For an absurdly low inclusive price they had seafood soup, baby sole and 'flan', which the British recognise as creme caramel. But their economy was humbled by the elderly man at the next table. He had few resources but great dignity. He took only the seafood soup and ingeniously turned it into a three-course meal. First he spooned off the liquid part, making his first course a consommé. Then he separated the remaining solids into two piles: rice and seafood. He did this with great care and it took nearly twenty minutes. Then he daintily ate the rice with his spoon. Finally, after a few moments' silent reflection, he had the seafood, dibbing into clams with a fork, shelling prawns with his teeth, spooning up mussels. In truth there were no more than three clams, five mussels and a couple of prawns but poverty and imagination had transformed them into a feast. "Remind me to write a poem about that," said Mark when the elderly man got up to leave, bowing ever so slightly towards everyone in the restaurant in turn.

Darkness had fallen as gently as snow while they were eating and now they wandered the lamplit town imagining themselves a hundred, two hundred, four hundred years in the past. Finally they turned back towards their hostel and its timbers really did creak as they made their way upstairs.

In the morning Mark decided to go jogging. The citadel was just the right size and shape for running round, its promenade affording spectacular views all the way. Pippa arranged to meet him as he returned along the Atlantic side near the cathedrals.

Cádiz had two cathedrals which faced each other across a small square near the beach. The new cathedral, Pippa discovered, despite a promisingly golden Byzantine dome, was conspicuously decrepit; the old cathedral was even more so and bore notices warning people not to approach it, so imminent, apparently, was its collapse.

As Pippa was poking around the buildings she became aware of shouting coming from the beach below the new cathedral. Curiosity drew her round the corner where she was startled by the sight of three people struggling. In the centre, a white-haired man was trying to maintain control of his money-belt which a swarthy young man was trying to pull off from the front while another dark youth tugged at the man from behind. It was difficult to take it all in. Were there two assailants or had one of the young men come to the old one's rescue? Pippa looked around her helplessly. Why wasn't Mark here? Suddenly she found herself running towards the little scene, shouting, "Let him go, let him go!" in English and Spanish. The frontal attacker looked up at her, he raised an arm. Something landed with a clatter at Pippa's feet. She looked down at it. It was a knife. Appalled, she looked back at the group of men but it had broken up. The knife-thrower had disappeared and the other two were sitting on a rock together; the young man, Pippa guessed, asking the older one if he was all right. She came up to them and quickly discovered that the young man was Spanish and the other a German who spoke neither Spanish nor English. The Spanish boy walked off almost at once, presumably thinking that the two foreigners would be best left together. Pippa was able to ascertain by gestures that the old man was not hurt and then to indicate that she would walk with him at least until they were away from the beach. Why was Mark taking such a long time?

They climbed the few rough steps to the promenade and then Pippa got her second shock of the morning. Mark was approaching along the promenade limping extravagantly and holding on at each step to the waist-high sea-wall for support.

"Whatever's happened?" she called out to him, forgetting the elderly tourist at her side.

"I fell into a hole. The workmen hadn't covered it." Mark did not sound amused.

"Then you won't be able to do the football," Pippa said, suddenly absurdly angry. "You promised."

"What football?" Then Mark remembered. Pippa's two classes of seven-year-olds were due to play each other at soccer. Pippa was to have been the hapless referee, until Mark had chivalrously volunteered to do it for her. He was feeling less chivalrous now. "Damn the football.Get Jeannette to do it. Ask James. I'm hurt."

"I will not put myself in Jeannette's debt," Pippa almost shouted. "And I don't imagine James plays football for a moment."

"You're totally wrong." Mark was yelling too now. "I've seen him play. Every year. Staff versus students. He's damn good."

Pippa felt a touch on her arm. Her silent companion had taken a two-thousand-peseta note from his rescued money-belt and now he pressed it firmly into her hand. With a polite nod and a flick of the hand he dismissed himself from their company.

"Just what in God's name is going on here?" Mark demanded.

Above them the great bells of the new cathedral opened their bronze throats to call the faithful to mass and simultaneously Pippa burst into tears.

## Seven

In the end it was James who refereed the battle of the seven-year-olds the following Thursday. Mark was still limping painfully though he had sustained nothing worse than a sprained ankle. The story of the weekend in Cádiz had drawn chuckles at work and James had retold it to Borja. "It seems to have done them no harm, though," he reported. "Their relationship is blooming as never before."

"They probably had their first row," said Borja sagely.

James available to referee a football match meant James not going to Jerez that Thursday. Paco was too busy arranging the Chamber of Commerce affair to have a lesson anyway and James, who would have to introduce William to Borja later that evening, was greatly relieved not to be spending the day with his new friend. A little breathing space was necessary, today, between them.

The reason for the Federación de Comercio dinner was not apparent to Borja or James. Perhaps it was simply to have a good dinner which, when they thought about it, did not seem such a bad one. Nevertheless, the pair set off with mixed feelings. For different reasons.

Borja felt awkward at being singled out from among his colleagues to dine with the top-brass of the tourist board. A formal dinner with the bosses did not promise to be a relaxing experience and especially not with his partner there. The fact that the invitations had come, out of the blue, from Paco Ybarra did nothing to reassure him either. Would he and James be seated far apart (which would be a pity) or close together (which would be worse)? He voiced these thoughts as they walked the two hundred metres from their flat to the Ayuntamiento, the town hall.

James made light of Borja's apprehensions. But his own misgivings were, of their very nature, impossible to share. He tried to visualise himself introducing Borja and William but his imagination balked at it. It would be the first time the three of them shared a space smaller than Andalucía, and he too had troubled thoughts about the possible permutations of the seating-plan. Still, neither of them had been invited to a civic dinner before or even set foot inside the Ayuntamiento. And now, as its sixteenth-century stone facade came into view, all barley-sugar mullions and caryatids, with smartly dressed men and women filing soberly in through the grand front entrance, their nervous doubts were stealthily supplanted by a sense of excitement; and the youthful scorn they both instinctively felt for the formalities of establishment junketing was swept away, as they passed beneath the arched lintel, by the idea that the occasion really was rather important and that, by extension, maybe so were they.

Once the doorman had scrutinised their invitation cards, they were waved up a staircase of film-set magnificence and into a salon full of people trying not to be mown down by waiters carrying knife-sharp trays of drinks. About half the men wore dinner-jackets and the other half lounge suits; this was a relief to Borja and James whose wardrobes extended only to the latter. The women on the other hand were wearing dresses of every conceivable colour, length and style; it was as if their invitations had said: come not as you are but as you would wish, on the strength of this one evening, to be remembered.

The drinks on the trays were copitas of fino the colour of bleached hay. Guests from the sherry companies were immediately identifiable as they sniffed their glasses with frowning, anxious, concentration.

Was this their own product they were being offered, or that of one of their competitors? How should they react to the first sip? Other guests, in contrast, quaffed their aperitifs with unclouded enjoyment.

Suddenly William was at James' elbow and with him the moment that he had so long imagined, dreaded and tried not to think about; the moment when he must introduce one lover to the other. "Hallo, William," he said. "This is Borja." It seemed a moment for understatement.

William held out his hand. "Hi. I work for Paco Ybarra at O'Donnell's. I should be Irish, I suppose, but I ain't. Bog-English, that's me." James had never heard such gibberish pour from William's mouth. Obviously he was suffering as acutely from nerves as James was. But it was evident only in what he said, which Borja, not knowing him, might not immediately identify as nonsense. William's manner, James thought, was impressively cool, calm and... James, in his agitation, could not think through to the end of the cliché. He prayed that the next ten seconds would go as smoothly as the first. And then the next...

Borja was smiling. It had not occurred to James until this moment that Borja might find William attractive. "Are you one of those assistants that James has spoken of – who take him off to the beach and get him drunk at lunchtime?"

"Could be."

Borja laughed. "Well, I suppose... it might have been the same with us had we been there."

"Hey," said William, surprised. "Shakespeare. Neat!"

James suddenly saw the three of them together on the beach at Chipiona. It was a powerful picture. That was how it should have been, he thought. That was how it must be. The three of them, just the three of them, playing together, chastely. Well, fairly chastely. How happy they could all be.

Ybarra stood among them. "Hola, Borja, we met before." He spoke in Spanish. "It's very good to see you again. I was going to introduce you to my assistant, William, but he seems to have done it for himself. This could be a useful evening for you, I thought. You could do yourself some good."

"In what way, precisely?" Borja asked.

Ybarra touched him lightly on the nose with his forefinger. "Don't be prickly." He smiled. "It'll happen. Just let it." He looked round at the others. "Now for the seating arrangements. You will find we are all seated separately. Safer that way. People put two and two together." He winked at Borja, who bristled in response.

A moment later a bell tinkled, a man who was too short to be seen through the crowd made an announcement that nobody could quite hear, and everybody trooped through another grand doorway into the banqueting room.

Borja found himself next to a youngish man with one topic of conversation: the respective merits of Betis and CF, the city's two football teams. Borja was happy to go along with this for a while but after a few minutes his own conversational stock on the subject was exhausted; he had no real interest in football. He was just considering the possibility of putting an end to the discussion brutally with a declaration of his own support for Salamanca when there came a face-saving intervention from his other neighbour, a grey-haired man of about fifty. He used the advantage of his years to, first, snuff out Borja's previous, unpromising conversation and then to interrogate Borja on his background and work in a way that Borja would not possibly be expected to reciprocate. Yet, in spite of himself, Borja found that he did not mind. His interlocutor seemed friendly enough and took a knowledgeable interest in what Borja had to tell him. This should not have surprised Borja. He quickly remembered that half the people in the room were in the tourist industry. Then it dawned on him that he must be talking to the Jefe de Turismo for the whole region of Andalucía, Diego Imendia, his boss's boss's boss. This discovery did not cause him to lose his tongue: on the contrary, he began to feel that he was making quite a good impression.

"Maybe we are too regional in our thinking," the older man replied to one of Borja's observations. "We don't think enough in terms of Spain as a whole – the whole rich experience. How many of your colleagues, for instance, know much of Spain outside their own region?"

"Well..." began Borja.

"Very few, I imagine. Yes, you've raised a good point. Of course you have a head's start over them already, coming from Salamanca as you tell me you do. You have two regions under your belt already."

"I suppose I could say that."

"Of course we want to hold on to our tourists here in Andalucía: don't get me wrong. Tourism is a major plank of our economy. But too many people see Andalucía and think they've done Spain. Next year Italy, maybe, or Morocco. Yet why should there not be someone in the tourist office who can say to them: wait, you've seen our lovely region; next year try Toledo, see Galicia, visit the Prado in Madrid....? And is informed enough to sell the idea to them."

"I see."

"What's in it for Andalucía, I hear you asking? Directly, not a lot. But Spain is a family of regions. Andalucía is large and poor. But if Spain grows richer Andalucía will grow richer too, just as in a real family: if the father gets more money the children will eat better. Are you married?"

"No," said Borja.

"It's early yet. Now, wouldn't it be a good idea if we had at least one member of staff in each main centre – Sevilla, Córdoba and Granada at the very least – who was familiar with the whole country and could give our visitors comprehensive and informed advice?"

"You could be right," said Borja.

"We'd have to train you up of course. Send you about a bit. Learn the territory." Diego Imendia paused and tasted a piece of fish. "It's a good idea of yours. Leave it with me. I'll think more about this, then I'll get back in touch. How do you find the sea-bass?"

Borja could hardly believe how the interview had gone. Diego

Imendia would be in touch. Already he heard the office phone ringing. The sea-bass tasted excellent.

\*

James, for his part, was sandwiched between a young secretary from González Byass in a flamingo-coloured dress and a middle-aged man whose provenance James couldn't quite catch. His Spanish was under maximum pressure at occasions like this. The young lady was oddly shy, considering the way she was dressed, but the man more than compensated with a cheerful loquacity. "Tell you a funny story," he said to James. "Friend of mine, he owns a few properties dotted around Seville. Well, you know, things get old and need replacing – kitchen fittings, woodwork and so on. So he's always got a team of workmen going the rounds, you see."

"Wish he was my landlord," said James. "He never has anyone free to deal with a problem."

"Anyway, there's this old widow-lady living just off Calle Sierpes and she needs her window-frames replacing. My friend tries to make an appointment with her to get the job done. He rings, he calls, but he never manages to get hold of her, so in the end he sends the workmen round with a spare set of keys to get cracking. She's out when they arrive but they get on with the job and take out the frame and chuck it away. Then the woman comes back. Doesn't know who the men are or what they're doing. She's in a right old state. 'Where's my window?' she asks. And for a joke, one of the men says: 'Oh, the maricónes have taken it.'"

James felt himself go hot and his mouth go dry. He put down his fork. "Why should they say that?" he asked evenly.

"Simply because they had another job on their work-list, also replacing a window, in another flat nearby where two men are living together. It was the first thing they thought of. But she, the old widow, says: 'Do you mean those two in the Plaza del Salvador?' And before they can stop her she's gone out the door and round the corner to face them with it. Quite funny really. Of course, by the time she comes back the new window's in and the workmen are making good. And that might have been the end of the story."

"And was it?" James asked, trying for nonchalance. His palms were sweating.

"No," said the other. "It gets better. Seems she told everyone she passed on the way to San Salvador where she was going and they egged her on: told her to ask for her window back. And later, learning from the builders that the maricónes' window was due for replacement a few weeks later, the neighbours decided to have a bit of a laugh themselves: they ripped out the window the weekend before the work was due to start, intending to tell the maricónes the old lady had done it."

"Not an especially brilliant joke, I would have thought," said James coldly.

"Well it didn't quite work out. The maricónes called the police before anyone had a chance to involve the old lady."

"And did the landlord, your friend, know about this?"

"Not at first, of course. But he heard the whole story soon enough. It was all round the town." The story-teller chuckled.

"I see," said James. "But how did the people get the window-frame out? Without entering the house, I mean. They'd have looked like criminals. Which, you have to admit, is what they were."

"No, no. It was harmless fun. They did it from the inside. The woman in the ice-cream parlour round the corner had a key, apparently. They only had to ask her for it."

"I never knew..." James came to a stop. He felt bludgeoned.

"What?"

"I mean, I should have guessed. Now, sorry to spoil your story but I didn't find it especially funny. Forgive my English lack of humour."

The other shrugged but did not seem put out. "Suit yourself," he said without animosity and turned away towards his other neighbour.

Miserably, James speared a piece of sea-bass. It felt like cotton-wool in his mouth.

Coffee and coñac were served in the salon where they had met earlier. Paco held the floor; William let him talk: an hour of chatting in Spanish to strangers had tired him out. Borja was not going to recount in public the gist of his conversation with Diego Imendia – though he would share it later with James in detail. Still, Borja seemed to James to be radiating a new-found self-confidence as he listened to Paco, casually adding his own comments to Paco's stories. Borja would need all the self-confidence he could muster if he learned about the window, James thought. He, James, would never tell him. Certainly, not while they lived at that address. He felt terribly responsible for Borja. It was he who had told Borja that coming to live with him would bring him no harm, had promised that their new neighbours would accept them just as they did in other big western cities. Borja had believed him in the end and now for three years they had shared that... that delusion, it turned out. Because those neighbours they talked and laughed with – or some of them – (yes, but which?) – had not only been happy to laugh at them but also been prepared to break into their house and ruin their weekend in order to laugh the longer. And the lady in the ice-cream shop, the nice lady he used to gossip with, had helped them do it, and never said a word. No, Borja must never know. James looked at him and saw again the beautiful, serious boy he had met on that train journey to Madrid. He'd shared his water bottle with him, then later, his life. Now was not the moment to be playing around with William.

"You're miles away," Paco said suddenly.

"No, I'm not," James and William answered in chorus, each thinking the question meant for himself, and the other two laughed at their subsequent embarrassment.

"Are you two going back to Jerez tonight?" James managed to ask.

No, they were staying in a hotel. James wondered if he could ask them back to the flat for a nightcap first and decided he couldn't.

Maybe a bar on the way home? James suggested Morales as it was nearby, and Borja did not veto the idea.

The pavements were narrow and Borja found himself walking next to Paco and not really objecting to his company. He felt he had his measure now and could deal with him, though whether that was the result of his conversation with Diego Imendia or the coñac would be hard to say.

"Borja's great," said William, walking behind with James. "And cute with it. I can see why you chose him."

"I'd better take care to try and keep him, in that case, hadn't I?"

William seemed taken aback. "How am I expected to answer that?" A new thought struck him. "Are you trying to tell me something?"

"Like what?"

"Like, how shall I say, like you won't be coming to Jerez on Thursday?"

"Well..."

"Well, it's a business trip. Whatever happens, or doesn't, between us."

"I think 'doesn't' is going to be the order of the day from now on," said James.

"I see. Well, if you want to cool it a bit, what can I say? We can always meet for a drink or something. Borja couldn't possibly object to that."

James thought he saw the logic of this.

They arrived at the bar. Paco ordered four coñacs. Meanwhile Borja had something to ask James. "Paco was telling me you are teaching in Jerez now on Thursdays. You never told me. Is it true?"

William moved swiftly. "Starting next week, isn't that right, Paco?"

"I was meaning to tell you," James said.

"But last week..." Paco began, puzzled.

"It was decided very suddenly," said William. He put his arm momentarily around Paco's shoulder. "Sometimes Paco doesn't know what day it is." James suddenly wondered, though he had lost his opportunity to find out, if Paco and William would be sharing the same hotel room.

The drinks arrived. Everyone drank to one another's health and then, because it was William's first visit to Morales' bar, the others made a great fuss of pointing out all its antiquated fittings and furniture: the ancient posters, the ceiling-high amphorae in the cobwebbed back room – all things which he could see for himself. They didn't stay for a second drink. After exchanging friendly farewells the two pairs of men went their separate ways.

"You didn't tell me about William," said Borja as they crossed back over the Plaza San Francisco. "I like him. But perhaps that's not so surprising. At times he looks quite like you. Maybe you never noticed."

# Eight

Alexa explained to her parents on the telephone that she would not be coming home for Christmas. They were not entirely understanding. Her father had fought in the Second World War and, though he had no hard feelings towards Bach and Beethoven, found the idea of his daughter spending Christmas in Morocco with a German guitarist oddly threatening. He was not quite able to put this into words when challenged to do so by Alexa. Still, she promised to visit England in the new year which slightly mollified him and her mother. It was not an easy phone-call, especially as, tipping coins down the chute, you never knew when you might be cut off. Alexa wasn't on this occasion but it was a call of expensive duration all the same.

Autumn was fading softly into winter. Washing hung wet and listless on the rooftops for longer than usual before it could be taken in. Sometimes there was even rain. Pippa invited Mark to spend Christmas with her parents. He accepted with alacrity: he had never been to England.

"The Christmas juggling act," James said. "Same thing every year. Who goes where? Who with? Who feels left out?" He was stretched naked on William's bed. A shaft of warm December sun glanced across his stomach and groin and made him glow with warmth in a way that never happened when he was clothed. William, similarly unclad, emerged from the kitchen with two glasses of post-coital tinto. It was

Thursday. Their resolve to transform their regular meetings into chaste café conversations had lasted about twenty minutes, each one its own individual agony. That had been two weeks ago now and there didn't seem any way of going back.

"That looks nice," said William, looking down at James' sunlit contours for a moment before joining him on the bed.

"So do you," said James. He sat up and drew his legs under his chin to make room for William who adopted the same position, facing him, at the other end of the bed, as if they were sharing a bath. Telling William he looked good was a very pleasurable thing for James to do: it was very much an affirmation of his own physical desirability. But he tried not to think too hard about that.

"So what are you going to do at Christmas?" William asked.

"Borja's going to his family over Christmas itself – for as short a time as possible. Then he wants to spend a few days seeing old friends in Salamanca. We meet up again for the Tres Reyes. That's our Christmas. Most Spanish people have their presents and things then anyway."

"But what about you?" William persisted.

"Same thing. A couple of days with the parents, and I'll probably look up a few mates in London... My parents are sending me the air-fare," he added a little sheepishly. "I can't possibly not go."

William stroked James' calf with his toes. "I'll be in London too," he said with quiet deliberation. "We could meet up. Spend time together. I've got friends where we could both stay."

The significance of this was not lost on James. He had never spent a night with William, never actually slept in his arms, never woken to see his head on the pillow beside him in the morning. He felt a surge of excitement which communicated itself (who knew how?) to William and in an instant they had both sprung forward and were all over each other, wrestling, exploring, sharing their warm nakedness. What was going on in William's head James could not be sure but he for one was fighting madly for control of a mind and tongue which wanted desperately to blurt out that most irretrievable cry: 'I love you'. Their untouched glasses of wine were jolted to the floor where their contents trickled unheeded along the joins between the tiles, making a grid as if for a crossword. The words would come in time.

\*

Mark went all unsuspecting to New Maldon. He had been prepared to find England rather small and drab but his expectations were wondrously exceeded. "Little houses," he complained to Pippa, "little shops, little streets, little people. And the damp. The chill, chill damp. People steaming like kettles when they speak to each other in the street. And it gets dark at lunchtime. It's worse than Canada."

For her part, Pippa was surprised to discover that Mark seemed diminished by being away from Spain. He looked smaller in himself and his clothes seemed shabbier, his trousers more frayed, his shoes more down-at-heel. She could almost fancy that he wore a hunted look, though, as she could not think why this should be so, she dismissed it from her imagination. Mark had a catchphrase that he used to use all the time in Spain: 'I think I can handle it.' But now he was in Britain he had stopped saying it. Perhaps Britain would be something he couldn't handle easily. Pippa warned herself to tread carefully.

Pippa's parents were quite taken with Mark. Her father in particular approved of his quiet courtesy, her mother was more appreciative of his charm and eyelashes. Like her daughter she noticed his unusual green eyes, flecked like blackbirds' eggs, but she saw in them the same hunted look that Pippa had noticed and was puzzled by it, not knowing that the look was as new to her daughter as it was to herself.

On their second to last evening, Pippa's father detained Mark at bedtime with the offer of a malt whisky. And as soon as they were alone together he pounced. "Would you like to tell me, young man, what your intentions towards my daughter are?"

Still unsuspecting, Mark replied: "Perfectly fine, sir. All open and above board."

"I don't think you quite understand me." The temperature in the room seemed to drop perceptibly. Perhaps it was the time when the central heating went off. "You are living together, are you not?"

Mark gave what he thought was a disarming smile. "You weren't supposed to know that, sir."

Pippa's father stood up. "Jesus Christ Almighty," he said. 'I wasn't supposed to know!?' What kind of damn fool do you take me for? I can read the signs, for God's sake. I was your age once, don't forget. Now listen. Pippa's mother doesn't know. It's important that she... I mean... I don't mean...."

"No, of course she's not. I mean... I know what you do mean."

"The point is, I mean the point is, what steps are you going to take to regularise the situation?"

"What sort of steps?" Mark asked, genuinely confused.

"You surely know what I'm talking about. Even across the Atlantic there must be some glimmer of understanding about the honourable course of action expected of a man in your position."

"Honourable course?" echoed Mark. He felt the blood chill in his veins as he finally understood. "I suppose," he said in a thread-thin voice, "I suppose I should ask you for her hand in marriage. If she'd have me, that is." He took a sip of whisky and thought of all the times he had heard, even used, the phrase 'I need a drink' without ever suspecting that it could have real meaning.

\*

Pippa responded well to the news of her engagement. She suggested going up to town in the afternoon. Mark had not yet seen central London and she wanted to show it to him, just as, two months before, he had shown her Seville. And while they were there they could look at the price of rings.

It was getting dark by the time they got to the West End. Mark was moderately impressed by the Christmas lights but he had somehow expected that London would offer something more subtle or sophisticated. Oxford Street was frankly disappointing, in spite of its surreal superabundance of red double-decker buses. Still, he was cheered to see the famous curve of Regent Street where it swoops upon Piccadilly Circus and he admired the sober grandeur of the streets around St. James. Wisely, Pippa did not even dawdle near the jewellers' shops in that particular quarter but took him on the top deck of a bus to the Portobello Road. Mark enjoyed its anarchic bustle, found it quite an agreeable surprise and began to modify his opinion of London. "London's kind of full of the unexpected," he was just saying, when the very unexpected almost bumped into him on the pavement.

"Good God," Pippa said. "James." For it was he. With someone who might have been his brother.

James looked extremely surprised to see them. More than that, Mark decided, he looked like someone caught out.

"What a coincidence," said James.

"Small world," said William.

And everyone was duly introduced. Pippa suggested heading for the nearest café for tea and cakes but was overruled by the two Englishmen who pointed out that the pubs were already open.

"You'd better be the first to know," began Pippa, then stopped and looked at Mark. "Can I tell them?"

"You'll have to, now," said James.

"We're engaged."

"Since about midnight last night," added Mark. And perhaps because rings were on his mind at that precise moment he noticed with a sudden shock that James and his not fully explained companion were each wearing a simple gold circle in their left ear. "You never had an earring before, did you?" he said.

James and William involuntarily half-turned towards each other, not with a laugh, not even a giggle, but with a faint shared snort of breath that made Mark suddenly quite certain of the situation that existed between them.

"We just had them done," explained James. "Just down the road here."

"They do tattoos as well," William said.

"But don't worry," James continued the thought-line. "Neither of us wanted to go in for one of those."

Did Pippa realise, Mark wondered? James had said lightly that William was an old schoolfriend. Yet Mark had a vague feling he had seen William somewhere before. He was puzzled and uncertain. How would he and Pippa talk about this unexpected meeting? If they even did talk about it. The moment became fraught with meaning. On the very day when he and Pippa had put in motion the machinery that would lock them together for life, why did they have to meet one of their closest acquaintances apparently unpicking the fabric of his own shared life and shackling himself with two slender gold links to a stranger?

*

Returning to Seville after her English Christmas, Pippa found a second Christmas waiting to happen. Spain was gearing itself up for the Epiphany, the feast of Los Tres Reyes, it being the Spanish custom to give presents on the twelfth day of Christmas rather than the first. Tall palm trees standing outside the big stores had been converted into Christmas trees by the superimposition of painted hardboard frames, lit with fairy-lights and hung with presents made from polystyrene and paint. The Three Kings themselves could be seen from time to time in the streets, complete wth Arab costumes and blacked-up faces. They even had a real camel with them, alive and belching. The pageant attracted crowds of children wherever it passed, and the kings threw them handfuls of sweets as they went by.

Reactions to Pippa's news were instructive. Her cousin Sophie gave her a warm hug and congratulated her fulsomely, but Pippa sensed an underlying feeling that for Sophie some of the magic had departed the scene now that the situation had been formalised in this convention-al way. Perhaps, Pippa thought, it reflected what had happened in her own case with Pablo.

Jeannette was for once full of enthusiasm. Pippa's engagement seemed to make everything all right between them for the first time since she had met Mark. Jeannette liked to see things wrap themselves up tidily. Also, there was now another girl living at the flat again so the rent was being taken care of. But Jeannette did sound a note of caution. "Don't let the engagement drag," she said. "You're so young still, and you're both very different." Pippa frowned. "I mean," Jeannette amended, "your backgrounds are different. What I wanted to say was, now it's all formal and your parents are happy, don't wait for ever before booking your place in front of the altar. Do you see?" What Pippa saw most clearly, and for the first time, was the extent to which people's responses to you were mirrors of what they felt about themselves. And no more so than in the case of Alexa.

Alexa made all the right noises but Pippa could feel that at heart she did not share in Pippa's joy at her new situation. It was not long before she turned the conversation towards music, sat down at the piano and said: "Listen to this." Still, it was a rare enough invitation and Pippa was delighted to oblige. She had only heard Alexa play once before.

The window-shutters were half-open now as it was January and the sun was warm rather than hot. It fell in gently slanting shafts across Alexa's piano as she played, and lit the back of her head. Pippa noticed that it made her long red hair almost the same colour as the rosewood instrument, as in a Vermeer painting. Alexa's face was in shadow.

The music was by Schumann and unfamiliar to Pippa. She didn't find it as easy to like as the Beethoven and Mozart Alexa had played on the previous occasion but she enjoyed the power and passion of the playing. She said as much when Alexa had finished. "Beautifully,

beautifully, played. But I don't think Schumann is ever going to be one of my favourites."

Alexa smiled. "To tell you the truth, I don't think he's one of mine either." She smiled again, mischievously this time. "Now listen to this. But first you must close your eyes."

Pippa was surprised. The instruction sounded childish and untypical of Alexa. Still, she obeyed. There was a pause, some movement and then, as soon as Alexa began the next piece, another surprise. Alexa was not playing the piano but the guitar. Pippa opened her eyes at once. Alexa was still sitting on the piano-stool but with her back to the instrument, her face and her guitar – if it was hers – full in the sun. She was playing a slow-treading sarabande, not attempting anything fast and showy, but the sounds she made exploded and resonated in the room with all the energy and feeling she brought to her piano playing. Pippa was almost physically shocked.

"Well?" said Alexa, putting the guitar down when the short piece was finished.

"I'm astonished," said Pippa honestly. "I didn't know you..."

"I didn't, until last month. I'm a virtual beginner."

"You didn't sound like a beginner. You've got real... style. Is Karsten teaching you?" It was the first time Karsten had been mentioned.

"He taught me a little at first, because I asked him. And perhaps soon I'll ask him for some serious lessons. At first I was just curious. But then I worked at it on my own. Karsten doesn't know I can play the piece you've just heard, for instance. Do you know who wrote it?"

"Bach?" suggested Pippa.

"Warm. Handel. It's one of his. I mean it's one of Karsten's. Part of his repertoire."

"And you're not sure of his reaction to your playing it?"

"Perhaps. The thing is, I'm getting hooked. When I should be working at the piano I keep breaking off and reaching for the guitar.

Do you think that's crazy?"

Pippa thought for a moment. "Well, no. But, if the piano's your career and the guitar isn't, it might seem crazy from a professional point of view, mightn't it?"

"You're right. But there are other things than careers that matter. As you know."

Pippa thought she had found the thread. Some time over Christmas, she guessed, Alexa and Karsten had ceased to be just good friends. But maybe things hadn't turned out so well. That would explain Alexa's brisk dismissal of Pippa's own news. The key must be Morocco. "So tell me about Morocco," she said.

Alexa was happy to. "Fabulous," she said. "Even crossing the straits was wonderful. The sun was going down, with the mountains of Africa in silhouette to one side and Spain on the other. There were dolphins. I felt so free. Last time I crossed the sea, I had a piano on board, remember. It was like... like a ball and chain." Pippa sneaked a look at the instrument.

Alexa went on to talk about Marrakesh: about how its red walls glowed at evening; about how the story-tellers and snake-charmers thronged in the great square, sitting round charcoal fires after dark. She giggled. "There was a madman, completely naked, standing on a high wall, peeing down into the street. Nobody seemed to bother. We stayed in a little room over a shop."

"Does Karsten speak Arabic?" Pippa asked.

"Just a few words. But he speaks good French. The Germans put us to shame, they're such good linguists."

The Germans, Pippa noticed. Not one German in particular.

"You know, the great thing is that Marrakesh is so like Seville, or rather, it gives you an impression of Seville as it must have been six hundred years ago. It gives you a new perspective on the place. The minaret there is just like the Giralda here in Seville – they were built for the same sultan. Coming back, you realise that this really is an Arab town and all the Christian bit is just an overlay on the top:

something that could easily be rolled back again."

"Is that how Karsten sees it too?" Pippa wasn't getting the story she was after.

"Oh yes. In fact it was he who made me think about it in that way. You should go there with Mark some time. I had a really good time."

I now, not we. Maybe yes, maybe no, Pippa thought. She was none the wiser and Alexa clearly wasn't going to give anything away. Pippa gave up. "Marrakesh sounds a bit different from New Maldon, certainly. I don't think Mark really took to London."

"Won't that be a problem?" suggested Alexa. "I mean, in the long term."

Pippa smiled confidently. "I think I can handle it," she said.

\*

"It was fate, I suppose," said Mark. He was talking to Karsten for the first time since Christmas. They had met by chance in the street and drifted into the Arco for a beer. "Do you believe in fate?"

"I have no reason to. I was brought up a strict Catholic. We were taught to believe in – what do you call it – freewill? But now I'm not a Catholic any more. I don't believe in all the impossible things they ask you to accept. But sometimes – against my good judgement – I do think there is a thing called fate."

"Hell, you're so serious sometimes," Mark complained. "It was only a rhetorical question."

Karsten hit back. "Then maybe you are too rhetorical and not serious enough. Maybe your attention was caught by the coincidental symmetry – engagement rings, earrings – and you exaggerated that into a feeling of fate."

"Maybe I did. But that wouldn't explain the way I feel now."

"How do you feel?"

"Depressed. Deflated. Anxious about the future. I'd always felt perfectly happy about Pippa and me. That it could go on for ever. I didn't mean I thought there would never be problems, but I felt that, together, we could handle anything that life might chuck at us. I was kind of buoyed up by that thought. Now I'm not."

"But maybe it's not that that's getting you down. Nobody can be certain about the future. Maybe you are actually troubled by something else."

"Like what?"

"It is very common to mis-identify the cause of our negative feelings. For instance, how many people know that you met James in London?"

"Only Pippa. And now you. No-one else."

"And did you and Pippa talk about it?"

"Not a word. I didn't refer to it in case she'd seen nothing amiss. She didn't mention it either."

"Perhaps for the same reason. So the reason you are upset may have less to do with the idea that you've been given a glimpse of the future – I mean one possible future, the break-up of a relationship – and more with the fact that you are friends of both James and Borja and so your loyalties are divided. You have one friend who feels compromised and would like you to keep his secret and another who maybe deserves..."

"Yeah, OK," said Mark, irritated at hearing Karsten spell things out with such plodding deliberation. "If you want to know, I don't plan to say anything to Borja. There's a small chance I may have read the situation wrong, though I don't think so. And in any case, it's their life, or lives. Other people can't sort things out for them. So I'd be kind of glad if you didn't..."

"That's sure. I wouldn't. Don't worry."

"Anyway, I wanted to hear about your trip to Morocco. How was it?"

"Very cool," said Karsten. "We had an extremely cool time."

Mark thought how difficult it was to use slang in another person's language. It never seemed to come out quite right.

\*

Borja, on his first day back at work after his Christmas break, answered the phone on his desk. He was startled to hear the voice of Diego Imendia, though the head of regional tourism was only keeping his word. Borja had been selected, Imendia told him, to take part in a new training programme. It would take him to a number of important centres of tourism in Spain, sharing information with his counterparts in the other regions. "You've struck lucky," said his immediate boss when they discussed it later. "I'd say it amounts to six expenses-paid short holidays. It's never too soon to learn the importance of sitting next to the right people at dinner." He offered Borja a small cigar.

Borja was excited by this development; when telling James about it he ran out of breath, forgetting to punctuate his sentences. James was pleased for him, and jealous too, for he had visited only a few of the places Borja would be going to. Half of him wished he could be going along for the ride. The other half saw at once the opportunity that Borja's absences would afford him for spending more time with William.

Initially, it was a shock for James, adjusting to intimacy with Borja again after three days with another man. For three days he had been a part of William and William a part of him, sharing a bed, sharing their bodies, becoming more like one person than two. Now, returning to Seville, it was disorientating to rediscover the identical intimacies with Borja. And then it came as another surprise to find that he did not love Borja any less now that he also loved William. (Yes, by this time he had told William so and William had used the same three words to him; neither would ever remember who had said them first.) If anything, James felt his love for Borja enhanced by his growing feelings for William and found himself exploring Borja both physically and emotionally like a new person.

James' account of his Christmas had necessarily to be short on detail, though he did talk of his meeting with Pippa and Mark in the Portobello Road. He mentioned in passing that he had been with an old friend he had met for lunch. If Mark chanced to let slip to Borja the fact that James had not been alone, then Borja would not be alerted by James' silence on the point. And James felt he knew Mark well enough to be sure that he would not dwell on the subject or mention William by name. Even if he did, lots of men were called William.

Borja in his turn mentioned one or two old friends he had seen in Salamanca. He had spent a couple of nights at the house of one of them who was now married. That was what he said and James had no reason to doubt him. In the end you just had to trust your partner or life became impossible. That was what James thought in general, and he was too preoccupied now to notice any irony in applying the idea in present circumstances. Instead, and against all logic, he drew the comforting conclusion that, since he had no suspicions about Borja's behaviour when he was out of sight, then Borja was unlikely to be suspicious of him.

# Nine

Borja's arrival at his parents' farm for Christmas had coincided with the arrival of the first lambs of the winter. This was good: it gave him an excuse to be busy. He could spend the days driving round the hill-pastures with his father and brothers in the Jeep, checking on new births, and punctuate the long evenings with visits to the barns where the weaker lambs, the abandoned ones and the orphans sheltered and were bottle-fed. The few ewes among them would stand to attention on the men's arrival and gaze dully into the light of the lanterns they carried. On Christmas Eve half the family went to midnight mass in the cathedral, the others, Borja included, went at noon on Christmas Day in the deceptively bright sunshine: deceptive because this was not Seville; the air carried a sharp upland chill.

Borja was not sure to what extent his family knew about him: about him and James. When he had settled in Seville with his lover, he had announced baldly that he was going to share a flat with an Englishman, called James: a teacher. He had let them make what they would of it. They reacted with some surprise but not consternation. The youngest son of the family had always been odd and different; here was just one more odd thing; at least it would be good for his English. Borja had not attempted to tell the whole truth. He had only knowingly met three homosexuals before James and one of those he had not even spoken to. He had certainly never heard of anyone who had told their parents.

There were boys at school whom he had admired secretly, and there was one who had returned his affection: Carlos, who had said suddenly, bitterly, one day: "If the world were a better, different place I would marry you." Borja's world had turned upside-down when he said it but nothing ever happened between them, not even a kiss. Carlos, Borja now understood, was working in a hotel on Ibiza – presumably having found there the better, different world that he wanted.

At university Borja fell in love for the first time as a grown-up. Unlike the handsome, athletic Carlos, Miguel was small and delicate-looking, much more so than Borja. But like Borja, Miguel was a very religious youth. Despite his own scruples Borja once or twice tried, very timidly, to make a sexual advance to Miguel. But temptation was never allowed to turn to sin; Miguel's fear of hell-fire was greater than his own, and he would politely remove Borja's trespassing hand with a small gasp of suppressed feeling. Miguel talked openly about living together with Borja after university – without sex, of course – to show people that it could be done. Borja played along with this idea when talking with Miguel, though privately he felt sure it would be impossible. Loving Miguel chastely was painful enough now when they lived on opposite sides of town.

One evening, when Borja's love affair with Miguel had been going on (or standing still) for nearly two years, he was making his way home past the Monterrey Park when it suddenly occurred to him to walk through it. He never knew why: it was not as if it were a short cut. A man was smoking in the shadow under a tree. Borja stopped and looked at him. The man looked back. He took a packet of cigarettes from his pocket and held one out to Borja. Still not knowing why, Borja walked towards him and accepted it. No light was offered. Borja leaned forward and lit up from the glowing cigarette in the other's mouth. Then, with a sang-froid that astounded him at the time and that he could barely believe even all these years later, he efficiently undid the stranger's belt and dropped his trousers.

If the world had turned upside-down when Carlos had talked of marrying him, it did so again that evening, but this time horribly, leaving him appalled at what he had done, alone with self-loathing and a handkerchief. The man and he had exchanged no words, no smiles; after the initial contact of cigarette with cigarette their faces had not even met.

A small mercy was that Borja was returning to the urban bed-sitter where he lived in term-time rather than home to the farm. He could not have faced his parents that night. As for Miguel, Borja went round town avoiding him for several days and when, as inevitably happened, he did bump into him again it was immediately clear to Borja that nothing could be the same again between them. Their relationship died in an instant. Miguel realised this as quickly as Borja but unlike him had no idea why. Borja was unable to tell him.

Borja never visited the park again. Even to pass near it gave him the horrors. His first experience of sex with another person had become the worst event of all his life. He got on with his work and kept his head down. He was only too relieved, a year later, to finish university and put Salamanca behind him. When, escaping headlong on the train to Madrid, during the first few minutes of his new freedom, his life had collided with James', broken to smithereens and started again from the beginning.

It had not needed James – sexually experienced, at ease with his orientation, yet discovering love for the first time in his life – to tell Borja that sex-inclusive love was absolutely right between them: every fibre of his being believed and attested it. It was only his concern about the contrary view of the Church that caused those early, angst-ridden, post-coital conversations. James calmed him. Did he know, for example, that the sin of Sodom mentioned in the Bible had nothing to do with homosexuality, or even sex at all, but was a misunderstanding based on a mistranslation? No, Borja did not know that.

James had read it in a magazine article back in England. Borja thought hard about this. If such things were written about by journalists in more liberated lands, they were surely also known in the theological colleges. Known but secret: past mistakes, misunderstandings, not acknowledged from the pulpit; the faithful kept deliberately in darkness. If the Church could keep quiet about this one small thing – yet big for him because it affected him most fundamentally – how much else might it be hiding? On how many other matters might it be mistaken? Borja did not lose his faith all at once. But the Church's stranglehold on his mind began to loosen. By now, three years later, he was able to keep religion at arms' length, regarding it with what he considered a healthy and proper scepticism.

A couple of days after Christmas, Borja left his parents' house and went to stay with friends in Salamanca city centre. Marisa had been his friend and confidante at university. They had been so close that some people took them for boyfriend and girlfriend at first and then were surprised when Marisa married her real boyfriend, Alberto, at the end of the first year. Alberto was a little puzzled by Borja but, realising quickly that he posed no threat (though not at first understanding why), allowed his friendship with his wife to continue. Only after meeting James had Borja felt bold enough to tell Marisa about himself. She was the first Salamanca person he had ever told, and she made it easier for him by interrupting to say that she had already guessed. Presumably she then told Alberto, though his gruff but friendly manner to Borja never altered.

Marisa had married young and she started a family young, too. By now they had Carmen, aged five, and – yes – Borja, aged three. Marisa had never actually said that her first boy had been called after her old friend and he wasn't going to ask. Still, he felt flattered by the choice of name – it could hardly have been random after all – and it went a long way towards negating the uncomfortable feelings he usually had in the presence of young children. For he lived – and was obliged to live, if he was being truly himself – in a world without them.

Marisa and her family lived in a large house which Alberto had the remarkable fortune to have inherited. The rooms on the top floors were let out, to students mainly, and as most of these were away for the Christmas period, there was no difficulty in finding space for Borja. "You'd know one of the people who stays here from time to time," Marisa said. "Somebody you'd remember from university. Works for an airline now. Rafael." But lots of men were called Rafael and the one Borja now brought to mind was a lumpy, oafish character. Borja was not particularly interested in remembering him. He certainly didn't know anybody who had gone to work for an airline. "Talking of people we used to know," Marisa went on, "do you ever run into Benjamín? Now that you're both in Seville."

"Occasionally," said Borja. "Not often. We were never very close and we've gone rather different ways. Also, he's rather difficult to get hold of. You obviously can't expect to just run into him in a bar or something. Once I even had to make an appointment. Can you imagine? Still, you've put him in my mind. Perhaps I'll go and see him in the new year."

The new year came and Borja returned to Seville to receive his news from Diego Imendia and to find James with a new light in his eyes, a spring in his step and one gold earring. A few weeks later came the annual football match between the teachers at James' school and the students. Not all the teachers played; numbers were made up by boyfriends of female members of staff. But James took part every year religiously even though it was the only time he now played. Football was a part of his youth that he could not bear to part with completely. To say that he 'used to' play football, he felt, would come very close to admitting to middle-age.

Football had been an important fact of James' life. As an adolescent, learning little by little not only that he was different but also in what way, it was what he did to prove to himself and to the world that he was nevertheless a real man with manly interests, competitiveness and strength. Borja, not a footballer, put his stuntlike car-driving and those push-ups that not even James knew about to the same end. But Borja came, as he did every year, to watch the game. It was played on a patch of waste ground between the river and the Plaza de Armas station that, after dark, was given over to stranger pursuits than football.

James played well. He had never had tremendous skill but he made up for it with boundless energy and a terrier-like determination that could quite unnerve his opponents. Especially if they knew him. For James was not at all like that off the football field. Watching him this day with his usual proprietorial admiration, Borja suddenly noticed something. He commented on it afterwards, after the statutory con-gratulations were over. (Though the result had been a draw: three-all.)

"Those aren't your usual football boots."

James could easily have said that he'd brought them back from home after Christmas. But he was flustered by the question and told the truth. "I borrowed them from someone in Jerez." He cast about for a good reason. "Mine are so worn out. I've had them since I was at school."

"I see," said Borja and let the matter drop.

\*

Borja rang the bell of the Archbishop's Palace. "Is Benjamín in?" he asked when an old priest answered the door.

"If you mean Padre Garcia Diaz," said the priest, sounding stern but not looking it, "yes he is."

"I can't say Padre to someone I was at university with," objected Borja.

"Why ever not?" said the priest. "Wait here."

A much younger priest arrived. He was quite tall but seemed extremely so on account of his unusual thinness. His face was long and high-cheekboned, his cheeks cavernous beneath them. His eyes were narrow but smouldered darkly. He might have been a medieval cleric from a canvas by Zurburan but for an unexpected thatch of black hair that was more early Beatles than monastic tonsure.

"Well, what a surprise," said Benjamín. "We haven't seen you for months." His eyes twinkled. "Have you come for confession?"

"No," said Borja, "I want you to come for a walk with me. I don't need confession."

"Everyone needs confession."

"Not half as much as the Church needs people to confess."

"Don't be cynical. It doesn't become you. Now listen, I'm busy. I'm a working man. I can't just drop everything and come out. If I came to the tourist office it would be the same... 'Sorry,' you'd say. 'Can't you see I'm on duty?'"

"I've brought you some cigars," said Borja. "Good ones."

"You can't bribe Almighty God."

"I'm not trying to. I just want to bribe you."

Benjamín inspected the box. "All right. You win." It had been an easy victory. "Where do you want to walk to?"

"I don't know. The Maria Luisa Park?"

"That indicates a quite long talk. OK, let's go."

"Hadn't you better get your purple stole?"

"My confessional stole? Whatever for?"

"That way you can put it down as a business trip. You might meet some poor soul on the way with an irresistible urge to confess something."

"Quite right, Borja. And in any case, we never know if your own conversation might not take a turn in that direction."

They walked through the Barrio Santa Cruz, through the tunnel of the Juderia, along jasmine-scented Agua, then down the broad Paseo that separated the old quarter from the main thoroughfare and across to the park, with its shady avenues and exhuberant Art-Deco pavilions.

"I want your advice," said Borja, as they stopped to sit on a bright-tiled seat. "But not as a priest. As a friend. It's worth more. The thing is," he went on, "I'm feeling a strange sense of guilt."

"I'm glad to hear it," said Benjamín. "Why can't you make life easier for yourself and your conscience? Find a pretty Sevillana – God knows there are enough of them. Stop trying to thwart Nature's purposes – and God's – by trying to love a man."

"That's not what I mean and you know it," said Borja. "Talk to me properly or I'll confiscate your cigars."

"Of course I'm aware how attractive he is. James is a charming man. He must be a wonderful friend for you. But why can you not keep him as a friend, that and no more? Why this sudden necessity for sex? At university you were so rigorous, so ascetic."

"At university you hardly knew me. You were five years older."

"Still am."

"And why, now we're on the subject, have you changed so much, you who used to be at the centre of all the night-life, with all your girl-friends...?"

"You didn't know me either. Now tell me more about this sense of guilt."

"Priesthood begets prurience," Borja said. "But I have to disappoint you. I'm feeling guilty only because I find myself being suspicious. I suspect James of having an affair. I have no proof. I just feel it. I don't know what to do next. There's no-one else I can turn to for advice. All my close friends in Seville are his friends too. You know what it is to love another human being, I'm sure of that. Tell me what to do."

Benjamín looked at Borja and shook his head. "My dear young friend, you surprise me, and you flatter me more than I can say. What a tempter you are! You ask me to, first, look back at my life and tell you what a great lover I was, and then ask me to teach *you* how to be one. And with a man for a partner at that. Seville, Seville! You know what Saint Teresa said about Seville?"

"Yes, of course. When the Devil really wants to tempt someone he sends them to Seville. Well, the Church sent you here: you can't blame the Devil for that. And you can't blame me. I'm not trying to remind you of your love-life. I just want your advice. Mierda!"

"What do you want me to tell you? That God made you to be happy on earth for ever with a playmate of your own sex and nothing would ever go wrong?"

"You're not thinking clearly. You used to. Now you run one thing in with another. Of course we're not going to be perfectly happy in life: nobody imagines that. But if I were a married man you would be full of practical ideas to make the relationship work. The Church tells us to do everything in our power, to use every trick in the book to keep marriages together. Well, with James and me it's no different from marriage. Yet because my love – not my playmate, by the way – because my love is a man, you, and the Church, shrug your shoulders and say: nothing can be done; those relationships can't work; you shouldn't have been born like that in the first place."

"I'll ignore that if I may," said Benjamín. "You make a cheap point that doesn't deserve a reply. But let's be practical. What makes you think James is being unfaithful?"

"It's just a feeling I have. As I said, I've no proof. There are a few little things though – things that taken by themselves mean nothing but, taken together... I mean, he said his football boots were worn out when they weren't." This came blurted out, childishly, with some bitterness.

"I don't quite see..."

"Never mind, that's complicated. I'm starting at the wrong end. He keeps getting asked to go and work in Jerez, on what seems like totally spurious business, working for a man who is gay, by the way, and when he comes back he seems different, behaves oddly. He's usually drunk quite a bit and he's come back twice reeking of pot. He hasn't smoked that since I met him. And then I have dreams about him. About him and... someone else."

"Dreams are not admissable as evidence," Benjamín said gravely. "Not under any circumstances."

"Well then, there's another thing. More recently he's changed his walk."

"Changed his walk? How do you mean?"

"He's taken to raising his heel at each step and bouncing along on the balls of his feet." Borja got up and did a demonstration. He sat down again. "It's actually quite attractive."

"I see," said the priest. "Does he spend nights away?"

"Never," said Borja. "Except in England, over Christmas." He stopped as a new doubt tweaked him.

"But you think it may be the man who works in Jerez?"

"Well, maybe." Borja felt uncomfortable speculating consciously who it might be. From the point of view of age and appearance William seemed a more probable candidate. He was also more likely than Paco to be the owner of a pair of lucky football boots. But Borja hated to think it was William. He had been very attracted, meeting him, and had looked forward to getting to know him better... "Though it might be someone else." Borja became cross with himself. "Look, I really don't know."

"How long have you been with James?"

"Three years – and a half. Neither of us has ever... I mean, there's been no-one else for either of us in all that time."

"Three years – and a half," mimicked Benjamín, though not unkindly. I suppose that is a long time for you people."

"Us people? What do you mean? Neither of us is yet twenty-five. Three years is a long time for anybody of our age. Even Marisa has only notched up six years and she married at nineteen. You twist everything and help nobody!"

"Now you're sulking. You asked me for advice but every time I open my mouth you get angry. Maybe you asked the wrong person."

"Maybe I did." There was a pause.

"Maybe you'd like a cigar." Benjamín held out the box.

"Maybe I would." Borja took one. "Thank you." There was another pause. "But what do I actually do?"

They smoked very earnestly in total silence for the duration of a small cigar. Then Benjamín said:"To be honest, I can tell you only one thing that I'm sure of. If you try to trap him or surprise him you will succeed not only in damaging your trust in him still further but also his trust in you. And if your suspicions were unfounded, that damage might take a long time to repair."

"And if my suspicions are correct?"

"Time will provide the answer. If time passes and nothing comes to light then either there was nothing there or else it was a small thing that he has put behind him. Forget it in either case; the present will have become the past. But if his affair is serious, then you'll find out in due course. People invariably do. And if that stage is reached you won't be asking me or anybody else for our advice. You'll find you make your own decisions how to act more swiftly than you've decided anything else before." He paused. The last few sentences were the first in which Borja felt he heard Benjamín's real voice. He wondered if Benjamín was speaking from experience as well as from the heart.

"Well," Benjamín resumed, "I think that's all I can offer in the way of worldly wisdom."

"Oh," said Borja. He sounded disappointed. "You mean you're saying I should do nothing."

"Yes, I am. At least for now."

Borja was not quite sure what he had expected. Something more melodramatic, perhaps: a ritual casting out of demons? He dismissed the fancy. "I suppose I should say thank you then."

"Certainly you should. If I were wearing my purple stole I should be telling you that the right thing to do was to let James go and live out his life of sin; that in the improbable event his conscience told him it wasn't sin but virtue, then that would be his own problem and no business of ours." Benjamín stopped again and shook his head. A child was calling for its mother a short way off. "I can't, obviously – I don't – say that to you. James is a likeable man, attractive too. And for you he is obviously more than both those things. But maybe he is not a very good man, not very strong, perhaps, or not very principled. But the question you may have to decide, not now, not yet but maybe one day, is which of those qualities matter in him most to you." Benjamín took another cigar from the box. "Well, would you like to know something else: something that isn't easy for me to say?"

Of course Borja wanted to know.

"I think that maybe..." Benjamín was speaking slowly, the words not coming easily "... If I were someone like you – someone for whom eternal salvation has become less of a preoccupation than it used to be – then I think I too would want to keep him. So in that endeavour I wish you all the luck you need." He stood up. "Since, at your suggestion, we are calling this a business meeting I think I should at least be able to treat you to an ice-cream on Arch-diocesan expenses. One last thought. Would you mind treating our conversation as confidential?"

"You mean it carries the seal of the non-confessional?"

"Exactly so."

"Very well," said Borja. "But don't forget that off-the-record conversations are the most carefully remembered ones of all."

Benjamín rested a hand lightly on Borja's shoulder and together they walked off to one of the gaudy pavilions in search of ice-cream.

\*

In bed that night Borja fell asleep before James, his breathing slowing to a regular, cat-like purr. And, just as if Borja had been a cat, James reached out and stroked his warm, thick hair. Borja stirred and muttered something. James recognised the same two-syllabled murmur Borja had uttered once before, the night when James had returned from the beach at Chipiona in the turmoil of the start of his new affair. But this time Borja repeated the word more clearly – and James' heart stood still. For what Borja said, and had said before, all those months ago, long before he had met him or even heard his name was: "William."

## Ten

James went with Borja to the airport. Borja had affected nonchalance but James knew him better than to believe it; he knew that Borja
was seriously apprehensive about taking to the air for the first time in
his life. Airside facilities at Seville airport in those days were basic: the
departure lounge was a mere glass box in which fixed rows of hard red
plastic seats faced each other like those in a clinic. James already knew
this and so he distracted Borja with chatter over a coffee until the last
call for the Valencia flight came. Then he let him go.

Borja was on his own and feeling decidedly so. As he climbed up
the rear steps of the elderly-looking Caravelle, he found himself
wondering if this really could be him, doing this insane thing in
imitation of Icarus: preparing to fly. But once inside the cramped
cabin he found a great drama in progress, being acted by the cabin-
staff: a propaganda play whose message was about normality. With
great seriousness the actors opened and closed lockers and dealt
briskly, professionally, with the questions and uncertainties of
people whom fear had rendered either innumerate or fractious. The
stewards and stewardesses reminded him of hospital nurses whose
breezy manner always seemed to say: look, we're all alive; now just
pull yourself together and you'll live too. He found his own window-
seat unaided. But at once a steward leaned over and spoke to him,
smiling. "The check-in staff always give that seat to someone young

and fit-looking. Congratulations."

"How do you mean?" Borja was doubly confused. Doubly because, when he looked up at the speaker, he realised that he recognised his face.

"It's the emergency exit. In a crash-landing you'd have the job of opening the hatch."

Borja was aghast. His face showed it.

"Take it easy," said the steward. "It never happens." His name was Rafael, Borja remembered. Though he would not remember Borja. Rafael stopped smiling and looked at Borja. "Hey, don't I know you?"

"We were at school together." Borja felt unaccountably foolish.

"And at university too, I think." Rafael was studying Borja's face intently.

"Oh, right." Borja did not want to give Rafael the satisfaction of knowing that he remembered his name. Rafael certainly would not remember his.

"Your name's Borja."

Borja turned red. Rafael had been two years his senior. They had never spoken before. "And you're Rafael." Borja distracted attention away from his blush with a grinning smile: an old trick which he had almost forgotten.

"Well remembered. Look. Must go. Talk to you later."

Borja felt inexpressibly cheered by this encounter. He focused his attention on the system of red emergency handles beside him and was able, to his surprise, to examine them with dispassionate interest, reading the instructions both in Spanish and English and imagining himself following them coolly and efficiently. If anything went wrong. Which it wouldn't, he now realised. Not with Rafael on board.

Years ago he had admired Rafael from a distance. He had striking-ly good looks and an easy charm and seemed always to be surround-ed by an eager following of boys as well as girls. He had sometimes wondered in those days – or had it been mere wishful thinking? – if Rafael shared whatever that thing was (it didn't have a name then) that made him different. Now with the the knowledge and experience that had come to him with age and three years of living with James, he was almost sure of it. Why else had he (albeit obliquely) commented on his youth and appearance? Why else should he remember Borja's name?

Engines started but, as they were mounted on the tail and not the wings, their throaty whine was made to sound less threatening by their distance from where Borja sat. Then the plane began to move. Borja was astonished to see the wing-tips flex and wobble as the plane trundled towards the runway but he told himself they must have been designed that way. But the take-off was more violent than he had anticipated. As the plane first tilted him backwards and then bore him up into the sky, he observed most of his compatriots making the sign of the cross and, despite his diminishing belief in the efficacy of such rituals, judged it a prudent measure to follow their example just in case. And when the undercarriage was retracted with a resounding thud a second later the other passengers followed suit as well.

But by now Borja was entering a new world: one where awe and wonder found a place but fear had none. A landscape was rolling out beneath him like a green carpet. It had an irregular looping pattern in shining blue: the winding tributaries of the Guadalquivir. Borja twisted round in his seat to look back at where they had come from but the airport was out of sight now and of the city itself there was no sign at all. It was a cloudless day and the view extended without obstruction as the plane inexorably rose. Soon the green plain was framed with mountains and then the mountains, ruddy brown, were crowded all around and the whole of southern Spain lay underneath like one vast beaten-copper tray. A bloom of mist came and went like breath around the edges, hinting at the distant presence of the sea. Towards the rim the Sierra Nevada appeared, wearing its snowy cover like a mantilla of white lace. Borja could hardly believe it. It lay a hundred miles away.

"Enjoying the scenery?" It was Rafael. "Officially, do you want a coffee? How long will you be staying in Valencia?"

"Just one night. I'm attending a sort of conference." The phrase came out self-consciously. He had never used it before.

"I'm staying overnight as well. I'll give you a phone number. Black or white?"

The snow-capped mountains sat in the centre of the southern horizon for nearly twenty minutes without seeming to change position, while the blue mists licked their feet. In the middle distance something glistened among their sprawling foothills. The sparkle of sun on man-made objects indicated a city, though it was no bigger, seen from this distance, than the thumbprint of a god. Borja told himself it could only be Granada, the city of the mountains, the most beautiful place, till now, that he had ever seen.

They floated over a sharp sierra: a row of black dragon's teeth ripping up through the smooth tawny plain. Then Borja saw the ground beneath him refocus into a million black dots like an old news-photo. The dots grew as he watched and turned into olive trees. The plane banked and turned. The sea, the Mediterranean, rushed suddenly to meet him, filling his porthole with a shock of sparkling blue. Just as suddenly it withdrew again; palm trees waved level with the window; in the last few seconds of flight the speed seemed to grow frighteningly fast; then wheels met tarmac with a squelchy kiss.

"It was my first flight," Borja admitted later to Rafael. It turned out that they were staying in the same hotel. "It's fantastic. Like a metaphor for freedom."

"More than just a metaphor," said Rafael. "Flying is freedom. If you're gay." They had already clarified that detail. Rafael was 'between affairs' he said. He had a very small flat, but his own, in Madrid, though he visited Salamanca still from time to time to see family and old friends. Yes, he did stay sometimes at Marisa's; he was certainly the Rafael that she had mentioned. They swapped addresses.

Borja told Rafael who he lived with. "And still very happily after three years," he said. Which was not entirely true. As the weeks passed

Borja was feeling more and more uneasy about James but he judged it unwise to mention this to someone who had just said he was 'between affairs'.

"I'm surprised he lets you out on your own," said Rafael archly. "Attending conferences all over Spain without him."

"And I'm surprised you need to make cheap comments like that."

Rafael was stung but did not try to sting back. "I'm sorry. But I was only joking." He saw that Borja did not appreciate camp and made a mental note to avoid it in future. Damn the company of airline stewards.

Borja remembered Rafael as a sporting hero and a challenger to fights. At school he had even stood up and fought for bullied nonentities against their tormentors. Borja had never been bullied, never been a nonentity.

"You had a charmed life," Rafael said. "Rather serious, even religious, but so practical and kind."

"How do you know that?" Borja asked. "You never even spoke to me."

"You're forgetting that what we have in common now we had in common then. I knew you better than you thought."

Secretly flattered, Borja let the subject go. Rafael had left school a year early, Borja reminded him, and turned up at university two years late.

"I did my mili," Rafael said. He laughed at the memory. "Nothing very exciting. I was a security guard at the Admiralty building in Madrid." He risked a joke. "You'd have liked the uniform, though. Anyway, what about you?"

"I didn't have to do the mili," Borja admitted. "I used to have some sort of fits. Not epilepsy, exactly, but something a bit like it." He chose not to mention the visions of death that had usually accompanied them. "Of course I'd grown out of them by that time." He was careful to emphasise this point. "I certainly don't have them now. But back to you. The mili would have been two years. What happened to the third one?"

"I decided to try my luck as a torero. I went to the training school in Madrid."

"You were never a bullfighter."

"I was."

"What, with a suit of lights?" Borja failed to keep the jealousy out of his voice.

"No, that would have cost. It wasn't the big time, after all. We dressed like gauchos. Small fights, small towns, small bulls. There was very little money in it. At first you have to pay them to let you fight. Only after you've proved yourself does the impresario give you a cut."

"And did you get that far?"

"Once or twice – before the end."

"The end?"

"My parents didn't approve. It was all costing too much, what with the training in Madrid as well. You need total support from parents, friends and family. Otherwise it's just impossible." He spread his hands. "I couldn't afford to continue on my own. Also, I'd started late."

"Bad luck." Borja made no attempt to dismantle Rafael's excuses. He clearly hadn't managed to hack it as a bullfighter but Borja admired him none the less for that. At least he had tried to realise his dream.

"Then at university I discovered I wasn't very academic. I only lasted a year, if you remember."

Borja recalled how he had burst onto the social scene, dazzled for a while and then vanished.

"And finally I thought about the sky. I tried to be a pilot first. They gave me some tests to fail, which I did. So here I am."

"And you like your job?"

"Like I said. It's freedom. Who doesn't like freedom?" He grinned. "And as for meeting people..."

"I can imagine," Borja said.

It was Rafael (typically, Borja thought) who proposed an evening on the town and went round getting other people to join them. In the end there were nine of them: some from Borja's conference group and the others Rafael's fellow cabin-staff. It was the latter who knew downtown Valencia and led the way through the Jardines de Turia to the bars of the Barrio del Carmen. A long, lively evening ensued: one which was typically Spanish in that, though everyone drank enough, there was so much talking and arguing that no-one had time or opportunity to get really drunk. Tapas took the place of an evening meal and then, towards midnight, they swarmed off to a disco. Borja danced with all the girls of the party. Dancing was something he enjoyed more with Spanish people than with James' English friends. The English just weren't cut out for dancing, he felt. Even James, who at least did it with enthusiasm, would have done better to stick to football. Now, suddenly, here was Rafael dancing with him, not cheek to cheek but very publicly man to man. Borja looked quickly round the dance-floor. It was not a gay place. All the other couples were formed in the more conventional way. Yet none of them showed any sign of surprise or disapproval. And this in turn surprised Borja. Rafael saw this. "You don't very often dance with other boys, I think," he said.

"With James sometimes, in a gay club in Seville. He's got two left feet though, to be honest." He felt a bit disloyal as he said this. "But not with other men, no." He flashed Rafael a look that said: take the information or leave it.

Rafael took it. "Then I ought to feel a little bit privileged."

As he danced with Rafael, Borja's mind returned to their conversation about freedom. Flying was freedom, Rafael had said. And so was this. Borja was used to enjoying himself with James, his dancing notwithstanding. Now he was surprised at how much fun he could also have without him. But was it right that he should be enjoying himself like this? He guessed that James was having an affair. He might even now be dancing the night away in Jerez with... He tried to block out the image of James with William. But maybe he wasn't. Maybe he was at home in bed after a quiet evening alone as he had told Borja he would be. Even if he were having an affair, that did not give Borja licence to have an affair himself. Dear God! What was he thinking? He was just having a night out with friends. He told himself not to project the warmth of this pleasant evening absurdly into the future.

Back at the hotel, which they entered with some noise and fumbling with keys and locks at half-past three in the morning, good-nights and good-byes were said. Rafael would be gone when Borja got up; he had an early flight out. They were on different floors; Borja was sharing a room with another member of his conference party: a stolid individual who had not joined them on their evening out. "But we'll catch up again, don't worry," Rafael assured him. "Now I've got your number." He stopped and smiled, risked a moment's camp: "I meant telephone number."

Borja held out his hand and began to shake Rafael's rather stiffly. But Rafael had a better idea and broke off the handshake to give Borja a quick, tight hug. Then they walked away to their respective quarters. When Borja got back to his room he found his room-mate asleep and snoring loudly.

The conference lasted the best part of four days. That first day Borja and the others had been lectured to and shown videos about historic Valencia and the beach resorts of the Costa del Alzahar. The next day they were bussed up the coast as far as Tarragona where they were given a guided tour: it proved as ancient and as romantically crumbling a city as any that Borja had seen. In the late afternoon the bus took them on to Barcelona where they were scheduled to spend the night. Now it was Borja, inspired by Rafael's example, who took the initiative in suggesting an evening in town, doing the Ramblas. Expecting to enjoy himself as much as last night, Borja was disappointed. He missed the lively presence of Rafael and became annoyed with himself when he realised this. Towards midnight he pleaded tiredness and, leaving the party still fizzing, made his way back to the hotel alone. He had a room to himself this time, which pleased him.

The following day was all about Barcelona. The head of tourism for Cataluña gave a presentation on the region that might have been dull but was enlivened by the fact that his slides were shown, to his apparent unconcern, in reverse order. So his elaborate discourse on the building of the Sagrada Família was accompanied by shots of sunbathers on the beach at Sitges, while pictures of Gaudi's famous church accompanied a description of wild-boar hunting in the foothills of the Pyrenees.

On the last day they made a pilgrimage to a ski-resort in the mountains where the snow had failed for the third consecutive year. Everyone was asked to shut their eyes and imagine the scene as it should have been – and would have to be sold in the different tourist offices all over Spain. Then they caught their planes home. Borja would have to change in Madrid. Although he had a window-seat again, Borja's second flight was disappointing. Thin cloud had slid down from the mountains during the night and all but hidden the ground they travelled over. Borja passed his time watching the stewards at work and wondering whether a change of job might suit him. Was Rafael's really a life of freedom? Anyway, freedom from what? From whom?

Descending into Madrid, Borja's plane left the clouds behind him and drifted between brown, table-topped mountains. It was like the moon, Borja thought. He had been to Madrid many times but had never seen its setting look like this. Flying certainly made you look at things in a new perspective; who knew what other lessons it might have to teach?

Then, boarding the plane for the last leg of his return to Seville, Borja walked straight into Rafael at the cabin door. "Here we are again," said the steward. "Just as I said."

Borja did not reply to this. He did not want to think that fate was drawing them together. But he was pleased to see Rafael again all the same.

"Who were you chatting to as you got off the plane?" James asked when he met Borja at the airport. He had watched the disembarkation through the plate-glass.

"An old school-mate, Rafael. He works as a steward."

Normally James would have made some ironic comment at this or raised an eyebrow expressively. But, conscious of his glass-house situation, he decided not to. "I missed you," he said instead. And as he said it, and despite the fact that he had spent two out of the last three nights with William in Jerez, he discovered that he meant it.

*

Easter fell early that year. Passiontide had long been a very special celebration in Seville, the pageantry of Semana Santa drawing crowds into the city from all across the world. For Pippa and Alexa, new to Seville, it promised to be one of the highspots of the year. Even for old hands like Mark and James it was a time of some excitement. For weeks now the confraternities of the different churches had been preparing the elaborate floats which they would carry through the streets in torchlit processions during the nights of Holy Week itself. Madonnas and Christs, some many hundreds of years old, were repainted and reclothed and the pasos decked with candles, flowers and coloured bands.

Semana Santa was still a religious occasion, even if its deep-felt passion seemed more Pagan than Christian. But it was also the most wonderful excuse for a great non-stop party during which the bars would stay open most of the night. Even as the slow-moving processions flowed along the streets with their white advance-columns of hooded penitents, glasses and bottles were handed in and out of the scrum of men, the costaleros, who bore the heavy statue-laden floats upon their shoulders. Bands played as they marched: strange Arab-sounding airs from long ago; haunting, melancholy songs that raised the hairs on people's necks. Drumbeats kept the marching feet in step and a horizonless sea of people, native

Sevillanos plus the thousands of tourists who had filled the hotels to bursting, washed up and down the streets of the city.

"Like Marrakesh or Fez," said Karsten to Alexa. "As if Seville had been recaptured by its past."

Nobody seemed to be at work. The schools were shut. Even Alexa did not attempt too much music practice. The competition was too noisy, the atmosphere too intense. Only Borja seemed to have other things to do. The tourist office had sent him away to witness lesser festivities elsewhere, in Toledo and Madrid. He would be back on Easter Day, however; arriving Saturday night.

It was the early hours of Good Friday, though, that provided the most powerful and spectacular highlights of the festival: the throwing open of the doors of the Macarena Basilica at midnight to allow the weeping statue of the Macarena to take to the streets, and the arrival at the cathedral of the most solemn procession of all, El Silencio, with its centipede of penitents, all bowed heads and dragging feet.

Mark and Pippa, Alexa and Karsten had managed to find a place in the cathedral to watch the procession come in. The total silence in which it arrived was like nothing they had experienced anywhere else. It was eerie, chilling, but more than that, it had a sound all of its own. Every moving being creates sound: the rustle of cotton on silk, the slide of shoe on paving, the tiny scratch of intaken breath. And how many people were standing, or clinging to aerial perches, there in the cathedral that night? Fifteen thousand? Twenty? Thirty thousand and more? It was impossible to guess. Seville cathedral is the largest gothic structure and the largest cathedral in the world. Its fifty-plus ribbed columns soar a hundred and thirty feet to reach the arching vaults. It covers an area of thirty-six thousand square feet. How many echoes were there in that vastness to pick up and multiply those countless rustles, whispers, scratches? The rush of noise was numbing, disconcerting, directionless, disorientating. Alexa fancied she was hearing a sound as old as time itself: the sound of the universe being born.

Pippa might not have felt it quite so keenly but she was awe-struck just the same. She clasped her lover's hand. And as she did so she caught sight of someone else she knew, just a few feet away, and was surprised she had not noticed him before. It was James, and with him was the man she'd met with him in London. The man called William. They too, almost unnoticeably in the throng, were holding hands. Pippa gave a start, blatant enough to cause Mark to turn and look at her. Then she realised that this was not the second time she'd seen William but the third. He had given them their guided tour of O'Donnell's when they went to Jerez.

"Why didn't you tell me before?" protested Pippa later. "If you knew."

"I only thought I knew," said Mark. They were part of a crowd, drinking and celebrating, in the Bodegón Torre del Oro. Flamenco dancing was in progress at the far end of the room. It was four in the morning.

"You talked to Karsten about it. You must have been fairly certain."

"I didn't want to... say anything to upset you. Especially at that particular time."

"Oh I see. I'm a weak-minded woman, is that it? We can't be allowed to share the alarms that disturb our menfolk. Too much for our poor little heads to take."

"Darling, you're being unreasonable. I talked to Karsten because he's an old friend. Contrary to popular belief, men do have friends – even straight men do – who they confide in. We're not the heartless planks you take us for."

"Then why were you upset so much you couldn't talk to me?"

"I can't explain," said Mark through half-clenched teeth. Neither of them was angry exactly, just exasperated with each other. They were both relieved when Karsten and Alexa returned to them through the crowd from where they had been watching the dancing and obliged them to cease their bickering.

"Did they see us?" Alexa asked. She and Karsten had clearly been discussing the same subject. "And do you or do you not tell Borja? You three, I mean. I don't include myself. I hardly know him."

"And I know James much better than I know Borja," said Pippa. "It's hardly for me to tell him."

"So the question is for Karsten and me," said Mark. "And we already agreed we wouldn't. I don't think anything's changed since then."

"You forget one thing," said Karsten. "You gave the reason before that you were not certain you were right. Well, now you are." They had all seen James and William leaving the cathedral together and exchanging a quick and – they must have imagined – unseen kiss as they disappeared into the uncondemning, celebrating multitude.

"The answer's still no," said Mark. "Unless anything else happens to make me change my mind my mouth stays firmly shut."

"Then I must say the same," said Karsten. "We'll have another drink. La Penúltima!" he commanded the barman, and the city danced around them as it would do until dawn.

# Eleven

It was not until early May that one of Borja's business trips coincided again with a weekend and this one was only arranged at the last moment. James telephoned William. "Get over here at once. We're going somewhere."

"It's Friday morning, Jacobite. I've got to work."

"Find an excuse. I did. Borja's away unexpectedly. In Jerez, funnily enough. Not back till Sunday evening."

"Yeah, but... oh, what the hell."

"Tell Paco your father's had a stroke or something."

"I'll think of something. OK."

"Be at the station at twelve."

"Wow."

"You've got to." James paused for a second. "Love you," he said, then put the phone down.

The day was already hot when William arrived at the San Bernardo station in Seville. "Where are you taking me?" he asked James.

"Granada," said James. "Where else for a May weekend?"

"Granada! I haven't even brought a toothbrush."

"I expect they sell them there," said James laconically. "I haven't brought one either."

Their train wound its leisurely way south, doubled back for a bit, and then turned east towards the province of Malaga. The landscape was wide and lonely, making the ranch-houses that dotted it look remote and vulnerable in the vastness. Once an eagle rose from nowhere to vanish again in the infinite sky. Cosy it was not.

At last, in the middle of the afternoon, the train drew into Bobadilla junction. At this hour all the trains in Andalucía seemed to converge on Bobadilla, everyone had to change, and for half an hour there would be chaos. Sandwich-sellers bawled their wares in emptying trains while in the station buffet there was a six-deep scrum jostling for attention and snacks at the counter. But for the rest of the day Bobadilla would be deserted except for the yellow mongrel dog that lived there and scavenged for abandoned sandwich-crusts between the tracks. For the station was in the middle of nowhere, topography alone dictating that all trains should pass this spot.

"Thank God for Bobadilla," said William, back on the Granada train one beer later. "I thought I'd die of thirst."

The landscape altered. Hills rose, scrub-covered, and became mountains. Imperceptibly they wound their way higher and then at last the valley they were climbing opened out onto the broad plain of the Vega where sugar cane waved tall between stands of poplar. The Sierra Nevada, still patchily snow-capped, lay ahead while in the foreground – and James and William were not the only passengers to crane from the windows to see it – Granada and the Alhambra hill appeared, magnificent and ruddy in the evening sun. William threw an arm casually across James' shoulder as they stood, leaning out.

It was a longish walk from the station to the old quarter of the city and the train passengers set out along it like pilgrims. Many were young travellers loaded with backpacks and James immediately felt superior in his unencumbered state. William and he were travelling like the birds. Just one other pair of travellers shared their condition: a waif-like young man with a mane of unkempt hair and a teenage boy without shoes. Their combined luggage amounted to a flute and a blanket.

They found a hostel easily enough a short way up the Cuesta de

Gomérez on the side of the Alhambra hill – family run, rooms at rock-bottom prices. The front door was opened by a long rope operated by the feet of a bare-legged youth lounging on the first floor landing inside the stairwell. It was a disorientating entry, followed immediately by a problem. The management wanted their passports as security against eventual payment. Neither of them had thought to bring one. "No somos turistos," William objected. "Vivímos en Andalucía."

"Relax," said James. "I've got cash. We only have to pay for the two nights in advance and the problem disappears." So they paid and were rewarded with a flashing smile from the bronze-thighed son of the house.

It was too late to visit the Alhambra. While daylight lingered they set about exploring the Albaicín, the hilly Arab quarter, instead. It was a place of near-vertical steps, of secretive cypress trees, of white-walls and an atmosphere of melancholy. "I'm not just imagining it, am I?" James asked his companion, willing him to share his thoughts. "Don't you feel it's almost tangible, the sadness of this beautiful place?" He needed William to feel it too.

"I do feel it." William said no more but stopped walking and leaned back against the whitewashed wall beside them. In the absence of traffic the sound of running water could be heard: the River Darro far below them in its thicketed ravine. They might have kissed each other but the silence was abruptly broken by the brittle buzzing of a moped and a shout nearby. The moment passed and they moved on.

Eventually the labyrinth of Moorish lanes disgorged them at the bottom of the hill, back in the post-reconquest part of town. Sightseeing gave way gracefully to bar-crawling as the evening advanced. They fell in with a group of students who took them to places they might not have stumbled upon otherwise: small back-street bars where wine was absurdly cheap and tapas were included in the price. You didn't need dinner, their companions said, provided you drank plenty. They moved on to a larger drinking-shop where hashish was quite openly being sold right beneath a printed notice forbidding it and William took the opportunity to replenish his supply.

"Do you know," said one of their new friends, "there are people in Morocco to this day, in the town of Fez, who keep the keys to properties here that were abandoned by their Arab ancestors when they fled? Against the day they believe will come when the Moors get Granada back."

"Fantastic thought," said James and visualised the ancient houses in the Albaicín they had just been walking among. He wondered if the keys would still fit the locks.

Then, as suddenly as they had become part of the crowd they had left it, or it had left them, and they were on their own. It was after midnight and they walked on pavements that shone like marble under the moon. Perhaps they really were marble. A twist in the street brought them to yet another bar and they entered almost automatically.

The bar was a rather smart one and they were alone in it except for the waiter. "Muy caro *(very expensive)*," he warned, indicating a row of bottles of superannuated Rioja impaled head down on complicated dispensing machines of nautically polished brass. They settled for one of the more modest vintages.

"Formidable," said James in a cod-French accent – for no other reason than that he was getting pleasantly drunk.

"Français," beamed the waiter, suddenly alive. "J'aime bien les Français et la France *(I love the French and France)*." There was no chance to put him right as he went on in animated French. "How good to see French faces. I thought, as soon as you came in, that you were French. Always we have German tourists up here, English tourists from the coast..." He swatted the imaginary visitors away like gnats with a contemptuous flourish of his tea-towel and put an additional glass of wine in front of each of them plus a dish of thyme-flavoured olives. James realised that they would have to talk French for as long as they stayed in the bar if they were going to avoid general embarrassment. He spoke the language tolerably well but had no idea if William did. Their 'host' had worked for several years in Paris and Bordeaux and not only had much to tell but, worse, many questions to ask. James was soon relieved to hear William rise to the occasion in fairly fluent French, then immediately appalled by what he said. They were from Bordeaux themselves, William smoothly told the man; they had been at school together. James had never visited the region in his life. Still, after a minute or two, James felt safe enough to join in the deception and found himself inventing shared recollections of people and places along with William, though he was unable to look at William as he did this. They stood side by side, facing the waiter across the counter.

James was full of admiration for William's gift for invention; his web of imaginings was so much more elaborate, and yet much more believable, than his own. Then a thought struck him. If it came so naturally to William to invent a new background whenever the need arose or if he simply felt like it, what about the story of his life as he had told it to James on the beach at Chipiona? About his father being a bishop, about running away to sea, about his ex-girlfriend, about Pieter... But it was too late to question it. They were here now.

Somehow they got to the end of their drinks, paid for them (rummaging in pockets not without difficulty) and fled into the street, running along it like children, laughing hysterically in each other's faces.

By the time they had calmed down they had passed by the door of their hostel and were halfway up the hill to the Alhambra. "Let's go on a bit," said James. "See where we end up." Actually an idea was forming drunkenly in his mind but he was not sure if it would work. Soon they were in thick woods though still on a made-up road. William began to have doubts.

"Where the hell are we?" he queried.

"Just keep going." An old street-lamp loomed surreally out of the dark trees. "We're in Narnia," James said.

His pose of confidence paid off. A few minutes later, the woods gave way on their left to a scrubby hillside which was crowned in stone by the rugged outer wall of the Alhambra. Where the building ended a high bridge arched over a ravine. "If we could scramble up the side of this gully and get onto the bridge..." said James.

"What, get into the Alhambra?"

"I don't think we could. There are big gates. But go the other way across the bridge and you're in the Generalife Gardens."

It was a long hard climb up to the bridge. There was many a slip and many a swear-word. But the moonlight saved them from real danger. The last bit, through a tangle of brambles, was the worst but by then the bridge lay only six feet above them and they were in no mood to go back. At last they hoisted themselves over the parapet.

They were not alone. On the other side of the bridge a young man stood. He wore white jeans which were bright in the moonlight and his cigarette glowed red but as the rest of him was dressed in invisible black the effect was decidedly spooky. "Buenas noches, maricónes," he said, quite politely. Then he added: "There is an easier way up. You could have taken the left-hand path and followed the wall round." He chuckled. "Might come in handy going down." They recognised him. He was the boy who had opened the door to them at their hostel.

Leaving him to whatever it was that brought him to that remote spot at two in the morning, they climbed up the gentle slope that led into the gardens. The sky was clear and the moon, which was nearly full, showed them the towers of the Alhambra coming into view below them. It was warm, considering the hour and altitude. A mixture of scents rose around them. There was orange blossom and, momentarily, something that might have been dead dog. A bird burbled suddenly in the ravine beneath.

"So that was the purpose of the visit, all along, was it?" said William. "To seduce me to the sound of nightingales."

"Something like that," admitted James, "though it's a bit bloody late to use the word seduce."

"Anyway, I thought it was me that seduced you," said William.

"No way," said James, laughing. "It was definitely me."

"Impossible." William punched him lightly.

"Well, if we don't know who started it," said James, "then certainly no-one else does." Though it did cross his mind for an instant that he might have been wrong about that.

Once the one bird had started there was no stopping the others. As they strolled into the gardens the tremulous solo grew into a vibrant chorus; it was as if you could reach out and touch the sound. Hawk-moths purred around them and probed like hummingbirds into vase-like nectaries. Bats skittered overhead.

They sat under a wall by an ancient broken cypress. "Under this tree," said James, "the Sultana Zoraya used to meet her lover Hamet. Or so the story goes."

"Did the Sultan find out?" William asked.

"They were executed." James tried to suppress the memory that the story had first been told to him by Borja, sitting in this very spot two years ago; tried not to find in it a lesson for himself.

"There's another story," James went on instead. "It's in Tales of the Alhambra. In it an ice-gatherer, Tio Nicolo, falls asleep among the mountains. When he wakes up it's night but as he looks down over the city roof tops he realises he has been transported back in time. He sees the cross is no longer on the bell-tower but the crescent moon instead."

"And what happens to him?"

"I don't remember the rest of the story. But, hey, you can almost make it happen for yourself."

"How do you mean?"

"Half-screw your eyes up like this."

They both tried it and, squinting through the pale night, convinced themselves they saw the Moorish emblem replace the great cross atop the palace.

"We haven't got anything to drink," said William.

"When I last came," remembered James, "there was a party of tourists drinking wine by the fountains there, keeping the bottles cool in the water."

"Maybe someone'll have overlooked one. I'll go and have a look."

"You're mad. That was years ago."

"I didn't mean the same tourists, wally." William went trotting off. A few moments later he gave a stifled shout, then he was back.

"It's white, I'm afraid," he said with mock regret. He was holding out a glistening bottle, almost shaking with surprise.

"I can't believe it. You really are a magician. Oh hell. No corkscrew."

"We have been here before," said William. He placed his metal corkscrew in James' hand. It felt warm from his pocket. "Never knowingly without one."

"No toothbrush but he brings the corkscrew."

"And a supply of dope. Don't forget that – if you really want to see Moorish crescents by moonlight."

"But you forgot the wineglasses."

"So? We have nightingales." William tousled James' hair.

"Open the wine," said James.

Long before the bottle was finished they had slid from their seat onto the ground and made love there, though without undressing each other completely – it was not that warm among the mountains. It was a little later that William said: "This moment should last for ever." He sounded so young sometimes, James thought. However it was exactly what he had wanted to hear. He put an arm round William. They had a smoke and finished the wine while one by one the nightingales fell silent, the damson sky grew cobalt blue and blackbirds woke and sang to take possession of the morning. When they made their way down the hill at last the sun was pointing up the caps of the sierras.

*

It was late morning before they roused themselves from their hostel bed. They were let out by the same boy as yesterday, back in his shorts now and tugging on the door-rope with his bare feet. "Buenas dias, señores," he wished them courteously, adding nothing except a smile, not even a wink.

First they descended to the Plaza Nueva in search of coffee. They also had another errand: shopping for toothbrushes and paste. "Get one of those spray breath-fresheners while you're at it," said James.

"And try for some Alka-Seltzer or something," said William. "For such mundanities are mornings-after made." It wasn't the sort of thing he usually said. It was the kind of laborious English aphorism that Borja took such pride in coining. William had never reminded James of Borja before. Now, watching him disappear into a shop, James felt a sudden panic. He did not like to think of Borja when he was with William. Not now, since they had both declared they were in love. A feeling of foreboding came over him, heavy as a stone yet empty as a void. But then William emerged from the shop into the sunshine and with an effort James willed the abyss away.

Later they climbed back to the Alhambra, paid and went in. Though he had been there before, James was physically shocked by the assault on his senses. Turning into the rampart garden under the Vuela they confronted the city spread like an ant-hill before them: the white Albaicín stiff with cypresses; the distant Vega shimmering with heat and husbandry; the mountains all around, hung with falcons and crowned with snow. At their backs, on a warm red wall, bees buzzed among fruit blossom. James felt his eyes fill up with tears. He could not look to see if William shared them, nor could he trust his voice to speak. For a moment he was angry with himself. The world was full of things to weep over. Why had you to cry at this?

Indoors and outdoors here were one. Mountain breezes blew through the Alhambra's patterned chambers. Its courtyards were fountained salons upholstered with hedges of box and myrtle.

"I've never been anywhere more beautiful," said William. They kissed, observed only by the stone lions that drooled around the fountain.

They drifted from room to courtyard, from courtyard to room. William read from a notice in the Hall of the Abencerrajes: "Here sixteen princes were murdered in revenge for Hamet's seduction of the Sultana. The stain in the fountain is supposed to be their blood."

They looked. Sure enough, the marble basin bore a liver-coloured stain. "I'd forgotten that," said James.

In all the beauty only one note jarred. The yellow jib of a crane overhung one range of low buildings, peering in from outside. Attached to its lifting-gear was a pallet-load of stone slabs resting on the ground in readiness for Monday morning. They chose to ignore it, following the sign to the Washington Irving apartments. "What a great place to have lived for six months," said William. "The lucky sod."

Entering the apartments was like stepping into a dream. A dream furnished with carved cedar ceilings and tiled walls, with lattice windows opening onto distant hills, a hundred feet of empty air between them and the ground beneath. Street sounds drifted up, clear as bells but coming from another world. "I could live here," said William suddenly. "Couldn't you? I mean, couldn't we?"

"Stop now," said James. "You make me cry." But at that moment he saw that there were tears in William's eyes also. There could be no turning back. William was his, now. They would be lovers for ever.

Later in the day, after a longish siesta, they explored more of the city; gazed at the austere tombs of Ferdinand and Isabella, chastely apart in death in the Capilla Real. And then they fell in again with the group of students they had met the previous night, did the round of bars with them and got invited to a party in a room over a shop in the Albaicín. At about one o'clock William said to James: "Come on, let's go."

"Anywhere in particular?"

"Yes. Tonight we do my idea. OK?"

The winding alleys of the Arab quarter seemed more tortuous than before. But once they had crossed the Plaza Nueva and were again climbing the opposite hill it was obvious to James where they were heading. Sure enough, they soon stood in the courtyard in front of the Alhambra. "This is where we spend the night," announced William.

"And how?" asked James.

"Easy. The crane." They were just next to the small fenced-in area in which it stood.

"You're joking. We could get up it easily enough, I suppose. Even get out along the boom or whatever it's called. But you can't shin down a steel hawser. We wouldn't have any hands left." He paused for effect. "Or were you thinking of starting the engine and riding down in the bucket?" He caught hold of William and gave him a mock-punch.

"Neither, actually, Mister Clever Dick." He put the accent on the Dick. "Look up. It leans right over the roof-ridge. You wouldn't even have to jump – just step down onto the roof. The slope's gentle enough. There's trees and scaffolding on the other side. All the windows will be open. What do you say?"

"Darling heart, you wouldn't dare."

"You mean you wouldn't."

"I bloody would," said James. "Maybe you wouldn't come with me."

"You reckon?"

Spontaneously they both leapt upon the protecting wire mesh fence and scrambled up it. But as they reached the top, their weight tipped the panel forward and they fell together into the compound, face-down on the flattened fence. They jumped up at once, unhurt as only drunks and children know how to be, and sprinted to the crane. Somewhere an electric bell began ringing. Neither of them connected it with themseves.

James jumped up onto the rim of a great wheel attached to the side of the crane and hauled himself between its spokes into the inside of the girder column. William was right behind. Climbing through the lattice structure they began to race each other effortfully to the top. After twenty feet or so the going got easier; they made contact with a ladder, the one the operator would use in the mornings; presumably the bottom section was removed at night to deter trespassers such as themselves. At last they emerged onto a horizontal surface, a platform that ran like a balcony around the top of the column. Above them was the wooden floor of the driver's cabin which would give them access to the jib. Entry was through a trap-door. They pushed at it. It was padlocked shut.

"Looks like this is as far as we get," said James. "And we didn't even bring a bottle."

"We can have a smoke at least," said William. "Admire the view."

There were clouds tonight and the full moon came and went, lighting the town intermittently. Below, some of the Alhambra's towers were floodlit. Round one of them a white owl hunted. The bell had stopped now. A distant motorbike retched and, just like last night, the nightingales began.

"Neat," said William.

"Pretty good," said James, then quoted: "If 'twere now to die..."

"...'Twere now to die most happy," finished William. And this time the words cut James like a knife. It was Borja who always finished off his Shakespeare quotes. Especially that one. It should have been Borja now. He had been going to touch William's hair. He found he couldn't.

A car drove suddenly into the square, quite fast, and pulled up by the broken fence. Two men jumped out.

"Oh no," said James.

"Fuck it," whispered William.

There was silence for half a minute. "What do we do?" William hissed in James' ear.

"I think the next move's theirs, don't you?" James whispered back.

The crack of a pistol shot. Surprisingly muted. Something zinged against the crane. They felt the vibration through their feet. They grabbed each other's arms involuntarily. "Jesus Christ!" said William.

"Firing into the air. Just to scare us."

"Then they're lousy shots. They missed the air and hit the crane. It'll be us next."

"Maybe it's time to go down," said James.

"Abajo, abajo," shouted a voice below.

"You're right," said William. "Let's go. Hey." He squirted some breath-freshener in both their mouths.

Slowly they clambered down and prepared to emerge from between the spokes of the wheel. "Should we go out with our hands up," wondered William, "or would we just look pathetic?"

"We'll look pathetic anyway," James said. "This isn't Butch Cassidy."

With both hands raised above their heads they walked slowly towards the waiting policemen.

\*

"Happens all the time, people trying to get in there." They were in the car now, heading for the police station. "Lovers mostly, people on honeymoon." The policeman stopped. A thought had struck him. "Well, who'd have thought it." Then both the policemen began to laugh, deep and slow.

"Passports. Here!" demanded the officer at the desk.

"At home," said James abjectly. "We're very sorry."

"No passport, no go home," explained the officer, stone-faced.

"How can we get them if we can't go home?" asked William.

"Someone must know where you are. Let them bring them."

"But they can't do that tonight," James said. The policeman treated himself to a smile. "That doesn't create a problem. You weren't going home tonight in any case. Check them for drugs," he called to a junior officer. "And find them a nice little room for the night."

They were strip-searched. It was rough but not brutal. "Why are you doing this?" demanded William. "It's not necessary."

"Leave it out," James told him in English. "Unless you want a beating."

"We thought you'd enjoy it," said one of the policemen. "Little maricónes."

"Maricónes," echoed a voice from behind a door. "Little friends of Lorca."

"Shut it," came another, harsher voice, "or I'll break your balls."

James was glad the cells had solid doors rather than the zoo-like grills he had been fearing. Wrapped in blankets they were promptly bundled into one. Learning to be thankful for small mercies, James was relieved to find they had it to themselves.

"Our clothes," objected William.

"Mañana." The officer laughed. "Sleep well, pretty boys."

James tried to bring some order to his chaos of anxieties. "What about your stuff, Orange? Was it still in your pocket?"

"No way. I wedged it between two girders halfway down the crane. Nobody'll go looking for it and they wouldn't find it if they did. Dogs can't climb cranes."

"Thank God for that at least."

"Yeah, but they got the corkscrew."

James snapped: "Don't joke." Then he relented. "Sorry, I didn't mean that."

They were sitting opposite each other on beds as hard and narrow as shelves. They were each wrapped in a coarse green blanket. A night-light burned dimly. There was no way to switch it off and the bulb was protected by a metal grill. At the far end of the room a shower fitment projected mossily from the wall over a hole in the ground. Next to it was another hole. Which stank.

"Fuck it," said William.

"Ditto," said James. "Look, we're going to have to let Paco in on this. Ring him at home in the morning. Get him to send someone over with the passports. They can get into my flat easily. The woman in the ice-cream parlour has a key. Borja won't be back till evening."

Or late afternoon? Even if all went well James wouldn't be able to make Seville till nightfall.

"We can not ring Paco," William said fiercely. "It's not an option. I told him my mother had died and I'd gone to England. I'd be out of O'Donnell's in a flash. Paco is my job. Borja's in Jerez, you said. Ring him."

"You told Paco what!?" James had suggested William's father having a stroke as an acceptable white lie. Pretending one's mother had died, on the other hand, seemed a fib too far. "I hope that never comes back to haunt you."

"Well, you gave me the idea." It was not an unfair reply.

"OK." James changed tack. "Paco is your job, you say. So we can't ring Paco. But what do you think Borja is to me? No skin off your nose, though, if we ring him. My difficulties don't count. Paco is your job. Well, Borja happens to have been my life for the last three years."

"Then why," said William in an even tone, "have you been telling me for the last three months that you loved me? Or doesn't that count?"

"I do love you," said James uncomfortably. He wasn't sure if he still meant it. "Now keep your voice down."

"OK, if not Borja, who do we call? Your two friends we met in London?"

"Mark and Pippa? No way. The fewer people involved the better."

"Then it must be Borja."

"No. Absolutely not. Ring Paco."

"Borja."

"No."

"Toss a coin," said William.

"Don't be an asshole," James said angrily.

"We haven't even got pockets," said William.

Then they both began to laugh, loudly, hysterically, until shouts and curses from their neighbours silenced them. They lay back on their boards.

"No nightingales tonight, James."

"Go to sleep. We'll decide who to ring in the morning."

"Sleep with me, Jacobite?"

"There isn't room, Orange."

They touched hands for a moment across the empty space between them and then let each other go. James thought hard and long. It was his fault they were here, not William's. He had suggested lying to Paco. He had started the affair. Why should William have to take the rap? There was no way now that anything could be hidden any longer from Borja. It might as well be got over with quickly. James would ring him in the morning. A word popped into James' head just then, unbidden: an old-fashioned word, one he had never used. But once there it would not leave him but beat at his skull without mercy. The word was folly.

## Twelve

It was about seven when Borja was woken by a knock on the door. It took him a moment to remember that he was not at home but in a commercial hotel between the town of Jerez and its airport. More confusing still, a voice was calling him to the telephone to take an urgent call from Granada. The only person he knew in Granada was his aunt Ana.

Borja threw on a T-shirt and jeans and ran downstairs barefoot. Early risers were eating in the breakfast room and, as he hurried through, Borja was further surprised to see Raphael at a table with a little group of young people – cabin crew, no doubt. He hadn't seen Rafael since that first trip out of Andalucía two months ago. Rafael looked equally surprised, gave the hurrying figure a half-wave of greeting, and Borja responded with a telephone gesture as he pattered on his way.

Five minutes later Borja was back. He headed directly for Rafael's table. Rafael got up. "Qué pasa?" he said. "You look as if you've seen Death."

"Worse than that," said Borja with some authority.

"Come over here," said Rafael, catching him by the shoulder and propelling him towards another, empty table. "Digáme."

"James is in a police cell in Granada. Some drunken idiocy got him into trouble. They won't let him out till I fetch them his passport." He paused.

"Well? It could be worse."

"It is."

"He's not alone."

"How did you know?"

"I'm twenty-four and not slow for my age."

"Someone I met once called William. He lives in Jerez. James wants me to get his passport too."

"Cheeky. Will you?"

"I think I must. Since I'm in Jerez anyway. But what are you doing here?"

"Stopover."

"On an internal flight?"

"We had some engine trouble. We can't fly out until tomorrow night. Tell me about William."

"Mierda." Borja was unable to continue.

"Sorry. Wrong question. We'll be practical. Where do we go from here?"

"Looks as if I've got to trek into Jerez right now, look for this rat's passport, then traipse over to Seville, get James'..." He broke off. "It'd take the whole weekend." He shook his head.

"I could come with you," said Rafael. "That is, if you'd like that. You look as if you could do with some support."

Borja nodded.

"Is there any way we can get them out before we arrive? Like bail or something."

"Hardly. Oh wait a minute. Just had a thought. Remember Benjamín?"

"The Don Juan who gave it all up and joined the Church?"

"He's based in Seville. We keep in touch."

"You think he could sort something?"

"It's just a possibility. If he has contacts in Granada."

"And if they're on good terms with the police. Bit of a long shot. But go ahead. Ring him now. And maybe I could fix something too."

"Like what?"

"Like a helicopter?"

"Don't be crazy."

"Phone your priest. I'll see what I can do."

They met again five minutes later. Rafael was shaking his head. "No helicopter, sorry. But there's a light plane going to Granada from Seville at twelve o'clock, delivering documents for a court case. We're on it. Free. OK?" He looked down at Borja's bare feet. "Coffee first, or shoes?"

*

James' phone conversation with Borja had been the worst one of his life. The threadbare blanket he was draped in seemed almost too obvious a metaphor for his situation. "I'm sorry, it was just one of those things," he heard himself saying.

"But why with William?" Borja asked several times during the conversation, quite unnecessarily. He already knew and James did not even attempt an answer or excuse. The sub-text was plain to both of them and both knew it would have to be explored at painful length in due course. Now they sought comfort in practicalities: William's address, the geranium under which his key could be found at the top of his steps, the drawer beside the bed (yes, bed) where his passport lay. It was a relief when the conversation came to an end.

When he got back to the cell, James found his clothes had been delivered, along with two mugs of black coffee. William was already dressed. "I'd kill for an aspirin," he said.

"Did you shower?" James asked him.

"Hell, no. That can wait. There isn't a towel and using the blanket would defeat the object." He dived into a pocket and flourished something shiny. "But we got the corkscrew back."

It was impossible to feel angry with William for more than a moment, James thought. Impossible not to have fallen for him in the first place. But he no longer felt comfortable with him. Not after last night.

James had assured the policeman on duty that the passports were on their way and would arrive at six. "And then can we go?" he had thought to ask. "We'll see," the policeman had said. Now, as he thought about it, even six o'clock seemed a terribly long time ahead, a very long time to share with William.

They drank their coffee in silence, sitting on their beds, facing each other across the space that separated them. What would it be like to spend six months in prison, James thought... or life. Even a day was a day too long. James threw himself back on his bed and closed his eyes, aware only that William had chosen the identical moment to make the same movement. Perhaps he had been thinking identical thoughts.

A knock woke them. It was nine o'clock. "Someone to see you at the desk. Come now."

Rounding the bend in the corridor they were startled by the sight of a rotund, elderly clergyman wearing a white lace surplice over a red-buttoned cassock and carrying a broad-brimmed purple hat. He was addressing the officer on duty.

"Good Catholic boys," he was saying. "Guests in our great country. Friends of a personal friend. Sunday observance. Obligation..." William, whose Spanish was still not as fast as James', wanted to know what was going on.

"Good news and bad news," said James. "We're getting out of here. Bad news: I think we've got to go to mass."

\*

Borja and Rafael managed to get a lift into Jerez and located William's flat. Taking the key from under the flowerpot they opened the door and went in. "Pray no-one sees us," said Rafael, "or we'll all end up in the nick."

It was a curious sensation, Borja discovered, to be in your lover's boyfriend's flat. The place was neither tidy nor beautiful. Yet it had a certain character. The posters on the wall seemed somehow familiar, like lost friends... Borja realised with a little jolt that that was exactly what they were; they had hung on the walls he shared with James when they first moved in together; James had transplanted them here. In a corner were the famous football boots that had featured in the school match back in February. Oyster shells served as ashtrays: a nice touch, Borja had to admit. By the bed (there was no avoiding it; that was where the passport was) Borja's eyes were drawn to the small mirror on the shelf – so small that there was room in it only for his own troubled face. How often had James seen his own features reflected there, he wondered? William's room, William's bed. The private sanctuary of another human being. To his surprise Borja found that he could not hate William even now. Here in this intimate place he felt instead an unexpected empathy with him. He could not imagine why. Especially when he found a pair of jeans of James'. Jeans that even smelt of James. Borja had been wondering where they'd got to.

"Here it is," said Rafael, holding up the passport. "Actually," he said, looking into it, "he's not that bad-looking."

"He looks like James," said Borja flatly.

They turned back towards the open door. It was blocked by a stout woman. "Who are you," she asked. "What are you doing?"

Rafael began to explain. "It's complicated. William needs his passport but he's in Granada. Borja here is a friend of William's who happens to be going to Granada today. I am just a friend of Borja's."

"How do I know this is true?"

"Sometimes you just have to trust people," said Borja, thinking bitterly that perhaps it was impossible to trust anybody. Even he was now engaged in backing up Rafael's efforts to warp the truth.

"When is William coming back?" the woman wanted to know.

"Tonight," said Rafael.

"Good," said the woman. "He is late wih his rent. What is he doing in Granada?"

"Another friend is showing him the sights," said Borja.

"Why does he need his passport for that?" There seemed to be no end to the questions.

"The hotel," said Borja. "You know he's a foreigner. Hotels need to have a passport number to put in their register."

"Is that true?" said the woman. "I wouldn't know that. When you see your friend," she addressed Borja sternly, "remind him to pay his rent or he will find his belongings out there on the steps."

"I'll tell him." Borja could barely believe what was happening to him. In the course of an hour he had had it confirmed beyond doubt that William was his rival, he had rushed around Jerez in search of William's passport and now he had to lie to his landlady and accept a ticking-off on his behalf for non-payment of rent. And the day was hardly begun.

The woman let them go. They walked down the steps while she re-locked the flat. Then she replaced the key with conspicuous ceremony in its secret hiding-place under the geranium.

"Right," said Rafael. "To the station. There's a train at eight-thirty. I checked. We can make the plane easily."

"But only if we make the train first," said Borja. "We'd better run."

People in the streets, going to church or on their way to the bakers', looked up as they passed. Not many people ran through the streets of Jerez on a Sunday morning. One man looked up with more surprise than the others. "Hola! Borja! What are you doing here?" It was Paco.

They didn't stop. Borja swore. "Who was that?" said Rafael.

"Long story," said Borja. "Tell you on the train."

Two hours later they stood in the front room of James' and Borja's flat in Seville. "What a great place," said Rafael, looking round it.

Borja looked and suddenly it wasn't great any more. It seemed a dingy, unappealing little place, changed like his own life, overnight.

Borja thought of the house in the Bible that the foolish man built on sand and that, when the storm came, was all washed away. He heard again the words he had learned as a child: 'And the rain descended, and the floods came, and the winds blew, and beat upon that house; and it fell: and great was the fall of it.' Borja felt himself starting to cry.

"I know," said Rafael, "I know." Then he took Borja in his arms and held him for a minute in silence. "Come on," he said at last. "Get James' passport and let's get out."

Having mastered his fear of flying in an airliner, Borja was now confronted on the tarmac with a single-engined, four-seater Cessna. But by now he felt as enthusiastic about the experience of flying as Rafael did, and when he was offered the front seat next to the pilot, accepted readily. Which pleased Rafael. With any luck the new experience would distract his thoughts and give him no time for brooding. And Borja was even more distracted than Rafael anticipated. After they had taxied out to the main runway in a peculiar, waddling, progress, the pilot handed an instruction manual to Borja without ceremony and said: "Read the final checks, would you?"

So Borja found himself intoning: "Gyros, turn and slip" (whatever that meant) "engine temperature, engine pressure. Call tower", like a litany only with the most extreme concentration. Then the pilot slipped the brake, they rattled down the runway, slid disconcertingly to the left as they gained lift, then without warning leaped into the air.

In the cloudless blue, Borja felt himself suspended between two realities: the turmoil of the morning he had just lived through and the daunting prospect of the confrontation that was yet to come. It was a short, charmed time of peace. Was that what freedom meant? Below, the plains gave way to Málaga's brown mountains with the Mediterranean glinting in the gaps between, then snowy peaks appeared ahead and the pilot, apologising for the abruptness of the descent, banked sharply to line up with something that looked no longer than a football pitch: Granada's airfield.

"At least we landed in one piece," said Rafael, adding when Borja did not respond: "But maybe that was the easy bit." Borja looked grimly ahead of him as they walked from the plane. The distant town glowed like hot coals in the lunchtime sun. There were no buses or taxis to take them into the city, but there was a courier waiting to pick up the document and happily he had a car rather than a motor-bike. The pilot, who wanted to go into Granada to get something to eat, persuaded the courier to take them all with him. The pilot was also prepared to fly them back to Seville provided they were back at the airfield when he was ready to go. "Would you be able to take three?" Rafael asked cheekily. The pilot thought not; the extra fuel consumption might draw attention.

They were deposited in the Gran Via de Colón. Did Borja know where the police station was, Rafael wanted to know?

"I did once, but I've forgotten. Anyway, Benjamín said he would try to arrange for James to be invited for lunch at the priests' house – to win the confidence of the police. In which case they would still be there. And that's probably just over there." He pointed. The cathedral and the Capilla Real loomed at the end of the street.

"Lunch," said Rafael wistfully. "That's more than we've managed."

"I'm sorry, but I couldn't," said Borja, "but you..."

"No, forget it." Rafael wished he hadn't brought the subject up. "Let's go."

Borja led the way, his face a mask of desperate resolve, and then a middle-aged woman came out of a side street and turned into their path. "Jesus wept," said Borja.

"What now?"

"It's my aunt."

\*

James and William had little appetite for lunch either. They had not been badly treated though. They had been taken to the lodgings of the cathedral priests and allowed to shower before being escorted to high mass. This was quite a long affair but James found himself not minding. To his surprise he found the solemn singing and the smell of incense quite soothing. But he noticed that they did not have the same effect on William who was more than usually restless and fidgety.

When the service was over, they were taken back again to the priests' lodgings and sat down in a large bare room whose predominant colour was brown and whose liveliest occupant was a large ticking clock. But conversation did eventually get going between the six priests and James and William: mostly, as it happened, on the subject of football. James was surprised at how interested the mostly elderly clerics were in the game and how well informed. They managed to put questions about English teams and players that James and William between them were hard put to answer. A glass of wine helped loosen tongues but James could do little more than toy with the dish of fierce-looking mussels that began the meal or the pork stew that followed it. But he was grateful – extremely grateful – that no-one displayed the slightest curiosity in his and William's circumstances or wanted to know how they had become overnight guests of the police in the first place.

As the clock ticked comfortably on towards two o'clock, James began to take an unexpected comfort from the spartan room and unusual company and experienced a disinclination to leave it, just as people in waiting-rooms feel reluctant to go in to a difficult meeting. After all, outside this place only two things awaited him in the immediate future: a police cell and the moment when he must face Borja. It came almost as an unpleasant shock when the canon who had secured their release that morning rose from his chair and offered to take the two young men for a walk in the sunshine before returning them to the care of the police.

\*

Borja could not avoid his aunt. The pavement was narrow and she had already seen them. "Borja," she said. "What a surprise." She flashed a look at Rafael. "But what are you doing in Granada?" She grabbed her nephew's wrists. "Is it true?"

"Is what true?"

"That you live with another boy. That you are like his husband. Or, God forbid," she looked up at Rafael, "like his wife."

Borja felt his scalp go hot and his tongue dry. He had so much to deal with today. Why did God have to give him this? "Tía Ana..." He was struggling for sufficient breath to speak with. "... You ask so many questions. This is my friend Rafael from Salamanca. I don't live with him. I live with an English boy called James. Not like a husband, or like a wife. Why does everyone have to be so interested in the mechanics? Look, it isn't the best moment to be saying all this. We live together because we love one another, that's all." Borja didn't dare try to catch Rafael's facial reaction to the last announcement. "Now do you know where the cathedral priests live?"

"I was going there myself," said Tía Ana. "We can go together." And so they did. But Tía Ana would not let go of the earlier subject. "What will your poor mother do when she knows?"

Rafael interrupted. "Perhaps she knows already. And if she doesn't, maybe she prefers not to. Do you plan to tell her?"

"Well naturally. It is a family matter. In Borja's family we are all very close. You would not know that. You are outside."

"I know it isn't my business, Tía Ana..." Rafael knew what he was doing; in spite of herself Borja's aunt was mollified by being called Tía Ana by this handsome young stranger. "... But think before you speak. Truth is a powerful spice. A little can go a long way. Too far, sometimes. I'm sorry to be impertinent but there it is. You will probably never have to suffer me again."

"Thank you," said Borja. "Now I think we're here." They had arrived at a large door at the front of a blank-faced building. The cross-keys of Saint Peter were carved in stone above it.

A thought struck Tía Ana. "Why are you going to the priests' house of all places?"

"I think my friend may be there," said Borja calmly. "I think he may have been invited to lunch."

"Madre de Dios!" Tía Ana crossed herself. "An English maricón invited to lunch with the priests!"

"Tía Ana... Anyway, why are you going to the priests' house?"

She opened the shoulder-bag she was carrying and pointed to a large book. "The life of Saint Teresa of Avila. One of the priests lent it to me. I promised to return it. Oh, but it was so long! You can't imagine."

"You did well to get through it, Tía Ana," said Borja.

"Oh but I didn't. I never finished it." She looked at her nephew in sudden alarm. "You won't tell the priests I didn't..."

"Of course not. Why should I do that?" He paused to let this sink in. "It isn't always necessary to tell everybody everything."

None of them had thought to ring the bell they were standing next to but the next second the door was opened from the inside and James and William and the white-haired priest spilled out to join them on the pavement. There was a tense silence among the four young men, some surprise on the part of William and James who knew nothing about the aeroplane and could not imagine how the others had beaten the train by nearly four hours, and puzzled glances between the priest and Tía Ana who knew each other at least by sight. Borja's eyes met James'; their glances ricocheted apart again, hard, like billiard balls.

Rafael grabbed the passports from Borja's hand and gave them to the two Englishmen. "At least you have these now. I don't know which belongs to who. My name's Rafael."

"Good," said the priest. "We were going to take a walk to kill some time. Now we can go directly to the police station."

"The police station!" Tía Ana was now in a mood to be shocked by everything.

"A little formality," said the priest. "Foreign visitors and their papers. The police are unnecessarily fussy about these details, I often think."

"Are you coming with us?" Rafael teased Borja's aunt gently. Her face suggested she would dearly love to satisfy her curiosity but she could not find any reasonable excuse to abandon her original errand now that she was already on the doorstep of her stated destination.

"You will come and see me later, won't you?" she asked Borja.

"Today I can't," he answered. "I must get to Seville tonight. To start work tomorrow. We all must."

She looked disappointed. Borja melted. He hugged her and gave her a kiss. "I'll come again soon to see you. When life is less... you know. I promise."

They left her, small and solitary, ringing the bell (for the door had closed again) at the priests' house.

The priest talked amiably of this and that as they made their way towards the police station. If he was aware of the stony silence of his companions and the tense atmosphere between them, nothing showed it. They arrived at last. "I took them out," said the canon to the duty officer, "I have brought them back in person. Otherwise you might not trust me again." He chuckled. "They have been to mass and are once again in possession of their papers. What more could you ask for?"

The police who last night had seemed most reluctant to release their charges seemed now only too pleased to get rid of them. No doubt the presence of the priest helped. On presentation of their passports the two criminals of the previous night were waved away as if they were of no more importance than thistledown. "Vayan con Dios," said the policeman on duty. It was an ending for him. For Borja and James it was just a beginning.

"I will say good-bye, now, too," said the priest. "I do not want to be curious, but I cannot help noticing that none of you seems to be particularly happy this sunny day in this most beautiful of cities. If you do not know why you are unhappy you need first to find out. And if you do know – then it is surely possible to put right. You are young and have everything in front of you. Adios and good luck." He shook hands quickly with each of them, then turned and left them.

"Let's get out of here," said William. Everyone nodded. It would be the only moment that day that found them all in agreement.

Rafael spoke next. "We came by plane. There's room for two to go back the same way. The other two will have to take the train." He turned to Borja. "Do you want to go back in the plane with James? After all, Seville is where you're going. William and I both have to go to Jerez. Is that OK?"

There was a general feeling of relief among the other three now that this had been decided for them, though James couldn't help feeling that William, able to travel with a total stranger, had done best out of the deal. He fished in his pocket for the return half of his train-ticket and handed it to Rafael. "If you're really sure that's OK?" Rafael nodded. He was nice, James decided.

Good-byes were mumbled, perfunctory, and the two pairs of men turned away in different directions. There was nothing to be gained by staying together any longer.

"We'll need a taxi to the airport," Borja said. It was the first thing that he had said to James. "We got a lift in. We can't easily get one back."

"There'll be a bus, surely," said James. His first words to Borja.

"I don't think so. The airfield's such a little place. They don't have regular services to anywhere as far as I know. So I think there can't be a bus."

"Taxi it is, then. Where do we look for one?" Their conversation clung tenaciously to the details of their immediate arrangements. Both were trying to stave off as long as possible the painful exchanges that would have to come.

Arriving at the airport Borja was relieved to see the small plane still on the apron, their pilot drinking coffee beside the vending machine in the nearly deserted airport building. "The documents got delivered OK then?" Borja asked.

"What documents?" James wanted to know.

"Something to do with a court case," Borja said. "I don't know what kind of a case it is."

"Murder," said the pilot.

James realised, as they walked out towards the Cessna, that this would be the first time he and Borja had flown together. With a sick feeling in his stomach he caught himself wondering if it would also be the last. He was impressed by the asurance with which Borja climbed in beside the pilot, then more than a little surprised when he picked up the manual and read out the pre-flight checks without waiting to be asked.

The flight was uneventful, silent save for the machine-gun din of the plane; the window a blaze of blue. The pilot announced quite suddenly that they were landing at Seville, startling James who discovered that he had been asleep.

Arriving home, they had a pizza from the fridge and a can of beer each. James put the television on. They saw two game-shows and then a film which seemed to make no sense. It went on till past midnight and they watched it, yawning, to the very end. Anything, it seemed, was better than talking. Finally, bed-time could be put off no longer. And then Borja said it: "Sorry, James. I can't sleep with you."

"Darling, don't say that. You don't know..."

"I know what I feel, that's all."

"Come here..."

Avoiding the arms which were trying to embrace him, Borja grabbed a pillow and a blanket from the bedroom and retreated to the living-room, pulling the door shut behind him.

## Thirteen

The cake was embarrassingly large. Mark had been bullied into collecting it from Sophie's kitchen and balancing it on the back of his scooter all the way through the traffic to the María Luisa Park. It would never have got there otherwise. And it certainly surprised Pippa.

"I didn't go for an exact number of candles, dear," said Sophie, "but rather for an impression. So don't count them. Just blow them out."

"I think I might take that to heart for future birthdays," said Pippa. "Not admit to an exact number of years but just give an impression."

"Quick," said Karsten. Mark had had a job lighting the candles in the open air and their small flames struggled against the breeze. Pippa blew, and everyone sang Happy Birthday – quite tunefully, thanks to the presence of Karsten and Alexa.

It attracted quite a lot of attention, this English birthday tea, served on two blue-tiled benches beside the carp pool in the Plaza de España. The tea had come in Sophie's thermoses, the sugar in a screwed-up paper bag. "It's just like home," said Pippa. She meant it. She was very touched. She also thought how typical it was of Sophie: fiercely Spanish in all things (her visiting card announced her simply as Sra. S. Nuñez) but relapsing into extreme Englishness on occasions of emotional significance such as the birthday – or arrival – of a cousin. Pippa remembered the Bisto and Bird's Custard.

It was a perfect day. In late May most days were. Jacaranda was in full flower, colouring whole avenues of trees surreally, blazing blue instead of green. The sun, not yet delivering the overpowering heat that would come in the months ahead, picked out the bright clothes and bicycles of children playing in the park, making them look cleaner than they were. White pigeons strutted on the sandy orange paths among the palm trees or, sailing just overhead, clapped their approval at the air.

Four of Pippa's colleagues from work were present, not counting Mark. Jeannette was there, James was not. Because of the arrangement of the benches everyone was forced to perch side by side like swallows on a wire, jostling and changing places every time a cup needed refilling or a conversation ran out of steam.

"His May baby, he calls you," said Jeannette, squeezing into a space next to Pippa and quoting Mark. "And his what-month bride? Or is it still not decided?"

"No, not yet." Pippa meant to sound breezy but it came out more like a sigh. "The thing is..." She struggled again to make this sound upbeat. "... Mark really feels we should spend a second year in Seville together. Even if that means..."

"Postponing the wedding for a whole year?" Jeannette was horrified.

"No, I wasn't meaning that. I was thinking about university. Postponing my final year."

Jeannette did not think this wise and said so. "... Weddings or degrees. Sorry, but that's what I think. Strike while... anyway. But maybe I'm thinking about my own situation. I haven't told you about Felipe, have I?"

"Not recently."

"He told me when we first started going out – or at least he let me think – he'd already done his mili. But in fact he's been putting it off for years. Now they've sent him an ultimatum and he's had to come clean about it. He's got to go at the end of the summer. They could send him anywhere. It's their policy in fact to post people as far away from home as possible. And here's me with a job to hold down in Seville. Two years apart is no joke. We should have got married before."

"I'm so sorry," said Pippa. "I'd no idea. But there'd be weekends and things, wouldn't there?"

"You don't know Felipe," said Jeannette darkly. "You don't know Spanish men."

"Mark's half-Spanish," Pippa half-bridled.

Sophie leant across to Pippa from the other side. "I was hoping James could come. It is a pity."

"Thursday's his day in Jerez," said Jeannette. "He's been going there every week for months. Cushy little number if you ask me."

Cushier than you know, thought Pippa.

"Though this week he's been behaving very oddly," Jeannette went on. "Very oddly indeed."

Mark was nodding his head. James had come to work on Monday with an ashen face and had avoided all but the most essential conversations with his workmates, not even looking them in the face if he could help it. Mark had made a point of suggesting a drink together after work and James had flatly refused: a refusal which was unprecedented in Mark's three years of knowing him. As for Borja, who would normally be seen regularly in the Bodegón or the Casa Morales with James, Mark had not seen him all week. Pippa and he had exchanged guarded comments on this: guarded because they found that any discussion of the James, Borja, William situation tended to become heated; neither of them was very clear why.

"As for his boyfriend," Jeannette continued, "he seems to have disappeared off the planet. If you ask me there's something wrong between them."

"Oh no," said Sophie. "That would be sad." She turned away and busied herself with a knife and cake and paper plates.

"Spanish men for you," said Jeannette.

"Nothing to do with Spanish men," said Pippa hotly. "If you really need to know, James is seeing an English chap..."

"Pippa!" protested Mark.

"... in Jerez. That's all. Simple as that."

"But it isn't your business to go telling people!" said Mark.

Pippa coloured. "I don't like people drawing wrong conclusions, that's all. It's so unfair."

"No arguments on birthdays, please," said Karsten. "Most of us here knew already. No doubt Borja knows also by now."

"I'm afraid it does rather prove what I've always maintained," said Sophie. "Those relationships are inherently unstable. Sorry but that's the way it is." She began distributing portions of the cake. "Have this one, dear, it's got icing."

"They haven't had time," said Karsten. "I mean same-sexers learning to make relationships work, the way oppo-sexers have always had to. Over the centuries it just was never possible before now. Especially so in Spain. Who knows yet if they can last or not? Borja and James are part of an experiment, are they not? In their own way they are pioneers."

"Or rather were, it now would seem," said Jeannette.

"Oh come on," said Mark, more crossly than he intended. He had found the impending split between his two friends surprisingly upsetting. Now that it seemed to have actually happened he felt worse about it than ever. It was as if it touched in some way his own relationship with Pippa. It made him feel isolated, adrift on a sea of doubts. He made a conscious decision to change the subject. "Alexa, when are we going to hear you play?"

"What?" Alexa was startled. She had not contributed to the last conversation but she had been following it intently. "Play what?"

Mark laughed. "The piano, of course. Did you think I meant baseball?"

"You've heard me play."

"In private, yes. When are you going to give a concert?"

"You mean a public one, here in Seville?"

"Yes. Why not?"

"Great idea," said Pippa, glad herself that the conversation had changed tack.

"I have been trying for some time to persuade her," said Karsten.

"It isn't that simple," said Alexa. "It's not like taking a guitar into the plaza, sitting down and playing. Piano concerts are difficult things to set up."

"Difficult is not the same as impossible, dear," said Sophie.

"No," answered Alexa, "but it is the same as expensive."

"There are too few classical concerts," said Sophie, ignoring Alexa's point.

Alexa smiled. "From my point of view there are far too many. I sound very negative, don't I? I'll make a bargain, though. If anyone here cares to organise a concert and promote it – then I'll play." She looked at her watch. "For the moment, though, I have to leave you. And so has Karsten."

"What?" said Karsten.

"Surprise," said Alexa. "You are summoned into the Presence. In other words we have both been invited to Eulogio's."

"Me? Why?" Karsten was trying not to feel flattered.

"Another surprise. But bring your guitar." Alexa stood up. "Pippa, enjoy the rest of your birthday." Then she moved towards her and whispered something in her ear.

"I'll try to remember that," said Pippa.

*

"What did you say to Pippa as we left?" Karsten asked Alexa later.

"Don't fall out over other people's problems. It's not worth it."

"Probably good advice," said Karsten.

They were sitting in the enclosed patio of Eulogio's old white house. It was like a tiny cloister court. Yellow and blue earthenware crocks full of flowering plants were arranged in the centre around a miniature fountain while leather armchairs sat in the shade of the overhanging first floor. Eulogio had gone inside to find some manzanilla and glasses. His wife had not joined them, pleading urgent business in the kitchen. She always did this: something which Alexa privately deplored.

They had only a moment ago come out into the patio. Eulogio had just listened to Karsten play the guitar for the first time and expressed unqualified approval. Then, to Karsten's chagrin, Eulogio had commanded him to demonstrate his skill at the piano, handing him his own, much written-in, score of the Mozart sonatas to play from. With painful self-consciousness Karsten had had a heroic stab at the C minor Fantasy. He was pleased now that it was over.

Eulogio emerged into the patio, holding a bottle and smiling through his opera-curtain moustache, while his wife made a cameo appearance behind him, delivering three dainty glasses on a tray before vanishing again into the kitchen.

"Never stop playing the guitar, Karsten," Eulogio said, stooping to pour the manzanilla. "You have much joy to give to many people. And enjoy the piano too. But keep it for your friends." He winked. "But I think you know all this. I asked you here today not only to charm us with your Scarlatti but also because Alexa has asked me a difficult question and I need your help to answer it. Here is a young woman who plays the piano better than most of my former students in London ever will but now she is wondering if the piano is really the instrument that she would like to spend the rest of her life sitting at. Maybe, she is wondering at this admittedly late stage, if her true talent lies with the guitar."

This was news to Karsten and his face showed it.

Eulogio went on. "Am I to blame for this, I ask myself? I told her to listen to the street boys strumming. Then later she met you.

Mea culpa." He turned to Alexa. "Which guitar do you prefer: the classical or the flamenco?"

"To listen to or to play?"

"Both. Take listening first."

"I love listening to them both. I adore the sound of the flamenco."

"And have you heard the cante, the real flamenco song?"

"Yes. In a tablao."

Eulogio pulled a face. "Yes, all right. But that's not the best. It can not be. There are fixed schedules, the tourists to entertain. The real cante..."

"Yes I know," said Alexa. "The real cante just happens spontaneously in some little bar up in the hills or in the backstreets. Only I never seem to be there when it does."

"It's only a matter of time. Don't worry. You'll hear it one day. Now to the classical. Who have you heard?"

"Segovia, but only on record. Ypes, ditto, Julian Bream and John Williams. And Karsten of course."

"You must hear more. I will give you some names later. Now about playing. Flamenco or classical?"

"I'm still a beginner."

"Forget that a moment. Which do you like to play?"

"I think," Alexa began slowly, "if I am to be serious there is no real choice. Flamenco I could only approach from the outside. I could do it, I'm sure, but like an actor playing a part. But the classical style is already a part of me. I already know what's what. Being realistic I'd have to – like Karsten – choose the classical."

Eulogio, who had been busy first cutting and then lighting a cigar during this speech, now drew on it slowly and exhaled the smoke. "I think you are wise in that. Also, remember that true flamenco guitar playing, the tocque, is inseparable from the cante. They are carne y uña, flesh and fingernail. But the toque is handmaiden to the cante: the flamenco guitar is not a solo instrument. And you are not 'cut out' (is that the expression?) for a handmaiden's role, I think. Am I right?"

"I would say so," said Karsten who was learning more about Alexa this afternoon than he had discovered in six months.

"Well, Alexa," Eulogio continued, "if you are wise in one decision – to choose the classical over the flamenco – perhaps you are not wrong in your other idea: to choose the guitar in preference to the piano. After all, it is not as if either will make you rich. Karsten, what do you think?"

"She should choose to be happy. That is all."

Eulogio sighed. "Ah, the wisdom of the young. Tell me now, who did you study with in Córdoba?"

"With Manuel Lozón."

"Take Alexa to see him. Let her play to him. I love the guitar, but with the heart only; I am no expert. If Señor Lozón judges that you have talent," (he spoke now to Alexa) "I will surrender you with a good grace. Otherwise I will teach you the piano with pleasure for as long as you need. I had to make a choice too, when I was young. The piano was a demanding bride for a young Andaluz. She condemned me to a life of grey skies and northern cities. Oh, England was all right." He looked round his sky-ceilinged living-room. "But I must have loved the piano very much. Decide which way you want, Alexa, as in the end only you can. But let your talent be your only guide. Beware the small voice that simply says the grass is greener."

"And people are saying I should give a concert," said Alexa, shaking her head. "On the piano. Now of all times."

"Why not?" said Eulogio. "Maybe now, of all times, might be the best of times. And now, perhaps, it is time I played to you." He got up and led the way in off the patio.

*

James and William had not contacted each other since parting outside the Granada police station on Sunday. James had thought constantly about picking up the telephone; the thought had pricked at his uncertainty like a needle. But he knew that nothing could be sorted out on the phone. He did not know now what he wanted, or even who. On the train to Jerez this Thursday, he felt as miserable as he ever had in his life.

Paco had rarely had the time or inclination for an English lesson since he had engaged James six months ago. Even when he did, it only took up a part of the day and James had been free to spend the rest of his time with William. William was usually the first person he saw at O'Donnell's, once he had passed reception, sitting in Paco's office in the almost invariable absence of his boss. But today, on entering the office braced for his re-encounter with William, James was doubly disconcerted to find Paco behind the desk and, standing in the small space available to them, three young ladies. The ladies looked glum but Paco was beaming. "At last I have a real class for you," he said. "These three beautiful women all want to learn English."

"Gosh," said James, moderating his reaction in the presence of strangers. "When do they want to start?"

"Well, now," said Paco.

"You mean this minute?"

"Yes, of course. There is no problem, is there?"

"What's their level, Paco?" He turned to the women. "How much English do you know?"

They gazed back, mute.

"They are beginners all," said Paco with pride.

"For God's sake, Paco!" At least they wouldn't understand what he was saying now. "This isn't very reasonable. At no notice. You could have telephoned."

Paco looked as startled as a child who has heard the word 'no' used in earnest for the first time. "But all the schedules have been changed to make them free now at the same time. Surely..."

"Paco, I haven't even brought a book." James felt like a doctor caught out on a house call without his medical bag.

Paco was puzzled. "You don't use a book when you teach me."

"I know, Paco, but you're not a beginner. Plus I've known you for three years."

"Please help me," said Paco. "Say that you'll do it. I did make an effort, you know, to increase the student numbers. So that you can keep coming here to Jerez. It is nice that you continue coming here. For everyone. No?"

"All right, Paco. I'll do what I can. Just find me a room."

"Thank you, my friend. Thank you, thank you. I am happy now. That you say yes. Even if the lesson can not be as good as..."

"The lesson will be good," said James curtly. "How long do you want it?"

"Just two hours."

"The first day, one and a half."

"Only?"

"Just for today. And with a break."

"A break?"

"Paco..."

"OK. A break. I tell them."

Mentally James rolled up his sleeves.

He did not have a moment to think about William until the clock allowed him to say good-bye to his new class. ("Good-bye. See you," they chanted as he left the room. The lesson had been all right.) It was almost a surprise to run straight into him in the corridor. "Oh," they both said.

There was a silence as they looked at each other, briefly examined faces, noticed clothes. They might have been meeting for the first time. In a way they were.

"Good to see you," said James. His tone was muted.

"Feel like a beer?" William sounded uncertain.

James smiled. "Best idea so far," he said.

They were well known by now in most of the cafés nearby. By unspoken agreement they picked on one this time where they could be strangers.

"Borja won't sleep with me." James came to the point quite quickly. "Hasn't done since Granada."

"Are you surprised?"

"I don't know if I am or not. Should I be? I mean, I'm not just talking about sex. He won't sleep in the same bed. Not even the same room. He spends all his time avoiding me."

William was sympathetic. "It sounds pretty miserable. I'm sorry."

"It is miserable. I feel just... stuck."

"We should never have allowed ourselves to get caught like that. It was stupid. On that crane we were like rats in a trap. And that was mostly my fault."

"Lots of things were stupid. Not just the crane. Not just you."

William did not pursue this. "What are you going to do? I mean, what do you think will happen?"

"Look," said James, "I was wondering... do you think I can stay with you?"

William looked startled. "Well, sure. I mean, yes. But for how long?"

It was James' turn to look startled. "Well... at least for tonight. And... till the weekend. I'd commute to school in Seville. I just don't feel I can face sharing a flat with Borja like two strangers. I think he needs a few days to come round." He risked a joke. "I've brought a toothbrush."

"Of course you can stay," said William, "but I honestly don't see what it is you're trying to do. On Sunday you were all for rushing back into Borja's arms. Putting me – putting 'us' – behind you. You didn't say that in so many words but it was there between the lines; I could sense it pretty strongly."

"That's not quite fair, darling. If you remember, we only got in touch with Borja because you wouldn't risk phoning Paco."

"Not true. You rang Borja because it made sense: he was in Jerez at the time. You were refusing to ring him at first."

"Because I didn't want to involve him! Look, we're going round in circles."

"I know. Not a very good start, is it?" said William.

"Start of what?"

"Well, if you're moving in with me that's the start of something, isn't it? Of a new phase. Whatever it may be."

"Better drink to it then." James struggled to say it with conviction.

Later that afternoon, after Paco had had his lesson, James rang Borja at work. At work because there would not be the opportunity for any wrangling – supposing Borja felt like it. James said he would be staying in Jerez for a night or two "until things sort themselves out." He meant, until Borja begged him to come back. At least, he thought that was what he meant. "I do want to come back, you know," he added. "And I still love you."

But it was not that simple. James was no longer sure what he felt about Borja, or about William. There were moments during that first evening of a different, more mundane, intimacy with William when he wished he could be a thousand miles away from Spain, away from both his men, starting life afresh.

They drank a lot that evening, doing the rounds of the bars. They tried to get drunk but without success. The wine flowed like water, but it was water off a duck's back. They talked as much as usual but laughed much less. "I don't know," said William at one point. "Why can't it be like it was at the beginning?"

"Because it can't. It never can be. We have to start again."

William brightened. "Well, there is one good thing: it'll be nice to have someone to cook for for a change. You didn't know I was an ace cook, did you?"

James did not, but the idea that William looked forward to cooking for him touched him and cheered him unexpectedly. There was something he wanted to ask William, something he was curious about, but, long as their conversation continued, he could find no easy way to get round to it. He dearly wanted to know what William had made of Rafael during the enforced companionship of their six-hour return journey to Jerez last Sunday. What had they talked about on the train? In the end he had to leave the question unasked. Perhaps he would never know.

Later that evening, with only a toothbrush for a dowry, he moved in with William. William did not cook that night. They put off going 'home' until as late as possible because neither of them knew what the word now meant. But once they had undressed for bed and faced each other naked across the familiar little room, the possibilities began to look more promising and when they got into bed together they found it easier than they had expected to make love.

## Fourteen

The following Thursday when Borja was preparing his evening meal, a sort of hash of rice, tomatoes and tinned tuna fish, he unthinkingly set two plates on the table instead of one. It was the third time he had done this since James moved out. The first time he had felt upset. The second time it had made him angry and he had thrown the offending plate to the floor where it provokingly refused to smash and lay there till he picked it up. This time he laughed, though he was far from finding it funny.

At heart Borja felt anger and humiliation. Anger but also unbearable loss. His house might have been built on sand – his own folly, that – but that made its thunderous collapse no less awful; its shelter seemed no less irreplaceable for having proved impermanent. James, however badly he had treated Borja, had been loving and warm, protective, beautiful. And was gone.

He had not become a total hermit. He did have friends apart from the ones he shared with James: colleagues from work mostly; and he had joined them once or twice in the evenings, visiting a bar or two or just walking by the river. These friends knew James up to a point and tacitly accepted Borja's relationship but it was not something any of them would have discussed with him or even thought too much about in private. That they knew something now was wrong was signalled by a little more attentiveness in their dealings with Borja rather than by any curiosity. That Borja was not really feeling sociable this week they also accepted as a matter of course and did not comment or show surprise when, on each occasion, he took an early opportunity to slip away home by himself. Where he still found himself laying up for two.

It did not take him long to polish off his supper. He had almost forgotten over the last three years how brief mealtimes could be when you lived alone. They didn't have beginnings or endings even but merged with other activities like cleaning the stove and watering the plants. The flat felt stuffy this evening, even with the windows open. The warmth of May was giving way to real heat which lingered in the stonework of the city through most of the night. On an impulse Borja stepped out of his flat, descended the stairs and went out into the plaza. He would take a walk to the Bodegón. If James' friends were there, so be it. He was ready now to face them.

All around the Plaza del Salvador, café tables buzzed with conversation as people came and went like bees. Then, just for a moment, as he cast his eyes around the scene, death was present and conversation stilled. The great crowd of people was mown down, falling like grass-stems onto the tables and the pavements in between. They made little noise as they fell, a rustle not a rattle; dead things were so light. Borja's encounters with death were growing fewer. In the last few months he had scarcely experienced them at all. Perhaps it had to do with his slowly waning religious faith, or maybe, like his outgrown childhood fits and his fading power to visualise unseen objects, it was simply part of growing up. But for whatever reason, the transformation of the Plaza del Salvador this evening affected him less than it would have done two weeks ago. So here was death? Big deal, really.

The Bodegón was unusually empty. That was relative, though. It was such a big space that a mere twenty customers did little more to fill it than three or four. But standing at the far end of the counter were Pippa and Mark, Alexa and Karsten. Borja's solitary state was emphasised by the emptiness of the place and as he came in through the open doorway they all turned and stared at him. It took him about ten seconds to reach them though it felt more like ten minutes.

For Pippa, Borja's entrance was that of a boxer stepping back into the centre of the ring after a punishing slam against the ropes. What he would say, do, in a few seconds' time, she thought, would set the course for the rest of his life. For the first time ever she imagined herself in the same position. At some level below the conscious she knew she must learn and profit from the moment. But consciously it suddenly occurred to her, most painfully, that whatever Borja was feeling now would be hers to feel one day.

Alexa had met Borja only a few times and didn't know him well. She had few preconceptions against which to measure him this evening. What came into her mind now was the cartoon by Hoffnung on her teacher's wall, of the pianist-matador entering the arena to confront his bull. And Karsten, seeing Borja's familiar trim figure approaching but dressed untypically in open-necked white shirt and jeans, was so startled by the thought that crossed his mind that he banished it at once.

Borja challenged them. "Why are you all looking at me like that?"

Mark answered. "I'm sorry. I knew I was looking at you like that. I didn't know we all were. Fact is, we'd just mentioned you and in you walked."

"In what connection, mentioned?"

"Business, as it happens. We were talking about organising a concert – Alexa's giving a piano recital – and we realised we couldn't get very far without involving the tourist office. And that's where your name came in. It seems your star is riding high there at the moment."

"Thank you," said Borja. He really meant 'Thank you' for their conversation not being about him and James. He looked around him. There had been a slight change in the decor: strings of garlic now hung from the beams in addition to the usual hams. "Have they been having problems with vampires?" he asked, deadpan. "Stay away for ten days and everything changes." The ice was broken.

"They're all more enthusiastic than I am," Alexa said. "They don't have to play the bloody thing."

"We were suggesting," said Karsten, "that she might do a two-piano recital with Eulogio, her teacher. His name would sell more tickets."

"That's very true," said Alexa, "but I don't know if he has a headful of two-piano pieces. I've never heard him play any. And I certainly don't have any in my repertoire. Also, I wouldn't be able to practise with him. We each have only one piano and they're a bus-ride apart."

"Perhaps," said Borja, "he could be persuaded to share the concert with you. You know, you do one half and he does the other."

"That's more practical," said Alexa. "Though he still might not want to do it."

"Don't be defeatist," said Pippa. "You can only ask."

"Hey," said Mark, "this guy doesn't have a drink yet." Borja chose a beer.

"The other thing is," Alexa went on, "Eulogio is simply much better than me. The difference would show."

"It wouldn't matter," said Karsten. "He's forty years older. People who know enough to notice a difference would also know enough to expect it."

"Whereas you," Mark said, "have the advantage of being forty years younger." Alexa pulled a face. "And vastly more attractive."

"There's nothing wrong," said Pippa, "with exploiting your natural advantages."

"Where will the concert be?" asked Borja.

"We haven't got as far as a venue," said Mark.

"Why not go for the Patio de las Doncellas," said Borja. "You know, the centre court of the Alcázar." They all looked at him.

"It's a brave idea," said Mark. "Reckon we could get it?"

"Why not try?" said Borja. "If I could get Diego Imendia

interested we'd be halfway there. He's the head of tourism for all Andalucía. I get on well with him." This struck his own ears as an exaggeration.

"At least I've met him once or twice," he amended. "When will it be?"

"As soon as," said Mark.

"Wait a minute," said Alexa. "There's just a little question of preparing the music. September or October would be the earliest."

They were interrupted at that point by a man with a suitcase full of furry toy fighting bulls. He wound one up with a key and made it dance on the bar counter. Pippa dealt with him, telling him in Spanish that he was not among tourists and his wares were not wanted. Too surprised to resume his sales pitch he moved away.

Discussion continued for some time. They talked about having tickets printed specially but rejected the idea as being too costly; a book of cloakroom tickets would do just as well. They discussed advertising. Borja said he knew very little about it but would investigate. He was fairly certain though that concert promotion in Andalucía would bear little resemblance to its equivalent where they came from.

Quite a lot of drink was consumed, by the men at least, and Borja found himself walking home at two o'clock in the morning with his head swimming slightly but, now that he had offered to help organise Alexa's concert, full of a new purpose. It hadn't been necessary to mention James once during the evening and when he got home he found, for the first time since James had left, that he was able to confront his reflection in the bathroom mirror with a smile.

Having done that he picked up the phone and dialled Rafael.

Who was surprised but not unpleasantly so. "In all my life you've never telephoned me. Now you do it at three in the morning."

"Sorry, but you were never famous for going to bed early. Look, can I come and see you at the weekend?"

"Mierda, I'm going to be in Salamanca."

"It would take me all weekend to get there." Borja's voice betrayed his disappointment.

"I might be able to get you a flight as far as Madrid. Can't promise now. Have to fix it in the morning. You'd be OK in the jump-seat, I suppose?"

"That's not the same as an ejector-seat?"

"Crazy boy. Ring you in the morning. Dream well."

Midday Saturday found Borja stepping out of a train in Salamanca station. The jump-seat, the foldaway extra seat in the cockpit of a passenger jet, had been a great experience, despite one moment of embarrassment at the beginning when Borja, whom Rafael had passed off as an off-duty steward, had to be shown how to attach the elaborate safety-harness by a puzzled flight-crew. But the views were brilliant and by the end of the flight Borja had had lessons in fuel economy, instrument landing and V.O.R. navigation. By the time they touched down in Madrid he was feeling as if he could have flown the thing himself.

Rafael was waiting on the station platform, wearing sunglasses and looking fit and tanned. They shook hands. "You're looking good," they both said in unison and then laughed at themselves. "Marisa's expecting us to lunch," Rafael said. "But we can go and get a beer first, don't you think?" Borja agreed and they headed for the Plaza Mayor, for both of them the scene of many a lively student evening. Only now the students were a sea of unfamiliar faces, some of them looking disconcertingly young.

"I haven't told James I'm here," said Borja, once they were settled at a pavement table. "That's a very significant step for me. Do you see why?"

"Not immediately."

"Well, it's not because I don't want him to know I'm here. It's because I no longer live with him in any sense. I really don't care any more what happens to him. It's over."

A waiter brought their beer.

"You've reached that stage rather quickly, haven't you?" said Rafael. "Where is James now?"

"As far as I know he's living with his lookalike friend in Jerez. That's where he went to nine days ago and, except for a phone-call to tell me where he was, we haven't contacted each other since."

Rafael frowned. "I wonder if you've given him a proper chance to put things right. I'm sure that's what he really wants. That's the feeling I got when I met him that day."

"Granada, two weeks ago. It could be a lifetime. But I'm not interested in whether or not he wants to put things right. There's no way he can do that. Not with me."

Rafael took off his sunglasses and laid them on the table. "Listen, Borja. I don't want to make light of your situation or of your feelings in any way. But these things happen to people sometimes. To married people, to lovers, to women, to men. And they do get put right. When both people want it. Which I am sure is the case with you."

"And I tell you most seriously it is not the case. If James wants to have me back why has he gone to live with William? Not that I even want to know the answer to that. Because I do not want him back. Not at all."

"What happened to Christian forgiveness? Maybe it's Benjamín you should be talking to, not me."

"Forgiveness doesn't come into it. I can forgive him as much as he likes or as much as the Church requires, but that won't make me want to be his lover again or even his friend. Do you see that?"

"I hear what you say. But I still think you're not giving yourself enough time. Time changes feelings."

"In some cases yes. With some people yes. But not in this case. And not with me."

"Have you ever thought," said Rafael, and he took a sip of beer, "that you take yourself a little bit too seriously? Now drink up; let's go and meet Marisa and the kids – one of them's named after you, by the way, I now realise."

Borja was not sure why he had come to Salamanca on the spur of the moment. It was true that there had been a question he wanted to ask Rafael, but now he was here it seemed too silly to bring up. Rafael had shared six hours of train journey with William. What had he learnt about the man in that time? What had they said to each other? But he found he could not put the question. What would Rafael make of such a petty preoccupation? Even to ask would make the answer seem important. Borja swore to himself it was not important and never would be. He would not ask. Yet it was good to be here; sometimes spur-of-the-moment decisions could be good ones. And it was great to talk to Rafael, even if he didn't always agree with everything you said. "It's not myself I take seriously," he said later, defending himself. "It's my relationship with James. I took that seriously. It seems he didn't."

They talked a great deal as the day went on. They looked up old friends, played snooker in a café, strolled into the cathedral and sat for a time in the gloom. Borja thought about praying: a habit that had come easily to him as a child; too easily, he now realised; suspiciously easily. Now no thoughts came to him and if there was a God there was no sign of him here this afternoon.

"I've come to a decision," Borja said some time later. "The flat has got to go. It's too expensive for me on my own. James doesn't earn much more than I do. He won't be prepared to go on paying for a place he doesn't use."

"Where will you live?"

"Like anyone else in the same situation. Throw myself on the mercy of friends with floors while I look for a room of my own. Yes, a room of one's own." He said it again, this time in English.

"What's that?" asked Rafael.

"Title of a book. It has a nice sound, don't you think? 'A Room of One's Own'."

Marisa, her husband and the children joined them for the evening paseo, but made a diplomatic departure for home and supper when Rafael suggested taking Borja to a gay bar. A gay bar in Salamanca? Borja was astonished. Seville was one thing and he and James had sometimes visited a gay club near the Plaza de Armas, but Salamanca! How quickly things could change.

As it turned out, the gay bar was not a hit with Borja and quite soon Rafael took him away to a more conventional disco where, as Borja said, "at least people look as if they're having fun even if they are straight." He had found the gay bar full of sad, uncomfortable people, not at home with their identities and unsure what they ought to be wearing and how they should behave.

"Don't be hard on them," said Rafael. "It's different for you and me. We belong to an international scene: you with your Englishman, me with travelling. Here in Salamanca it's only just beginning. It was probably the same in England ten years ago." But he had to admit that Borja looked more comfortable now, and more relaxed than he had ever seen him: dancing, or leaning back in his chair with a cigar in his hand, laughing. Not a simple character, Rafael thought and made a mental note to be careful with him.

The evening receded; friends and acquaintances, drinks and tapas that had been like a tide engulfing them had drawn away and at two in the morning they themselves made their way up the stairs of Marisa's by now silent house, to Rafael's room on the top floor. It was the same room Borja had slept in after Christmas. There was no room empty this weekend. Rafael let them in. There was the bed and there was the floor. "You know..." said Rafael.

"I know." Borja smiled. "But the floor will do fine."

The next morning they had coffee and tostados in the Plaza Mayor along, it seemed, with the rest of the city. "This is the first time I've ever come to Salamanca without visiting my parents," said Borja, wondering at himself a little.

"Is this a sign that you're growing up, do you think?" Rafael was enjoying the feeling of being two years older.

"It could be. Hey, supposing we went to mass in the cathedral and bumped into both our families. Might that be interesting?"

"Don't even think of it. Marisa has invited us for a paella, remember, and after that I have to put you on your train back to Madrid. Don't you think you've got enough on your plate just at the moment without your family? That is, if Tía Ana is in any way representative. I'm being your big brother this weekend – I think that's what you wanted when you phoned me though you didn't exactly say so – and in that role I'd say this morning was one for sipping coffee in the sun, maybe strolling in the gardens if we have the energy, but nothing more ambitious than that. OK?"

Days with time limits were sometimes the best ones, Borja thought. When you knew you had to catch a train at four...

They walked through the Monterrey Park, the first time Borja had set foot in the place since his traumatic night there years ago. He looked almost disbelievingly at the tree under which he had taken a cigarette from a stranger. So much had happened since that time. He didn't tell Rafael the story. Maybe one day, if they got to know each other better.

The paella was judged a success, especially by the children. Borja the younger had to be physically restrained from throwing the empty mussel-shells through the window at some small friends in the street. Then at last his older namesake had to break up the lunch party in order to go to the station.

"I'll come with you," said Rafael, and asked Marisa to save some brandy for him on his return. But, having secured those few minutes of privacy, walking with Borja, he found that neither of them could find much to say. There was the sunshine, the familiar sights also of the city centre they had both known all their lives, but also, for both of them, a sense of something new, beginning now. When they reached the station, Rafael waited till Borja's train came in. And at the last minute they both found it the most natural thing in the world to kiss each other on the lips by way of goodbye.

Borja flopped into his seat. The Caudillo, Franco, was barely dead two years and here was he, kissing a man on, of all places, Salamanca station, scene of so many departures throughout his life, in full view of crowds of people: some, for all he knew, the neighbours of his childhood. You could get arrested for such a thing. Salamanca station! So many departures. So many beginnings.

There was no flight back to Seville for Borja; Rafael's magic wand had not managed to extend that far. Borja was obliged to take the overnight train and present himself for work in the clothes he had been wearing for the past twenty-four hours. This was a new circumstance for him and one which he would normally have found unsettling. Yet strangely he felt bright, almost elated, starting work that Monday morning. He performed his tasks with more than usual cheeriness and energy and dodged home at lunchtime for a shower and a change of clothes. There he found an electricity bill, plus a note which had been pushed under his door. He read the note while he was taking off his shirt. It was written in Spanish and he was a little surprised to discover that it was from Karsten: he wanted to know if Borja could meet him later for a drink. Karsten's note named the Gipsy Bar, the Gitanilla, which suggested to Borja that he wanted a private chat for some reason, without the usual Bodegón crowd. Or maybe simply, without James.

Intrigued, Borja took himself off towards the Barrio Santa Cruz at the appointed time. It was over a year since he had been in the Gipsy Bar, though it was only a fifteen-minute walk from where he worked. But really there were no fifteen-minute walks in Seville. That was the essence of the place. You met people on the way, talked to them, changed direction, forgot where you were supposed to be going, forgot what time you'd said.

It was still light when Borja arrived at the Gitanilla. A swarm of young people hovered around the entrance like bright insects; the sound of a guitar thrummed out into the alley. Last time Borja had come here, with James, it had been to hear Karsten play, sitting on his usual windowsill. Now, though it seemed a lifetime later and James no longer a part of it, there was Karsten, sitting on the same windowsill and entertaining another delighted crowd. Maybe the same crowd. Maybe the crowd was always the same, delighted or otherwise.

Borja recognised the music. Foreign though it was to Andalucía, it sat happily enough on Karsten's guitar strings. It was something by Schubert, though Borja could not have said exactly what. Karsten did not look up when Borja entered: people were coming and going all the time. This gave him a chance to observe Karsten without Karsten seeing him. For the first time since he had known him he noticed that Karsten was really quite nice-looking. It had never crossed his mind before. He would have had to be blind not to notice the beauty of Rafael. But Karsten? Was that what freedom meant? For a moment he was afraid that death would take possession of the whole scene and destroy it for him. But that didn't happen. Karsten just stopped playing. The piece had ended.

"Hola Borja," said Karsten when he looked up. He beckoned to him through the crowd. "You don't mind sitting in the window? There's nowhere else."

First the jump-seat, now the windowsill. "So long as I don't have to play."

Karsten ordered a drink for them both.

"I don't know if you wanted to talk about Alexa's concert," said Borja. "But I haven't had time to do much about it. I was away all weekend. One or two other things to deal with."

"Don't worry. It's not about the concert. At least, not directly. Perhaps it's just as well you haven't done too much about it. Now, how to say this? I wanted to talk to you because... (our English friends would find a better way to say this; I just have to do it direct like a German)... I think that you and James may have split up. So that maybe you have more expensive accommodation than you need. Maybe I have too, for reasons I will explain in a minute. Maybe we could be useful to each other in that way. Do you see?"

"I think I see."

"La musica," called voices in the cramped bar. "La musica!"

"Momentito," answered Karsten. He turned back to Borja. "You see, my flat is only temporarily mine. The time is up at the end of next month. I had once thought that Alexa and I..."

"I still did think that," said Borja.

"Well, no, as it happens." Then: "Double-bugger it," he added in English. They had been speaking Spanish up to now.

"I never heard that one before," said Borja although he was accustomed to Karsten's habit of swearing in English. "James never uses it."

"I think I may have made that one up. Anyway, Alexa's moving to Córdoba – at least for several months."

"Good God. Why? And what about the concert? What about her piano?"

"The last question is the easy one. She wants me to move into her flat to keep an eye on it. She daren't rent it out to some stranger and she can't take the piano with her. The thing is, there's plenty of room for two people at her place. And if you needed somewhere just for a few months, somewhere that wouldn't cost a lot... well, there you are."

"Thank you," said Borja. "I'll have to think about it. Have to talk to James." And the thought came to him unbidden – and he certainly did not put it into words – Have to talk to Rafael too.

"I was right, wasn't I? Thinking you'd split up."

"Oh yes. You're right about that."

"Maybe you'll tell me about it some time. If you want to. Now you don't have to move. In fact, please stay. I have to play them another piece. Then you must tell me about your weekend. And if you have time to stay for a second drink I'll tell you about mine."

"La musica!" called the impatient crowd. And with Borja sitting next to him in the window, silently facing the expectant audience, Karsten began to play.

## Fifteen

At first Karsten had been all in favour of Eulogio's suggestion. Alexa was the doubtful one. To Karsten nothing could have seemed more sensible than that Alexa should go to Córdoba and play the guitar to his old teacher, Manuel Lozón. But Alexa reminded him that she was a beginner. It would have been like sending a child prodigy to play to Horovitz, without the twin shields with which childhood protects its prodigies: innocence and a thick skin. Karsten had pointed out that she was being equally negative about the projected piano recital. "You can not wait always for everything to be exactly right before you commit yourself."

Reluctantly she accepted his point. She allowed him to arrange an appointment (or two, Karsten had said mysteriously) in Córdoba on the Saturday Borja had been in Salamanca. Karsten, telling this story to Borja, still in the Gipsy Bar but now at floor level, had just listened to Borja's account of his weekend. "Of course we didn't have the gift of wings," Karsten said. "We had to take the train like ordinary mortals."

Karsten had very much enjoyed Córdoba when he had lived there, studying with Lozón. He always liked returning there and now it was an additional pleasure to show the city off to Alexa. Córdoba was particularly beautiful in May when all the streets competed to have their balconies and housefronts most lavishly decorated with flowers. That morning, as they walked down from the station into the old quarter, they found the city as fantastically garlanded as King Lear. Trailing geraniums and morning glory overflowed their balconies to brighten the outlook of downstairs neighbours' in unselfconscious gestures of sharing. But Alexa was only half able to enjoy the prettiness. Although it was Karsten who carried the guitar across his shoulder, it was she who would have to play it in due course. Nervousness was weighing heavily upon her morning. Nevertheless, she did stand still and stare when the maze of narrow lanes ejected them right in front of the Mezquita, a sprawl of ancient, unembellished stone. Was it the largest medieval building in the world, she wanted to know, or just in the Arab part of it? Karsten thought it was both and promised to show her the splendours of the mosque's cavernous interior later, when they were less preoccupied. "Right in the middle of it," he told her, "is a cathedral. Quite a big one. But it's so dwarfed by its surroundings you hardly know it's there."

They reached a small square. The statue of a colt stood in the centre. Here also was an inn where Cervantes had stayed and later written into the story of Don Quixote while the colt, el potro, gave the square its name. But Karsten turned his back on the statue and indicated a tall and narrow yellow house. "That's where I studied," he announced. "Let's go in."

An old lady in black led them up dark stairs, opened a door into a room ablaze with sun and there a portly, balding man was standing, hand outstretched.

"Señor Lozón," said Karsten, "may I present Alexa from England?"

"By no means," said Lozón, bowing. "But you may present me to Alexa."

Karsten tried to cover his embarrassment, but only added to Alexa's, by passing her his guitar as soon as hands had been shaken. Lozón took this as a sign that Alexa would play immediately. He pointed to formal, uncomfortable-looking chairs, and then sat down himself, quite heavily, in expectant, frowning silence. Alexa had no choice. She must play. Now.

"I will not try to impress you," she said to Lozón. "Let the music explain where I've reached." Lozón gave no sign that he had heard her. There was silence. So Alexa played. She played a prelude by Bach in her own arrangement. It lasted about two minutes. Lozón did not look at her while she played but stared down at the floor. He maintained this position after she had finished, in a silence that endured longer than the piece she had just performed. For Karsten it seemed like an eternity; for Alexa, several times that long.

Then Lozón looked up. "Come back this afternoon," he said. "Then we will talk. Right now you are expected somewhere else, I think." His face relaxed a little, though not quite into a smile. "By the way, though Bach explains your progress very well, you did also manage to impress."

Flushed, Alexa stood up. Then she and Karsten were politely shown the door. The meeting had lasted four and a half minutes.

"But he wants you back this afternoon," said Karsten. "That's the main thing."

They had left the Plaza del Potro and were walking up one of the streets that led off it. The 'somewhere else' of their next appointment was the rather sunless ground floor of a building on the next corner. It housed the workshop of Javier Mendez, guitarero to the most emminent guitaristas. The door was open and they let themselves in. After the brilliance of the street the gloomy interior offered them nothing at first except smells: the heady scents of cedarwood, varnish and glue. Then gradually they made out the shapes of guitars, some finished, some incomplete, hanging from the rafters in profusion, the way the hams did in the bars. Two work-benches came into focus, cluttered with an assortment of spokeshaves, clamps and planes. There was a rustle of shavings underfoot and Señor Mendez himself appeared, a shadowy figure in the gloom, wraithlike and aproned. But as the moments passed he became more human, and once he had fully materialised he invited them both to touch and try the instruments.

Anthony McDonald

"Here is a flamenco guitar I am working on," he said to Alexa. "And there is a classical. Pick them both up."

Alexa obeyed. "The flamenco is lighter."

"Quite so. Notice the taper of the neck. See the narrow fingerboard."

"And the bridge is lower."

"Well noticed. So that the strings lie closer to the mouth to give the typical flamenco sound. See also how much darker the classical one is in colour. That comes from a wood called palo santo. The flamenco is made only from cypress and pine; that gives it a faster, less sustaining, sound. Now come and look here." He led them to the other work-bench and showed them another guitar, still in pieces. "Each guitarero has his own way of building up his instruments. Myself, I begin with the top, the tapa. Here it is in two halves. It is cut from two slices of the same piece of wood, opened out like a book. The grain is in symmetry on both sides, you see. Next I add the embocadura, the decoration round the mouth. Then the bottom, the fondo, and then I shape the neck, attaching it here like so." He went on to describe the bending of the aro, the long strip of wood that forms the sides of the guitar; it was done by hand, he said, over a hot fire. Then he pointed to strips of ebony and rosewood and went through the rest of the process down to the final varnishing and stringing. "But in the end," he said, "no two will be the same. Each one must be adjusted and readjusted to find its true voice, the inner voice, the pulse within the wood. No two voices are the same. A sound that sits well on one instrument might sound rough or throaty on another. We must adjust and keep adjusting and hope to find the instrument's true nature. For the voice of the instrument is also its soul."

"As with pianos," said Alexa. "At least with good ones. No two are ever the same."

"Like snowflakes," suggested Karsten.

"Like snowflakes," echoed Señor Mendez. He smiled. "How apt, how beautiful an analogy." Then he shook his head, almost sadly. "Of

214

course, a snowflake is something I have never seen."

Borja, listening to Karsten's account, thought it rather wonderful that the old Córdoban had never seen a snowflake. But he liked Karsten's comparison too. "Mathematically perfect, yet each one perfectly different."

"Hmm," said Karsten. "Alexa liked the snowflake comparison too. Maybe a bit too much."

"How do you mean?"

"We went for a drink and a sandwich. At least I had a drink and a sandwich. Alexa was in too much of a state to eat anything. But she talked about snowflakes. About how the beauty of a snowflake was bound up with its setting; that there was a place where it belonged."

"In the plains of Andalucía," Alexa had said, "a snowflake has no place. That is why Señor Mendez has never seen one. But other things, I now realise, are out of place here."

"What things?"

"My Bechstein piano, for instance. The music I play on it. Beethoven."

"Don't say that." Karsten was deeply dismayed to hear Alexa talk in this way. He began to worry about where this conversation was leading. Alexa soon showed him.

"I've just found out today that I must make a decision and make it soon. I've discovered that I can no longer pursue both piano and guitar. If I choose the piano then I must go back to England, as Eulogio himself went, years ago. But since I came here something's happened to me. It began when Eulogio made me listen for the sound of guitars in Beethoven. Little by little the music spoke to me more strongly. I heard it everywhere, the voice of the guitar, the voice of Spain. And little by little I fell in love with the guitar. And I realised I'd fallen in love with Spain already. Perhaps that happened when I crossed the Pyrenees the first time in the lorry with Colin and George, though I didn't know it then. I fell in love with Andalucía. I couldn't have imagined, just eight months ago, that anything so strange would happen. But now I don't feel I ever want to return to England. It's not as if I even know if I have a talent for the guitar – I mean the potential to play really well. I certainly don't know if I could ever make a living at it. But suddenly I know I must decide – or the decision must be taken for me – very soon. I can't stay undecided. So very strange. Such a short time ago there was nothing to decide."

Karsten's face had reddened "Dare I ask," he ventured, "if I come into the equation in any way?"

Alexa hesitated a second before answering. "I am so sorry... when your friendship means so much to me, and when you've helped me so much more than you even know, but I'd be lying to you if I tried to pretend 'yes'."

Karsten related this to Borja, almost word for word. Borja was touched by Karsten's willingness to tell him about such an intimately painful moment. He did not know Karsten especially well; they had certainly never talked about things like this.

"I'm sorry," Borja said. "That's really bad luck." To his own ears the phrase sounded horribly, coldly, English. Where had it come from? Too much literature? Too long living with an English boy? England was no longer Borja's promised land; its inhabitants were dissembling and heartless. To dissociate himself from such people and their empty sentiments he patted Karsten's knee, hoping to show that he still had southern sensibilities and could empathise with the pain of a man who had been unlucky in love. But Karsten flinched away, to Borja's mortification. How careful you still had to be, he thought, with people who knew something about you without really knowing you: who knew, or thought they knew, what you were but did not yet know who.

"I suppose I should have expected it," said Karsten. "I can't say she gave me much encouragement. Only we all have dreams."

"And the guitar," said Borja. "Remember what Lorca said: 'The guitar makes dreams weep.' That's what it is for. And that gift you still have. But back to Córdoba. What happened in the afternoon?"

"The rest of the day was surreal. It was a dream; but it was like eavesdropping, if you like, on someone else's dream, a dream in which you had no role or share. We went back to my old teacher. He had a friend with him, a flamenco singer. Lozón praised Alexa to the skies to the singer: she had the greatest potential, he said, of any student he had ever met. He did not ask her to play again. He was in a mood to play himself, he said. They both felt the duende at that moment. So they sang and played for us, cante and toque, carne y uña. I have to say I seldom heard it better. They performed for three hours."

Borja nodded approvingly. "Three hours. It must have been good."

"Mendez, the guitar-maker, joined us halfway through. After it was over they offered Alexa a deal. Lessons at half-price. Introductions to all the big people. A flat for free at the top of Mendez's house. They didn't need to suggest she bought one of Mendez's guitars. She's already decided. Whatever the cost."

"Does she have that kind of money?"

"She put down a deposit. She intends to sell her piano."

Borja whistled. "What did you say?"

"What could I? It's her business, not mine."

"But the piano surely belongs to her parents."

"Apparently not. It was a gift."

"With no unspoken quid pro quo? They're surely not going to like it."

"I don't know Alexa's parents," said Karsten. "I know that mine would go ballistic."

"Mine too, I think," said Borja.

"She came back to Seville with me that night," said Karsten, "but only to pack. She left for Córdoba again yesterday evening. She says, for good."

"Strange creatures, women," said Borja. "Though they're more your province than mine. Maybe I don't have the right to an opinion on the subject."

"I don't see why not," said Karsten. "I have opinions about men. I think they're pretty strange creatures too."

Borja did not want to be drawn on that just then and changed the subject, although not very much. "I'd better phone James tomorrow and arrange about the flat."

"That's tomorrow," said Karsten. "What do you think about the rest of this evening, though? Maybe we should unleash the old sow for a bit."

"Is that a German way to say: 'let's do the bars and get drunk'?"

"You could show me some bars I don't know, and I could show you how to drink beer like a German."

The last idea would have appalled Borja even just a few days ago. But at this moment it appealed to him. All possibilities seemed interesting, attractive. He was enjoying Karsten's company and, if he was going to share a flat with him, it seemed like a good idea to get to know him better. "OK," he said. "You're on."

*

James was not entirely surprised to receive a phone-call from Borja at work next day but neither was he exactly expecting it. An unprecedented inertia had settled on him. Instead of controlling his own life as he always had done up till now, he found that life was happening to him: he was merely the passive recipient of whatever it might throw at him. It was as if, in making a bid for freedom and control over his own destiny by embarking on his adventure with William, he had ended up losing those very things. He had not run into Borja in the streets of Seville, despite the fact that they both worked in the same small quarter between the cathedral and the river. On the other hand, he had not deliberately avoided him – although he had got into the habit of making straight for the station directly work finished. He simply had not met him, a fact that he accepted as fatalistically as the eventual phone-call. He thought back to the beginning of his time with Borja: how he had taken matters into his own hands then, and wrestled destiny into doing his bidding. How could he have changed so much?

"Borja wants to give up the flat," he told William that evening. "I suppose it's inevitable."

"I suppose it is," said William without emphasis. "You're welcome to stay here of course. At least, for as long as I'm here."

"Thank you for that, anyway." James touched his hair, then gave him a kiss. He was no longer in love with William. Nor was William with him. But they still got on together. Their domestic life worked well, for one thing. When William had said he was a good cook it had not been an idle boast. He had taken it on himself to do the shopping and cooking on all the days when James had to travel to Seville. When James had lived with Borja they had shared the cooking, a task in which both were reasonably competent (a necessity for men unlikely to marry) but which neither particularly enjoyed. But William, to James' pleasurable surprise, positively liked being creative in the kitchen and could knock up imaginative dishes from what seemed to James the most unpromising combinations of raw materials. Another thing on the plus side of their relationship was that they still had wonderful sex together; the physical part of their being together had lost none of its intensity.

And yet James felt as though they were simply drifting along together on the same tide; neither of them actually choosing to be together, neither of them determined to make a new start. And in the odd moments when he couldn't avoid thinking about it, James found himself admitting that they lived together only because neither of them had anywhere else to go.

The day after Borja's phone-call James finally spoke to Mark, apologised for his behaviour over the past ten days and invited him out for a drink when they finished work. The streets were beginning to be oven-like now; summer was starting in earnest. But Seville would get hotter yet. It was as if an excess of coal had been heaped on a fire.

You knew what was going to happen and could only wait helplessly for the inexorable increase in temperature. Not for nothing was the nearby town of Écija known as the frying-pan of Europe. James and Mark walked slowly, clinging to the shady side of the street. It was a relief to plunge into the cool interior of the Bodegón.

"I did know about William," said Mark, when James had given him an idea of his present situation. "But I guessed I wasn't supposed to."

"You guessed right. Though there's no point keeping it a secret now. Who else knows?"

"Pippa, of course. Alexa and Karsten – I'm afraid they saw the two of you together in the cathedral during Semana Santa – and I'm sorry but Jeannette knows too."

"In which case we shan't need to put announcements in the press," said James.

Pippa came through the door at that moment, looking for Mark. She stopped when she saw that he was with James.

"Join us," James said. "It's OK now. It's all been said."

But Pippa guessed that very little had been said. Men told you so little about what was really going on inside them. She would have liked to have known if James would go back to Borja, given the opportunity. Did he still love him? Or did he now love William instead? How could men be so changeable; so dim when it came to knowing what they wanted? Perhaps Sophie had been right: men were totally, heedlessly promiscuous by nature; the failure of gay relationships spotlighted this most starkly; it was only the woman in a straight partnership that could keep things on track. But Pippa was learning not to blurt out such unpalatable thoughts in mixed company. Instead she told James about the plan for Alexa to give a concert. It was almost the only thing she could think of that counted as news.

It was a surprise to James. He had heard from Borja that Alexa had moved to Córdoba to take up the guitar and was selling the Bechstein. This in turn astonished Mark and Pippa. As they talked over the implications, James' gaze and his attention strayed out through the open door and across the street. There stood the building where Alexa had lived but which would house Borja in a couple of weeks' time. He was staring at his ex-lover's new front door, one which he would have to pass a dozen times a day. He tried to imagine their first encounter. Tried but could not. His mind refused to cope with what he might say or how he might feel. Inertia of spirit had grounded his capacity to imagine as well as to act. Was that what was meant by despair?

For a couple of weeks nothing new seemed to happen. James got up, took the train to Seville, taught all day and took the train back to Jerez in the evening, sometimes stopping off, now, for a chat with Mark and Pippa on his way to the station. He hadn't managed to make his one day's work in Jerez expand to more. On the contrary, he had the impression that Paco was becoming tired of the existing arrangement and would cancel it at an appropriate opportunity. After all, it was costing O'Donnell's quite a lot of money to hire James for what had turned out to be very sporadic bouts of work. James was still not sure why Paco had brought him to Jerez in the first place. Even before that first visit Borja had believed that Paco fancied James. Yet in nearly a year Paco had shown no sign that this was so. Paco was friendly towards him and was also gay but that did not amount to the same thing.

As for the little group of beginners James had had to teach the day he had moved in with William, there had been no further sign of them. Once or twice Paco had threatened James with a repeat session with them and he had arrived on standby, armed with books and pictures. ('Is it still morning in the second picture? No. So what does Mary say?') But they had not showed up. "Sorry, so sorry," Paco had said. "No problem, no problem," James had replied. He filled the time quite pleasantly in William's office with William and a half-bottle of fino. William now had his own fridge. Then, one day when James was least expecting it, the three beginners were on hand, with pencils and paper, and expecting a lesson. This was perhaps just as well: William was out on some errand and James had been debating with himself whether his standing at O'Donnell's was high enough for him to make use of William's office and fridge in his absence. At least he was armed and ready for a class.

But the lesson had only been in progress for ten minutes when Paco knocked and entered. "So sorry to disturb you, but I think you can help. Telephone call. The Obishpope of Saffon Wallon to speak to you."

"The who, Paco?"

"William's father."

"My God."

"It's international call."

"Yes, of course. I'm coming." James hurried along the corridor in a state of agitation. His own parents knew little enough of Borja, let alone anything about William. But William's father had clearly heard of him. He really was a bishop, it now seemed. And he wanted to speak to James. What on earth about? Was he going to give James an earful for seducing a bishop's son? With a sermon on divine retribution to follow? Entering Paco's office he braced himself and picked up the phone.

"James, we meet at last," said a friendly voice, "albeit only on the phone. I hear so much about you from my son. I think it excellent that he has a friend like you. He has needed for so long a stabilising element in his life."

James could hardly believe what he was hearing. "So you really are a bishop," he heard himself say.

"Yes, for my sins," said the other, sounding a little put out. "Shouldn't I be?"

James wanted to ask: but what about William's running away to sea; what about Pieter? But managed instead to say: "William's not in the office today. How can I help you?"

"It's his birthday in a few days, as I'm sure you know. The thing is – and this is why I'm so glad to be able to talk to you – I see him so little. I have no idea what to get him that he might appreciate. It was so easy when he was young, of course: model cars, model trains, Lego, that kind of thing. But now, when they're grown up... of course you know all this; you must have parents of your own..."

"I think," said James, "if my advice is of any use at all, and I don't claim too much for it, a shirt might be a welcome gift. A bright blue, perhaps. Collar size fifteen and a half."

"Well, thank you," said the bishop, sounding a little surprised. "You've been most helpful. I hope we'll meet face to face one day. And I do thank you for being such an asset to my son."

How little parents knew their children, James thought as he put the phone down, and the better they tried to be as parents the less they seemed to know them. But he was delighted with the blue shirt idea; it was the first bright idea he had had for ages. William looked great in blue; it did magic things for his eyes. And if William didn't like the shirt he could always pass it over to James. Fifteen and a half would be a perfect fit for him too. He arrived back in his makeshift classroom with a smile on his face.

William had actually plucked up the courage to ask Paco to dine with them on his birthday and when the day came they borrowed the necessary third chair, knife and fork from the landlady downstairs. Perhaps it had been a sensible idea to invite Paco this particular night. Making William's birthday an intimate evening à deux with James might have looked like setting a seal on a domestic arrangement that neither of them now wanted to become too much of an institution.

Paco, for once in open-neck shirt and jeans, looked younger than James had always thought him. He might be less than forty, perhaps no more than thirty-six or thirty-seven. But as he was no longer slim, and dark-complexioned, he was at a disadvantage when it came to looking younger than his years. Although even thirty-six still seemed nearly middle-aged in James' eyes, he was growing conscious that the time when he could allow himself such a viewpoint was fast running out. He would be twenty-five later in the year. William was twenty-four tonight.

Paco had arrived on time and taken in his surroundings with a practised glance. If he hadn't already deduced that James was living with William the evidence was now all about him: James' denim jacket next to William's on the two nails in the wall (there was no wardrobe), the practised way in which James found glasses and bottles from the fridge, a dozen other tiny, telling details. Nevertheless, he made a point, almost at once, of saying: "What a pity Borja could not join us tonight. I did look forward to see him."

"Have some fino," William said. "You have to guess the brand. It's not O'Donnell's."

Paco tasted. "You're teasing me," he said. "It isn't fino de Jerez at all. It's manzanilla. And, I think, La Gitaña, no?"

William nodded, eyebrows raised, impressed.

"I saw Borja a few weeks ago," Paco continued, undeflected. "Running to the station here in Jerez at eight o'clock on a Sunday morning." He looked at James. "In the company of an extremely handsome young man, also."

"Yes, that was Rafael," said James airily. "He's an airline steward. They were on their way to meet us for the weekend. N'est-ce pas?" The switch to French was a coded message that begged William's collusion. Which came in the shape of a nod.

"An airline steward," said Paco. "Borja should be careful, James, you know. And so should you."

Happily for James the conversation was sidetracked at that point by the imminence of dinner. William had cooked baby squid in oil with hot pepper and garlic, and this was followed by lamb cutlets cooked with lemon, anchovies and thyme. Paco was highly impressed by William's cooking and James cheered himself with the thought that, in the mess that was his personal situation, not everything had turned out badly.

It was a few days after this that Paco's warning came back to haunt James. He met William in the café across the square to have an aperitif or two. Or three. No-one was counting. Dinner, of which James had his usual high expectations, had been left to simmer softly at home. They talked about their working days as they usually did. But

James saw something different in William this evening. His usually clear blue eyes had a clouded look and there was an unfamiliar tightness at the corners of his mouth.

James had had the feeling since Borja's phone-call of being becalmed, of getting through the days but making no progress with his life, of getting no nearer to resolving anything. But now he thought he could read in William's face the approaching end of this present phase. He half-welcomed, half-dreaded it, and sat out the evening in that state. Dinner was well over and it was quite late when James finally managed to ask the question. He put down his can of beer. "What's wrong, Orange?"

The song of canaries sounded loudly, too loud almost, beyond the open window. Then William answered. "I suppose I have to tell you. But you won't like me for it."

Expecting to hear it was no protection. James' blood ran cold. He had known things would not go on as they were; this limbo could not last for ever. But he did not actually want to hear William say that things were coming to an end, now that the moment had arrived. Nor had he wanted it to be William who chose the timing. "Go on," he said.

"It's just that I won't be living here much longer."

"Oh?" said James flatly. "Why?"

"I mean you could stay on if you wanted, I'm sure." William took a small gulp of beer. "The rent's not that much, after all."

"Screw the rent. I mean: why?"

"I've been offered a new job. Or rather, an additional job. Paco wants me to look after his house for him."

"He what?"

"Just what I said. He wants me to look after his house. Do the cooking and so on."

"And that's not compatible with living here?"

"Obviously not. He needs someone to live in."

"You amaze me."

"What's wrong? Everyone takes up the offer of a new job for more money. It's normal."

"So how much money, then? It must be quite a packet."

"Don't sound so bitter. It's not that much money actually. But it's a cushy billet. No bills, no rent to pay, everything provided, use of the car, not so many hours at O'Donnell's but the same money there."

James could hardly take this in. "You fucking little tart. Is that how you see yourself? A rich man's little houseboy? A catamite for Paco? What do you think you're doing?"

"Look," said William sharply, "I intend to take the opportunities life presents me with when it presents them. It's my life, not yours, so I don't need your sermons. Clear?"

"You live with me," James blurted out and immediately wished he hadn't.

"I do not. You live with me, but as a guest, it so happens, since Borja chucked you out. You can't do the wronged spouse bit on me." He paused and added more gently: "We don't have those claims on each other."

"I suppose we don't," said James. "Silly of me to go remembering a time when we thought we did."

"Did we really think that?" said William. "I mean, really think it?"

"Yes we did," said James emphatically. It seemed desperately important at that moment to remind William it had been so.

"Well, maybe we did. For a few days in Granada, perhaps we did."

"Certainly we did," said James. "No perhaps. And in the weeks and months that led up to it. You cried real tears when you thought about the two of us living together in the Alhambra."

"You shed plenty of tears over me at around the same time," said William, "but they soon stopped when we got to the police cell with Borja on his way the next morning."

As this was true, James said nothing. William got to his feet and made a thoughtful circuit of the room, beer-can in hand. "You are right of course," he said after a moment or two. "I did think I loved you. How quickly, strangely, we forget these things. Unbelievable that one has to be reminded. In my case, I fell for you very early on. That first day in Jerez I surprised myself. I'd never met a man I wanted so much before. I didn't even think I was gay, really. Perhaps I still don't. Even with Pieter it was nothing so strong as that. But then that day on the beach when you and I touched each other for the first time, that day I knew it was really on. I didn't sleep at all that night. I saw how clearly it was beginning, how it would develop. It was all so clear. And yet I couldn't guess, couldn't begin to guess, how it would end." William took another sip of beer. "Only I wasn't in love with you, was I? Any more than you were in love with me."

"What do you mean?" James' voice was a whisper.

"Come here." William put down his beer and pulled James to his feet and led him to the other end of the room. They sat down side by side on the bed. William reached out to take the little mirror from the shelf, then adjusted its position in his hand. With his other hand he pulled James' head towards him until they were cheek to cheek. And cheek to cheek their reflections appeared in the mirror. Indeed they overfilled it. The effect was startling, the more so because of the pain and trouble on their faces, or rather face. There came to James' mind the image of a two-yolked egg overflowing the receptacle into which it has been cracked.

William spoke. "That's the truth, isn't it?" he said gently. "For both of us." James nodded. William kissed him. "Maybe not tonight, but sometime soon will be the last time. We both know that." He kissed James again. "Now come to bed."

## Sixteen

"Flip a coin," said Karsten. "I really don't mind."

"Heads I get the bedroom, then," said Borja, but tails it was and he took possession instead of the spacious put-u-up in the room where Alexa's piano was. Still, it was a nice big room.

On the whole Borja liked the new flat. He was especially pleased when Karsten showed him the roof garden with its views across the city; he hadn't realised it existed. On the other hand he had found parting with his home of the past three years unexpectedly painful. Every stick of furniture, every scratch on the paintwork was its own story and a small part of his. He did not in fact have much to move, though it was more than would go into a suitcase. Angel, his colleague at work, had lent him his car for the occasion. "You could have come to stay with us for a bit, you know," Angel had said, which was kind of him. But he and his wife had a baby and no second bedroom and Borja knew that the invitation could not possibly have been taken up.

Karsten helped with the move and, realising that this was a difficult day for Borja, did so with more than his usual briskness. "I shall be Teutonic today," he had announced; though, seeing Borja's look of apprehension, added, "but only for today. You will find me a more or less Hispanic flatmate."

"I'm not too sorry to have moved," Borja admitted later, when the actual, wrenching, process was complete. "There was some bad feeling from the neighbours where I was before."

"What sort of bad feeling?" asked Karsten.

"Do you remember all that fuss and mystery last year about the stolen windows? It turned out it was all a practical joke played by people who we thought liked us. And just because we were maricón."

"How did you find out?"

"I overheard two people talking about it in a café. They weren't exactly being malicious. They just seemed to think that because we were different it was a legitimate prank."

"Amazing how cruel nice people can be," said Karsten. "Though you only have to study a little history. Did James know about it?"

"No, I never told him. He had such confidence in the neighbourliness of the Sevillanos. Being English he couldn't read between the lines like I could. He'd have been too upset for words if he'd discovered."

Karsten clocked the discrepancy between Borja's sentiments and his use of tenses but did not refer to it. "I did wonder why it had all gone quiet, I must admit," was all he said.

If Borja had any anxieties about the practicalities of sharing a flat with Karsten – the 'that's-my-toothpaste-ness' of flatshare – he need not have done. Karsten's natural orderliness outdid Borja's own. His clothes were always folded and put away, plates in the kitchen stacked in order of size, windows opened and shut as sun and ventilation demanded. So much so that Borja feared that, after nearly four years of being the tidy one of a pair, his role was now going to be reversed.

They didn't coincide too often at the flat – which suited them both. Sometimes they ate together, sometimes not. If they sat down to talk in the evening it was often of serious matters, as if, conscious that their period together would be a short one, they should really try to put the world to rights in the time they had. They talked about life, about love (more gingerly), sex (more gingerly still), about death, about religion. Especially the last. Karsten tried to show Borja that they had both travelled the same path, from childhood faith, through youthful scepticism, to mature agnosticism. Borja was inclined to agree, though he thought that he had somehow missed the middle stage. Borja had not often talked of religion with James since their early days together. He found conversation with Karsten refreshing, yet there remained a distance between them that Borja could not quite explain to himself. Maybe it was the simple fact that he was gay, Karsten straight. At any rate he was content to leave the distance be; something told him it would not be a good idea to try to shorten it.

Karsten, for his part, could not help noticing how often the name of Rafael cropped up in Borja's conversation, even more than James'. He knew, of course that Rafael was the friend Borja had visited in Salamanca and had heard a little about his part in the flight to Granada. Now he began to be curious about him.

Since Alexa's departure, the subject of her possible piano recital had been quietly dropped. Still, Borja had not forgotten it entirely; after all, he had offered to help organise it. Perhaps that was why he found the presence of Alexa's piano so oppressive. For him it was the one big drawback to the flat. Although Karsten occasionally played Mozart on it quite charmingly, it was for most of the time a silent sentinel in the room where Borja slept. It seemed to be mutely reproaching Alexa for her neglect, and at night its silhouette bulked uncomfortably large in the room while its profile disconcertingly resembled a bull with lowered head. One night Borja dreamed it really was a bull; its back was stuck with banderillas and it bled. Borja saw its eye come close to his. He woke with a cry and in a lather of sweat. The dream had vanished but the brooding presence had not and for some time he didn't trust himself to go back to sleep, just like a frightened child, in case the furniture should transform itself again.

The very next day, at work, Borja received a phone-call that threw him into a panic. It was from Diego Imendia. He had almost forgotten that in his first flush of enthusiasm for the recital project he had left a message on his chief's answering machine about it. Now came the reply. Yes, the tourist board would be delighted to have a concert in the Alcázar. How advanced were Borja's plans and could he commit them to paper in some detail together with costings?

Borja managed to stall Diego Imendia with a promise of something in writing within the next few days. "But what do we do?" he said to Karsten later. "If Alexa's lost all interest in the piano and nobody seems to have even approached whatshisname – her teacher."

Karsten felt he should accept some responsibility for the situation. "Can it wait till after the weekend?" he said. "Alexa's asked me to visit her in Córdoba. I'll talk to her: get a definite answer one way or the other. Then I could approach Eulogio. Maybe if Alexa won't play he'd consider coming out of retirement to give a solo recital of his own. Especially in the Alcázar."

Borja had been going to mention the weekend himself. He had had another phone-call that day, from Rafael. He had arranged to be working a flight that landed at Seville on Friday afternoon and another one that took off from Seville on Sunday evening, taking a gamble that Borja could spend some time with him and put him up over the weekend. It was easier for Borja to broach the second matter with Karsten now that he knew he was going to be out of the flat during Rafael's stay.

"He can have my bed then," Karsten said, adding: "assuming he wants it," as an afterthought. "Pity I won't meet him. He sounds OK."

"You may still meet him. Unless you're leaving very early on Friday."

No, Karsten would not be leaving especially early.

In the event Rafael arrived while Borja was still at work and it was Karsten who let him into the flat. Rafael liked the flat but was surprised by the bulky presence of the Bechstein. Yes, Borja had said something to him about it – and about its owner having left for Córdoba – but he somehow hadn't realised it would be so... well, so big. How long did Karsten think Borja intended to stay there, he asked cautiously?

It depended, Karsten answered with equal care. He offered to make

Rafael a cup of coffee.

A coffee would be nice. Was there any sign of a reconciliation with James in the near future, then?

Not that Karsten had noticed. Though Borja had not confided in him very much on that subject. Rafael had met William once, hadn't he? What was he like?

"Like James to look at – though you probably know that. Quite good-looking, though not so handsome as to make you feel uncomfortable."

It would take quite exceptional looks to make Rafael feel uncomfortable, Karsten thought. He was impressed in spite of himself. Did Rafael take sugar?

"And he has a stock of charm too," said Rafael. "He's – how should I put it – puppyish. One sugar – thank you."

"Borja's quite curious about William, you know. I suppose people always want to know about the people they consider their rivals. You must have got to know more about him, travelling all that way back from Granada together."

Rafael laughed. "I'm sure he's curious. No doubt he'd like to know what we found to talk about on the train. James too, probably. But then I'd dearly like to know how Borja and James got on on the plane. Coffee's great, thanks."

Karsten realised he had been gently rebuked for being nosey; he headed the conversation towards more general topics. Then it was time for him to leave.

Borja arrived a little later. He had been in two minds as to whether to make Rafael's visit a very private one or to let him meet his other friends, in particular those like Mark and Pippa who were also friends of James. He was still undecided about this when he let himself into the flat and Rafael, hearing him come in, or perhaps having seen him from the window, came bounding downstairs to meet him. It was a novelty to be welcomed home by Rafael but they restricted their greeting to a warm handshake and shoulder-claps.

"Can we go for a beer somewhere?" Rafael suggested. "I've been a prisoner here for nearly twenty minutes since your flatmate left. I'm parched." Karsten's coffee clearly didn't rate as a thirst-quencher. "What about the place opposite? It looks OK from the window."

The place opposite was the Bodegón.

"Well..." said Borja doubtfully.

"If you're worried about James being there, don't be. He left about ten minutes ago, heading for the station I suppose. I saw him from the window. Don't worry: he didn't see me. I'm surprised you didn't pass him."

"I think he cuts down a backstreet. He must do, because I never see him."

Rafael grinned.

"I know it's a bit ridiculous, the two of us walking down parallel streets at the same time each evening. OK, the Bodegón it is. So long as you don't mind running into a crowd of English people."

"No problem. I actually quite like English people these days – though I realise you may have changed your mind about them."

So Borja and Rafael made their entrance into the Bodegón together, and found almost the entire staff of James' workplace celebrating the arrival of Friday evening. Borja headed towards Mark and Pippa. Although Mark was a close friend of James, Borja found himself more at ease with him than the others. Perhaps it had to do with his being half-Spanish. And, now that he was actually doing so, he found that showing off Rafael in public was rather fun. "Meet Rafael, a friend of mine from Salamanca." It was quite a heady sensation.

"You've been to Seville before, I guess?" Mark asked Rafael once he had a glass in his hand.

"Of course," said Rafael.

"That's just as well. I was wondering how Borja was going to show you the whole city in a weekend."

Rafael smiled. "You thought it might be my last visit as well as my first?"

"Sorry," said Mark good-humouredly. When he made a gaffe he never tried to bluster his way out but accepted the fact with grace. It was one of his charms.

Rafael turned his attention to Pippa, discovered who she was and flattered her by praising her Spanish. "But will you be married here or in England?" he asked.

"Here," said Mark. "Of course."

"England," said Pippa, simultaneously. They stared at each other.

"Well," said Rafael awkwardly, "it'll be a great day wherever it is," and then changed not only the subject but the language it was expressed in as if he hoped that by speaking English they might avoid the conversation becoming a minefield.

Hearing Rafael speak English for the first time Borja was genuinely impressed. "I didn't know you could do that," he said. "All I've ever heard you say is: 'fasten your seat belts'."

"Because I've never thought it necessary to speak to a fellow-Castillian in English. But perhaps in your case I was wrong." A mischievous look came into his eyes. "Maybe it's the only language you can be – how to say? – courted – in."

Now it was Borja's turn to look embarrassed and Mark's turn to change the subject. He asked Borja if there was any news on Alexa's concert and Borja explained that Karsten had gone to Córdoba to discover exactly that.

"Funny people," said Rafael. "A concert in October and they plan it in June."

After one drink Borja and Rafael made their excuses. Quite normal in Spain; there were other people to see, other bars to visit. Mark said that he and Pippa would be eating in the Casa Ruiz later, adding that they were welcome to join them there. Maybe, they answered, maybe.

"Well," said Pippa to Mark once they had gone. "What do you make of that?"

"What do you want me to make of it? They're friends, that's all we know. We don't know if Rafael's gay."

"He's an air steward."

"You're outrageous. That proves nothing. He may be married with children."

"He used the word 'courting'. I know it was partly a joke but even so..."

"Well, whatever. But just one thing: if Borja wants to tell James his friend was here that's up to him, not us. It's easy to put two and two together, make four or five or six, but after the James and William business... quite honestly it's something I'd prefer not to think about."

"For a poet, for a creative person, you have a great talent for closing your mind to things."

"What's that supposed to mean?" Mark demanded.

"Nothing." Once again Pippa found herself wondering why even the briefest mention of James and William led inevitably to tension between them. She asked him, as a matter of habit, not expecting a reply, what he was writing at the moment.

"Something good, I think. In a week or two I might just be able to let you look at it."

He always said this. Pippa was used to it. But this evening it gave her a particular feeling of dissatisfaction. She decided to keep the discussion about where they would get married for another time.

\*

The Casa Ruiz was an old-fashioned restaurant across the river in Triana near the Ceramica Santa Ana. You stood by the bar for your aperitif and tapas and then, if you asked to eat, the counter would be raised like a drawbridge and you went through the servery into the kitchen where gas-jets blazed and frying-pans hissed like dragons. From there you passed under an arch into the comedor where all was peace, quiet and white table-linen. You ordered meat, fish or both. No vegetables. Vegetables were for wimps.

When they arrived, towards ten o'clock, Pippa and Mark had the place to themselves. Spanish people dine late but once they start arriving the place fills to capacity in a matter of minutes. Much later everyone leaves almost as quickly and then the restaurant closes. After years of living in Seville, Mark's antennae for the exact arrival time in various restaurants were finely tuned.

As they anticipated, it was a matter of moments before the place began to fill. They did not really expect Borja and his friend to join them and were a little surprised when one boisterous party of about a dozen turned out to have Borja and Rafael at its centre. As tables were pulled together to accommodate them all, Borja waved across and motioned to Pippa and Mark to leave their table for two and join them. Which they did.

Mark was in his element at this kind of Spanish gathering. Pippa watched him enviously as he told jokes, took off different characters and flirted with those women whose age, in Pippa's eyes, rendered them safe. She herself found such occasions hard work and not just because her Spanish was still not as good as Mark's. She had learned from experience that the energy you invested in these moments never produced a return. No new friendships grew for her out of these meetings, these sparkling evenings. They sparkled for her, yes, but like water as it runs away. It was always so... (she allowed herself to think the word)... so superficial.

Right now, for example, Pippa was surrounded by a Conchita, two Pepes and a Carmen. Conversation had followed a familiar pattern. The two Pepes had expressed interest in her country of origin and background but seemed unable to follow the thread of what she told them about these, more impressed by the originality of their own questions than by her answers. Next, Conchita explored her interest in Seville, inviting her to agree that it was the most beautiful city in the world, its tapas the most tasty in Andalucía and its men likewise. Thirdly, Pippa discussed with Carmen at length the rival merits of the sea and the mountains as holiday destinations and fourthly, the two women hoped that she would soon be married and giving the world more beautiful children – for, if born in Seville, beautiful they were bound to be. And that was that. That was always that. There was never more to it.

The interesting people tended to be the ones who were different – people who could meet outsiders on their own terms because they were outsiders themselves. Mark, of course, was different – being half-American – but, as he was her fiancé, he didn't count. Borja was far from superficial and certainly different. He was not only Castilian but gay. But gay. Then there was the newcomer, Rafael: strikingly handsome, clearly very fond of Borja... but she had hardly met him. He was, sadly, now at the other end of the table so whether he was interesting or not she would have to discover another time.

After the party ended, in the small hours, when their companions had flown away like noisy birds and she and Mark were walking home, Pippa found herself forming a question in her own head, one she had tried not to ask before: Was there no more to Seville than this? Was this all there was, a social ambience in which everyone but she could get caught up but which, like the bullfight, she could only ever observe as an outsider? If Mark had his way and she ended up staying longer in Spain, would life always be like this: a long evening that ends at daybreak, new people who remain always new? She also asked herself for the first time: Was Mark happy walking home alone with her? He always said he was. No doubt James had said the same thing to Borja, and to himself, before he went off with William. Men seemed hardly to know themselves. Was there not a part of Mark that wished tonight that he were part of that chattering, laughing party who had gone on 'somewhere else' wherever that might be?

\*

Of course there is no somewhere else that parties go on to. They all break up in the end and their participants are left alone: alone singly or alone together. And so Borja and Rafael finally found themselves confronting each other in the room where Alexa's piano stood.

"It's still hot," said Rafael.

"There's a roof-garden, did you know that?" said Borja. "Come, I'll show you."

Rafael dived into the kitchen and returned with two glasses and a half-bottle of manzanilla. "I put it in the fridge earlier," he explained. "Now show me the garden."

A moment later they were peering over the low parapet through a lattice of television aerials and wires. They overlooked other balconies but were overlooked themselves by none. Two blocks away the cathedral towered above the housetops, a gigantic confection of stone. Beside it, bathed in the same lemony floodlighting, the Giralda pointed the way to heaven. In the other direction the Torre del Oro with its ring of date-palms stood sentinel beside the river. Beyond it the orange lights of the San Telmo Bridge shimmered in duplicate, thanks to the dark water below.

"It's beautiful," said Rafael.

The sound of brass instruments, exotically tuned, came from the river. "They practise under the bridges for the acoustic," Borja explained. "For Semana Santa, I think." The music drifted, strange and melancholy, on the night air, sending shivers down their spines.

Rafael uncorked the manzanilla and passed a glass to Borja. "It's still hot," he said. Then he unbuttoned his shirt. Borja watched him till he had thrown it down, then he felt himself unbuttoning his own. He was mesmerised by the sensation; it was as if someone else, not he, were doing it. His shirt joined Rafael's. "You're beautiful," Rafael said.

Borja placed the palms of his hands on Rafael's chest. It was broader than his own. "So are you," he said.

Very slowly they undressed, without speaking. Neither could take his eyes off the other. It was as if each thought the other might disappear like someone in a fairy-tale if they stopped gazing at each other. At last Rafael looked down. "And everywhere," he said. Then he dropped down to his knees in front of his new love and took him gently in his mouth.

In the short time before dawn they made love in as many ways as their energies would allow. And those were considerable; both had gone hungry for some time.

The first flash of sunlight caught them unexpectedly asleep. They had happily lain naked under the gaze of the stars and the night-birds but the sight of the risen sun, of whirling swifts, of sky-threading skeins of egrets, made them feel suddenly vulnerable, as if compromised, and they migrated downstairs, only to nestle together again in Borja's bed until nearly noon. Rafael slept soundly, but Borja was less easy. The piano beside them now seemed to have become a judgemental presence. As he drifted in and out of sleep it changed itself from time to time into the bull he had dreamed of before. He saw its eye again: this time it seemed to be all-watchful, all-knowing.

At about twelve o'clock they crossed the road to the Bodegón for toast and coffee. But it was a different Bodegón from yesterday's: changed, in Borja's mind, by the fact of last night. He imagined himself a camera in which a new colour filter had been placed across the lens.

Rafael spluttered on his coffee. "Wrong moment to giggle," he said. "I suddenly thought, I want to stand up and shout to everyone in the place: 'I slept with this wonderful man last night'."

"So do I," admitted Borja.

They passed the afternoon lazily, lying among shady reeds on the river-bank, trying to hold onto every moment, experiencing every sensation, even the giant grasshoppers that whirred past on rickety wings, with a new keenness. Even the furtive meetings between cruising men along the tow-path seemed, absurdly, ennobled by being observed by the two of them in their euphoric state.

"Tell me," Borja asked at one point, out of the blue, "about when you were a bull-fighter. Were you never hurt?"

"Tossed once, and I don't remember the landing, but never punctured, never gored."

"Wasn't that frightening?"

"Strangely, no. When it was actually happening it passed like a dream. Like the men who run with the bulls at Pamplona. They are never frightened when they actually do it. It is a moment of stillness. So it was for me when I worked with the bulls in the ring. Only – I was afraid before. Everyone is." He stopped, picked a grass-stalk and chewed it. "Except perhaps you would not be. You strike me as someone who is afraid of nothing."

Borja laughed. "Either you're joking or, if not, your impression deceives you as much as it flatters me."

Rafael ran a finger down the nape of Borja's neck. "What could possibly frighten you, then, little one?"

"What could not? Fighting bulls, for a start. Fighting anyone at all, come to that. Pain. Dying. I used to be frightened of flying – until I did it – and you're mostly to thank for that."

"Perhaps you won't be frightened of dying either, once you've done it."

"A thousand thanks. But you asked a serious question."

"Sorry. Go on."

"Judgement."

"The four last things? Death, Judgement, Hell and Heaven?"

"No, not those."

"Then what judgement?"

"My own, perhaps? There being no other? Oh I don't know. Ask me next week."

The luxury of that last thought. There would be next week. There would be a future in which to split hairs over the difficult questions of life and death. They were both conscious of that thought; both shared it; both knew they shared it, and the echoes of that joint realisation reverberated in a great chamber of being that, for the first time, they inhabited together.

"Do you know something?" said Rafael. "I used to be scared of flying, before I did it, just as much as bull-fighting. Maybe that's why I took them both up. Come on, let's move. I've got an idea."

They took a pedal-boat out onto the river. "I haven't been in one since I was a child," said Rafael.

"I never have," said Borja.

Steering took some practice. Initially they rammed another boat which was crewed by two children and had to lean out and hold onto it until it had stopped rocking. They apologised in embarrassment – embarrassment that was perversely pleasing, for being shared.

"The longest day of the year," said Rafael, "or thereabouts."

May it be the longest day of ever, Borja thought just then. May I always feel like this. He would not, of course. The bull would return to him in the night to menace him with guilt and doubt. The hard and complex realities of life would conspire to change the way he felt. Today, last night, might some day be repeated but would never come again...

That evening was not one for doing the round of bars where they might meet up with the likes of Angel and his friends, or Mark and Pippa: it was an evening to be savoured just by two. Borja showed Rafael the Casa Morales instead – Rafael was impressed by its Rip Van Winkle atmosphere – and then they ate at a place near the Alameda de Hercules where Borja was sure that no-one he knew would ever come.

By midnight they were back on the roof-terrace again and in each other's arms. Part of a poem came suddenly into Borja's head. It was in English.

Every farthing of the cost...
...Shall be paid, but from this night
Not a whisper, not a thought,
Not a kiss nor look be lost.

He clasped Rafael more tightly to him.

If Saturday had slipped away like quicksilver then Sunday disappeared like smoke. It was time for Rafael to catch the airport bus.

It left from the bottom of the road. They walked down together, their silence almost palpable. At last it was Rafael who spoke. "I don't want to presume on two nights. But I have known you for all my short adult lifetime. I'd like to think we could be something for each other. For the long term, that is. You know, I've never said this before – to anyone. What's happening?... I don't know if you could ever feel the same."

The silence returned. Neither of them could look at the other. Then: "I just don't know," said Borja. "It's all a bit quick. Soon after James. Mierda! Why am I saying this?" (It had all seemed so simple yesterday by the river.) "Why can't I just say yes, when I want to?"

"Think it over, then say yes. Take your time. I understand why you need it. But not too much time. And in the meantime I may be persistent. Like phoning you. Is that OK? Inviting you for a weekend rather soon?"

Borja smiled. "I think I could cope with that. But about the long term, no promises just yet. Do you mind?"

"I think I'll cope too," Rafael said. But Borja suddenly heard another voice in his head, one that had spoken to him at this precise spot eight months ago. Then, and now, it said: "But how could you possibly lose a window?"

They were at the bus stop. Other people milled around them waiting for the coach. Above them a half-opened shutter revealed the impassive face of an old woman, staring at them. From her lonely vantage-point it was her role in life to be the witness to an unending pageant of good-byes. Rafael turned to Borja. "I love you," he said, surprising them both by his emotion. The coach arrived. They kissed unashamedly among the crowd then the coach took Rafael and he was gone.

Borja did not know, as he walked up Calle Santander, if he wanted to sing and caper up the road or hide away and cry.

## Seventeen

"I'm really sorry about that," said William. He was phoning James at work unexpectedly on Monday. "I'd no idea she'd re-let the place so quickly." William was now definitely moving out, and in with Paco, at the end of the week. He had told his landlady so the previous day. It was now apparent that James would become homeless at the same time.

"It doesn't matter," said James. "I wasn't going to stay on in Jerez anyway. It wouldn't make sense." He had already taken his old posters down.

"Have you got somewhere you can stay in Seville? I mean, I'm sure we could..."

"No, thank you. I've got a couple of irons in the fire here." Which was not true, though James hoped it would be soon. He had not meant things to end like this. Of course the break with William had to come but he had wanted it to be at a moment of his choosing or else by their mutual agreement. To be dumped in favour of an older man – albeit a rich one – was an indignity that went beyond his worst imaginings. He didn't tell Mark anything about Paco when he had a drink with him that evening in the Bodegón. But he had to tell people he was splitting up with William if he was going to have a bed at the weekend.

"What a bummer," Mark said. "Where'll you live?"

James took a sip of wine. "That's the problem. I've no idea."

"Look," said Mark, as James had hoped he would. "I'd have to check with Pippa, of course, but I'm sure you could stay with us till you find somewhere. It couldn't be for ever and it would only be a sofa but it'd be better than under a bridge."

James had already considered the bridge option. With the hot nights of summer already upon them it seemed both a romantic and a practical possibility. But only at first. What did you do with your valuables while you slept? What kind of people roamed the river bank by night? What did you do with your bowels in the morning? Were there rats? "Thank you," he said. "If it's OK with Pippa I'd be really grateful."

Pippa arrived just then, in the company of Karsten, and Mark laid James' situation before her at once. She agreed quite readily to James' coming to stay with them though, as he was standing right beside them, it would have been difficult for her not to. It was settled that he would move in on Friday night.

Pippa's arrival with Karsten was coincidental: they had met just outside the door. Karsten was returning from Córdoba with news of Alexa – news he repeated to Borja later in the evening as they sat on the roof-terrace, refugees from the heat of indoors. "She wanted me to apologise to everyone," he said, " for any inconvenience caused by her pulling out of the concert."

"It hardly needs an apology," said Borja. "We haven't exactly been overworking on the project."

"She also said: 'Give my love to Mark'. Not to Pippa, not to you. I found that curious."

"Why? She knows Mark better than she knows me. I've only met her once or twice. Anyway, the concert's definitely off, then, is it?"

"Yes and no. It's off as far as Alexa's concerned. She won't play if she doesn't practise the piano. And that she won't and can't. She hasn't got a piano of any sort where she's living. And she's totally besotted with the guitar. Works at it night and day. Harder than I ever did."

"She started older than you did. I suppose she feels she has to catch up."

"It's more than that. There's something driven about her. I wasn't like that with the guitar. She wasn't with the piano."

"I'd have said she was. Coming all this way."

"She was certainly committed. All right, driven if you like. But not to the extent she is now. Not in the same way."

"And has she talent?"

"Yes, yes, yes. Even as a relative beginner. I can see that now. Lozón saw it the first day. I'm afraid she's ten times better than me."

"You're jealous?"

"Of course I am. But not in any competitive sense. We're not thinking about the same league. I've had my own kind of success, as a guitar teacher and a street musician – and in Seville of all places, despite the handicap of being a foreigner. I'm proud of that and I don't ask for anything more. But she wants something else. She wants to be one of the great ones. You know. Up there with Narciso Ypes and Segovia."

"Wow. Is that really a possibility?"

"I worry about that. I'm afraid for her. It's not just a question of talent."

"You're talking about being a late starter? About being English?"

"Both of those. And other things."

Borja nodded his understanding. "She's a woman."

"Exactly. And in Spain..."

"Quite. Just as gay boys don't often become toreros."

Borja had referred to bullfighters several times in the last few days. Karsten wasn't sure why. "I suppose so," he said. "But what you need to know is this. The concert's going ahead. Alexa and I both spoke to Eulogio on the phone. He's going to do it. He says he finds retirement boring without Alexa to teach. Now there's a torero for you." Karsten tapped his pockets absently. "Shit. I'm out of cigarettes."

"There are some cigars in the kitchen. Rafael left them." It was the first time Rafael had been mentioned in the conversation. Karsten had almost forgotten.

"Oh right. Did you have a good weekend together?"

"Yes, very good." Borja coloured slightly, thus answering Karsten's question more completely than he had intended.

"Well, you'll be able to have the place to yourselves again soon. I'm off to Germany on Saturday week for a fortnight." He let this sink in for a moment. "I haven't seen my parents for ages, that's the first thing. Secondly, I think I know someone there who might buy Alexa's piano."

Karsten explained that pianos like Alexa's were not easy to sell. Most professional concerts were given on Steinway instruments and the people who gave them naturally liked to practise on a Steinway at home. But a few people still preferred the more colourful tone of the Bechstein and were prepared to pay well for a good specimen. Someone whom Karsten's father knew was looking for just such an instrument, he thought. Karsten actually had a tape of the Bechstein being played by Alexa herself in a flattering acoustic. It had been made by a friend of hers on the occasion when Alexa had played the Emperor Concerto with her local youth orchestra. He thought a friend of his at the university would be able to make a new copy, toning down some of the more alarming idiosyncracies of the youth orchestra.

Borja felt quite cheered by the prospect of the piano's removal even if it wasn't imminent. Its presence in his 'bedroom' had become even more irksome since it had witnessed his lovemaking with Rafael. It was the first time in four years he had slept with anyone other than his partner and as the weekend receded he was having mixed feelings about this new development. Even if you stopped believing in God you still could not help weighing your own actions and wondering a little.

*

Jeannette, whom Pippa saw every day at school had taken the unusual step of inviting her to her flat – the one where Pippa had spent her first days in Seville – for coffee. Pippa was getting on better with Jeannette these days. Since Alexa's departure Jeannette had begun to take over the role of Pippa's confidante. Pippa could hardly remember why she had disliked her at first. Not because of her looks, surely. It was always nice to be the prettier one of two. Perhaps it was simply the fact that Jeannette fatally lacked style. Associating with her might have somehow tarnished her own image in other people's eyes or dented her own self-esteem. But none of that mattered now. Pippa had what she wanted and had a ring on her finger to prove it. Admittedly, what she wanted was not yet in quite the right place: Mark was still being vague about the question of when they would go to live in England, but that would be resolved in time.

Pippa arrived at Jeannette's door, dabbing at her neck with a handkerchief. This heat. She rang the bell. She had not noticed anything particularly urgent about Jeannette's invitation to coffee this afternoon but it was clear from her face when she opened the door that she had something she wanted to say and as soon as they were upstairs she said it. She was pregnant.

"Wow. Well, congratulations... if that's appropriate." Jeannette's demeanour suggested that commiserations might have been a better word.

"Thank you," Jeannette said. "It wasn't planned, of course. Felipe's furious. As for his family..."

"What about yours?"

"They're not so near at hand. I haven't told them yet."

"My God. What will you do?"

"I just don't know. Sophie thinks I should have it. That's easy for her."

"Does she also recommend you to marry Felipe, or to go it alone?"

"Marrying Felipe isn't an issue. I don't want to marry Felipe."

"Sorry if I'm not being very clever but I always thought you did."

"I thought I did. Now I see I don't. Simple as that. I've been mad, Pippa. Living in a fool's paradise. Now I've got to pay the price. Whatever price I choose. I can have a baby I don't want, or an abortion I'd have to live with afterwards, or a husband I don't want either. I can even have two out of the three."

"I don't know what to say." This was true. Only the most banal expressions of sympathy came into Pippa's mind; she fought them back. What messes people got themselves into, she thought, and wondered for a second if modern freedoms – so welcomed and trumpeted by the likes of Sophie – were not overrated. And as this thought flashed through her mind, a little tremor of doubt shivered its way through the solid fabric of certainty she had built around her own situation. She squeezed Jeannette's hand. "I'll make the coffee," she said. She turned towards the familiar rickety stove and saw to her surprise that it had been replaced by a new one. "Oh," she said. "That's an improvement."

"Yes." Jeannette half-smiled. "There's a pair of pliers going begging if you want them."

*

Friday night coincided with the end of the month which meant a long evening in the Bodegón for James and his colleagues, waiting for Ignacio to issue the pay-packets towards midnight. Quite by accident then, the evening became a sort of Welcome Home party for James. It gave him mixed feelings. He was back in Seville, that was true, but home had got lost somewhere. He glanced at the door from time to time, wondering if Borja would walk in. He half-hoped he would, half-dreaded it. It wasn't so much that he had left home, he thought, but that home had left him. "Home is where your toothbrush is," he told someone drunkenly, late on in the evening, and produced his from his pocket with a laugh. He did not mean it, of course. It was his own fault entirely that this had happened. If only he hadn't flounced out of Borja's life when he – temporarily – hadn't felt like sleeping with him. If only he had never met William. "If only you'd gone to Jerez that first day instead of me," he said to Mark.

"Jesus, what are you talking about? I've never seen you like this," Mark said. Later he and Pippa had to manhandle James onto the sofa and remove his shoes, leaving him to snore in T-shirt and jeans throughout the night.

Saturday didn't count as a day: James was too hung-over to make much sense of it, let alone do anything with it. But during the days that followed, James found himself tuning in for the first time to the relationship between Pippa and Mark, or rather, tuning into the stage it had now reached. Pippa talked all the time about England, to him, to Mark, to both of them together. Although she had agreed to postpone her return for a year she had a very clear idea about what would happen when they did get there. They would rent a flat in Leicester while Pippa did her last year of university. Mark could teach English to the Asian population while continuing to write his poetry, if that was what he really wanted to do. James listened to all this politely; he actually found it hard to imagine Mark writing poetry in Leicester, let alone teaching immigrant schoolchildren. But Mark didn't seem to hear Pippa. He talked only about making the most of his final year in Seville. There was Alexa's concert for a start. Then there was the summer itself to enjoy. It was July now and the school would soon be closing. Classrooms were already half-empty as students stayed away on the coast at Rota and Chipiona. Sometimes classes didn't even happen at all. "Seville in summer," said Mark, "is a furnace of passion." (Furnace of Passion was the title of one of his poems, although the poem itself had yet to be written.) He reminded James of a child during the last week of school holidays trying to blot from its mind the imminent return to study lest the prospect spoil the radiant, precious, but shrinking, present. Pippa seemed not to realise this.

In fact Pippa was not standing up to the heat too well. It made her both lethargic and irritable. She told James slightly too often how pleased she was that he had come to stay so that he got the message that she really felt quite the opposite. Then, a few days after he moved in, choosing neutral territory, she spoke to James at work, finding a moment when they were alone together in the staff-room. "I know you'll say it's none of my business," she said, "but I can't not ask you: do you think you'll be getting back together with Borja?"

James was taken aback by her directness. "I don't know," he said. "In the long term, I think yes, but it's not something that can be rushed." She wants me out of her flat, he thought. "These things take time."

Oh, but you haven't got time, Pippa wanted to say. There's Rafael now and it may already be too late. "I know," she said, "but you ought at least to try and talk to him soon." She had taken seriously Mark's warning, which he had repeated several times, not to mention Rafael.

"I don't see why there's a rush." James resented Pippa's sudden interest and found himself digging his heels in.

"People change," Pippa said. "Even Borja. He might find someone else."

"He might, I suppose. But I wouldn't expect him to be in too much of a hurry." He permitted himself a moment's vanity. "He's very choosy."

"I'm sure he is. But he'll soon know you're back in Seville if he doesn't already. He'll expect some contact. If it doesn't come it'll give him quite another signal."

Reluctantly James was forced to agree with Pippa on this point. And although he was not enjoying the conversation it was at least forcing him to confront the truth: he did want Borja back. Even thinking the words brought Borja's presence to him; he seemed to feel him physically, small but muscular, wrapped around him; experienced the comforting smell of his hair. "I want you more than anything," he silently told him. "I love you." Seville, the seat of southern warmth and light and the scene of three years' happiness, had gone dark for him and he wandered it like a blind man. His voice was unsteady when he replied to Pippa: "Yes, I see. I will talk to him. But I'll have to choose the moment carefully."

"Good," said Pippa. "And good luck." James saw that she meant it, but another teacher came into the room just then and the conversation had to end.

\*

James did not have the chance to choose his moment to talk to Borja. The moment chose him later the same day. He was taking a long-cut to an evening class through the shady alleys of Santa Cruz and as he passed through the vaulted tunnel of the Judería he ran into Borja on the blind corner in the middle.

"Hi," they greeted each other, both too startled to say anything else or to feel any emotion for the moment.

"I heard you were back," Borja said. "Karsten said you're staying with Mark."

"And Pippa," James instinctively corrected. For all his otherness Borja had the macho Spanish habit of speaking as if the womenfolk did not count. "Look," James went on quickly, "I want to talk."

Borja was caught off guard. "Do you mean now?"

"No better time."

They eased their way out of the claustrophobic tunnel into the little open space beyond it where the crenellated walls of the Alcázar rained down showers of bougainvillea and a fountain whispered in a corner.

"I want to come home, Borja."

Borja looked at James. He was thinner. There seemed something crumpled about his face. His hair was not as clean as usual. Neither, perhaps, were his clothes. And something else was different: the earring had gone.

"What do you think of me, James?" Borja asked.

"I love you."

"That's not what I mean. What sort of man do you think I am?"

James was puzzled. "I don't know what you mean. Talk properly."

"You mean tell you what you want to hear. Of course. But I can't. Do you think I'm an idiot? Some silly child of the sunshine who won't notice if you run away with another Englishman? Who then won't realise when he's kicked you out, or won't ask you why you suddenly turn up and say 'I love you'?"

"No," said James feebly.

"I wasted time loving you. Three years of my life. You burnt them up in smoke."

"It wasn't serious with William. I was serious with you. I loved only you."

"No doubt you said the same to him. When you say 'I love you' to one person you mean it and when you say it to another you don't. But how are those two people to know which of them is being lied to? Or if they both are?"

"No." James shouted this loudly enough to stop Borja in his tracks for a moment. But only for a moment. Borja was growing angry. He continued in Spanish:

"I thought it would be possible with you. To break the mould. To have a sexual relationship with a man that would not be a sin."

A couple passing near them looked up as they turned into the next alley, unsure if they had overheard aright.

"I wasn't born to love a woman," Borja went on. "I wasn't born to be a bullfighter. I didn't want the things the others did."

"Not born to be a bullfighter?" James had never heard Borja talk like this.

"Our love, our making love, was meant to be a sacrament, not a plaything to be exchanged for something else: for a pair of nice blue eyes and a new cock. When you got tired of your little Spanish boy. Maybe you should try Mark next. He's only half-Spanish."

"Try Mark?" James was outraged, bewildered. "You're not letting me speak. I only want you. I only ever have. I made a stupid, stupid mistake. You haven't even let me say sorry. Can't you see, we're only human, you and I?"

Something on Borja's face made James think he had scored a point.

"What happens to me now?" Borja asked. "I've lost everything I believed in. You took and destroyed it all. First my religious faith. For a time I had you. Then you took yourself away too and left me with nothing. I used to believe you loved me. But people like you know nothing of love; you are capable only of sentiment, sentimentality." Borja's face was screwed up into an expression James had never seen on it before. "You took everything and left me with nothing." He shouted this refrain like a furious child.

"Then take me back and I'll spend the rest of my life giving it back. I devote the rest of my life to you."

Borja was moved in spite of himself but he had worked himself into too much of a rage and was under too much pressure from other feelings to give the answer James wanted, now, so desperately. "It's too late," they both heard Borja say. "You can't affect me now. I've put you behind me. And now I've somewhere to go and I'd better move along." He held out his hand stiffly.

Not quite believing how the scene was ending, James took the hand and shook it half-heartedly. "We'll see each other around?"

"No doubt." Borja half-turned to go. "I suppose you'd better know from me." He said this heavily, without either enthusiasm or malice. "I'm seeing someone else." James' mouth dropped open. "You met him once. Rafael."

They stood looking into each other's eyes for what seemed to both of them a very long time, each thinking that they knew the other completely at last, and for the very first time. Then, both equally shocked, they turned apart and continued on their separate ways.

## Eighteen

Borja had been busy during the past ten days. He had telephoned Eulogio himself to discuss his fee, rung round the removal companies for quotes to transport Eulogio's piano the two miles to the Alcázar (he was amazed at the cost: "I don't want to *buy* a piano," he protested) and put all this in writing to Diego Imendia. In reply he had got Imendia's blessing to go ahead and set things in motion with the Ayunamiento, who managed the Alcázar. It was expected that a date would be fixed in late September. He would receive an increase in his salary for taking on this responsibility and was given a budget for publicity, transport and so forth. He was rather excited by all this. He had never had a budget before.

During this time he was acutely conscious of not phoning Rafael and of not hearing from him either. Then he had had his run-in with James in the Judería and, by coincidence, Rafael rang him later that same evening. Borja did not mention James during the phone-call. Rafael was ringing, he said, because he had the next weekend off and a couple of flights that involved Seville. He could arrange it so as to spend Saturday and Sunday in Seville, or else Borja could fly with him to Madrid on Saturday night and spend a couple of days there. Borja chose the second option. Partly because it fitted in with his own schedule, partly because he didn't feel quite ready yet to entertain Rafael in Seville under James' nose, perhaps bumping into him in bars... No, Madrid would be better. And also, there would be no grand piano in Rafael's bedroom.

As it happened, one of Rafael's Seville flights was the one Karsten would be taking to Valencia, to catch a connecting flight to Düsseldorf. Rafael told Borja he would look after Karsten on board – then return to pick Borja up at Seville airport in the evening.

*

"I'll come and talk to you once we get going," Rafael greeted Karsten as he boarded the Caravelle on Saturday morning. "We're not very busy. Sit where you like."

The day was airless and sticky. Even the aircraft's air-conditioning system was struggling, at ground level, to make the cabin bearable. Karsten chose a window-seat over the wing. He had never fallen in love with flying as Borja had but even he found himself enjoying the views as they climbed out over the Guadalquivir basin. But the distance he could see was limited today, the Sierras nowhere to be seen. The heat-haze of the summer had seen to that.

Despite being (as he had coined it) an 'oppo-sexer', Karsten felt obscurely flattered when the steward, taking a break, slid into the empty seat beside him. It was as if good looks could be catching somehow, induced by close proximity, like measles.

How had Rafael enjoyed his weekend in Seville? Karsten asked him by way of small-talk. Rafael gave him an edited account of it. Karsten had already had a similarly edited account from Borja. "I like your roof-garden though," Rafael said. "It made me very jealous. Just the place for weather like this." He paused. "A place for late-evening, sharing confidences." That was as far as he dared go. He was caught between two strong but conflicting desires: to hoard secretly the memories of his nights with Borja like precious private treasures, and impulsively to make them public at the risk of making them cheap and absurd. It was not as if Karsten was a close friend, even. He found relief from these opposing impulses by forcing a change of subject – though the new topic was hardly one he would have chosen otherwise. "Last time we met, you asked me a question I didn't want to answer," he said, almost wildly. "Remember?"

"Really?" Karsten tried to recall.

"About William and the train journey from Granada."

"Oh yes." (Oh yes.)

"I don't want to create a mystery by not answering questions. I don't want there to be things hidden between Borja and myself."

"You're pretty serious about him, then."

"Never more so with anyone. So I'll be honest with you. William and I didn't talk a lot on the train. He was feeling pretty down and needed someone to cheer him up. So we had sex. That's all. The carriage was empty, I need hardly add."

In spite of himself Karsten was shocked, both by the grinding gear-change of the conversation and by Rafael's revelation. Rafael saw this.

"Oh come on," Rafael said. "You can tell Borja or I will. I wasn't in any way his partner at the time; I wasn't supposed to be being faithful to him. As for William, his allegiances, if any, were his own responsibility, hardly mine." Rafael paused a second. "I'd never had an English boy before. He was very nice." The plane bounced for a moment in a rough bit of the air.

"I can not understand you when you speak like that," said Karsten. "If you think Borja will appreciate that story you clearly don't know him well enough. I don't think you should have told me either."

"You asked," Rafael replied reasonably, though privately he was wondering what on earth had made him blurt the thing out to Karsten. "It was only sex, for God's sake, nothing more."

"If you are really serious about Borja you won't be able to do that kind of thing any more. 'Only sex' is not a concept he'd appreciate. He mustn't be hurt again like James hurt him. Do you see that?"

"I'm coming to see that, yes. Getting to know him is changing the way I feel about lots of things – how I feel about myself, for one. He's not only become very important. He's made me feel that perhaps I'm in love for the first time. You know? And that everything before was... Have you ever had that feeling?"

"I'm not sure," said Karsten, slightly uncomfortably. "I don't know really, if anyone can relate their experience to someone else's."

"You may guess – you obviously realise – that we've slept together. But that's only ever a beginning. I don't know even now if he wants me... long-term."

There was silence for a moment. Then Karsten said: "Were you ever a bullfighter, Rafael?"

"Yes." Rafael was surprised at the question.

"I can't tell you yet if he'll have you for keeps. Only that he thinks about you a lot and thinks a lot of you. Things he says. Looks on his face. I wish you luck, I suppose, though I should warn you that James is back in Seville: he's split with William. But come and stay as often as you like." He paused, then added: "Yes, I did realise my bed had not been slept in."

Rafael had to return to his duties then. They were beginning their descent into Valencia. The heat haze below them developed into cloud: at first filmy, then milky and at last, as they neared the coast, candy-floss thick and growing rapidly into pinnacled towers. It was a violent ride down through them – as if a toy were being bumped downstairs by an unheeding child. It grew darker by the second and there was an almost tangible feeling of relief among the passengers when they broke out of the turbulence and saw the ground beneath. A twist of funnelled wet spun rearward from the wing-tip. It looked sharp and silvery like the bit of a high-speed drill. Rain, thought Karsten, and wondered what the weather would be like in Düsseldorf. Going home was always a fraught affair; your parents vaguely dissatisfied as ever with your progress in the rat-race; your friends perversely uncomprehending of your success in a far-off place, shaking their heads in wonder that you had been away so long.

The plane banked sharply. Karsten peered out. The runway they were making for was clearly visible ahead, offset. It looked very close, foreshortened, like a welcome mat at an odd angle. The wing-tip pointed to television masts on the tops of tower-blocks.

Suddenly black tentacles of cloud uncoiled across the view then enfolded the plane in a tight embrace. The plane leaped and plunged – how could water vapour do this? – reared and floundered – became a torero tossed by a bull.

People screamed. Karsten hoped he had not been one of them but could not be quite sure. The captain's voice came over the speakers: "Please keep your seat-belts fastened. Cabin crew: your seats for landing." The words were reassuring but Karsten was conscious of an edge to the captain's voice.

The battering went on. Strangers held on to each other. An overhead locker spilt its contents with a shock of noise. Then there was Rafael, moving up the aisle, clutching at the seatbacks. He seemed to be wading, as if in a river torrent. "Some people at the back need cheering up," he said to Karsten.

"Sit down for Christ's sake," called Karsten.

"Back in a moment." He passed on.

A glimpse of ground showed a golf course zooming frighteningly close below. Then the plane rode up again as if released by a giant hand. The captain's voice: "Thirty seconds to landing. We have control." Then suddenly: "Brace, brace!"

The hairs were standing up on Karsten's neck. You had to lean forward... The giant hand now smacked them down; somewhere a voice cried 'help' in English... You overlapped your fingers on top of your head. You mustn't interlock them. You might never play the guitar again...

"Brace!" Now it was Rafael's voice, loud and clear from the back of the plane. Then they hit. An enveloping roar, sudden darkness, and everything shifting; heavy things falling, shouts and yells. Karsten tried to shut his eyes. He could not. Brilliant light trailed outside he window. Flames? Sparks? His seat thrust him forward; the seat in front collapsed.

Almost to his disappointment, Karsten's life did not flash before his eyes like a cinematic obituary. Neither did he feel a sense of resignation: this is it. Instead he felt only the absurdity of the moment, the ill-luck that brought him here to face extinction in a careering, disintegrating, metal cylinder in a cacophony of bursting rivets and the crying of the equally unprepared.

Movement slowed to stillness. He was sitting next to the emergency hatch. His two hands were twisting the red levers. The panel opened. It was not hinged but came away in his hands and the weight of it practically dragged him out of the plane. He stood upon the wing and walked along it. Most of it was still there though the end was torn and jagged. The smell of kerosene was overpowering. Never had he been so glad to be in torrential rain, walking in a thunderstorm. The lightning would not dare to touch him now. He was not high above the ground: a metre or two at most. The undercarriage had not survived. Other people would need his help. He turned, still clutching the escape hatch like a shield.

"Idiot," someone shouted. His sudden turn had nearly felled the people following him. He tossed the hatch over the edge. He saw Rafael standing on the wing beside the exit, handing people down to someone on the ground below.

"Need any help?" he called, wondering how Rafael had arrived there quite so soon, but Rafael didn't answer, so he turned again and joined the line of people walking to the quivering wing-tip and jumping, lemming-like, from its ragged end.

He jumped too, felt searing pain in foot and chest, stumbled into long wet grass, half-falling, turned to view the wreck behind him. The plane, or most of it, sprawled like a downed game bird, its tail blasted away. Half a mile back something was burning dully, like a sulky bonfire. The pain intensified. He fell, unconscious, under the rain.

## Nineteen

Marisa telephoned from Salamanca during the afternoon. Borja was at work. She had terrible news, she said. Rafael's sister had rung her with the information from the airline: Rafael had been killed in the Valencia plane crash. There was no radio in Borja's office; he had not heard about the accident. He put the phone down. Death had gatecrashed his party. He had the sensation of a great silence, such as he already knew from his visionary experiences of death in the past. He felt nothing else just yet: only silence and – on this scorching day – a numbing cold.

A minute later came another phone-call. A woman's voice he could not immediately place. It was Alexa. She had heard on the news. There was a number to ring for information. She had rung it, then rung the hospital where Karsten had been taken. Incredibly, she had been able to speak to him. He had some broken bones but nothing worse. He had wanted her to tell Borja he had seen Rafael alive just after the crash although he had no further news of him.

If Borja's spirit soared it was only as a torero soars when he is tossed by the bull, uncertain how he will land. He's dead, he told Alexa. His family was told he was dead. Alexa was appalled. She promised to check and ring back. Borja went outside for half a minute, needing solitude and air. Then he rang the information number himself. Yes, Rafael's death had been confirmed. Alexa rang later, tearful with apology for raising Borja's hopes. She would be passing through Seville the next day on her way to see Karsten. Could she meet Borja? He said yes.

He couldn't bear to go home, at the mercy of well-meaning friends. People like Mark and Pippa would want to call with tentative condolences. Even James might feel obliged to seek him out. He could not deal with that. He asked his colleague, Angel, to let him stay the night. Angel said yes. Angel was the kind of friend whom Borja appreciated the more for the questions he didn't ask.

Next morning Borja went to the Plaza de Armas station to meet Alexa, a small politeness which she found unexpectedly touching. There was some time before her coach left for the airport. They went up to the roof-garden. "Be my guest in your own apartment," said Borja. They sat in silence for a moment, listening to the caged canaries all around them. "Can you tell what key they sing in?" Borja asked.

"Yes, at first. But then they keep changing it. And they sing so fast. It's difficult to follow." She paused, then said more slowly: "I'd never heard of Rafael before yesterday. Karsten told me a little. You must feel very... torn apart."

"What do you think happens to people when they die?" Borja asked, though he was hardly addressing Alexa.

Alexa pointed across the roof-tops to where the Charity Hospital stood behind its guard of palm trees. They both knew the inscription over its door by heart. Domus Pauperum et Scala Coeli. "They go to heaven," she said.

"Do you believe that?"

"Does anyone?" She changed the subject. "Tell me about your future."

"I've got a concert to organise."

"I'm being serious. I mean your future life."

"Then I have to say... it depends..." Borja faltered. "It depends on who I meet."

"Really," said Alexa in wonder, though her next remark unintentionally sounded like a put-down. "It really isn't possible for you to think about your life except in terms of someone else?"

Borja thought for a moment and decided to make his reply a moment of dignity. "Yes," he said. "That's what I'm like."

"I envy you," said Alexa, adding quietly, not expecting an answer. "I wonder who taught you to be like that?" She appeared to change the subject. "I saw William once, you know."

"It's not hard, then, for you to realise what James saw in him."

"No," said Alexa. "Like likes to look for like and likes its likeness."

"Very good," said Borja. "Who said that?"

"It's a thirteenth-century proverb. You said 'saw'."

"I said what?"

"You talked in the past: what James saw in William."

"William kicked him out." Borja's face registered a faint smirk of satisfaction. He was only human.

"And where is James now?"

Borja told her.

"Some likenesses are superficial," Alexa said. "Some go deeper. Sometimes they lie almost too deep to be perceived as such. I wouldn't... Can I say this to someone I know as little as you?... I wouldn't rule James out of your calculations entirely."

Before Alexa left, Borja asked her if she would like to check on her piano in the room below. "No," she said. "I don't need to. I know it's being well looked after."

Borja's face fell. He had not really meant 'check'. He rephrased his request. "In that case, could you play something for me? I've never heard you play the piano and perhaps I'll never have the chance again."

Alexa smiled. "I can't very well say no, then. But I think it must be Bach, don't you?"

Borja went with Alexa all the way to the airport. Not so much for her sake but... He didn't really know why. Of course he had nothing else to do. "You're not afraid of flying? I mean, after yesterday?"

She rebuked him gently. "Don't be silly. If we didn't do things just because we were afraid..."

Borja kissed her good-bye at the departure gate, then walked away feeling somehow grown-up: matured by Rafael's death, strengthened by Alexa's visit.

When he returned to Calle Santander he found a note pushed under his door:

I called but you were out. I wanted to say sorry about Rafael. His name was in the paper. You'll remember I met him once. He was a good guy. There are other things I have to say sorry about too – but they will have to wait till you are ready to see me. Living without you is no life at all. It is a glimpse of death – and you of all people now know what that means. I love you with all my heart. James.

\*

Borja went by train to Salamanca. It was a long, solitary journey: exactly what he needed. He didn't tell his parents he was going; it was too complicated. He stayed overnight at Marisa's. The funeral was next day, in a church he didn't know, on the outskirts of the town. He sat with Marisa near the back. By now he knew just how Rafael had died. It had been in the paper. For a day or more he hadn't been able to read the account of the crash, but eyed the front page with dread. In the end he had been unable not to know. He had read the report through several times, trying to squeeze meaning from every word, trying to find Rafael, trying to share those last moments with him. Rafael had been at the rear of the plane although his allotted seat for landing was at the front. The tail had sheared off on impact and one of the engines had burst. The occupants of the last three rows of seats (just six passengers and Rafael: the flight was not full) had spilled out like shelled peas, passing through a blizzard of shrapnel before hitting the tarmac. The report said – everyone said – death had been instantaneous. Borja asked himself: how long was an instant?

The priest who paid tribute to Rafael clearly hardly knew him:

probably no fault of his own. Sitting near the front was someone who, from the back, looked startlingly like James – or William. Borja studied the head closely and with apprehension but was relieved when it turned slightly at one moment to see that the resemblance went no further.

An instant later an image came into his mind that was vivid, shocking and breathtakingly inappropriate for a funeral. He had a sudden vision of Rafael and William, on a train seat and locked in the most intimate of embraces. Logically, the picture was not difficult to conjure. He had been in the same position with Rafael and as for William, he was practically James' double anyway. But where had the picture come from? And why now, at the funeral of his friend of all places? Death seemed as ready to mock your seriousness as life was. The two had more in common than was generally supposed, he thought. And what if it were true, this anarchic flash of his imagination? Then it occurred to him that, whether it reflected an actual event or just his own darker imaginings, the idea – and its grotesque timing – was also comical. So be it, he thought. He found himself having to suppress a smile.

Borja had never met Rafael's parents; they in turn had never heard of him. But Marisa knew his sister and through her they were all introduced. The parents were touched at Borja's travelling so far, and puzzled too; the in-laws of homosexuals rarely recognise themselves in the role. Still, they had other things on their minds. The reception in their small suburban flat was a low-key affair and Borja left quite early. He had a train to catch.

Karsten arrived back in Seville the next day. His parents had wanted him to go on to Germany, arguing that if he was well enough to fly all the way back to Seville he might as well come to them and be looked after properly. But he was not prepared to waste one of his rare home visits having to move at a snail's pace and on crutches. Besides, he felt concern for Borja, felt that he ought not to be left alone too much just yet.

Karsten had broken a bone in his foot and cracked two ribs. He could do everything for himself – except sneeze – but very slowly and carefully; he felt well but fragile. His return in this condition was, as he had anticipated, very good for Borja; having someone who needed looking after was precisely the therapy that he himself needed. Although he tried not to fuss over Karsten too much when he arrived, by taxi from the airport, he was attentive to him and watchful, climbing the stairs just two steps behind him in case he should stumble and need to be caught. Karsten was aware of this and was touched.

"I don't know how much you know about Rafael's last minutes," Karsten said, once he was installed in an armchair and alone with Borja.

"The newspapers were pretty explicit."

"I would say he was courageous. He didn't have to be where he was. He'd been told to take his seat but he went back when he heard people in distress. He wanted to comfort them. It was more than just doing his job."

Borja thought about this for a minute. In a way that tied up with what he had imagined happening between Rafael and William on the train. Rafael had had a talent for comforting people. And a particular way of doing it. As he knew.

"But Alexa said you saw him after the crash."

Karsten looked pained. "Yes, I did think I saw him. And not only me. Other people in the hospital thought they'd seen him. Obviously they didn't. He was already dead and his body half a kilometre away. Yet it seemed to be him, clear as day. So who did we see? Or what? I had plenty of time to think about this in the hospital, believe me. And I learnt a lesson from it."

"How do you mean?"

"I mean that speculating, or trying to imagine something super-natural, if you like, was a waste of time. It doesn't matter who the helping figure was, or whether he existed at all. It matters who it should have been."

"And who was that?"

"It should have been me."

"I see," said Borja. He paused before adding: "Yes, I think I understand that."

"Though lots of us were taken to hospital only a very few were seriously injured. Most of us escaped lightly. There was one couple, not badly hurt – like me – but inconsolable. The plane broke in two just behind them. Their son and his young wife were in the row behind. They were killed, of course. The old people lived. It seemed so arbitrary, so unfair. I felt I must say something to them. I couldn't think what. Then a line came into my head: 'When that day comes, one man shall be taken, one left, as they work together in the field; one woman taken, one left as they grind together in the mill.' I felt I owed something to whoever it was I saw standing on the aeroplane's wing. I started talking to them about God."

"God?"

Borja's incredulous interruption made Karsten smile. "Honestly. And about the afterlife, the Divine Plan for mankind... all the stuff I'd been taught to believe in as a child and dismissed years ago as nonsense. It all just came pouring out."

"But you don't believe any of it," Borja objected. "You were telling them lies."

"Listen a moment. Some strange things soon began to happen. First of all, it did them a lot of good. Even physically. They left hospital at the same time as I did. (I've promised to keep in touch with them, by the way.) The second thing was that... all the things I was talking to them about – all the Christian mythology, all the Catholic propaganda – began to have an effect on me. It seemed, for the first time in my life, to make some sort of sense. And following from that, the third thing is... I think you have a friend here in Seville who is a priest?"

"Benjamín."

"I should like you to introduce us. I need to talk to someone like him. You see, I think I have a vocation to be a priest."

Borja's mouth opened but no words came out. He stared at Karsten in astonishment.

"I can see you think I'm mad. Allow me to confirm your suspicions. For me the whole happening, the crash, the time in hospital, was like a tap on the shoulder..."

"A twitch upon the thread," said Borja in English.

"Pardon?"

"It's a quote from a book, quoted from another book. It goes something like this. 'I caught him with an unseen hook and an invisible line – one long enough to let him wander to the ends of the world and still bring him back with a twitch upon the thread.' I see. Does Alexa know?"

"Yes. She also thinks I'm mad. She talked – as you are just about to if I don't stop you – about my talent for the guitar. About wasting what God had given me. Funny how everybody talks about God in the end – and almost always it's in order to tell you that He agrees with what they think."

"I see," said Borja. "I think I can promise you never to do that. God and I don't seem to have thought much along the same lines for years."

"You are developing a very English sense of humour, I notice. Which could introduce a (maybe welcome) change of subject..."

But Borja did not want to change the subject just yet. "Becoming a priest. Have you thought what that means? You'd be expected to believe in things like the virgin birth, the physical resurrection of your own body, the assumption of the Blessed Virgin... who knows what else. It makes no sense. We belong to a generation just struggling, just learning, to grow out out of these things. And now you of all people want to climb back in again. There are other ways to help people; you don't need to become a priest. Will people like me have to suffer you in ten years' time denouncing us from the pulpit for the sin that 'cries to heaven for vengeance'?"

"Well, I promise not to do that. And you're right, of course. I don't believe all those things. Not yet. But maybe I shall come to, little by little."

"That's absurd," said Borja. "And awful."

"But in the end, does it matter exactly what I believe and what I don't? Supposing the world becomes a better place. One in which, little by little, people feel safer. Where wars become less frequent, famine is conquered, more and more people die painlessly in their sleep. Then there may be no need for religion, ours or any other. But suppose it goes on being an impossible place to control for long, a world in which civil wars can erupt in the most unexpected places, where a crop failure can ruin a prosperous people in one season, where a landing aeroplane can split a family in two, two to die, two to live, where death can separate two men who were just beginning to love each other... Well, as long as the world went on being like that, there'd be a need for people like me – I mean the new me, the person I want to become."

Borja was shaking his head. "It's very hard to talk to someone who's been born again. Especially for those of us who're just getting used to being who we are in the first place."

Karsten smiled. "Introduce me to your priest friend. The sooner you do that the sooner I can spare your ears all this."

"I do think you're mad," said Borja, "but I'll phone Benjamín for you. I'll phone him first thing in the morning. It should get his weekend off to a good start. There's some beer in the fridge. Want one?" Borja went to fetch it.

"I really did want to change the subject just now," Karsten called after him. "But you wouldn't let me. I wanted to ask: have you heard anything from James?"

Borja returned from the kitchen. "He wrote me a note when he heard Rafael had died."

"Was it a nice note?"

"Yes. Very."

"And have you answered it?"

"Not yet."

Karsten drank a little beer. "Take him back, Borja."

"There would be a nice symmetry in that. Very much in keeping with your new calling. OK. I know he's a nice man. I know that his cheating on me doesn't make him any worse than the rest of us. But there's just one thing. I loved him. For more than three years I loved him more than any other human being – probably more than any one in the future. But I don't love him now. It's that simple."

"You can learn to love him again. I know that."

"You're getting like a priest already. You presume to know me better than I know myself. I don't much like that."

"And I don't really care if you don't. I'm a different person from the one you knew a week ago."

"Evidently."

To Borja's surprise Karsten leaned forward and grabbed Borja's two hands. "I'm not speaking from personal experience. I'm talking about a certainty that goes deeper than that." He chuckled. "If personal experience was all I had to go on..." He stopped.

Borja considered this for a moment. "Are you telling me you've never been in love?"

"That's right."

"Not even with Alexa?"

"Not even with Alexa. I thought for a time that I might be. But I wasn't. And there's another thing, while we're on the subject. I've never been to bed with anyone. Not a woman, not a boy."

"That's nothing to be ashamed of," said Borja more gently.

"Yes, I know that now. But it used to be something I felt ashamed of. Like not being a real man."

"Being a man doesn't depend on having a sex life." As an afterthought Borja added: "Any more than it depends on what gender you're programmed to fancy." There was a moment's silence.

Karsten withdrew a packet of cigarettes from the neck of his T-shirt and lit one for them both. "Shall I tell you something?" he said, his tone indicating that he was going to say it anyway. "There were moments – there have been moments – since we moved in together when I thought... but this embarrasses both of us... that you and I..." He stopped.

"There were moments," Borja admitted awkwardly, "when that crossed my mind too." He looked at Karsten's face. "Now I see that we both are embarrassed." He stared down at the floor for a minute, then looked back at Karsten. "Well, you're going to be a priest now, you say. Perhaps it's just as well we didn't try any... lifestyle experiments we'd soon be regretting. We'll just forget it, shall we?" He got up and planted a kiss on Karsten's forehead. It was the most platonic place he could think of.

"Perhaps," said Karsten, "it would be civil of you to at least acknowledge James' note."

# Twenty

It was like her hair, Pippa thought. Just as odd, just as sudden. It stayed the same for ages, then one day, or even one lunchtime, it was suddenly too long, too dirty, and could not be borne like that a moment longer. So it was with Seville, with her life, with Mark. She went to see her cousin Sophie.

"We just go on from day to day," she explained. "I can't live like that. Mark says, stay another year here and then we'll go to England. I've given up my place at university. Supposing next year he says stay one more year, and then another. What then?"

Sophie looked at her with an expression Pippa had never seen before. It was as if she had drawn a veil over her face. "I don't understand you, dear. You're in Seville. Is that not good enough?"

"Yes. But, I mean, for ever?"

"Why not? It's good enough for me. Even though Pablo is no longer here to share it with. I would never think of going back. It's the heat making you feel like this, that's all. You'll be going back to England for August, won't you? Well, you'll feel fine again when you come back."

"You don't understand. It isn't just Seville. It's also Mark. I haven't admitted it before. He's lovely – in bed and in every way – but he has no goals. I mean, has he? Part-time teaching, chatting in the bars and writing poems he makes no effort to get published – he doesn't even polish them enough to be read by me, for God's sake! – those are the limits of his ambition. He has no get up and go."

"But in Seville," Sophie said, "in Spain, why should he get up and go when he's arrived? And so have you arrived. It crosses my mind that you don't know when you're well off. Are you thinking that perhaps it's you who should get up and go?"

"Not without Mark," said Pippa emphatically. "Don't imagine that. I want him with me. But it has to be somewhere that has a future for him. For his own sake."

"I wonder if you might not be asking for something that is in no-one's power to give. My dear, if I may give you one piece of advice, it's don't be in a hurry. Don't do anything, don't say anything – to anyone, let alone Mark – don't even think anything until you've had a holiday and come back. Now tell me about something else. What's happening with that boy you have staying with you, James?"

It didn't make life easier, Pippa admitted, having James almost permanently underfoot. He had been with them nearly a month now and there was no sign of a reconciliation with Borja, or James taking any step in any other direction.

"Of course, Borja's friend being killed so tragically like that won't have simplified matters. Deaths which appear convenient on the face of things to outsiders rarely are." Sophie shook her head. "And yet that might have been a wonderful pairing too. So romantic. He used to be a bullfighter, you know." Pippa had not known. Sophie seemed to know everything about everyone.

"It would be nice, of course," said Pippa, "if James and Borja could get back together. But nothing seems to work out like that here. There are no conclusions to anything. Maybe it's the climate. Everything just stagnates." She saw the veiled look cross Sophie's features once more.

"Talk to James," Sophie said. "If things won't happen, make them. Or maybe I'll talk to him." An idea was forming in her mind. "I could invite them both over. Effect a public reconciliation."

Pippa's mind recoiled in horror. "I'm not sure if that would work." She was being as diplomatic as she knew how. "Leave it with me. I'll talk to James. Meanwhile, I was on my way to have a look at the Triana market. Come with me?"

Later that day Pippa re-ran the conversation with Jeannette. She too favoured knocking James' and Borja's heads together but took a very different line on Mark. "Get tough with him. I should have done with Felipe but didn't. They walk right over you, men do, however gentle their natures. But give them an ultimatum and they'll come to heel. Trust me. Tell him everything's off if he won't come to England with you."

It sounded high risk to Pippa, but it had an appeal nevertheless. "Yes, but if it doesn't work?"

"It will. But don't worry. In the end it's everyone's privilege to change their mind. Whatever the result, you won't lose him."

Six months ago Pippa would not have taken Jeannette's advice on any subject, but Jeannette had matured greatly recently and Pippa thought that, on balance, her present suggestion was a good one. At least it would force matters to a head. That evening, after supper (it had been James' turn to cook) she suggested a visit to the Bodegón. This was a code (understood and accepted by James) which meant she wanted to be alone with Mark. James rarely came to the Bodegón in the late evening just as Borja rarely went there early on, and for the same reason. Now, he said, as Pippa expected him to, that he wouldn't come with them, he had some homework to mark, but, less expectedly, that he'd join them at ten o'clock if they were still there.

The way to the Bodegón from Virgen de la Luz lay through the Barrio Santa Cruz, and Pippa chose carefully one of the most beautiful sections of the journey, where a tiny street opened into the miniature square of Santa Cruz, with its orange trees and rose bushes and its wrought-iron cross in the centre, to say: "Mark, I need to talk."

Mark's heart sank. He really had no idea what she wanted to talk about, had no idea that a storm was brewing, but his heart always did sink, always had done, when people said they had to talk.

"What about, darling?"

"About being here. About being here and about us."

"I see," said Mark. His eyes flicked quickly round the square as if in search of some distraction or diversion. "Should we sit down?" They sat on the steps below the filigree cross. A guitar was being played softly, invisibly, behind an open window. The sun still lit the upper storeys of the houses brilliantly; at street level it was already dusk.

"You know how happy I am here," Pippa said.

"Yes."

"And how happy I am with you."

"I hope so."

There was a pause before Pippa said: "Don't you feel there's got to be something else, though? That we ought to be making some sort of progress in life?"

Mark was puzzled. "No, not really. Why?"

"I know it's wonderful, the life we lead here: the sunshine, no real responsibilities."

"And being together," Mark added.

"Yes. But in Seville for ever?"

"For one more year," said Mark. "I never said for ever. You want to go back to England. Then I want to, too. I only want what you want."

"Then let's go this year. Let's go now. Please. We must. Otherwise..." She had a sudden picture of the English countryside in winter. Bare trees... You never saw that here.

"Otherwise we never will? Well, what's wrong with that after all? Staying here for ever. Teach the whole population English."

"It's stagnation, Mark." Things she missed. Bare winter trees. The smell of new-mown lawns in summer. Marmite...

"It's living."

"Yes, but..."

"No, it's really living. Perhaps it's something you don't understand. Perhaps you never have."

It was Pippa's turn to feel her heart sink. "But you're not going anywhere."

"Going anywhere? Where could anyone possibly want to go after Seville?"

"I don't mean geographically," said Pippa. How could he be so dense? "I mean your life. Your poetry. None of it ever sees the light of day."

"Getting poetry into print..."

"Yes, I know how hard it is. But you don't even try to get into print. And maybe you don't want it in print. But you could at least complete the poems. Or at the very least finish a provisional draft good enough to share with friends. Share with me."

"They're never good enough for you."

"You make things impossible."

Mark looked round the square again. There was no-one, nothing to rescue him. The old-fashioned street-lights were coming on. "I've never faced this before," he said. Saying it seemed to hurt him. "It could be that we've never understood each other after all."

"Mark..."

"My darling, listen. Have you ever really understood that everything I am is here? I recognised Seville as home when I first set eyes on it when I was twelve. Back in the States I always wanted to get back here. And now here I am again." He stood up. "Let's walk. And I'll tell you a story."

They walked out of the plaza and into the Jardines de Murillo. "Or rather, two stories," Mark said. "When I was here first time – I'd have been about sixteen – one night during the Feria I danced all night with a girl, just one girl – and only danced, you understand: my parents were there. In a caseta and then under the stars. I was in love that night, more than I'd ever been before, more than I expected to be ever again. We danced till the sun was up, more than up. And we were exhausted. Of course I never saw her again."

"You never told me about her," said Pippa, not unkindly. Mark had told her a little about his previous loves – or some of them, it now appeared. "What was her name?"

"I don't think she had one."

"Mark..."

"Or if she did, I never knew it. Or if I knew it, I forgot."

"You're crazy."

"And that brings me to the second story." Mark pointed to the Moorish battlements ahead of them. Beyond them rose the trees and blossom of the Alcázar Gardens. "I used to spend my time in there when I was a kid, walking among the fountains or sitting writing the kind of stuff you write at sixteen. One day in early summer I'd been there later than usual. My parents were away somewhere. It was getting dark. A bird started singing in one of the lemon trees. I sat there listening. Then the moon came up, glinting through the arrow-slits in the battlements and eventually rising above them. It was a round full moon, not the Moors' thin crescent like we have tonight. It lit the gardens silver.

"I realised it was late suddenly. I was quite alone. I made for the gates but they'd been locked for hours. I hollered for a caretaker or someone but no-one came, and the bird stopped. So I stopped shouting and after a while the bird began again. And I thought, my parents were away, no-one would panic if I didn't go home."

"So you spent the night?"

"In a palace garden with a singing bird. I slept eventually – on a compost-heap behind the gardeners' huts. I had the most wonderful dream of my life."

"What did you dream about?"

"About... nothing. It wasn't that sort of dream. It just had a texture, composed of night sounds: the breeze ruffling the palm-tops, the water whispering in the fountains... it was like quicksilver, as beautiful and even more elusive.

"In the morning the gardeners woke me and the dream vanished in the sunshine, leaving only that half-memory. I wanted to get that dream back, wanted it for years. And now tonight you've made me realise something. That I have got the dream back. I've been living it for three years. Oh, you've been part of it during this last year; you've been the best part of it ever. But now you're about to wake me up again like the gardeners did. And then I shall lose it for ever. I can't let you do that. There won't be a third chance. And now I see that you can't stay part of it with me. I can't make you happy here. You'd be forcing yourself all the time into shoes that didn't fit. And if I left Seville with you I'd be nobody. I wouldn't be any good to you – an unemployable poet in New Maldon. I wouldn't be me any more."

"Then supposing I stayed," said Pippa. It was what she wanted, suddenly, this moment, more than anything.

"Then you wouldn't be you any more," Mark said with a crushing certainty that Pippa had never heard in his voice before. She had the feeling again that cracks were running through a building, only this time the cracking didn't stop. Everything was crumbling. Mark went on. "Everything good we've had would get washed away by disappointment. Let's just say it's over now, while the memories are still so fine."

"Over?" Pippa sounded incredulous but she knew it was true.

"Now do you see why the girl had no name? She didn't need one. She was Spain."

"I need some time to think," Pippa said quietly. "You go on to the Bodegón. Meet James. Let me go home." She turned abruptly back to the square. Mark watched her, unable to decide whether to go after her or call her back. Though what was there to say? She disappeared from sight, and Mark turned away, along the street named Water.

\*

"I wrote ten o'clock," said Borja. He was standing at the long bar of the Bodegón with Karsten, drinking red wine.

"What else did you write?" Karsten wanted to know.

"Nothing. Just that I'd be there. He wanted to talk. I've given him the opportunity, no more than that."

"No forgiveness, no terms of endearment?" Karsten was stepping over a boundary that pre-crash Karsten would have considered sacred.

Borja didn't seem to mind. "We'll see what happens. If he comes."

"Just make a sign and I'll disappear," said Karsten. "He won't want to talk to me, that's for sure."

The door opened. Borja stiffened. Mark walked in.

"Hola," said Borja when Mark reached them then, registering the expression on his face said: "Qué pasa, what's the matter?"

"Pippa and I just split up."

"Oh fuck it, no," said Karsten in beautifully enunciated English, to his own surprise as well as the others'.

"I'm so sorry," said Borja. "Manolo," he called across to the barman, "pone una copa para Marco."

The door opened again. This time it was the wind-up bull man who set his furry clockwork toys on the counter in front of them, where they did a nerve-shredding Muffin-the-Mule dance. Untypically it was Borja who yelled at him: "No somos turistos!" and he went off with the hauteur of rejected salesmen everywhere to try his luck among the tables. And suddenly there was James beside them. "Borja," he said.

"Hallo James."

Then something happened which Borja might have predicted but which mightily surprised the others. James burst into tears.

"You can't do that here," Borja said. He meant it seriously but, hearing himself say the words, realised they sounded both ridiculous and mean. He smiled, trying to pretend it had been a joke. Then he had no alternative but to pull James towards him and clasp him in the kind of embrace they had never before shared in a public space. Neither was wearing more than a T-shirt; Borja had jeans on, James only shorts. How familiar, and yet how wonderful James' body felt. And in touching it Borja found himself in contact not only with familiar flesh but with something like a net or web made up of shared experiences, shared confidences, commitments and trust which, however badly holed and damaged, could never be unpicked; in touch again with three-plus years of joined-up life which could never be unlived. Borja held him tighter and wondered whether perhaps the ceiling might fall on them, garlic-strings, smoke-black hams and all, or whether Manolo would order them out and call the police. Would they be arrested for public indecency and he become the second person to share a police-cell with James that summer? But none of that happened. As he stood there, silently stroking the back, then the hair, of the person who meant most to him in the world, Borja realised that nobody cared ten pesetas what he did: that if he was happy then so was everybody else. And he felt at that moment that death had withdrawn its shadow and that he would never be frightened by anything in the world again. He kissed James on the lips. Nobody batted an eyelid.

Except James.

"I think we'll go now," Borja muttered to the others. "If you don't mind." He whispered to James: "Come home." Then the two of them made their way towards the door, a little unsteadily, each trying to walk, for the first time, with an arm around the other's shoulder.

Karsten looked at Mark. "I don't think I'll be going home just yet." He ordered himself another drink. "Tell me what happened, if you want to. Or if you know it yourself."

## Twenty-one

Sunrise was the coolest time of day. Now August was upon the city, fierce and hot-breathed as a lion and Seville operated during daylight hours behind white walls and shuttered windows. Only in the evening did the heat retract its claws. As if a curfew had been lifted, the citizens emerged to party; a breeze stirred near the river and the scent of jasmine came and went among the streets. The street party went on till dawn for many. And sunrise was the coolest time of day.

James and Borja lay naked on the roof. They had spent at least a part of every night up here during the week since James came home. At first there had been an awkwardness about their lovemaking together, a certain holding back. For both of them more recent sensual experience kept getting in the way, like layers of gauze between them. But it had been the physical presence of James, the touch, the scent of him, that evening in the Bodegón that had reawakened Borja to the man he knew, had woken him up to the fact that he had never stopped loving him. And as they continued to rediscover each other's bodies, not only through sex but in the routine intimacies of living together, the gauzes melted away, revealing to each of them a person known but also new, a partnership that was unchanged and yet transformed, not only old and tried but also just beginning and full of every possibility for the future.

Most other mornings there had been work to go to but this

morning there was none. Not only was it Saturday, it was holiday time as well. Dates had been synchronised months ago when there had been no thought of Borja and James holidaying apart, but plans had been left unmade when there seemed no possibility of their spending the time together. Now they had been made quickly, and to Borja's total satisfaction; all apprehensions were on James' side alone. What would his parents make of Borja close up and under their own roof? They vaguely accepted the gayness of their eldest son when it was two thousand miles away, and the unknown Spanish friend as well. It might still be a phase he was going through. But soon now they would have to confront James and Borja for the first time as the item they were. And how would Borja go down with the lads in the pub? With James' brother? As for the means of transport that would get them from Seville to Sussex, James had the greatest misgivings. But Borja had decided and so that was that. At least the trip would be free.

Borja was getting good at organising things, James noticed. The concert was nearly all fixed up already and there would still be six weeks in which to step up the publicity when they got back. And by then they would have the flat to themselves. "Is Karsten up yet?" James asked.

"He went out to get some bread," said Borja.

It made James smile: Borja wandering around the flat stark-naked, chatting to Karsten unconcernedly about bread; that was something new; he'd better not do it in Sussex. "We can stay up here and sunbathe," James said.

"You'll burn." Borja put his hand on him. "I mean there."

"Only for a little while. Just till breakfast. The sun's not hot yet."

"Shall I tell you something?" Borja said.

"Please do."

"Wait for it," said Borja, "and try to relax. Take a deep breath. I want to try to become a pilot."

James sat up sharply. "You what?"

"I said relax. And I said 'want' and I said 'try'. We're not there yet."

"I know but..." James snatched at a thought. "Darling, it would cost a fortune... to train."

"Yes, I've thought of that. I'd need a private pilot's licence only. Maybe my parents could run to that. Then once I'd got accepted by an airline they'd see to the rest."

"My boy's gone mad," said James. "What if your parents can't pay – or won't?"

"Then I can volunteer to do my mili. In the air-force. See if they'll have me. Then I'd get trained free."

"Your mili? Correct me if I'm wrong but they let you off that when you were younger because you had fits."

"That was when I was younger. Do I have fits now?"

"But you don't believe in the army. You're practically a pacifist. You even have mixed feelings about the bullfight – the only Spanish male I've ever met who does. What's got into you?"

"Take it easy. The military would only be a means to an end..."

"Ask any dictator!"

"The end is flying. Freedom."

"Freedom from what? From me?"

"No. From the past. From everything that's gone before. Freedom from myself if you like. But I think of it more as freedom with you. A new beginning for us."

James was not convinced. "With me but in my absence? Funny kind of togetherness, that."

"I might not get accepted anyway. I might not have the aptitude to be a pilot. I might not pass the medical, the sight tests... Rafael didn't make it..."

"Light is dawning," said James.

"... And if I don't, then OK, I'll be a steward instead."

James sighed. Had he got Borja back only to lose him again? "I see." A pause, then: "Do what you have to then. Everyone must fight his bull in the end, I suppose." There was another moment's silence. "You must have loved him a lot."

Borja considered his answer, drew the words out carefully. "I don't think I'd got quite that far along. Rafael was always more immediate than me, more headstrong."

"It seems to have rubbed off," said James.

"Perhaps I would have come to love him very much in time. But there wasn't time." Which was fortunate for Borja's relationship with James. This crossed both their minds. Neither said it.

"Why," James asked, "why did it need someone's death to bring us back together?"

"That's a question for Karsten, I think," said Borja. "Not for me."

"Are we all just lightning-rods for other people's destinies? Is that what it's all about?"

"Again, ask Karsten. He likes answering questions."

James, who had been sitting propped on one elbow now moved till he knelt astride Borja. With his fingers he traced the familiar palm tree of hair that, growing from its shady roots, rose, interrupted only by his navel, to fan out in two broad fronds across his chest.

"Don't! Somebody might come up."

"Señora López doesn't do her washing on Saturday mornings, the couple from the ground floor are only ever up here in the afternoon, and as for Karsten, he's seen you the way you are within the last half-hour."

"Yes, but he hasn't seen us actually..."

"Who says we're going to actually...?"

"You know what I mean."

James lay forward, flattening the palm tree into a warm carpet. It was familiar, comforting, tickly. He put his mouth over Borja's.

"Private party or can anyone join?" South London accent, rather loud.

Like startled hares they flicked apart and round towards the voice, both adopting a protective crouch. Borja wanted to grab for a nearby garment but there wasn't one; he told himself he looked more dignified as he was.

Staring at them and grinning broadly were two young men, quite muscular, in working boots and shorts. One had tattoos on his forearms, the other an earring. "We're a bit early," said the one with the earring.

"Holy Moses," said James. "Who let you in? We weren't expecting you till the afternoon."

"Looks like it. We met your friend with the crutches on the doorstep. He said to find you up here. 'Course he was hardly to know..."

"I'm Colin," said the tattooed one. "He's George. We'd better let you get dressed. Unless you're into nude heavy lifting." They both laughed, not unkindly.

Half an hour later, downstairs, dressed and breakfasted, Borja and James were learning how to un-leg a grand piano and ease it onto its side on the handling-shoe. Karsten had volunteered to help but was firmly told not even to come near the operation and was reduced to making unhelpful suggestions from the sidelines.

"Seems a shame," said Colin, "Alexa giving it all up like this." They had paused for breath at the top of the stairs.

"It isn't giving up," said Karsten. "It's a question of moving on to other things. She's a brilliant guitarist. She's studying in Córdoba."

"You should have seen her father's face, though, when he came round to organise the pick-up. Unsmiling wasn't the word."

"I was hoping to spare him that," said Karsten. "I thought I had a sale fixed up in Germany. It's a pity that it... er..."

"Fell through," supplied James. "I'd love to know how you got the thing up here in the first place."

"Some blokes were digging up the street outside with pick-axes. Shoving a piano onto the first floor was like a holiday for them...Once we'd shown them a couple of bank-notes."

They turned their attention once again to the piano, wedged in the angle at the top of the stairs. It did not feel like a holiday just now.

"Twist it this way," said Colin, "then ease the shoe down the first

flight. And I mean go easy. We've got to catch her at the bottom."
They hauled the instrument round and obediently it sledged down
the stairs, securely strapped to its wood and metal shoe. Everyone had
a cord to hold and as it neared the bottom of the flight, "Pull," said
George and, like magic, the piano stopped.

Karsten went down to open the grill that led to the street and the
waiting lorry. "Last flight," said Colin. "Get the shoe round." It was
easier this time. Too easy. Nobody was holding onto their cord and the
piano suddenly slipped away from them.

"Look out," yelled James to Karsten. George leaped for one of the
cords but was dragged downstairs and tripped by the escaping piano.
Reaching the bottom, the piano met the trolley that was put there to
receive it and slid the short distance through the grill, just missing
Karsten, and onto the narrow pavement. The rear corner of George
and Colin's lorry stopped it with a crunch. A pianissimo chord came
from the piano like a sigh. "Christ Almighty," said George.

The accident drew a lot of attention from passers-by and some
snippets of advice from two draymen who were delivering beer-kegs
to the Bodegón opposite but the damage was relatively minor. A
moulding below the piano keyboard had been gashed and would need
repairing; a tail-light on the lorry had smashed. Once the piano had
been effortfully loaded on board, Colin and George went off to buy a
replacement fitting: you couldn't cross three countries without rear
lights.

"I met Pippa in the baker's," said Karsten when he was alone with
James and Borja. "She had two news." (James just managed to stop
himself from correcting him.) "Jeannette's going to marry Felipe after
all – and obviously keep the baby. Once Pippa's gone home they'll
have the flat to themselves."

"It still makes me sad," said James. "Not about Jeannette, of course:
that's great news. But about Pippa. And about Mark. She came here
with such high hopes. Met Mark. Everything seemed great. And now...
And Mark back on his own again. On the very evening that I move out

from under their feet, Pippa moves out too. I feel sorry for him. Well, for them both."

"Pippa's young," said Karsten. "She's going back to university. Anything can happen. And Mark... You didn't let me give you the second..."

"...Piece of news." James got it in quickly.

"Alexa's invited him to stay with her in Córdoba." Karsten let this sink in. It did.

"Wow," said James.

"Somehow I'm not surprised," said Borja.

"You don't mean you saw it coming," James challenged him.

"No, not at all. It's just that... sometimes people have more in common than they realise: things that are not obvious or superficial; things that lie deep. 'Like likes to look for like and likes its likeness'."

"Where did you get that from?" asked James.

Borja smiled. "From Alexa."

Karsten looked at his watch. He had an appointment at the hospital: just a routine check. There were three good-byes to be said to Karsten. Good-bye because James and Borja would probably have gone by the time he got back, good-bye because he would soon be off on his own, delayed, holiday to Germany, good-bye because, after that, he would be 'trying his vocation' and staying six months in a monastery near Ronda while he did so – experimenting with a life in which it would be his destiny to be a repository of other people's secrets but not have any of his own.

Then there were just the two of them, at least until Colin and George got back. It still seemed crazy to James: travelling home in a lorry with a piano, Borja sharing the driving with the two young men. But everything was crazy now: he back together with Borja, Borja wanting to be a pilot... and yet everything was possible. A thought struck James. "You don't see death any more, do you?" he said.

"No," said Borja. "Perhaps I no longer need to. Perhaps it was Rafael's death I was seeing all along. I don't know. Maybe death will leave me alone entirely now – at least until he comes to find me finally."

James did not pursue this – it seemed a morbid thought: part of the old self that Borja was now trying to put behind him. He thought for a moment, then set off at a tangent. "Will this place suit us, do you think?" He looked around the flat.

"I hope so," Borja said. "I had a bad feeling about the other place. Ever since the neighbours..." He stopped himself.

James looked at him. "Are you thinking about the window? I didn't know you..."

"I wasn't going to tell you," Borja said.

"I wasn't going to tell you either." They looked at each other for a minute while they digested this. "Come on," said James. "We have a date with the ferry to Newhaven."

"Newhaven sounds so romantic. Is it?"

The question floored James. He had never entertained so peculiar a notion. Then he remembered suddenly his first sight of a foreign country as a child. Taken to Dover Castle on a visit, he had put a coin into a powerful telescope and seen a foreign shore, seen foreign cars in silhouette upon a clifftop road, seen the great clock-tower, even made out its hands... which told a time that was different from his own. His heart had leaped, he had not known why, but now he understood. For that had been his first discovery that not everything was the same everywhere, that different people set their watches to a different mean. It was a discovery that stood him in good stead later when he began to learn about his own nature. Eventually it had brought him to Spain – and to Borja. For Borja it was obviously the same.

"Yes," James said. "Newhaven is romantic. It's a dull little nine-teenth-century town but it's magic just the same." He described its position in a fold of the chalk downs, told how the big ships threaded their way like eels into its narrow harbour. He told Borja about the road up from the port, the Firle Beacon with its plunging views, the gleaming Seven Sisters, the oak-beamed pubs in Alfriston, bluebell woods, the smell of English gardens under summer rain...

"Oh brave new haven," began Borja. Then he stopped abruptly. James watched his eyes fill up with tears.

\*

The sky was cloudless. Pippa peered down. Spain was rolling away beneath her at a steady nine miles to every minute. Eventually it would all be gone. From such a height it looked like rough unpolished gold, a vast jewel-box in which towns and cities nestled like trinkets. Impossible to think that people really lived down there, getting on with strange unfathomable lives. Even her own life in Seville, ended just one hour ago, now seemed as remote and distant as her childhood, unreclaimable as a dream. So much had happened to her and yet it was as if nothing had.

A mist appeared and turned to cloud. The Pyrenees lay just ahead. The plane adjusted its heading by a few degrees. Now the clouds lay thick below her, finally obliterating Spain. On the other side of them lay all the uncertainties of her future, alarming yet exciting. There also lay that most mysterious of destinations and the most elusive: home.